INTERNATIONAL BESTSELLING AUTHOR

JACKIE IVIE

Giselle

Cover Design and Interior format by The Killion Group
http://thekilliongroupinc.com

DEDICATION

To Jennifer Jakes, for your wizardry.
Thank you.

CHAPTER ONE

On the eve of her twentieth birthday, Giselle finally found out why her own family disliked her so much. Not that anyone would speak of such a thing. The idea would cause a sensation if she were to mention it. After all, Giselle was surrounded by every luxury known to mankind and used to being protected and pampered like a princess.

It wasn't surprising.

She was the only daughter of the *Comte* d'Antillion.

Such distinction should have given her access to every soiree and fest. She should be the center of attention, surrounded by envious friends and acquaintances, her social calendar filled to the last hour. But instead...she was ignored. Overlooked. Forgotten.

Her mind screamed at the injustice of it while her hands stayed piously crossed in prayer. She hadn't any envious friends. She hadn't any acquaintances she could name; at least, not any in the social world. She didn't even know, for certain, what a social world was.

She was never going to find out, either. Her father, the *Comte* d'Antillion wouldn't allow it. She didn't know what she'd done to make him detest her so. She'd tried to be a good daughter, ladylike, silent as a mouse, and as still as a shadow, but it wasn't enough for her *pere*. Nothing she did pleased him.

There was no one to be jealous of her because Giselle wasn't allowed to be seen, let alone envied. She'd been imprisoned in this wretched wing of the chateau for years!

Years!

The intensity of her thoughts would've been noticeable, as much as she gripped to the skirts of her gown, but no one commented on it. Her maid, Isabelle, and the fat priest had themselves to think on. That...and God.

Isabelle was a pious woman, much more so than Giselle would ever be. Giselle didn't know how to make the envy disappear from her body. She didn't know how to find a feeling of peace, piety, or devotion. Prayers rarely helped. All they did was torment her further.

If there was a God who cared, surely He would see that I had some contact with the outside world, wouldn't He?

She asked herself that often.

She never got an answer.

Giselle's lips twisted as the priest's voice droned on and on. She was failing at patience, too. Her governess, Louisa, should give up trying to instill it. Patience may be a virtue, but Giselle was far from feeling it. She'd been patient, enough! *It isn't fair!* Louisa could come and go as she pleased while Giselle was imprisoned, restricted by the confines of her station.

How she longed to be a commoner.

She dreamed of an unfettered life, free of the rules and stricture that no one saw anyway. If she were a commoner, she wouldn't have to dress for sup. She wouldn't have to sit board-straight in a high-backed chair while she practiced her *petit-point*. She wouldn't have to....

Giselle stopped her thoughts. It was a lie. She didn't truly wish to be a commoner. It sounded horrid, too. Her maid, Isabelle, had told her how harsh life was outside Chateau Antilli's white stone walls.

Mama had spoken to Giselle for years about the history and pageantry of the Antillions. The second *Comte* d'Antillion had died in battle against the English in the twelfth century. It was he that designed the chateau, Giselle, Mama had told her. 'We have him to thank for the shape of it, the flagstaffs at each tower, and the white stone. It was designed that way, to be a beacon to all of French dominance.'

The way Mama had described the history, made it seem real.

But now, it seemed even Mama had deserted her only daughter. Giselle wondered what she'd done to deserve that. Mama hadn't been in to visit for over three months, and it was maddening. There was nothing but the walls to look at and the windows to look from, the huge bedstead to lie in and dream from, and the altar to kneel in front of.

Giselle sighed from her position beside her maid. She caught Isabelle's glance over at her, and practiced showing nothing on her face. If Isabelle had glanced down at Giselle's skirt, she'd have known of the other's inner torment, however. Giselle didn't realize she was holding her breath until Isabelle turned back to the priest.

She couldn't concentrate, but it wasn't entirely her fault. Louisa had filled her head with chatter about the upcoming betrothal of her ten-year-old brother, Francois, the oldest of her six brothers. Giselle knotted her hands into fists on the skirt. She hadn't even seen him since before Christmas Mass! She hadn't seen anyone that mattered.

She would almost welcome a visit from the *comte*.

Giselle closed her eyes. It wasn't to pray. It was to bring the image of her father to her mind. The *comte* was the most regal and handsome man in the world. She'd thought so since she was a child, and she had none that could compare. Of course, she'd been isolated from the world for so long, she was no judge.

What was she thinking? Welcome her father? She'd as soon welcome her own judgment day. The *comte* had no warmth for his daughter. Every time he came it was an ordeal. Giselle didn't know why. She would speak when spoken to, act gracious when serving him, show him her latest tapestry for any words he might speak, and still he detested her.

Giselle felt the tears swelling, and she quickly blinked them back. He wasn't coming. That was probably a good thing. He may be the most handsome man in the world, but he was also the coldest, most unfeeling one.

"Giselle!"

Giselle looked up at Isabelle' s loud whisper. Isabelle always whispered. Sometimes it was a soft, caring whisper, and sometimes, like now, it was a sharp, chastising sound.

"Pay attention."

She was holding out Giselle's rosary. Giselle didn't even recall dropping it. She knew Isabelle watched as she unfurled the fabric in her fingers before reaching for her beads. She couldn't meet the maid's eyes.

In the main rooms, far from her, they were celebrating Francois' union, gaily dancing to music she could only dream about. They'd be serving exotic foods, like the steamed peacock Louisa had described earlier.

Giselle tried to cleanse the envy from her thoughts, but her heart wasn't in it. She supposed God knew it, too. No one would remember that it was her birthday the next day. Even if they did, it wouldn't be mentioned or celebrated. That much, she already knew.

She smoothed down her satin skirts, working at the creases she'd put there. The fabric snagged on a fingernail as she waited for the priest to finish. She wondered how that had happened. Isabelle had given her nails a buffing with pumice just that morning after her daily cleansing.

"Amen. Come Child, it is time for confession. Have you any sins you would like to confess?"

Giselle looked at him with as much innocence as she could muster, and yet still show her disdain. It was such a useless question, and yet she was asked it daily. What sins could she possibly have to confess? The only one was envy. She even envied the priest. That fat atrocity of a man could even come and go as he wished throughout the countryside, while she...?

"No, Father," she said quietly, and knew Isabelle was pleased.

"Bless you, Child." The priest's hand hovered over her head for a moment, and then he, too, left her.

"Come, Giselle. Dinner will soon be served. It is time to dress for it. You selected the green flowered frock this morning. Do you recall?"

Giselle followed her, but her eyes were still on the priest. She watched as he knocked and was given freedom from her tower. Of course she remembered selecting the dress. She had no other pressing business this morning. Besides, she only had three gowns to choose from. One she was wearing, and the other was being laundered. What other choices did she have?

She gave one last look at the closing door before turning back. She shouldn't envy the priest. She was allowed out, too. Once a day. For her constitutional, as the doctors called it.

The *comte* had ordered it after Giselle had started fainting during her lessons last year. She hadn't asked God for forgiveness of her weakness. Why, if she'd known it would get her the chance to actually go outside – even it is was the chateau's outer sanctum – she'd have learned how to faint years earlier.

It was too cold to venture out now anyway, so she hadn't asked in weeks. Spring was always cold. Just like the spring day when she'd been born. April 18, 1730. And her father's disappointment was legendary.

Giselle had heard it from the dressmaker who had been hired for her when it became impossible to wear her old clothing any longer. Amid the fitting, pinning, and shaking of her head, the dressmaker had muttered about the scandal. There had been a row caused by the d'Antillion's first child's birth that was still talked about. Although she'd been fifteen at the time, it had still hurt.

Papa had wanted an heir for Antilli, and he believed Giselle's birth was a curse. After five childless years of marriage to the *comtesse,* he had a daughter, not a son. The villagers had spent many hours gossiping over his outburst at a *salon,* whatever that was.

The dressmaker's tone had been so filled with excitement that Louisa had exchanged glances with Isabelle. Giselle didn't even know why. Papa had been premature in his anger, though. He hadn't known then that his future held not one, but six male heirs.

Francois had been the first, followed by a succession of boys, each with his own private nanny and wet nurse. Giselle already knew how proud the *comte* was of them. His expression would change whenever he spoke of it.

"Your dinner, *Madame.*"

A manservant placed a tray at the table and removed the lid. He bowed before meeting Giselle's glance, then left. If she could have gotten a good look at him, she knew she'd have another comparison for Papa. The manservant wouldn't compare favorably, though. They would never send Giselle a comely servant. God forbid they send her someone nice to look at and perhaps converse with. That would have to be immediately corrected. The *comte* would have it no other way.

"Porridge? Again?" She couldn't keep the disgust from her voice.

"It'll keep the color in your face, Giselle, and you know it." Isabelle added honey to it as she scolded. "You know how the doctors fret if you don't eat."

"Oh. The doctors. Very well." Giselle sobered and walked to the table.

Her reflection in the chamber mirror stopped her for a moment. She was paler than usual, but that was probably due more to her own curtailment of exercise than lack of nourishment. She was always pale, anyway.

She was also very petite, much smaller than Louisa or Isabelle. That was one reason she hadn't needed a new wardrobe in five years. She had light brown hair that was strangely streaked with white strands around her face, high arched brows, and a large mouth.

Giselle knew she wasn't ugly to look upon. Louisa had told her she'd create a sensation if her papa would allow her to attend one of the Antilli soirees. Giselle bowed mockingly to her image, and watched as the firelight glinted on the white streaks in her hair.

"Your supper, Giselle?" Isabelle cleared her throat.

"I'm coming!"

Giselle was sharper than she intended. Isabelle would have to forgive it, but she could be such a nag, at times. As Giselle reached for her silver spoon, the large, emerald-shaped ruby of her ring caught at her eye. That reminded her of its presence and power. She grimaced. She didn't even care if Isabelle saw it, and scolded her later. The ruby was the cause of everything, she was sure. It was the mark of her real status.

Giselle was a married woman.

It wasn't her marital state that the Antillions disliked so much, although that was what she'd always suspected. Giselle had reasoned that her *pere,* the *comte,* didn't like that she was a *duchesse,* with a higher title than his. She was wrong — it was much more.

Isabelle answered a late visitor's knock at her door and came back with a strange sort of awe on her face. "It's your father, Giselle."

Giselle was ashamed at the way her hand shook as she replaced her wine goblet on the table. She had nothing to be frightened or ashamed of. She always had some wine before dressing for bed. It helped her sleep.

"Mon pere."

She bent into a low curtsy. *He came for my twentieth birthday!* She tried to hide her joy, but knew it wasn't successful.

"Giselle," he said gravely.

Her emotion died. She felt it. The warmth of her cheeks receded, leaving her feeling weak and chilled. She was grateful he didn't seem to notice, but that was stupid. The *Comte* d'Antillion rarely noticed his daughter, and when he did, it wasn't a good thing.

"You are well?"

"Yes, Papa."

She gestured him to a settee and seated herself with an elegant gesture in her usual chair. She watched as he eyed the structure for a bit before seating himself.

"You don't look well."

"I'm sorry, Papa." She looked at her folded hands.

"You're eating?"

"Yes, Papa." She straightened further against the chair's back. This was terrible! The meeting was going poorly already.

"That's good. Francois is now officially betrothed to the second daughter of the *Comte* Duisebonne. That was the best I could do."

Giselle wondered why he was telling her this. He never talked to her about the family before. She kept silent and waited.

"She has a dowry of seven-hundred acres of prime ground and a thousand *louis d'ors.*"

"That's a fortune, Papa!" She exclaimed.

"No."

His cold eyes appraised her after the one word. Giselle felt like an insect spread out for his inspection.

Despite her best intentions, gooseflesh rippled through her arms. She fought the urge to clasp them about her.

"It would take a dowry as rich for all my sons," his voice softened a bit in pride, "to make up for what you cost me."

He stood abruptly and turned away from her as if the sight was more than he could bear.

"But, Papa...."

"Don't speak to me, Giselle!"

She gasped and felt tears fill her eyes.

"Not until I've finished what I've come to say."

Giselle opened her mouth to say 'Yes, Papa,' like a dutiful daughter, but then closed it. She knew any word would give away her emotion, and he'd hate that worst of all.

"When you were born, I cursed you, and I cursed God. I drank until I couldn't walk, but nothing had changed. I still had a daughter."

Giselle wiped a tear as it escaped her eye on the tip of a finger. She already knew his feelings, so why bother crying?

"When you were small...a little over one year old, my neighbor to the south, Berchald, came to see me."

She watched Papa walk to the window and move the drape aside. She didn't say a word as he unlatched the thick-paned glass and pushed it open. Giselle shivered in the sudden draft, but he seemed unaffected.

"Somehow, he talked me into a betrothal. His nephew and heir, Etienne, was a lad of ten. God help me, I signed the agreement."

The drape fell back into place, shielding her from the cold of the elements, but not the chill of her father. His eyes, when she dared glance at them, were filled with disgust. She lowered her gaze instantly.

"Nearly a third! Don't you understand, Giselle? Somehow, that weasel of a man talked me out of Savignen Valley and all its riches!"

Giselle gasped, finally understanding how much he had lost. Savignen was renowned throughout France for its vineyards and wines. It had no equal. Giselle's betrothal price was Savignen Valley? She could scarcely believe it.

"I thought, since you were such a sickly child, you'd never reach marriageable age. I was crazed with anger, drunk with disappointment. I don't know which to blame. Perhaps a combination. It doesn't matter, really. I agreed. It doesn't matter why at this point."

"I'm sorry, Papa," Giselle whispered, looking up.

"Silence!"

He stopped her with a raised hand. Giselle's heart hammered loudly in her breast as if it had acquired a mind of its own. At least she understood why Papa had always looked at her with such an air of detachment. She actually preferred that to his full attention, now that she had it.

"I've sent notice to the *Duc* du Berchald that you're arriving within a sennight."

He turned his back on her again. "I've sheltered you since the marriage and sent good Antilli gold after bad, while all of Savignen's riches fill your husband's coffers. I'll do it no more."

"*Non,* Papa. Wait! I beg—" Giselle stood from her chair.

"Control yourself, Giselle."

She ignored him. She no longer cared if he admonished her. He was making the solid wood of the tower floor feel like it was sand, and it was nothing to him? She rushed to his side and reached for him. "Please Papa? I'll eat less! I'll make my clothes last longer! I'll do anything! Don't do this to me."

"It's too late Giselle." He pried her hand from his arm.

"But, Papa. Please!"

"Isabelle, give her a posset. She has taken ill."

He pushed from Giselle and walked stiffly from the room. She didn't know if he looked back either, her face was buried in her hands.

It was Louisa who opened Giselle's eyes. Her governess noticed the shock on Giselle's face the next morning. Or perhaps it was because Giselle wouldn't get out of bed.

"What happened, Giselle?"

Giselle turned her face away.

"Isabelle, why does she lay there as if her life were over?"

"The *comte* came last night."

Giselle knew it was Isabelle pulling the drapes open. Giselle longed to box the woman's ears, only she never had, and she didn't have the strength at the moment.

"The *comte?* What did he say?" Louisa's voice sharpened.

"Oh Louisa, how can I bear it?" Giselle cried out and buried her face into her pillows.

"If someone doesn't tell me what's happening, right now, I'll send for the doctors."

"Not the doctors!"

Giselle gasped. All those medical men wanted to do was attach leeches and drain her blood. She detested them almost as much as she did Papa.

"My father is...he's—." This was terrible. She caught the sob just as it sounded.

"Yes?"

"He's sending me to my husband's family." Giselle finished.

"Thank the Lord!" Louisa clapped her hands and started jumping in a little circle.

"How can you say such a thing?"

Giselle wasn't successful at keeping anger from her voice. Louisa was never anything but a champion. Giselle felt betrayed by the other's emotion.

"Because it's true! I've been praying to God every night for you for this very thing. I can't believe my prayers are finally being answered!"

Giselle stared. She couldn't believe it. Louisa must not care for her at all.

"It's a grand day, and you lay abed. Up!"

Of course it was a grand day for Louisa. She wasn't the one being sent away like excess baggage. She must be happy because her term of employment was over. Giselle had no idea how little the other woman must care. Giselle narrowed her eyes, and looked away from the sunlight. She'd ordered Isabelle not to let in the sun, but that command was disobeyed too. She was surrounded by people who didn't care. She tried to keep the emotion from her voice, and the words came out as flat as she expected.

"I'm being exiled, and you rejoice. My thanks."

Louisa laughed. "Don't be silly, Giselle. You aren't being exiled. You're being set free!"

Giselle's mouth opened, then shut. She hadn't looked at it like that.

"I've watched you wallow in self-pity for too long, already," Louisa continued. "I don't think you've allowed sunshine into this chamber in months. It's gloomy and depressing, just as your life has been. That's why I had Isabelle draw your drapes. It's a new day, Giselle. The start of a new life for you. The future is all yours. Just think of it!"

"I'm trying not to," she grumbled.

"You'll be chatelaine of Chateau Berchand, with many servants to command. There will be menus to decide, entertainment to provide, and don't forget, you can order any piece of clothing you fancy — at will! I look forward to seeing you in a new wardrobe, furnished with the latest in Paris fashions. I'm almost too overjoyed for words."

Wardrobe? Giselle wondered. *Entertainment?* "Aren't you forgetting something, Louisa?"

"What?"

"What? Are you so dense? I may be chatelaine of the castle, but I'm not alone. What of my husband? Well? What of him? I've never even laid eyes on him."

This time she was trying to keep fear from her voice, but fell woefully short. Giselle knew it as she met Isabelle's glance. The maid knew exactly what she was feeling.

"Oh, him? There's little to fear, Giselle. I promise."

Louisa's voice lowered and she moved her eyebrows up and down suggestively. Giselle stared at her. So did Isabelle, although she had to stop her infernal fidgeting to do so.

"Remember the wedding, Giselle, when you were six? You must remember something."

Oh...she remembered, all right. Mama had made certain Giselle wore her daffodil-yellow frock, complete with a lace pinafore on top. She was very excited, even if she had instructions to stay away from Papa. She didn't know why she'd been told that, for she loved him.

"I recall it, Louisa," she said.

"Then you must remember your cousin, Janelle? Remember how lovely she was in her white gown? It was a wedding gown. She was your stand-in."

Giselle hadn't seen Janelle since, but she still recalled how beautiful Janelle looked. She had kissed Giselle as she left for the town chapel, and called her *"Ma petit duchesse."*

After Janelle had left, Giselle had asked Louisa, "What's a *duchesse?*"

"It's a title, Giselle. You're being married by proxy today. The *Duc* du Berchald has petitioned for and been granted His Majesty's permission for the ceremony. Isn't it exciting? You'll be a member of the Berchald family. Your new title is higher even than your papa's."

"It is?" Giselle couldn't imagine that. Papa was so tall, she barely reached his waist. She had no idea what Louisa meant.

"It's wonderful, Giselle. I can't wait to see Chateau Berchand, and all its riches."

"I can't wed, Louisa. This is stupid. You're wrong, and Papa will stop it."

"Your papa? He doesn't like it, but I assure you, he can't stop the *duc* from marrying you today."

Giselle remembered that day, all right. And how it ended. She'd cried in her new chambers until late into the night. Papa couldn't bear the sight of her anymore. She was a Berchald, and Papa cursed them all.

She looked at those same chamber walls in the daylight, knowing and hating each and every stone. But she had to admit it. Louisa might be right. She *was* being set free.

"You do remember, don't you, Giselle?"

Louisa sat on the edge of the bed and took Giselle's hand. She nodded.

'Then how can you worry? You're the *Duchesse* du Berchald! Even your Papa can't take that away from you. Always remember that."

"What does he look like?" Giselle tried to keep her voice steady.

"Who?"

Isabelle even looked heavenward. "My husband!" She slapped the bedding.

"Who cares how he looks? He's the hereditary Master of His Majesty's Wardrobe. Your position at Versailles is assured, and he's the key to your escape from this prison. Just think of it."

Giselle had never known Louisa to be so vague before. She narrowed her eyes. "Louisa! You'll tell me this instant, or I'll..." The threat ended as Giselle gasped for breath.

"Don't upset yourself, so! Isabelle, assist me!"

Giselle didn't want assistance. She wanted answers. Was he ugly? Was that why he never came to claim his bride? Worse, was he deformed? Was he a simpleton, with an over-large head?

She was gasping for breath, as the women fluffed the pillows behind her, and made her sip at a goblet of wine.

"Forgive me, Giselle. I didn't know how much it mattered to you."

Giselle looked away from the speculative gaze. Of course it mattered. She had dreamed of him, thought of him — when she dared — but she'd never let anyone know. The thought was enough to give her further vapors. Papa hated the Berchalds. It would have been disloyal.

"He's very handsome, Giselle," Louisa said softly. She lifted Giselle's hand and waited until she looked at her. "So much so, that Janelle pouted at him throughout the ceremony, and he was but fifteen then."

Giselle felt her heartbeat quicken at the words. It was everything she dreamt about, like a fairy tale.

"He's very tall. All the Berchalds are tall, Giselle. He's fair, too, lighter even than you. But that's to be expected. They are of Norman descent, after all."

"They are?" Giselle hadn't known that.

"It's nothing to be ashamed of. The Berchalds proudly list their antecedents in the court heraldic lists, and now you'll take your place among them. Just think! It's a new beginning, and you've been a ghost for far too long."

Tall and blonde?

She pictured him in her mind and felt a shiver. Her husband. Etienne Berchald. A man so handsome even Janelle had flirted with him. It was exciting, dangerously so. Giselle closed her eyes and shut out the sight of her stone-walled prison, and ignored the unasked question.

If it was so perfect...why had he never come to claim his bride? Why?

CHAPTER TWO

"He's here! Isn't it exciting, Giselle?"

Giselle had to admit that Louisa's excitement was infectious. Ever since the Berchald family had replied to her papa's summons, she had listened nonstop to excited chatter. Her bedchamber was beginning to look heaven-sent. And if Louisa's emotion was bad, the seamstress was worse.

So much had happened in one week that Giselle could scarcely catch her breath. The *comte* had engaged a seamstress from Paris to clothe her.

From Paris!

Giselle was ecstatic. The *comte* wouldn't allow her to go to her legal family poorly clothed. It was the closest he'd ever come to showing he thought of his only daughter in any way. So, he'd ordered a new trousseau, because his pride was at stake. No nobleman clothed his children poorly. Giselle's mouth opened more than once at the thought of new clothing, even as she'd come to dread the fittings. The seamstress, *Madame* Broussard, had more than once commented on Giselle's fifteen-and-a-half-inch waist as if she wasn't even there.

"The petite *duchesse* will cause a riot in Versailles! The king has an eye for the ladies, he does, especially one as lovely as she. Why...I understand he's looking for another *maitresse en titre,* too."

She and Louisa had laughed, while Giselle huffed in silence. It mattered little to her if the king had an official mistress, or not. Giselle wasn't being outfitted for the king. She was being clothed for her husband, the tall, handsome, blond Etienne.

It had taken what seemed like forever, but now, he arrived!

"It's the *duc?*"

Giselle held in her breath as Isabelle finished hooking the corset.

"I don't believe so," Louisa answered. "He must be near thirty years old by now. The man awaiting you is barely your age, but he's definitely a Berchald."

"How do you know?"

"Please, Giselle, grant me some eyes. The Berchalds are very handsome. And he's definitely that. Isn't he, Isabelle?"

The maid shrugged.

"Let me see him!" Giselle begged. "Please? You've already peeked at him from the balustrade. It's not fair."

"You'll meet with him soon enough."

Isabelle lifted the new day gown as she spoke. Giselle turned to Louisa.

"Oh, please? You can't imagine how much I've longed for this! *S'il vous plait?*"

Giselle put her best innocent, guileless expression on. She knew it had worked when Louisa smiled.

"Very well."

The woman sighed afterward, but Giselle knew it was an act. Louisa would give in. She always did. It was Isabelle who was the tougher one.

"But not until you've finished your toilette. Come, Giselle. You must be perfection, itself. Isabelle and I expect nothing less."

Isabelle had never been so slow!

Giselle watched the mirror as the maid fussed and fidgeted with the folds of the new gown. Minutes passed. Giselle heard every tick of the clock. It was all she could do to keep the agitation from showing. Her hair had been dressed the previous day, and the mass of curls atop her head gave her some much needed height. The white streak along her face was theatrical, and she toyed with asking Louisa if she'd powder her *coiffure* like the *comtesse* sometimes did.

Giselle du Berchald had never looked so spectacular.

The gown was peach-colored satin, and it skimmed atop a mass of yellow lace petticoats. The skirt was slit open from the waist, allowing a froth of yellow to catch the light every time she moved. The sleeves skimmed her arms just to the elbow, where more yellow lace was sewn on. *Madame* Broussard hadn't allowed one bit of excess room in the waist, however. Giselle wasn't sure she could breathe once Louisa took the final stitch and pronounced her ready.

"*Madame* Broussard was right, Giselle," Louisa remarked as she met Giselle's gaze in the looking-glass. "I've never seen anyone to compare. Your waist is small enough for a man to span it with his hands. The *duc* will be pleasantly surprised, won't he, Isabelle?"

Giselle watched as Isabelle simply shrugged, but she knew the woman was pleased. It was in her heightened color.

"Now? Are we finished? *Oui?* Come! We must hurry."

Giselle followed the maid and governess she should have long since outgrown. They were all acting like schoolgirls. Louisa was right, though. It was exciting! Giselle was already having trouble breathing, and she hadn't even seen him yet.

She lifted her hem to keep it off the steps leading to her tower, but she couldn't stop the noise. The satin rustled no matter how tightly she held to it or how slowly she tiptoed. She didn't want to tiptoe, she wanted to run. She wanted to see him right away. Giselle hoped Isabelle wouldn't notice the noise and put a stop to the entire affair.

"Shush."

Giselle stopped moving, and waited as the satin dropped back into place. She was smoothing it down to take the worst of the wrinkles out as she neared. She was also hoping Isabelle wouldn't notice.

"There." Louisa stopped Giselle with a hand to her wrist as they reached the top landing. "We dare not go closer. He's standing by the fireplace. Do you see him?"

She did.

Oh my.

Giselle caught her breath. She'd seen knee breeches on Papa and the manservant. It hadn't been preparation enough. She had no idea a man's legs could be so long or muscular. Nor that his shoulders would be so wide. He looked extremely masculine, and she could only see the back of him!

"Is he handsome enough for you?" Louisa whispered.

"Hush," Isabelle said.

Giselle didn't answer. She couldn't stop looking. She caught her lower lip between her teeth as she looked him over. She could only pray her companions weren't watching her. The queue that grazed his back was definitely blond, a shade or two lighter that hers. His jacket was of dark maroon material, while the tightly fitted breeches on his legs were light green. He looked lean, strong, and very much a man, although she had little to compare him with.

He was also tall.

Good heavens!

Papa walked up to him and spoke, and Giselle's eyes widened when she saw that her papa barely reached the man's chin. Giselle would be a dwarf among such people. She barely ducked in time as the *comte* gestured toward the stairs and they both turned.

In that moment, Giselle saw his face and her heart sent reaction through her. She was afraid she might swoon. Louisa hadn't been specific enough. This man wasn't just handsome, he was beautiful.

"They're sending for you!" Louisa whispered. "Quickly!"

Giselle ran the steps and tripped on some lace, hearing it rip. The first such clothing she'd ever owned, and she'd already ruined it! Isabelle would be upset and she deserved the scolding, but Giselle didn't waste time worrying over that. Her mind was racing with other thoughts

A Berchald was here for her! And if her husband favored this man even slightly, she was a very lucky woman.

They reached her room before the summons came, but it hadn't been enough time to recuperate. Giselle was holding her hands to her cheeks when there was a knock.

"Madame la *Duchesse?"*

The manservant bowed, and Giselle smiled at first Louisa and then Isabelle. The former winked, while Isabelle simply folded her arms and looked strict. Giselle had to admit Isabelle's stance had a calming effect and it was a good thing. She needed to portray a calm, unruffled composure. That is what her father would expect.

Giselle hands trembled as she held her skirts, walking sedately to the receiving hall. She followed the manservant, but not too closely. She spent some time perusing his stocking-covered legs as they walked, sucking in her cheeks as she did so. She had been right in her earlier assumption. She giggled and clapped a hand to her mouth. This manservant wouldn't even compare favorably to the Berchald that was waiting for her.

Her new relative still stood by the fireplace. Giselle's glance went to him just as he turned. And then she dropped her eyes and bit her lip. Oh, how she wished she could whisk away this shyness. It was impossible! She'd never met such a specimen before.

"Monsieur du Berchald? My daughter, Giselle."

Papa came for her, and took her elbow to draw her closer. Of all her new experiences, that contact felt the strangest. She guessed it showed on her face as she neared her relative.

And then she was there, but still unable to look up. Giselle swept into a curtsy, watching the skirts billowing out elegantly. Then she stood to greet him.

Le bon Dieu, *but he's immense!* She barely reached the lace on his jabot, and she dared not look higher.

"This is Giselle?" he asked. "You're certain? She is much too small. This can't be her."

Giselle's welcoming smile dropped and she looked up. He wasn't addressing his words to her. He seemed to be ignoring her completely. That was rude and arrogant of him. As if she could help her size.

"Pardon?"

The *comte* finally said, breaking the silence.

Giselle was very proud of the way her Papa asked that, adding a slight edge to the word. He conveyed everything she wanted to shout at the man before her in one simple word.

"Enchanted, *Madame* la *Duchesse.*"

The man reacted from the rebuke quickly and she watched with wide eyes as he lifted her hand to his lips, although he had to bow in order to reach her.

"Navarre du Berchald. At your service."

His lips touched her hand, and she snatched it away. Her mouth dropped open. She didn't enjoy how gauche and naive she felt, nor the heat that rushed to her cheeks, either. Someone should have warned her. *How dare he be so charming? How dare he have such a deep voice? How dare he have such a lyrical name?*

She longed to stomp her foot and rant the questions, but remembered finally to close her mouth.

It was embarrassing, but it was more than that, too. Giselle dared a glance up at him, and as she did so, she felt the strangest whisper of movement within her.

His nose wasn't small enough to grant him the handsome visage she'd thought at first — for it was quite long and narrow. His skin was dark-toned and his eyebrows were a dark brown. And his eyelashes!

She was stunned into envy at his eyelashes. They were so thick, her own wouldn't compare favorably. When the light touched on them, they resembled small butterflies fluttering about his cheeks. He blinked and moved his glance to her. Eyes the color of a stormy sky met hers and Giselle gasped. She couldn't look away fast enough as another blush heated her cheeks.

She couldn't explain how strange it felt. It was almost like she'd stepped onto an icy spot during her winter walk and fallen without warning.

"*Monsieur* has just been explaining why his brother, the *duc,* couldn't come in person, Giselle," Papa said. "I'm certain you'll find the answer as interesting as I do, won't you, my dear?"

Papa had never spoken like that to her before. There was an insinuation in his tone that she couldn't place. This Navarre heard it, too. She watched Papa pour cognac for himself and drink it, purposely refraining from asking Navarre if he'd like one, too.

Although Navarre stood an arms-length away, she felt him stiffen at the insult.

"My brother, Etienne, would've come, but he's been...indisposed for some time, *Monsieur* le *Comte.*"

"Indisposed?"

Giselle spoke without meaning to, and she wasn't prepared when Navarre looked at her again. She couldn't tear her eyes away, although the sheen of dislike in his was easy to see.

"The *duc* suffered a riding accident when he was twenty-one, *Madame.*"

He bowed, then looked away again.

"A riding accident?" Papa asked. "He's not disabled, is he? We should've been informed earlier, *Monsieur*"

Giselle looked at Papa, seeing him as Navarre was, and she felt the shame. It was as if the emotion he'd always shown her was directed entirely at the man beside her. She was used to it, but it embarrassed her to see it exhibited. She stiffened and turned back to her new relative.

"When am I expected, *Monsieur?*"

She tensed for the strange power of his gaze, and wasn't disappointed. Purplish-blue eyes questioned her, and Giselle's heart pumped more color into her cheeks. She didn't flinch as she lifted her chin. He had no reason for his dislike of her. She wasn't an Antillion. She was a Berchald, just as he was.

He smiled slightly. "When your luggage has been collected, *Madame.*"

Mon Dieu!

Giselle couldn't continue looking at him if she couldn't control the reaction better. Her cry was audible as she looked away. She could only hope he wouldn't guess the cause.

"Chateau Berchand isn't far, *Madame* la *Duchesse,*" he said softly.

"Of course it isn't."

Giselle squirmed in embarrassment as her Papa interrupted rudely.

"It's on the other side of Savignen Valley. Just as it's always been."

She recognized the bitterness that filled his words for what it was. She felt a kinship with Navarre as they both looked to the *comte.*

"I must keep you no longer, *Monsieur.* I'll await my kinswoman outside."

He turned to Giselle, surprising her. She didn't have any experience on how to stop him as he reached for her hand again. She desperately tried to control her breathing, but confined in the dress as she was, all she could do was gasp for air.

"Don't keep me waiting overlong, Giselle."

Oh my! He'd called her Giselle!

She managed to nod as he released her hand and moved away. Her eyes followed him. She had to remember that he wasn't her husband. He wasn't Etienne. But how was she supposed to do that?

"Thank you for your hospitality, *Monsieur* le *Comte.*"

Navarre bowed stiffly to her father, an insult in itself, then he walked out the front door. Silence followed him. Giselle tried to control herself. Something was wrong. She was experiencing tremors. She had to stop the reaction. But how? She was still fighting her own pulse when her papa spoke.

"If this Etienne is disabled, you are to return home, Giselle. At once. Do you understand? The wedding will be annulled at once. At once, do you hear?"

Giselle caught herself almost nodding and saying 'Yes, Papa,' like she'd always done, but something stopped her. She knew what it was, too. It was the man awaiting her outside.

"This isn't my home, *Monsieur* le *Comte* d'Antillion. It's a surprise that you would say so, for it hasn't been for some time."

She curtsied formally to him, and felt sudden strength filling her. Louisa was right — she was free.

"Good-bye, *Monsieur le Comte.*"

She walked to the stairs, vaguely surprised that he had no reply, and that she had been so brave. She climbed the first flight sedately, but was racing them before she reached the chambers. And that was stupid. She was out of breath.

"Well?" Louisa asked.

"Well...what?"

"I saw how you acted. Come. You have to tell us. We're on tenterhooks, aren't we, Isabelle?"

Isabelle simply shrugged, and Louisa tossed her hands. "I will not tolerate this attitude. I want to know what you think, and I want to know now."

Giselle giggled, and it felt strange, too. Everything did. "I find this Navarre large, rude, overpowering…and extremely handsome. Does that make you happy?"

"Only if I get to see your face when you meet the *duc.*"

Louisa clapped her hands, as if she were responsible for the turn of events.

"As I recall, Etienne is even paler than Navarre. His hair is lighter. He is taller, too."

"No one could be taller," Giselle replied. "I'm dwarfed, I tell you. I won't stand for it."

"Oh, Giselle." Louisa chuckled. "As if he could change his size. You say the silliest things, sometimes."

She was right, and Giselle had thought much the same thing already.

"Hurry. Take up your *pelisse,* so you don't keep him waiting."

Isabelle assisted her with the light shawl, fashioned in the same yellow shade as her petticoats. Giselle watched her image in the mirror as the maid draped it over her shoulders. Then, she met the women's eyes. They both had the strangest smile on their faces.

"Aren't you coming?"

"Isabelle and I will follow with your clothing. You are a married woman. You've no need for a chaperon. We were informed that this Navarre came in a light chaise, and we wouldn't have fit, anyway. He's a nobleman, Giselle. Don't fret. You'll be well taken care of."

Giselle's eyes went wide.

"What? I have to travel with him…alone? I can't! You don't know—" She caught her tongue, before she spilled it. They didn't know how much he affected her.

"We don't know what?"

"I've never done this. How can you ask it of me?"

"Giselle." Louisa clucked her tongue.

"I can't do it, Louisa. I can't. What will I speak of?"

"Say nothing. Let him talk. That's what men enjoy most, isn't it, Isabelle?"

Giselle had never known Isabelle to have a man, so it was no surprise that the maid simply lifted her eyebrows and said nothing. Oh...Giselle was so woefully ignorant of such things. How could she possibly ride beside this Navarre? The sight of him stole her breath and gave her shivers. Being alone with him would be more than she could imagine.

"Go, Giselle. Enjoy your first ride. It's the first of many new experiences. You must tell me all about it the moment you arrive at the castle. Just think! You're riding in a new chaise, wearing a beautiful new dress with a handsome escort at your side. And before you go to sleep tonight, you'll meet your husband, Etienne. Isn't it exciting?"

Giselle's expression answered for her. She knew how worried she looked, for she glimpsed herself in the mirror before she left.

Louisa was right. Again. Giselle counseled herself as retraced her steps down the staircases. It is a new experience. She should feel excited and a little fearful. There's nothing wrong with that. Dare she tell this Navarre that she'd never traveled before? How could she? She couldn't even look at him. How could she speak with him?

Her chin rose.

She wouldn't tell him. It couldn't be that frightening, and if it was, it couldn't last long. And...she was going to meet her husband!

Giselle's heart skipped a beat as she neared the doors. That wasn't a good sign. Then she passed the *Major Domo,* and walked out and into such sunshine, her eyes squinted. And there was Navarre, standing beside one of his horses, stroking the animal's nose. Giselle gulped. He had a very large horse. Giselle would have been terrified, for it was so very large in comparison to her.

Oh...why wasn't she tall like Isabelle? She'd rather be statuesque, instead of tiny. It couldn't be helped. Giselle walked down the steps, across a red carpet, and approached Navarre.

"Ah. There you are. Come. Allow me to help you up," he said.

Giselle eyed him warily as he walked to the half-open door of the open carriage. *Help me up?*

"Have you no parasol? I'm afraid your skin won't last long in the sun." He looked around. "Perhaps you should send for one. Have you a maid?"

Giselle nodded and watched as he sent a servant off on the errand. She felt even more foolish. She should have thought of a parasol before she came down.

"You don't deliberately whiten your skin, do you, Giselle? I've heard of women who do, and it's a dangerous beauty secret. Come. I won't harm you."

Giselle longed to say something to his chatter, but she was afraid her voice wouldn't work. It had something to do with the immense hands reaching for her.

"You're very small. I'm not certain what Etienne will say about that. We're not used to such women. I'm afraid you'll break at any moment."

His hands easily encircled her waist, and Giselle couldn't help blushing. It was too intimate, but she hadn't any resource to tell him so. He lifted her high into the air and onto the narrow bench. *Oh my!* Her skirts made it even more strange. She'd never had such a volume of material about her. It made it difficult to feel the structure beneath her. It was also high in the air. She shut her eyes.

If I fall....

The vehicle swayed. Giselle squealed in terror and her eyes flew open.

"Giselle?"

He spoke softly, and glanced to where she'd gripped his arm. It was simply Navarre stepping in that had made the vehicle sway. Giselle waited for her heart to calm, the relief was so strong, she felt giddy.

"What is it?"

Giselle couldn't answer. He was too close. She could see muscles in his thighs! They were clearly defined through the green satin breeches. She'd never seen any man to compare. Oh. *This was terrible.* She had to concentrate to unlock her fingers from his arm as she studiously avoided looking anywhere near him.

"You're frightened? Don't be. It's not a terrible thing to be a Berchald. You'll see. Look. Here's your maid with your parasol."

Giselle looked down at Louisa, terrified again. The woman was so far below them.

"Enjoy your drive, Giselle."

The governess squeezed Giselle's hand. She tried to smile in reply, but it felt more like a grimace. Beside her, she heard Navarre cluck his tongue, and Giselle grabbed the rail beside her in surprise. The chateau moved past in a blur, and she tightened her grip. Perhaps, if she looked above the horse's head instead of at the ground, it wouldn't seem so fast.

"Is something wrong, Giselle?"

Her white knuckles gave her away, or perhaps it was the short gasps of breath she was taking. Giselle couldn't believe how stupid she must look. She shook her head and focused her gaze on a spot between the horse's ears. That seemed safe enough.

"This is the very latest cabriolet. I bought it in Paris only two months ago. It's very smooth and fast. You'll enjoy the ride, I think."

They'd reached the end of the driveway. Before passing through the stone gate posts, Giselle forced herself to be brave enough to turn for a last glimpse of the chateau. It had such beautiful white stone and such aesthetically pleasing architecture. She'd almost forgotten how marvelous Antilli looked.

It was a shame it was cold and harsh inside.

She turned back around just as Navarre flicked the reins. She was proud of the fact that she kept her squeal inside as the horse increased its stride. She'd never moved so fast before — or been so far off the ground. It felt like they were flying.

"I told you it was enjoyable," Navarre said from beside her. "How do you think it compares?"

"To what?"

He shook his head. Giselle saw the motion of his shadow on the footrest before them.

"With other carriages. I told you it was fast."

"I'm no judge. I-I've never ridden before, nor have I been aboard a...what did you call it? A cabriolet?"

"No!"

The word showed his astonishment, as did his shadow. She watched the movement of it, equal in size to hers due to her parasol.

"Never? I don't believe it. The Antillions are renowned for their excellent stable. I don't understand."

"It's true." Giselle shrugged.

"Why'd they keep you from such a thing? I don't understand."

She shrugged again, and his shadow turned away from hers.

"I suppose it's because of Savignen Valley, isn't it?"

Giselle moved her gaze up from contemplating his shadow on the footrest to the horse's head. She'd been told to allow him to do the talking. That was terrible advice. "Perhaps," she replied.

"If you don't wish to speak of it, I'll understand."

"It isn't that, Na...varre." Her voice caught midway through his name. She didn't dare look to him to see if he heard it. She took a deep breath.

"Why did the *duc* not send for me sooner, Navarre?"

CHAPTER THREE

Giselle was amazed at her own words, and immediately wished them unsaid as she felt him withdraw. Even though they were side-by-side, she felt Navarre pulling away. She dared a glance up at him and watched a nerve in his jaw twitch.

Will he tell me the truth?

Then she wondered how she knew what he was thinking. Giselle turned her attention to the view ahead. There were tiny buds on the tree branches, and the new green of spring grass was everywhere.

"Etienne...keeps his own counsel, Giselle. I'm sorry."

She looked at him and met the purplish-blue gaze she'd been avoiding. He truly looked sorry...and something else. Something incredible. She couldn't believe how aware and alive she felt. She was gloriously attuned to the surroundings, almost aglow. Her eyes widened at the moment his narrowed, and then he licked his lips.

Giselle reeled, her breath caught. Her mind stopped. Of their own volition, her lips parted. All of that was not only mystifying, but it angered him. He cursed, pulled his eyes from hers. Giselle fought the impulse to cover her ears at his words. She'd never heard words such as he used.

She watched the trees at the side of her as he controlled himself, after scooting as far away as she could. It didn't help that the dress didn't move with her, and she simply slid within the confines of the petticoats.

Navarre had finished and silence descended. Giselle listened to his harsh breathing, broken only by the slight creak of the wheels, the horse's occasional snort, and the twittering of birds in the trees. It was an uncomfortable silence, and she didn't know what to say.

She glanced over her shoulder at him. She'd been wrong earlier. His nose wasn't large at all. And that was a dangerous thought.

"Forgive me, Navarre...for speaking as I did," she whispered.

He sighed and looked at her, holding her gaze for a moment before turning back to his driving. "No. I must apologize. And hope you forgive me. I had a story prepared in the event you asked me about him, but I find I cannot lie to you, after all."

She watched as he transferred the reins into one hand.

"Etienne hasn't been the same since the accident. He...hides, you see."

"Hides?" Of all the scenarios she'd created, she hadn't thought of that one.

"I can't even say for certain if you'll meet with him when you arrive. He...keeps his own counsel."

"Oh."

She didn't know what else to say. Perhaps her husband didn't even know she was coming. That was a sobering thought. Perhaps he was disabled to the point her Papa had hinted at. Giselle's heart went out to her husband, hiding in his castle. She'd been doing the same thing.

"Thank you for telling me this, Navarre."

He relaxed beside her. Giselle couldn't tell exactly how — perhaps it was the shift of his shoulders. She smiled. For once, her height was an advantage. She

had the seat against her back, but Navarre was too tall
for it to be of use.

"I've arranged a light supper at the Minot
farmhouse. We'll change horses, and you'll enjoy
Madame Minot's cooking as much as I do, I'm
certain."

After endless meals of porridge, she would enjoy
anything different.

Navarre smiled as he spoke, and she followed the
motion to his eyes before glancing away. He had
incredible eyes. *Perhaps my husband is blessed with
such eyes, too.* Her heart quickened at the thought.

Louisa had said Etienne set Janelle to flirting at the
ceremony with his handsomeness. Giselle had to hold
onto that thought and ignore Navarre's bulk beside
her. That's what she told herself she had to do.

She smelled *Madame* Minot's cooking long before
they reached the farmhouse. She knew Navarre did,
too. It was a delicious aroma, like frying bacon or roast
pork, and she'd thought those smells long forgotten.

"Minot!"

Navarre shouted it as they came into the clearing.
Beside him, Giselle jumped at the noise. She hoped he
wouldn't notice it. People hadn't shouted around her for
years. The door to the home opened, and a woman
almost too large to walk came out. She was followed by
a rail-thin man. Giselle had to look away before they
saw her instant smile.

"*Monsieur* and *Madame* Minot, may I introduce la
Duchesse, Giselle. Etienne's wife."

Giselle turned back to the couple. She noticed that
Madame Minot was staring intently at them. It made
Giselle more self-conscious, and she had to look aside
again.

"Come, Giselle," Navarre continued. "*Madame* Minot
is well-known for her culinary skills, and I'm
famished."

The vehicle swayed again as he got out, and Giselle gripped to the railing until it calmed. Both Minots greeted him warmly, and the sight of his laughing face made her heart flutter strangely. He turned back to her.

Again, his large hands encircled her waist, although this time, he swung her into his arms and walked to the house. Giselle's eyes went wide and her breathing quickened. And he held her for the entire eleven steps! She knew the number. She counted each one. She'd never been touched by any man, let alone carried intimately by one! It was incredible. Amazing. Shocking.

"I couldn't allow your dress to touch the mud, Giselle."

He set her on the porch, explaining although she hadn't said a word. She was incapable of speech. She was trying to erase the memory of the feel of his chest against her breast, and his arms about her body. The seamstress, *Madame* Broussard, hadn't given Giselle enough material to prevent the sensations.

She couldn't raise her face and meet his eyes, because she couldn't stop blushing long enough.

"You're very pretty, *Madame* la *Duchesse.*"

Giselle smiled her thanks to the man who was so much thinner than his wife, it looked absurd.

"She's more than that, Jacques," *Madame* Minot said with a curtsy. "She is *tres belle.*" She motioned them into the house. "Sometimes I think that man of mine is blind."

The table before them seemed to groan under the weight of all the food on it. Navarre led Giselle to a separate table, elegantly covered with fine linen, placed beside a diamond-paned window. Giselle's smile widened and she turned her gaze to the view. She was going to dine...intimately with a *man*?

Oh my. Heavens! Louisa and Isabelle couldn't have foreseen this! Perhaps the sight of the grounds outside would calm the heat she felt rising through her chest and into her cheeks, but she doubted it.

After all, she had Navarre du Berchald as a dining companion.

The main course was roast pork, as she'd suspected, but *Madame* Minot glazed hers with a mixture of sweet and sour Giselle couldn't place. She watched with much interest as Navarre devoured it while she moved pieces of food about her plate.

He caught her watching him. "You don't eat very much, do you, Giselle? Is that how you stay so small?"

"I can't change my size, *Monsieur*,'" she answered in what she hoped was a cool tone. "But, as it happens, I'm quite replete."

It was true. She'd already sampled the first courses *Madame* Minot placed before her, and Navarre was right when he praised her culinary skill. Her *bouillabaisse* stew was exciting to taste, and so were her rolls. Giselle had decided she was tasting nirvana long before the main course was placed before her.

She waited for his reply, unable to look away even if she wished. Navarre lifted his napkin to lips moistened with glaze, and Giselle was amazed to feel the area behind both of her knees tingle. She couldn't prevent the widening of her eyes as he lifted one eyebrow at her words and dropped his napkin to the table.

Such eyes! Such lashes! Merde! She had to cease looking! There was no excuse for such behavior, and it was starting to make a knot form in the base of her throat.

He lowered his gaze then, freeing her to swallow, but it was more of a gulp. The waning sunlight tipped his lashes with gold. Giselle couldn't bear to continue looking, yet was unable to move her glance away.

"You're right, and I shouldn't tease, Giselle." He sighed and looked out the window.

Oh no! That was worse, if there was such a thing!

She found it difficult to follow what he was saying. In profile, he was even more handsome. She hadn't noticed before that his lower lip was so full, but it was obvious now as she watched him speak.

Oh! This was intolerable.

"...Antillions aren't known for their large size, it's just...." He stopped, as if searching for the right words. "You'll see when you meet Esmee. She's almost as tall as I am, but then, we're known for our height. It's something every history book refers to...."

Louisa should've told Giselle more about men. Then again, how could anyone have described this Navarre? What would Louisa have used for a reference? The only men Giselle had seen were menservants, the priest, and Papa. Navarre was from another realm entirely.

There was a faint shading of light brown on his upper lip. It wasn't a mustache, but perhaps the beginning of one. Giselle wondered if it would be noticeable...when he kissed someone.

He turned and caught her looking. Whatever he was saying stopped the moment his eyes met hers. Giselle gasped in dismay and dropped her eyes to her lap. The situation was impossible! She had just met this man, and he was her husband's brother. The *Bon Dieu* would never forgive the train of thought she'd been pursuing! It was evil. Illicit. Sinful.

"Perhaps we should be leaving."

He rose from his chair and she nodded. She was close to tears and shivering with the effort of stopping them. The peach of her dress blurred as she looked down at it.

"Have you no wrap, Giselle?"

She couldn't answer. He held out his hand. Any words would give her away. She shook her head.

"It'll be colder now, but I have blankets. Come, or we'll be late at the castle."

His hand was very warm. Giselle held to it briefly, releasing him the moment she stood, but she couldn't erase the memory as easily. She was being plagued with the new experiences, and she wasn't ready! It was worse than intolerable. And he would probably carry her back to his cabriolet! She didn't know if she could stand it, and he didn't give her any acclimate herself to it, either.

"Giselle, please. The horse grows restless."

He stood in the mud with his arms out toward her, but her feet wouldn't cooperate. Her entire body trembled with just the thought...of his touch. The intimacy of his arms about her. She didn't even dare look at him.

"I won't harm you."

Giselle raised her eyes and met his gaze. She felt the blood drain from her face, watched dark spots dance before her eyes, and held her breath. She couldn't faint! Not now. That would be more ignominious than she could imagine.

Giselle?"

She caught her lower lips between her teeth and walked forward two steps and into his arms. Navarre lifted her differently this time, cradled against his chest, while her arms wrapped about his neck for security. He smelled wondrous, too. How could she have missed that, earlier? Different from anything she'd experienced before. It was like sunshine on spring meadows, combined with the scent of the outdoor gardens after a rain shower...no. Perhaps it was more like the lingering smell of a warm fire combined with Savignen wine...no. That wasn't even the smell. She didn't know what it was.

He shifted her, as if adjusting her weight. Giselle squeezed her eyes shut. The arm beneath her knees felt like it was touching on bare flesh, and the feel of his hard, warm chest against her side was making her dizzy.

The walk seemed to take forever, the length to the carriage triple what it had been. Much more than the eleven steps from before. She wasn't trembling anymore, it had turned to shudders, and her hands gripped to the fabric of his jacket. The feel of the material sent gooseflesh roving her limbs.

"It's all right, Giselle. You're safe. Such a frightened little thing you are."

He whispered the words against her ear. Heat touched her neck, instantly warming and tickling, and then something more happened…something insidious and strange. A tingling sparked into being somewhere in her lower belly, and began radiating outward from there. Giselle tightened every limb to halt whatever the sensation was. She had them locked when she felt him place her on the wood of the carriage seat. It took an act of will to release her fingers from his jacket. Giselle moved first one hand to the metal railing, and then the other, grateful for the chill against her palm.

"Here, *Madame.*"

Monsieur Minot handed up a thick woven blanket, and Giselle watched her hands reach for it, and then somehow wrap it about herself. She didn't know what was wrong with her. Her hands didn't even feel like her own. Nor did the blanket help much. Her body was too warm. Too aware. Too…alert. Nothing felt cold. Everything about this odd commotion within her felt amazing. Intoxicating. Addictive.

"You really haven't ridden before, have you? Forgive me if it frightens you so. I can go slower if you like." Navarre offered it from his side of the carriage.

Slower? Oh no! Oh…yes!

What was she thinking? The experience of driving with Navarre was emblazoned on her senses. She didn't dare ask him to go slower…and make it last longer.

"*Non.* No. I'm fine, Navarre. Tru…ly."

She turned to reassure him, but, from her vantage point a few inches above his head, the intent went awry. Her voice dropped. He'd placed his hat back on, and the shadow of the brim fell to his lips. And her heart reacted with a leap.

She almost slapped a hand there. Oh, heavens! This was impossible! But it couldn't be all her fault. It was unfair for any man to be so comely. He smiled. Giselle gasped and turned away so quickly, it was probably insulting.

"It was a pleasure to serve you, *Madame* la *Duchesse.*"

Both Minots stood on her side of the carriage, and she smiled at them numbly. It felt like her mouth had joined the fray, and belonged to someone else, as well.

"The pleasure was mine," Giselle replied in a voice that trembled. "You are an extraordinary cook, *Madame.*"

The cabriolet swayed as Navarre got in. Giselle started, but didn't jump that time. The only reaction was the white knuckles on her hands. She was rather proud of that.

"You must visit again." *Monsieur* Minot lifted his hand in farewell.

"I'll make certain and bring her." Navarre flicked the reins. "Until then."

No. Oh, no.

He couldn't bring her again. She'd refuse. She couldn't let herself be this close to him ever again. She was a married woman, journeying to her husband. And this Navarre was far too attractive to her. Being near him was creating more than shivers. She couldn't allow this again. Everything on her body was sending a warning.

"Look, Giselle,"

Navarre spoke from beside her, interrupting her thoughts. She started and then looked out at where he was pointing. Savignen Valley. Her dowry.

"Isn't it beautiful? I always think so, especially so when dawn is just breaking. You can see that, can't you? I can understand the *comte's* hatred for us better each time I look at it."

"You know of his...feelings?" she stammered.

He chuckled. "All of France knows of his displeasure. He makes no secret of it. He's even tried to draw Jean-Claude into a duel over it — more than once."

"Jean-Claude?"

Giselle put her nose under the blanket for warmth. It was much colder, and she shivered. She wondered how Navarre could sit there so calmly without even a rug over his legs. He had only his hose and the green satin breeches to keep him warm....

Oh dear! She had to stop her thoughts!

"My brother, Jean-Claude, attends to court functions in Versailles. He's one of the king's favorite courtiers. Hopefully, you'll never—"

He stopped abruptly. Giselle waited, but he was silent. Navarre pulled on the reins, and the horse stopped.

"See those lights?"

He pointed again. Giselle forced herself to look beyond how his sleeve defined the strength in the arm before her. But she'd known he was strong. She'd felt it as he carried her.

Oh dear! She had to concentrate on where he pointed. It wasn't an easy task.

"That's the Chateau Berchand. We'll be there within the hour. Hold these."

He held the reins out for her. Giselle gripped the leather strips in both hands, trembling visibly. Luckily, the horse didn't move, for Giselle was woefully ignorant of how reins worked.

She watched Navarre strike flint and light candles in two glass boxes on either side of the carriage. The glow shed some light on the road, demonstrating how dark it had gotten. Giselle would have been petrified with fear if she were alone.

"Are we late?" She whispered it as the vehicle swayed again with his entrance.

"Not so much that anyone will worry."

He smiled down at her. Time stood still. The newly lit lanterns made it more than obvious. The light glinted on teeth. Of course, he would have the most stunning smile she'd ever seen, too. She would simply have to admit that to herself and then let it go, as well.

"What of my maid, Isabelle? And...my governess? They'll worry."

He chuckled and took the reins from her hands. 'They're behind us. The baggage wagon can't travel fast enough to overtake us. May I share your cover?"

Her heart stopped again. Her eyes went to their fullest, and he probably heard the gasp. Share the blanket? Together? *Oh...my!* She had yet to stifle how it felt when his fingers had touched hers while taking the reins! He kept up a running chatter, as if unaware of her reaction.

"*Madame* Minot is a great cook, isn't she?" he asked. "Not that our own Chef Aaron doesn't compare. Esmee would have my tongue for denigrating words. Still, I grow tired of lengthy courses rich with sauce. Don't you?"

Perhaps he was rambling to put her at ease. It was wasted breath. The feel of his leg against hers, even through her skirts, was stopping her thoughts, and giving her different ones.

Giselle started praying then, silently and in earnest. She couldn't ignore the effect this Navarre had on her any longer. It was unwise and unprecedented. She hoped Etienne's presence would be equally stimulating.

Stimulating?

Giselle reeled in place. She'd learned that particular word from a novel Louisa had sneaked in for her to read. Now, she knew what it meant. There was a feeling of expectancy, combined with...*mercy!* Could this be sensual attraction?

Sensual? Attraction?

Oh. This was bad. She should banish the thoughts! But...how?

"I paid the Minots well to provide for your servants," he continued. "Tell me, Giselle, why is it that you employ a governess? Aren't you too old for one?"

"I...I...." She was shaking too much to answer.

"You're cold! Here, move closer. I'll warm you."

Oh no! He can't possibly mean...

He started the horse moving with one arm, and Giselle was jolted against his side. And then she was held there by his other arm. It wasn't remotely cold. Her blushes overheated and frightened as she landed into the space beneath his shoulder. She couldn't stop the urge to snuggle and closed her eyes. It was akin to a dream. And even if it was sinful, it was wonderful, too.

CHAPTER FOUR

"Wake up, Giselle. We're at the gates."

She barely resisted the urge to giggle. She wasn't sleeping. She was existing, letting many wild thoughts fill her mind. One thing was certain. The next time she saw a priest, she'd have something to confess. She wondered what the penance would be.

Giselle sat up and stretched, although the gown left little room for the move. A stone gatehouse loomed ahead. Although there were two lamps on either side of the road, it was hard to see color, especially against the mass of light that was glowing from the castle yard inside.

"Am I presentable, Navarre?"

Giselle touched her curls and wondered how much damage she'd done as she snuggled against his side. The memory made her warm all over, until there wasn't anything cold. Anywhere. Perhaps that would be all she had to keep her warm in the future. That was a sobering thought.

He looked down at her, his eyes unfathomable in the shadow of his hat brim. She raised her chin.

"You mustn't ask that of me, Giselle. I've been trying to control myself all during this trip. I still don't know how I managed."

He turned away, and Giselle's eyes went wide. Her mouth followed. He couldn't have just said—? He couldn't possibly mean—? The waist of her new gown

wasn't the only tight part. The bodice was restricting all
the feeling hammering through it. Amazement followed
surprise as emotion filled her. Razed her. Tossed her
senses into the air somewhere so they could burst free.
It was brightness. Light. Joy. *Heavens!*

Light flooded the courtyard they entered. A mass of
servants surrounded the cabriolet on both sides. It
would have been frightening, but she was beyond that
at the moment. She was doing her best to control the
giddiness.

"*Monsieur* Navarre! Finally! You've arrived! This
then, is *Madame* la *Duchesse?*"

A groom opened the half-door and held out his hand
for her. Giselle looked at it warily, ignoring the woman
who'd spoken. It was Navarre who answered.

"*Oui,* Esmee. I've brought Giselle du Berchald.
Pardon, my good man. Allow me."

Navarre moved the groom aside and reached for her.
Giselle hadn't even felt the sway of the vehicle as he'd
left it. This time she leaned for him, and gasped as his
hands encircled her waist. The contact sparked. And
then it heated. Rapidly.

Her feet touched ground, but everything else was
soaring. She caught his eye for a moment and the push
her heart gave stunned and horrified. And thrilled. And
then she was facing a carpet stretched out for them.
Giselle placed her hand on Navarre's outstretched arm
as Louisa had instructed. Her hand trembled, while the
arm beneath her fingers hardened somehow.

Oh my! Louisa hadn't said a word about any of this!

"*Madame?*" the woman said. "I'm Esmee Denton.
The Blue Salon has been prepared for your arrival. Will
you follow me?"

Their sister had a different surname? Giselle
pondered it during the walk to the salon, keeping her
mind blanked to the arm beneath her fingers. It was
impossible! But somehow she must try. Each finger
thrilled to every nuance. The fabric of his jacket felt

sensual...and the arm beneath! *Merde!* She'd known Navarre was strong. Now she was getting another sample of just how strong. And it was heavenly.

No. It was wrong.

She must control her thoughts. Esmee was safe. His sister had a different surname. She was in apparent control of the estate. And she was extremely tall. Even Giselle's papa would have to look up at the woman. Giselle was dwarfed.

"We have champagne, tea, and several pastries that Chef Aaron has prepared for your arrival," Esmee added.

Giselle stood at the door, considering a white-and-blue striped settee and two chairs before stepping forward and settling into a chair. There was a mirror opposite her, taking up a large portion of the wall. She glanced at it, gratified that her hair was still presentable, although a few wisps of white hair had escaped and trailed down one cheek. It was attractive, but it looked contrived, even to her.

"Champagne, please."

Giselle couldn't force another bite of food past her lips, but a bit of champagne might help...if it didn't add to the effervescent sensation overtaking her entire body. She felt strange. Other-worldly. As if her skin was the only thing keeping her from floating away. It was incredible. Wondrous. Enervating. And Navarre was at the root of it.

She forced herself not to look at him.

"This vintage comes from Savignen, circa 1736. We felt it was appropriate, *Madame.*"

Esmee's voice was warm and welcoming. It appeared she was doing everything she could to be charming. Giselle inclined her head, waiting for the other woman to sit. She was beginning to remind Giselle of Isabelle.

"Why is that?"

Giselle lifted the glass to her lips and immediately felt the tension in the room. Despite her every effort, she exchanged glances with Navarre, and instantly she knew. *Of course!* That was the year of the marriage and their acquisition of Savignen Valley.

"Please. You must call me Giselle, *Madame* Denton."

The woman sighed in relief. *"Tres bien.* Call me Esmee. I'll accept no other name from you...Giselle."

Giselle watched her through the side of her wineglass. Esmee didn't favor Navarre much. Her hair was so blonde it looked powdered. Her eyes looked light blue, but Giselle couldn't be sure. Esmee caught her studying her, and Giselle had to look away.

Navarre sat in the other chair, and she glanced at him for the barest instant. She couldn't stand to look any longer.

She continued perusing the room. It was safer.

The salon had floor-to-ceiling bookshelves beside the fireplace that contained several slim volumes. The fireplace was of black marble — very effective against the blue-flecked fabric lining the walls. There were two long windows stretching upward to split the room. Giselle guessed that even if Navarre stood beside them, the windows might be taller. The drapes on either side were a darker blue than the rest of the room, and puddled onto the floor.

It was warm, inviting, and feminine. The table behind Navarre was beautifully carved, and flowers graced the top. The arrangement was very artistic. Several miniatures hung on the walls, but Giselle couldn't tell the subject matter from where she sat.

And then she did it. She couldn't prevent the pull of Navarre. Giselle gasped when she met his gaze and couldn't move. His eyes were no longer purplish blue, they were the color of storm-filled skies.

"Our aunt, the dowager *duchesse,* is responsible for decorating the Blue Salon, Giselle," Esmee said. "She had a hand in furnishing much of the castle, didn't she, Navarre?"

He shrugged and Giselle couldn't pull her eyes away.

"She looks forward to meeting you, Giselle. We all do. There hasn't been a new face for so long, I can't tell you how exciting it all is...."

Her voice could've been the buzzing of an insect for all the attention Giselle was paying. Navarre had said he'd controlled himself during the ride? Oh my! The words still thrilled. Stunned.

She watched him lift his champagne flute to his lips. Giselle swallowed with him, although she was simply gaining time. Not once did he even blink.

"Perhaps you'd like to see your chambers, Giselle? Giselle?"

"The trip was most...exhausting, Esmee."

Navarre turned from Giselle and answered for her. Giselle watched him. *Exhausting? No!* It was exhilarating! Amazing! Exciting!

"In that event, I should allow Giselle to retire. Giselle?"

Giselle forced her head to tilt toward the taller woman. "Thank you, Esmee. I would appreciate it immensely if I could be shown to my...bedchamber."

She blushed and looked down at her hands. The last word came out in a whisper, and Navarre choked on his drink. Perhaps she should seek a priest and ask penance before going to bed, but then she wouldn't be able to pursue her thoughts before she slept.

And that idea shocked her even more.

"Of course, Giselle."

Esmee clapped her hands, and a woman in a long black dress entered the room. She must've been waiting right outside the door. Giselle recognized her uniform as that of head housekeeper, just like the one at Chateau Antilli.

"*Madame* Dessard? The *duchesse,* Giselle. Please have her shown to her rooms."

Esmee dismissed the woman with a wave of her hand. Giselle wondered how well Esmee would take it when she was replaced as chatelaine of the Castle.

"If you'll follow me, *Madame* la *Duchesse*?" *Madame* Dessard asked.

Giselle said good night to them, but didn't dare glance anywhere near Navarre. As she left the room, she realized he was right. She was exhausted. The day contained more exercise and excitement than she normally saw in a year.

She waited at the bottom of the staircase for her weakness to fade. By the time she started up, *Madame* Dessard was near at the top.

Giselle slid her hand along the polished wood of the banister as she climbed. Her legs felt like lead, and her muscles like gruel. She hoped her rooms were on the second floor. If she had to talk farther, she might need assistance. It was an uncomfortable reminder of her frailty.

"*Madame* is well?" *Madame* Dessard came back down the stairs toward her. "You are weak, *Madame?* Wait one moment. I'll send for Navarre."

Oh no!

The thought of having him carry her up the stairs gave her needed impetus, and she reached the landing easily. If it hadn't been for the sconces high on the walls, the hall would've been black. As it was, Giselle was grateful *Madame* Dessard still escorted her.

The main rooms of Chateau Antilli were large, but the ceilings in Berchand were even higher. Giselle craned her neck to look up and still couldn't make out their height. A door loomed before them, taller than two of Navarre. It seemed like the entire home was built for giants.

Madame Dessard knocked, and they waited.

"*Madame* la *Duchesse,* we've been expecting you."

A young woman answered and almost fell over with the depth of her curtsy. Giselle hid a smile, and then forgot all about her at the span of space before her. The room was dark. Grim. It made her feel even more small and insignificant. Giselle walked in slowly, waiting for the impression to fade. When it didn't by the time she'd reached the center, her spirits lowered further. Perhaps it was because it was night, but the candelabra on the table barely threw enough light to see the size of the bed.

Giselle's gasp of surprise was drowned out by the housekeeper's explanation to the maid. Giselle ignored both of them. The bed was another monstrosity of immense proportions. Either it was the largest structure she'd ever seen, or it just looked that way because it was several steps above the floor, on its own platform.

The headboard seemed built for giants, too, because it ended in the darkness above the level of the light. Giselle followed the maroon shaded drapes on either side of the bed to the top of the headboard where they disappeared somewhere in the gloom.

"Your wardrobe has been arriving daily, *Madame.*" The housekeeper bowed as she left. "This is Gerty. She'll assist you until your own maid arrives. I'm certain you'll be comfortable, but, if you need anything, the bell is here." *Madame* Dessard walked to one side of the bed and showed Giselle the cord.

"*Merci.*"

Giselle watched the door shut, then she slid down a bed post to the edge of the partition on which the bed sat. The room overwhelmed her. The entire experience was beginning to, and she wished Louisa was here. She would've helped dispel the depressive atmosphere of the room.

"Would you like a bath before bed, *Madame,* or shall I order one for the morning?" Gerty approached where Giselle leaned against the post.

"The morning will do."

"Very good, *Madame.* May I unhook you? I'm certain *Madame* would be more comfortable in bed, *non?*"

Giselle longed to tell the girl that it was too much effort. Too much had happened. She just wanted to be alone, but she knew the gown wasn't going to unhook itself.

"Oh. Just look. You've been sewn into this. No wonder there's few wrinkles. There's some that would call this wasteful, but not me. I've got more to do than worry myself over the ways of the nobility. It's no problem, either. I've got my sewing-knife right here. Don't you worry, we'll have you out of this and into your nightclothes immediately, just you see."

Giselle leaned forward and let the girl unpick Isabelle's stitches.

"*Madame* is very petite. It'll be a pleasure to see *Madame* gowned. And such gowns! We didn't believe anyone could have such a tiny waist. The entire staff...."

Giselle raised her hands to her temples as the girl kept speaking. Finally, the bodice was opened and shed, and then came the skirts and then the corset. Giselle had forgotten how wonderful it felt to be able to take a deep breath again.

Gerty held out a wispy nightgown and Giselle nodded. She longed to say that it didn't matter, but the girl didn't need any encouragement to continue her prattle. Giselle watched in the mirror as her new maid combed out all the curls and braided her hair loosely. She looked as pale and drawn as she felt. Louisa had said Giselle looked like a ghost, and right now, she'd have to agree.

Giselle sat at the vanity table as Gerty walked over to her bedside, climbed the partition and lit a lone candle. The maid was going to take the candelabra with her, and Giselle nearly cried out to stop her. She'd never slept alone. She'd always had Louisa and Isabelle in their rooms beside hers. She would be isolated and so alone in that huge bed. Everything was strange. Her bed at Antilli was against a stone wall. She always slept with that at her back. She would feel unprotected in the monstrosity they'd given her.

"The *duc* is just beyond this door, *Madame*. It's usually kept locked, but we thought it—I can lock it if you like."

Giselle looked at the tall door and shook her head. If she dared to lock that door, the staff would spend endless hours gossiping about it. That much, she knew.

"That's not necessary, Gerty. You've been most efficient. *Merci.*"

The maid dropped another curtsy and left, and the light seemed to slide right out the door with her. Silence descended on the gloom of her new room, and Giselle looked to the ceiling again. She had time to say her prayers. She wondered where it would feel safest to kneel.

She told herself she was being ridiculous. It was just another bedroom — a bit large and dark, but just another room. She stood, and was walking toward her dressing table when angry voices came from the connecting door. One sounded like Navarre.

"I told you meddling fools I'll have no....!"

It was like Navarre, but not quite. By the sound she heard, the door wasn't completely shut. Giselle guessed the staff had left it that way on purpose.

She stood close to the door, holding her breath, as she realized the man who had spoken had to be Etienne. Her husband.

"...had to bring her here! I had no other choice. You should count your blessings she's as lovely as she is."

Now...that voice was definitely Navarre, she thought with a smile.

"Lovely? What do you know of it?"

Giselle heard glass breaking, cursing, and then someone sobbing.

"Etienne, if you'd listen—"

"Listen? You're all fools! And she can go to hell with the rest of you!"

Something struck the door, sending it against Giselle's nose. Tears started in her eyes at the shock.

He threw something at the door! As if he knew I was listening!

She turned to run to the bed but her toes caught in the hem of the nightgown, and she fell, stifling a squeal. And a moment later there was another slamming sound in the other room. Giselle didn't wait. It didn't matter how monstrous and strange her new bed was. It was safer than staying there.

CHAPTER FIVE

The connecting door was open when Giselle woke the next morning. She blinked to clear her eyes and wiped at them as she stared. It had been closed when she huddled beneath the sheet, heavily embroidered with lace. It was also closed when the only witness to her crying had been the sputtering candle.

It wasn't closed now, though. It was even more obvious because of the glow of dawn that came from in there. Giselle stared at the portal, wondering why Etienne's room was so much brighter than her own. It looked like the only light in Giselle's rooms came from the open door.

She wondered why it was open. Had he come into her room while she slept? And what must he think? He probably thought his wife was tiny. She barely showed since she'd slept with her back against the headboard. It was the only place in that massive bed that she felt secure.

Giselle slipped out, her toes flinching at the chilled floor. She was intrigued beyond measure. Why, after seeing his new wife, had he left the door open? There was an open book on the floor just inside his chamber. That must be the object he threw against it the previous night.

The light in the room dazed her, and she shielded her eyes with her hand as she ventured in. The view from his window was spectacular, and she saw Savignen

Valley just over the parapet. Navarre had said
Savignen was best when viewed at dawn. It was true.
And Etienne's windows were open, explaining the chill,
but she was putting off the inevitable. The view wasn't
why she'd come.

Giselle turned slowly back to the bed.

The ducal chambers were larger than hers, and much
brighter. Giselle wondered who had decorated it that
way. Etienne's bedding was of light material, almost
silver, frothy with black lace. Her eyes widened.

He slept front-down on his bed, and he hadn't
changed from his evening clothes. Perhaps he hadn't
changed in some time. For the first time, Giselle looked
carefully at the room and saw that it hadn't been
cleaned in a long time, either. If the windows were
closed, the smell would've been terrible. Wine decanters
lay about, some broken, some staining the carpets with
old wine. She'd never seen such filth before.

Etienne snorted and moved in his sleep. Giselle held
her breath and waited. His breeches could've been
gray, brown, or black. It was hard to tell the original
color from the condition of them. He wore a shirt that
was torn at one sleeve, and there were wine stains
down it.

*Is he a drunkard? Is that the disability no one speaks
about?*

He settled back, turning his face toward her and she
approached the bed slowly. She had to see how he
compared to his brother, Navarre. Etienne may be
taller, but not by much. The legs that stretched to the
floor were shapely, too, although his hose were streaked
with stains.

She stepped up onto the pedestal and held her
breath. He was blond, too, but it was hard to tell if the
lanky strands on the sheets were dark blonde, or as
light as Esmee's, due to the filth of him. He had a fine
golden beard on both cheeks, which narrowed his face. It

didn't look groomed. It looked more like he'd neglected to shave.

He was disgusting, and yet his nose was almost like Navarre's, and the eyelashes were easily as long. It was hard to tell, because they were so blonde. Giselle caught her breath as he stirred, and then she noticed his mouth.

He had the same full lips. That's when she decided he was every bit as handsome as his brother. With a bath, shave and decent clothing, he'd be stunning. Still, she was only guessing. After all, she was a novice at male beauty.

An eye opened, and she caught his glance. The eyes were vivid blue, not purple-blue as she'd expected. Giselle gasped and held her hands across her breast as he blinked, stared, and then blinked again.

And then he scowled, causing sharp lines to furrow down both cheeks. Giselle stepped back quickly, stumbling as she reached the floor. *Oh dear.* She shouldn't have come in. She should've waited. And she definitely should have worn a robe!

Giselle watched his gaze travel over her, revealed in the morning light through her transparent negligee. She covered her breasts with her hands, but that didn't fix anything. And one side of his mouth lifted at her movement.

"What...do you want?"

His voice was rough, deep, and filled with malice. He lifted himself up onto his elbows. His filthy mass of hair was in bad need of care and hung limply to the covers. If it were washed, it would probably be as blonde as Esmee's she decided, stupidly.

She stumbled back another step.

"Get out! Out! I won't be looked at in such a fashion!"

Giselle turned and ran, slamming the door and locking it the instant it shut. She didn't care if the servants talked. Let them. She refused to ever open it again. Etienne was horrid.

And he frightened her.

Giselle ran back to her bed and huddled beneath the covers. She was still there when Louisa came in to wake her for the day.

"Such a to-do your arrival has caused, Giselle," she said. "I swear they talk of nothing but la petite *duchesse* this and la petite *duchesse* that! My, but this is a dreary room. I've never seen such a dungeon. Why would they decorate your chambers in such a heavy fashion?"

Louisa walked to the window. With some effort, she pulled aside the drapes, letting sunshine flood the room. "Well? What do you think of this change in station, Giselle? Isn't it lovely to be free to do what you wish?"

"I hate it," she replied.

Louisa stared at her.

"Are you ill? You've not taken a chill, have you? I was hoping we'd be finished with the doctors. There's no need. You're no invalid. You never were."

"I want to go home." Tears filled Giselle's eyes again, and she couldn't stop them. "Oh, Louisa, I wish I hadn't come. I want to go back. Can you arrange it?"

Louisa climbed onto the bed, sat beside Giselle, and took her hand.

"Giselle, my dearest. I've been with you for over fifteen years. You must never wish for that. Your father kept you imprisoned."

"It's better than here."

"But why? Was your handsome escort rude to you? Did he frighten you?"

"No."

"Then, what?"

"I...I met Etienne." Giselle looked away.

Louisa sighed and released Giselle's hand. "I was hoping to talk to you before you met with him. It's not easy for a man of his abilities and looks to be so disabled. It must be a heavy cross to bear."

"He drinks, Louisa. What disability is there in being a drunkard?"

"Who told you that? I'm surprised at you, Giselle. The man's back was broken. He's an invalid. He cannot move his legs. He hasn't been able to since the accident." Louisa scooted from the bed and stepped down to floor level. "I heard rumors about it when it happened, but I refused to tell the *comte*. *Non*. He would have annulled the marriage."

"What's wrong with that?"

"Giselle, you've been treated unfairly for years, yet defend your family? I knew of Etienne when he married. He charmed everyone. I believe that man still exists. You'll just have to find him."

"You're wrong, Louisa. He's not charming. He's uncouth, cruel and...he frightens me."

"Giselle, surely you're being unfair. You frighten easily, don't you? Is it his fault he tried to claim his husbandly rights, and that you're little more than a child? That's what normally happens when a man and woman marry. I assume that's what we're discussing, *non?*"

Husbandly rights?

Giselle's mouth fell open. Then closed. She couldn't force the words through her lips. She shivered with distaste at the thought of intimacy with the unshaven, unbathed, hateful man in the next room. She'd rather die. Louisa had explained about intimacy, and the emotions Giselle would experience with her husband, but she didn't want that with Etienne.

If it had been Navarre, however....

Le Bon Dieu! She couldn't finish the thought.

"*Madame* is awake?"

Someone knocked on the door. Louisa answered and let in Gerty with a breakfast tray. Giselle didn't say a word as the tray was placed atop her lap. She was speechless at the array. She recognized grape juice and a poached egg, but she'd never seen pastries such as this Chef Aaron made.

"Where's Isabelle?" Giselle asked once Gerty had left.

"Don't avoid the subject with me, Giselle! I'm asking you to give it time. Perhaps you'll get over your fear. Only time will tell."

There was another knock. Louisa went to answer it.

"You ordered a bath, Giselle?"

She'd forgotten it until then. "Oh. Yes. I did. And I'd love a bath."

She watched as a hip bath was set in the middle of the floor. Two maids emptied buckets into it before curtsying and going out for more water.

"Finish your breakfast." Louisa told her. "You've so much to do. I'm certain *Madame* Esmee will give you instructions on the many duties of running the castle."

Giselle didn't want duties. She wanted her chambers back at Antilli. She wanted her safety back. *Still,* she reasoned, *if Etienne was an invalid, that explained his strange movement as he lifted up in bed.* It didn't explain his drunken, filthy condition, though. Nothing did.

Chef Aaron made flaky pastries. Giselle enjoyed as many bites as she could hold. If she continued eating this well, she'd soon grow out of her new clothes.

Isabelle came in next and held open the door as more maids returned with more water. Giselle supposed she had Esmee to thank for such efficiency. She'd never given much thought to running a household. Antilli seemed to run by itself. But she could learn it.

If Etienne was disabled, then he probably misinterpreted her curiosity. That could explain the ugliness of his words. Still, she could hardly tell him the truth, that she was comparing him to his brother.

While Giselle bathed, she tried to ignore the myriad of women intent on duties within the bedchamber. Before she'd finished she decided to unlock the connecting door. After all, she and Etienne were wed. They would have to reach an understanding of some kind. Louisa was right again, and Giselle was getting heartily sick of that.

She would give it time.

Giselle was exhausted before luncheon, and it was getting more and more difficult to disguise it. Esmee took her through the lower rooms, but Giselle was lost before the library, and definitely before they reached the Blue Salon again. The floor of the foyer that split the main castle was checkered with alternating black and white marble tiles. They were beautiful and highly polished, and continued into all the rooms opening from the foyer. The most commonly used rooms were to the right of the hall. There were drawing rooms, three dining rooms, the *duc's* study, and a morning room.

To the left of the hall were the little-used rooms — salons, ballrooms and weapons rooms. In the latter, Giselle was awed to see five full suits of armor on display. The kitchens were to the back of the castle. Giselle found it hard to believe that the chef made such extraordinary pastries in such dark and small surroundings.

"Perhaps you'll ask the *duc* if an expansion to the kitchens can be accomplished, *Madame?* It is a horror I cannot describe trying to reach culinary mastery in such a kitchen. I shouldn't complain, but I need room. I need light! I need more ovens. You do see that, don't you, *Madame?*"

Chef Aaron was taller than Giselle, but he easily accounted for two men with his girth. He was very earnest with his pleas, however.

"I will speak to the *duc* about your needs," Giselle answered.

She should have realized that comment would be gossiped over, and that she'd be open to all sorts of complaints. Giselle was surprised she'd been so naive.

"There aren't enough housemaids, *Madame* la *Duchesse.*" *Madame* Dessard added her list of wants quickly. "I can't clean the rafters without help."

Giselle smiled from her position at the end of the table in one of the small dining rooms. "Hire what is necessary, *Madame* Dessard. See to it that the ducal chambers are given a thorough cleaning, too."

A look of consternation crossed her face. That was almost amusing. Giselle knew the cause. She'd met him that morning.

"Perhaps I can make do without the extra help, *Madame,*" the housekeeper finished.

She was waiting to be excused, but Giselle wasn't about to allow that.

"*Non.* You're to see that the *duc's* rooms are cleaned, *Madame* Dessard…with or without the new help."

"How do you suggest I do that, please?"

Esmee looked to Giselle for suggestions too, and she had none, but she couldn't let them know that.

"I'll have the *duc* moved into my chambers in the meantime," she finally replied.

"Very good, *Madame.*"

The look she gave Giselle was a combination of bemusement and doubt, and she was right. How could Giselle get Etienne moved into her chambers? That news would spread through the staff quickly, she knew that much. She recalled how quickly they learned things back in Antilli. Giselle sighed. There was nothing for it. She'd have to speak with Etienne.

She stood. "What have you arranged for luncheon, Esmee?"

"I have made arrangements for salmon mousse and peaches to be served at half-past two, Giselle. I can have that changed if it's not to your liking."

"Excellent. It sounds delicious."

Giselle realized her luck instantly. Esmee was going to be a dear about it, when Giselle had been expecting dislike, anxiety, or worse, outright anger.

"I am in awe of your ability, Esmee. I will consult with you before I change a thing. I'm...very new to this sort of thing, you understand."

Esmee smiled and it made her look very like Navarre. Giselle had been doing her best to forget him, too. She had to look away.

She hadn't seen him all morning, although she'd kept expecting to, especially when they reached the Blue Salon. Giselle had glanced at the large chair he'd occupied, just to see if her previous reaction was there.

It was.

Perhaps it was better that he hadn't been there. After all, she was a married woman, and had no right thinking of another man.

"You're doing splendidly, Giselle," Esmee replied. "The staff has noticed, too. The castle feels different, already."

She wouldn't be as effusive if she knew how frightened Giselle was of approaching the *duc*. None of them would.

"Would you excuse me please, Esmee? I believe I'll rest in my rooms until luncheon."

Giselle had to ask a servant to direct her and felt like an ignorant fool. How could she have said she'd get Etienne to move? And into her chambers? She was mad to consider it.

Giselle lay in the bed, trying to rest. All she could think of was her dread of Etienne.

"He cannot move, Giselle," she told herself aloud, hoping to banish the fright. "If he's horrid to me, I can run. He cannot."

Isabelle had undressed Giselle from the deep purple morning gown she'd worn, so she could rest. She couldn't rest at all. A dressing gown lay across the bed, and she put her arms into it before tying it haphazardly about her waist. She would speak to Etienne right away, before luncheon. It wouldn't get less frightening if she delayed. It would only get worse.

Giselle stopped at the connecting door and watched her hand shake at the lock. She couldn't do it. He'd throw another book at her! He'd sneer at her again. He'd frighten and scare her.

She sighed, turned around, and went back to the monstrosity of bed.

CHAPTER SIX

There were twelve for dinner. Esmee took Giselle around the drawing room, introducing her to the castle's tenants. There was only one she remembered by sight because he was named Francois, like her brother. She spent most of the time conversing with Etienne' s aunt, the dowager *duchesse,* Mimi.

That, and attempting to ignore Navarre.

"I can't wait to see your portrait in the gallery, Giselle," the dowager *duchesse* said. "The Berchald line has always possessed beauty, but you're even more so. Then again, the Antillions are known for being comely. I was so proud when my husband, the late *duc,* arranged your marriage to Etienne, especially with your dowry."

Giselle murmured something inconsequential, but it didn't matter. Their aunt didn't seem to need encouragement.

"Etienne has angered me greatly during these past years. Why, when he had his coming-out, they came from far and wide just to see him. You can't imagine a more handsome physical specimen than my nephew."

Oh yes, I can, Giselle thought and looked over at Navarre.

He'd attended sup, dressed as if to draw everyone's attention. He wore a burgundy-colored jacket that made the color of his eyes stand out. And he had a small amethyst stone at the throat of his jabot. He'd

completed his ensemble with black silk breeches over
white hose. He was more than handsome, she decided.
He was a delight on the senses. Giselle couldn't have
kept her eyes from him if she tried.

The priest had already counseled her on her duties,
which were owed to her husband. Giselle was to light
three candles to Saint Mary to absolve herself from
further lustful thoughts. Giselle frowned.

It appeared she'd gone to confession too soon.

As if she spoke aloud, Navarre looked at her over the
rim of his wine glass. His eyes were dark purplish blue,
and he narrowed them slightly as he watched her.

"Then there's Jean-Claude," the dowager *duchesse*
continued at Giselle's side. "Such a waste. Almost the
moment my dear brother-in-law was buried, *Madame*
Berchald took him to Versailles, and it has ruined him!
They've turned him into the same kind of noblemen as
themselves. Always the parties with them. Always the
drink, the games of chance, and the trysts! Sometimes,
it goes on for days, I am told! He is just like the others
who are ruining France. Ah! For the old days."

Navarre sipped his wine and held Giselle's gaze
easily.

Why couldn't it have been Navarre?

"The Lord didn't bless me with any children, Giselle,
and I hope you and Etienne will somehow...oh dear. My
mouth does run away with me sometimes. I apologize."

"Pardon?"

Giselle pried her gaze from Navarre and watched the
dowager *duchesse* blush.

"Yes...where was I? Your new family is not so large,
oui? I've heard your own swelled to eight, is it? So
many sons! The *Comte d'Antillion* must be so proud."

Giselle murmured something. It didn't matter. Mimi
just kept speaking.

"Well, there's also Esmee. She was betrothed at
birth to the eldest son of the *Marquis* de Lingue. It
would've been such a union! One, I had a hand in

creating, I must confess, but alas, the boy died from a childbed fever."

"Then who was *Monsieur* Denton?"

"He was a commoner! A member of the bourgeois! Such a misalliance. He was a mere shopkeeper in Paris, a milliner. It was such a shock, and I still shudder to think of the repercussions."

She looked ready to faint. Giselle kept her eyebrows from rising, and was proud of that fact. And while she waited for the dowager *duchesse* to recover, she practiced ignoring Navarre's presence, just as the priest had advised her to do.

"Esmee's rather...large, my dear," the dowager *duchesse* continued. "Not that you'll ever have that problem but she was also too old. Why, she was over twenty when Monsieur Denton offered for her. He was tossed out for his trouble. Their father would never allow a marriage with a tradesman. Esmee had other plans, though. You see. She eloped."

Giselle was engrossed by the story of Esmee's elopement. She wouldn't have dreamed the woman capable of such a thing.

"Of course, *Monsieur* du Berchald, my husband's brother, disowned her completely. Cut her off without a *franc,* if you will. He had no other choice." She shook her head sadly.

I won't look at Navarre. I won't! Nothing can make me.

"She was in luck that Etienne accepted her back when *Monsieur* Denton died. Then again, Etienne was young...just sixteen, and he had other things occupying his life. He had just been wed with you, and received your dower."

With Janelle, you mean, Giselle thought absently. It was a moot point. She had still been wed. She was having a difficult time following the conversation. Navarre had moved from behind the pianoforte to the fireplace. Giselle somehow knew it without looking.

"Now, we are just the remnants of the great Berchald dynasty. What you see before you, is the only family I have. You'd think with so many nephews, I would have more babies to spoil...oh dear. I have done it again."

"What of Na— Um. The others?"

"Jean-Claude is wed almost eight years. That is his wife over there."

The dowager *duchesse* gestured to someone Giselle should have remembered. She looked over and saw a large, unhappy-looking woman. Giselle pitied her the stays of her corset, because she looked pinched in half. Giselle may have a small waist, but her own corset was driving her mad with the scratchiness. It was best to keep her mind off of it.

She was wearing one of her new gowns, complete with panniers to hold the skirts out at the sides. To sit and converse with Aunt Mimi, meant she was barely seated on the edge of her chair. That was the only way her skirts would fit.

"They have a daughter, but alas, no heir. Of course, Jean-Claude would have a better chance of that if he stayed at the castle instead of intriguing with his *Mama.*"

Aunt Mimi touched Giselle hand with the tip of her fan, as if she were telling the latest bit of gossip. And perhaps it was. What did Giselle know of it?

"My maid mentioned that Etienne sent for a bath this afternoon, my dear. I can't tell you how pleased I am about that."

Giselle moved uncomfortably on the chair. It wasn't due to her dress. It was because of her failure. Etienne wasn't sending for a bath because of his wife. She hadn't managed to gain enough courage to even speak with him.

"It would make my heart so proud to see his heir."

Giselle's eyes widened. Her breath stalled. She was amazed to still be seated, numbly listening to the woman's prattling.

"I was so hopeful that he meant to join us this evening. I haven't even seen him since the Christmas Mass, and he was so wrapped up, it could have been anyone. But come, Giselle, my dearest. Dinner is being served."

The dowager *duchesse* stood, surprisingly spry for her age and the amount of foundations she had to be wearing. To Giselle's consternation, she realized that Aunt Mimi hadn't said anything that mattered.

She hadn't said a thing about Navarre.

"I'm to escort you to dinner, Giselle."

She looked sideways and saw black breeches and above those, a wine-colored jacket. Oh my. Her heart started hitting painfully against her corset. She should've known it would be Navarre.

He bowed before her, and Giselle had to consciously stop her knees from knocking together as she looked at his arm. It amazed her that she had that affliction with as many garments as she was wearing. She had to clench her thighs to stop the motion.

Despite everything, the reactions still happened. It was intolerable. No matter how many candles she lit or prayers she said. Navarre still affected her.

"You look very beautiful, Giselle."

He whispered it as they preceded everyone into the medium-sized dining room.

Oh heavens! The instant joy had to be stopped. She must concentrate on her place. She must recall Scripture. Remember her duty. He called her beautiful! There wasn't enough material in the bodice of her dress to hide a blush. Giselle quickly looked at the table, and not at her escort.

There was a sculpture of a castle in the midst of the table, carved from ice. Giselle made herself see it and absorb its appearance. There was a peacock on the table as well, with steam rising through its arrangement of feathers. It was just like Louisa had described to her before at Antilli, and—

...he said I look beautiful!
I must keep my mind on other things!

Navarre led her to the head of the table, and a
manservant held the chair out for her. There was a
servant behind each of the twelve chairs. Giselle had
never been to a dinner like this. She thanked Louisa
and Isabelle for their lectures, then. They'd made
certain she always dressed for her lone supper and had
perfect table manners. She hadn't known what it was
preparation for, but she was grateful to them, now.

Navarre lifted her hand to his lips without touching
it. He didn't have to. His eyes sent messages down the
length of her arm. Giselle only hoped she wasn't
replying with her own.

He pulled out a chair to her left, and Giselle turned to
the other side, wondering what fool had seated him so
close to her. She had to stop it from happening again.
She wasn't to be near him. She wouldn't allow it. He
would just have to be seated at the opposite end that
Etienne left vacant.

Etienne...

That was something which she could concentrate
on. Aunt Mimi had mentioned that Etienne ordered a
bath. Giselle already knew it, though. The servants
were more than willing to tell everything they knew.
Gerty was a font of information while Giselle had
dressed. She had listened carefully while Isabelle looked
sternly at her in the mirror the entire time.

"You've been listening to Aunt Mimi, Giselle,"
Navarre spoke. "I should have warned you first."

Giselle turned to him, trying to look more confident
than she felt.

"She probably gave away all our secrets by now."

He smiled conspiratorially, and Giselle tried to return
it. She did. But the effort died on her face. In the
mellow yellow light from the chandeliers, the shadow
of his lashes reached to his lips. She'd known his were
full and pouty. She'd caught herself wondering what a

kiss from them would feel like. She was ashamed of herself and yet, unable to do a thing about it.

It was mad.

She already knew he was devastating. She knew all of it, yet despite her every effort she was unable to tear her gaze away.

"You mustn't look at me like that, Giselle," he said, and turned away.

There wasn't enough penance for the shame she felt. Giselle immediately turned to face the end of the table, the place Etienne should be. That's when the first hint of self-hate started, growing until it became an ache. Navarre shouldn't have to be the one to point out such things to her.

The first course was served. Giselle toyed with it. The second arrived. She lifted a bite and put it back down. It must be delicious. By the time sorbet arrived to clear their palates, everyone was eating. She barely managed to stay upright in her chair and hold onto her spoon.

"You must eat, Giselle," Navarre whispered. "You look ready to faint."

He motioned to her plate, and Giselle picked up a mouthful of something and put it in her mouth. Swallowed. She tried to stop a tear that slid from one eye but failed. It was more mortification that he saw it. She wondered how she was going to get through the entire meal. She'd never felt so lost and alone.

"Giselle!"

Navarre leaned toward her as if retrieving something he'd dropped. His head touched her skirt and Giselle closed her eyes, feeling two more tears make a path to her mouth. This was impossible. Horrible. She couldn't endure it much longer.

"Must you make this harder for me than it already is?"

He hissed the question at her skirt before sitting back up. She didn't see his movement. She didn't have to.

And for a moment, she thought she'd misheard him. *He couldn't possibly have just said....*

Giselle opened her eyes and was stunned by the deep, almost black color in his as he looked at her.

"Well?" He raised one eyebrow.

"No."

To her horror, the word came out in a giggle. Giselle lifted the napkin to her lips to hide what couldn't possibly be absolute joy. He hadn't been reprimanding her. He'd been asking for his sake. And that must mean...that he felt the same?

Oh sweetness!

Suddenly, the light wasn't mellow at all. It was bright and golden. The peacock tasted wonderful, and everything was superb and sparkled with perfection. She dared not look at him again, though. It was lustful, it was evil.

And it was wonderful, too.

CHAPTER SEVEN

She had been kissed!

Oh wonders! She had been held and kissed, and it wasn't wicked-feeling. It was everything she'd dreamt it would be. Giselle finally admitted it to herself as she passed by the five armored sentinels in the weapons room. It had been Aunt Mimi's fault, actually. It was her idea that Giselle see the portrait gallery, and that Navarre was the perfect one to show it to her.

Giselle had been listening to Jean-Claude's wife, Margot. She couldn't recall what they were discussing when Aunt Mimi entered the drawing room with Esmee.

"There she is," the dowager *duchesse* announced. "I've been describing the Berchald portraits to Giselle earlier, Esmee. Perhaps you could show them to her? It's the perfect time."

"Oh, I couldn't. Please don't ask that of me."

Her answer made Giselle narrow her eyes. Esmee looked very anxious. Over ancestral portraits?

"Then it will have to be Navarre. He knows as much about the artists and periods as anyone. Navarre!"

Giselle's heart began pounding loudly. She wondered if everyone could hear it.

"Yes, dearest aunt? Can I be of service?"

He lifted her hand to his lips, and Giselle's stomach turned. She tried to tell herself that it was the amount of food she'd eaten, but she knew she was fooling herself. It was because he'd kissed his aunt's hand, and she could almost feel it on her own.

"Me?" Navarre looked at Giselle for a moment before he turned back to his aunt. "Why am I being chosen? You know we decided—"

"You're perfect for the task, Navarre. That's why," his aunt interrupted.

Giselle looked from one to the other. Only Margot looked as confused as Giselle was. "I can see them some other time," she offered. "I'm feeling quite tired. Perhaps I'll simply go to my rooms...."

"Oh no, dearest Giselle. I insist. Navarre would love to show them to you. He would."

"Of course," he said. "I'd enjoy showing the *duchesse* where her portrait will hang. I'm honored."

He held out his arm to Giselle. She looked at it, afraid to meet his eyes. He didn't sound honored and pleased. He sounded angry. But everyone was watching, so she accepted his assistance. She placed her hand on his forearm and thought she detected a slight tremble in response. Her heart raced. He turned her and began walking. Two menservants opened the double doors for them and Giselle swept from the room with Navarre. No one said a word.

It wasn't a true portrait gallery. It was a long corridor ending in plateaus of steps. Another set of servants opened the doors for them to enter. Giselle didn't have time to thank them. She was having trouble keeping up with Navarre's strides while he spoke.

"The Berchald family actually goes back to the Capet rulers, when our ancestor was granted the title *marquisat*. No portraits exist from that era. Most of our holdings had to be fought over again during the Hundred Year War. Once the English dogs were defeated and sent back across the channel, King Charles the Seventh bequeathed the titles and holdings of *Duc* du Berchald to this man, Jean-Phillipe."

Navarre held the candelabra aloft so Giselle could better see the painting they'd stopped in front of.

"Painted in 1454, it was restored just before my uncle came into the title, but it won't last much longer, we fear."

Jean-Phillipe was painted strangely. Perhaps it was the dullness of the colors, but it looked flat and one-dimensional to her. The man was blond, but there the resemblance to her guide ended. The paint was rippled at the edges of his clothing and flesh. In some places, it appeared to be missing altogether.

"There is no portrait of the first *duchesse*," Navarre continued. "That tradition didn't begin until the fifth *duc,* also named Jean-Claude like my brother. That portrait is near the stairs. In the meantime..."

Navarre moved her to another picture, mounted on black velvet and Giselle held her breath. It could have been Etienne.

"The second *duc,* also named Etienne. He was killed in a duel, or so the legend goes. He didn't wed, so his title passed to his brother, and my namesake, Navarre."

He walked farther, passing by several paintings Giselle might have wanted to see had the situation been different, then he stopped before a life-sized one.

"He doesn't look much like you," she said.

Navarre's eyes flicked to hers for a moment. Then he looked away. "No, he doesn't."

"What are we doing here, Navarre?" she whispered, amazed at her bravery.

She was watching close enough to see him flinch at the question. She wondered if he would tell her the truth.

"We're viewing portraits, Giselle."

He walked to the first set of stairs, and she was left no course but to follow.

"The *Duchesse* Bertina du Berchald. She was painted in 1602 when she married Jean-Claude. Bertina was sister to the queen and had Spanish ancestry. You probably have noticed the resemblance to Esmee and myself."

Giselle saw it. They had the same nose. The *Duchesse* Bertina had been painted wearing an impossible collar affair. Giselle remembered seeing similar portraits at Antilli.

"Bertina was Jean-Claude's first wife. His second was the beautiful *Comtesse* Raniou, a widow. Her portrait was commissioned through Paris. It's said she was one of the King's mistresses, but that has never been proven. She brought immense royal favor to Jean-Claude, though. It was through his marriage to her that he was awarded the title of Hereditary Master of His Majesty's Wardrobe."

The *Comtesse* Raniou was a beautiful woman, at least for her time. She had a flirtatious smile on her lips and a very full bosom. The *Comtesse* Raniou wasn't blond. She had very dark hair, topped by a tight-fitting caplet, and her face was framed by a high collar, too.

Giselle murmured something, and they walked onto the first landing, four steps up. The staircase was as wide as the corridor. At each landing, more portraits graced the walls.

"This is my great-great-Uncle Pierre. He was more accustomed to spending time at court than attending to family duties, and it shows."

"He...looks a bit like you." Giselle stepped closer.

If it hadn't been for the prominent widow's peak on the subject's forehead, he resembled Navarre greatly. He was dressed in a foppish manner, but very like the man at her side.

"Why did you have to be so lovely, Giselle?"

Navarre spoke so softly, Giselle almost didn't hear him. And then she couldn't believe she had correctly. The image of the long-dead Pierre smiled at her while her eyes widened on his handsomeness.

Giselle dared a glance up at Navarre, holding her breath for the strange connection of his gaze. He wasn't looking at her, however. He was studying the same portrait while a nerve twitched in the side of his jaw. She'd never seen anything as stirring.

He sighed and looked down toward her. Giselle couldn't look away fast enough and spent some time looking at the gilded-wood frame.

"Come, Giselle. Let us get this over with."

He reached for her arm. She skipped to keep up as they passed three more landings filled with paintings until they stopped before Aunt Mimi's portrait.

"My aunt, as you must have guessed..."

He spoke so abruptly it was rude. Giselle wondered what she'd done to make him so angry.

"...and my uncle, the thirteenth *Duc* du Berchald."

He turned her to face a larger-than-life-sized painting. The man was clearly a Berchald, from the light blond hair, to the blue eyes.

"He was the most depraved man in France...unless we count my brother, Jean-Claude."

He released her arm and stepped back while she tried to assimilate what she'd just heard. "Depraved?" Giselle asked.

"Debauched, drunk, immoral. Wicked. Obscene. Need I go on?"

There was an angry, hard note in his voice. It felt like a physical blow. Giselle stepped back from him, bumping against an ornate table as she did so.

"Perhaps you should sit down, Giselle." He pulled out a Louis the Fourteenth chair, and Giselle slid into it. "My uncle nearly bankrupted the family, although we don't look it."

He probably added the last when Giselle looked up at him in astonishment. *Bankrupt?* she wondered. *That's absurd. The castle is filled with luxury!*

"Savignen Valley saved us," he continued. "Actually it was *you* that saved us. Perhaps that was what made me dislike you so much. I was only eight when the marriage took place, and it wasn't to his liking, I assure you. What handsome, strong sixteen-year-old with the world as his feet wishes to be tied to a baby?"

"That's not fair—"

Giselle began, but he interrupted her.

"I was young. Impressionable. Smitten with hero-worship. I listened to every word he cursed you with. He didn't deserve to be forced to wed with you."

"Forced?" Giselle choked on the word. "But I was only six, Navarre. I wasn't even there! How can you say such things to me?"

"You're right, Giselle...God help me."

She didn't see him reach for her, but she didn't have to. She felt the heat of his palms against her waist, and then his arms as they encircled her. And then she was hauled from the chair and held against him. The lace of his jabot scratched against her cheek when he spoke again.

"I cannot finish, Giselle. Forgive me. I can barely stand to be near you. I keep telling myself that you belong to Etienne. And even that fails."

His hand went beneath her chin, lifting her face. Her arms wrapped about his waist, putting the smooth silkiness of his jacket against her bare arms. It cooled the heat spilling through her. His hair fell forward as he bent his head towards her. Giselle closed her eyes, afraid of what he might read, and that it might stop him.

She felt the firm pressure of his lips at her forehead, and held the gasp as he trailed his caress down her nose. A sound escaped as she pursed her lips in expectation. She was unable to help herself.

But he didn't kiss her lips, despite how her entire frame yearned for it. Silently beseeched. Her neck craned upward, but he lifted his head away, sighing loudly enough it covered hers. Giselle opened her eyes to the most severe expression on his face as he watched her.

It made her want to laugh and cry simultaneously.

Then he disentangled her, reaching behind himself to unclasp her hands. Giselle couldn't have done it — she wasn't even aware she still clung to him. She collapsed back into the chair and tried to stop her knees from shaking.

"Forgive me again, Giselle. I didn't bring you here to show you these paintings, or to make love to you."

He turned and walked from her to stand under Aunt Mimi's portrait.

"Then...why are...we here?"

Giselle was hoping to keep her reaction hidden, but her voice gave it away. She watched him frown, and then he swiveled to look at the painting.

"I brought you here to ask you. No! I beg you. To save us again! The only thing standing between my brother, Jean-Claude, and the title.... This is too much to ask of me!"

He slammed a fist into the wall beside Aunt Mimi's portrait. Giselle jumped. Her eyes blurred with unshed tears. She belonged to Etienne. She'd just met Navarre. How was it possible to feel like this in just one day?

"Finish it, Navarre. Tell me."

"Etienne must...." He touched the frame of the painting as if he needed to draw strength from it. "You and Etienne must. There has to be— I'm sorry. I cannot finish it. Esmee will have to."

"Etienne and I must have a son."

Giselle said it for him. When she'd finished they were surrounded by complete silence. He nodded, but he didn't have to. She knew what they expected of her, but they didn't know how difficult it would be. Etienne was horrid. She shuddered now, from the recollection of meeting him. The idea of intimacy with him was revolting to her.

"He wasn't always as he is now," Navarre said, surprising her with how he'd read her thoughts.

"Perhaps...Jean-Claude...won't be as you suspect?"

He laughed, but it was a bitter sound. "You don't believe me?"

"No. It's not that. It's just I...."

She let the words simply end. How was she to tell him of her aversion to the brother, that by his own words, he hero-worshipped?

"Come, Giselle. It's late. I'll see you to your chamber."

He turned to her, and she shook her head. She was watching the floor at his feet. She couldn't face him. Too much was happening. She had no experience with men. Her senses were flying at the memory of Navarre's embrace, and yet reeling with the thought of allowing it to be Etienne. With such a confusing reaction, how could she begin to help the family? How could she begin to try if Navarre touched her again?

"Shall I get your woman?"

He knelt so she could meet his eyes. They were more deep purple than blue in the light and so gentle! They were going to haunt her.

She nodded and watched him go.

Her euphoric state lasted longer than she remembered. She recalled little of the rest of the evening. Louisa chattered at her while she undressed, but Giselle ignored her talk, and barely heard Gerty's unsubtle musings.

Navarre had kissed her! True, it wasn't on the lips, but still...

Giselle wasn't disappointed. She kept remembering what it felt like to be held so tenderly and almost-kissed. She'd wanted him to do it, too. She trembled to recall how it felt. The big bed didn't feel so large and over-powering.

"It is time for your prayers, Giselle."

Isabelle stood beside the bed-platform with Giselle's rosary in her hand. That was when the cloud over Giselle's thoughts evaporated, and everything came into perfect focus.

The candle was too bright as she knelt. Navarre was her brother-in-law. He had embraced her, which was a grave sin, but she was no less guilty, because she had enjoyed it. She had wanted more. Of course, it was normal to be attracted to the first handsome man she met, but that wasn't absolution. She had a duty to her husband.

Navarre was so handsome, though. Just the recollection made her fingers slip on the beads. It was wrong to feel this way. Wicked.

And yet, so wonderful.

Eventually, she finished, and dismissed Isabelle. And then Giselle climbed into the immense bed, covered herself to her chin, and stared with unseeing eyes at the rest of the room. Everything beyond the bed's pedestal was dark and menacing if she thought about it.

She didn't. She kept thinking of Navarre.

CHAPTER EIGHT

The connecting door was open again. Giselle lifted her head from the pillows to look. It wasn't very comforting to think of Etienne coming into her room at night while she slept, to look at her, but he had that right. And more.

She pushed away from the headboard and slid off the mattress. This time she remembered to put on her dressing gown. If Etienne had the right to look at her, she had the same right to see him. She went through the connecting door without thinking of the repercussions. At least he'd bathed. Perhaps he wouldn't be as offensive.

"Have you come to stare?"

He glared at her from the balcony and she considered running back to her room. But then she lifted her chin. She'd been a coward long enough. It wasn't helping the situation, and there was no reason for it. He was a self-pitying, self-destructive invalid, nothing more. She told herself she could handle him.

He sat in a strange looking contraption. Giselle's gaze flicked over it for a bit, before returning to his face. He didn't look pleased to see her, but he had bathed and shaved, and he had his hair pulled back in a queue. He wasn't as frightening-looking as before, but he wasn't assaulting her senses like Navarre did, either. He was eye-catching, though, even with a scowl on the full lips that so closely matched those of his younger brother.

Perhaps his rudeness was a defense against the world. She hadn't looked at it that way before, and she was slightly ashamed at herself. It wasn't her fault, for she'd never been around a handicapped person before, but she should've given him a little compassion.

"It seems fair to me," she finally answered. She gestured to the door behind her as she stepped toward him.

"I only wanted to see what price I have paid for that valley of yours."

He turned away and looked out at Savignen. Navarre had been more than right. The trees were tipped pink with dawn at the edges. Giselle held her breath and watched as the color fanned out. It was beautiful and stretched as far as she could see, stopping only when she glimpsed the river.

"Well...that is what I came to do, too," she replied.

She thought she was prepared for the look he gave her, but she forgot his eyes. They were bluer than the sky and twice as cold. Giselle tried to feel a tingle, a stirring of anticipation, a murmur in her heart, anything. He was fairly handsome. His hair wasn't as blond as Esmee's after all, nor was it as dark as Navarre's.

Navarre!

Giselle's heart cried the name, and she stifled the instant ache. It was her own stupidity that brought his image instantly to her mind. She was a fool, and her dreams had been just that. Navarre wasn't her husband, the man before her was.

"I suppose you've been asked to bear my son."

Giselle stiffened at his words. *How can he ask it so easily?* She fought the reaction, but knew she was blushing. As closely as he watched her, it would have been impossible to disguise.

"Well?" He sneered after the word.

She nodded.

"You'll have to do the work then. I am incapable of that sort of movement."

Giselle lost her color at his bluntness. She felt it. Oh! He was worse than horrid, he was uncouth and bestial. She must have made some sound, because he looked her over even more critically.

"You're different from what we expected, Giselle. You're smaller, and not near as monstrous as I was led to believe."

"Monstrous?" She choked the word out.

"Well, you hadn't been seen in years. Who knew why? I told myself you couldn't be as bad as I imagined, but the imagination runs amok without reins. Navarre was right. You're lovelier than anyone expected. Who knows? Perhaps we'll be successful in trying for a son after all. I look forward to it."

Giselle's jaw dropped, and she couldn't close it. His eyes roved her form as if—

She couldn't finish the thought. She ran to her room with the sound of his laughter following at her heels.

"Why is it you still cling to these hours, Giselle?" Louisa asked. "I wait for you to ring for Isabelle and myself, and you don't. Then, when I come to find out why, you've been up for hours. Don't you realize what this is doing to you? You're too weak, and you can't sleep through every luncheon...."

"Etienne came into my room again."

The words stopped Louisa's tirade. Giselle watched her suck in breath as if she needed more power behind her speech, but she said nothing. Giselle looked away. Louisa could wipe that speculative look from her face. Giselle wasn't partial to Etienne, and she wasn't likely to be, either.

"Well...this is excellent news, Giselle. It's just what this overbearing household needs, too. Since I'm too old to continue as your governess, a child would be a godsend."

She thought Giselle was up and gazing out her window because of...that? Ugh. Have a child with Etienne? She would rather die! And she wasn't weak! Giselle had paced furiously about the chamber for hours! That wasn't weak. That was a reaction to more imprisonment. The castle was consuming her. Closing in. And there was nothing she could do about any of it!

It wasn't fair! Her future had already been written, regardless of how she felt about any of it. She was expected to cleave unto the monster in the room next door, close her eyes on any emotion, and allow him to—

She stopped the thought and squelched a retching motion. He'd said she'd have to do the movements! She didn't even know what that meant. And she refused to do such a thing with him! Jean-Claude could just become the next *Duc* du Berchald, and the family would just have to survive how depraved, debauched, or wicked he was! Giselle wasn't going to help them.

"I need a companion, Louisa," she said. "That's what you are and have always been. You know that."

"Giselle."

Louisa clucked her tongue in the reprimanding fashion she had. Giselle wasn't going to allow that. Louisa didn't know Etienne. She didn't know one thing about it.

"Assist me to the chapel, Louisa. I feel the need for peace, and I'm not getting any here."

"You need to live more and pray less, Giselle, and you know it." Louisa put her hands on her hips. "You're the *duchesse!* You can have anything you want, yet all you want to do is cover yourself in sack-cloth and pray like the self-pitying waif the arrogant *Comte* d'Antillion created. Well, I refuse to stand by and watch! Come, eat this delicious breakfast, and decide your wardrobe for the day. *Madame* Esmee looks forward to continuing with you from yesterday. That woman can help you more than you can possibly imagine. You mustn't keep her waiting."

"Don't you listen? I don't want to tour the castle! I don't want any help with running it! I want to seek solace in prayer. Is that too much to ask from my companion?"

"You know the answer to that already. You can't change your destiny, Giselle. You can only bend it to fill your needs. How many times must we go over this? You're married to the *Duc* du Berchald. Nothing can change it. You're the chatelaine of Chateau Berchand, and your duty lies within. Show me a priest who would argue that. Well?"

Giselle sighed. Louisa was right again, and she was thoroughly tired of it. "You're not a very supportive companion, Louisa."

"You are so wrong, my love. And I'm the best friend you'll ever find. Between us, we'll find a way to make this work, you'll see. Things are never as bad as we think they are. What do you say? The sun is bright, you can go wherever you like, and do whatever you wish. Who knows? A child might be what the *duc* needs to bring out his charm."

"Charm? Etienne? You don't know the man." Giselle mumbled it, but she did start picking through the breakfast tray.

"No, but I heard he sent instructions for tomorrow's supper. You're more of an influence than you think. He might even join the family downstairs. Think of that! He hasn't joined them for dinner since the physicians sent by his mother gave up on him. That was years ago. Think of it, Giselle!"

Louisa shook her head while Giselle sampled her omelet, trying not to show how frightened she was at the thought. She was to dine opposite him? With the things he's said and the lustful way he eyed her? How would she manage to eat?

"And all you long for is to pray," Louisa continued. "A habit reserved for nuns, priests, and bedtime, I say."

Dinner was as horrible as she'd imagined.

Non, Giselle thought. It was worse than horrible, and she'd spent more than four hours getting ready!

Isabelle had awakened her from a nap with the news that a hairdresser was there to see her. Giselle would've asked who ordered his services, but knew she wouldn't like the answer.

"Ah, Giselle, good. You're awake," Isabelle said. "This is wonderful. There is a *Monsieur* Poinre here. He is a hairdresser. He finished with your new aunt, and is ready to assist you."

"You're a very lucky woman, Giselle. I hear he is the best at hair arrangement in all of Paris. We were lucky he came this far south on such little notice, weren't we?" Louisa asked.

Giselle met Louisa's eyes in the mirror until her smile faded. "I'm being prepared for sacrifice, and you dance with glee."

"Sacrifice? You have a vivid imagination, Giselle. I'm more than surprised at you."

"That's what it is," she grumbled.

"*Non,* Giselle. It's a fete, held in your chateau, and in your honor. It's just as I imagined for you all these years. Think of it. The *duc* gave instructions yesterday to prepare for his presence, and the invitations went out all day long. You should see the list of acceptances. It'll be the most entertaining evening the locals have seen in years."

"That's what I'm afraid of."

"There's no reason to be afraid. Why wouldn't they come? No one has seen you since you were a child, and who can blame them for their curiosity? You have no reason to be other than thrilled. I know I am."

"I'm being put on display, and you're thrilled?"

Louisa laughed. "Of course, you'll be on display, Giselle. What beautiful woman isn't? And you will be stunning. We'll make certain of it, won't we, Isabelle? You'll outshine them all. You'll see."

So. She was to be the entertainment...and worse. Etienne would be joining her at it.

"You'll be more than stunning. Everyone will notice you tonight, everyone. We will make certain of your enticement."

Such preparation was absurd. She knew why they were doing it. And who it was to entice. But they didn't know him! Etienne didn't need any encouragement. She shuddered again at the thought. Etienne was barbaric, bestial, and uncouth. *Disgusting! Revolting!*

"I have told this *Monsieur* Poinre that you're undecided about the powder for your coiffure. He's an aficionado of that sort of style, and very hard to dissuade, I'm afraid."

"You? Unable to dissuade anyone? I find that hard to believe," Giselle said.

Louisa smiled at her again.

"You will see him, won't you? You'll not hide away in your new rooms while the world rushes by you? You'll wear your new gowns and show all of them the beautiful *Duchesse* du Berchald in all her God-given glory?"

"Enough already, Louisa. You win. Show this hairdresser in."

Giselle waved her hand as Isabelle and Louisa exchanged glances.

Monsieur Poinre was as short as Giselle, and that was incredible. He brought a stool to stand on in order to do his work. She watched with as much interest as Louisa and Isabelle were as he applied some sort of greasy salve to Giselle's hair to make it shine. When she asked what it was, he laughed.

"I cannot tell the *petit duchesse* my secret," he said. "Where would that leave me? The court at Versailles swears by my formula. It has made me a rich man, and my services are in demand. I've considered hiring a helper, but then I'd have to reveal my secret, and it might be stolen from me. You're lucky I was available, you know."

Mon Dieu, Giselle thought. The man chattered throughout the arrangement, giving her a headache. When he had her hair slickened and thick-feeling, he fitted a strange caged contraption to the top of her head. Giselle was grateful it was fairly weightless as he settled it into place. Her eyes were starting to pound with the same painful rhythm as her head. She almost cried out as he teased her hair about the cage, pulling and twisting it into masses of curls.

He told her he'd given up two days of patrons in order to travel so far south. It was fortunate he was available when *Monsieur* Navarre spoke to him. But he had no idea the *duchesse* was so fair. He might waive his travel fee. It would make his reputation grow to have it known that he had dressed the *Duchesse* du Berchald's hair. It was a pleasure, and one he rarely received. Most of his patrons were either thin-haired, or ugly, or old, or all three.

He couldn't wait to see her finished.

The moment he mentioned Navarre's name, Giselle's heart had panged within her, and she cried aloud before she could prevent it. She'd suspected it was Navarre arranging for her to look beautiful...and that hurt. *Monsieur* Poinre assumed her reaction was due to the arrangement of waves he was creating to cascade down the front of her coiffure, and Giselle let him.

Navarre hired him, because he wanted her beautiful...for Etienne.

Giselle was grateful she hadn't been forced into her corset yet, because she needed to take deep breaths to still her emotion. It would never do to attend her first public outing with the traces of tears about her face. She wondered if she were strong enough to stifle it, and knew she had to. It was her fate. It was sealed. They wanted her to have a child by Etienne.

Navarre, too.

The thought hammered through her temples until nothing else mattered. Navarre had asked her to be intimate with her husband. How could he ask such a thing? How could any family ask such a thing? What strange intrigues the Berchald family attempted, begging the new *duchesse* to have her own husband's child! Had she mentioned it to her priest in Antilli, he would have crossed himself.

Giselle suspected *Monsieur* Poinre's formula contained grease, but it smelled faintly of roses. He worked with her hair until the cage was completely hidden. Giselle caught Louisa's look of delight, and Isabelle's lifted eyebrows, and tried not to scowl. They could look as pleased as they liked. It wasn't either one of them who were being dressed to titillate Etienne.

"If the petite *duchesse* will close her eyes for a moment?"

The hairdresser's request interrupted Giselle's train of thought.

"I'll be finished. Everyone in the castle will be in rapture over your beauty. Everyone in Versailles would be sick with envy."

Giselle wondered if he spoke to all his clients like that as he tipped her forward, so her face was atop her knees. And then rose-scented powder filled the air, making it difficult to breathe. She was coughing and choking, while tears rolled down her cheeks. She'd wanted her hair powdered, like her mama, the *Comtesse* d'Antillion, but after experiencing it, she changed her mind.

"There!" Louisa clapped her hands. "It's finished, and you look delightful. I'm astounded, Giselle. Really, I am. What do you think, Isabelle?"

"It's different," the maid answered, noncommittally.

Giselle looked up and caught sight of her reflection in the mirror. Isabella had been accurate. Her image had certainly changed.

"You would be such a hit at the palace," *Monsieur* Poinre said with a theatrical whisper. "His Majesty's eye for beauty is well-known, and you are *tres belle*. I do not lie. You don't even need the rice powder so many ladies use to whiten their complexions. Your skin is already so pure and unspoiled. You are lucky for that. I've heard some of the nobles have taken to using arsenic to whiten and beautify their skins, although it's very dangerous. I'm certain you'll never resort to such. You are so very lucky, *Madame.*"

Giselle's headache worsened the longer he spoke. She didn't care what the nobility did, or how they kept their looks. She only cared about one man, and he wasn't her husband.

She watched as Louisa tipped him. From the way he turned back and thanked the *petit duchesse,* it must have been a gracious tip. Giselle wondered why Louisa had pocket gold, while her own employer had no idea how to go about getting any.

"We should probably have asked him for a patch," Louisa murmured as she shut the door.

"A patch?" Isabelle asked.

Giselle turned her head to admire *Monsieur* Poinre's work. Her neck never looked longer or more sleek, and the lack of color made her shading stand out. Giselle's eyebrows still had high arches, but they were so dark against the rest of her complexion, they brought out her eyes. She hadn't noticed before how dark brown they were, and her lips looked as if she'd applied rouge.

"Patches come in several shapes and are applied to the face," Louisa explained. "I've heard of stars and moons for example. Not only are they interesting to look at, but they make one's face look even paler."

"I've never heard of anything so strange, but you heard *Monsieur* Poinre," Giselle remarked. "My skin is white enough. Isn't arsenic a poison? How can people be so stupid?"

"While it is true of you, I've heard that all follow His Majesty's pursuit of a clear, unblemished complexion. Most of the nobility weren't blessed with porcelain skin as you were, Giselle."

"Blessed? I've been hidden away. Is it any wonder I'm white? I rarely see the outdoors."

"Complaints still? Giselle."

Louisa clucked her tongue and Giselle glared at her through the glass. It didn't do much. The maid just continued in a chastising tone.

"Look at you. You have a full evening of entertainment ahead, a beautiful dress, and a new hairstyle. Besides, you can go outside anytime you like, anymore. Isabelle and I have talked of it. Why don't you pursue riding? The Antillions have long been renowned for their ability, and I'm certain that new brother of yours, that Navarre? He would teach you. Isabelle and I spoke on it."

"Which dress am I wearing?" Giselle spoke quickly to interrupt her.

"A new one, *Madame*. It just arrived from Paris."

Both women exchanged glances again in the mirror, and then Isabelle lowered her head.

"What's wrong with the dress?" Giselle asked. "Isabelle, answer me."

"There's nothing wrong with it, Giselle," Louisa said quickly. "It's the latest creation. There was a month of stitching done on the bodice alone."

Giselle swiveled in her chair, balancing the weight on her head carefully as she looked at them. They were endlessly trying to hide unpleasantness from her, while nagging her at the same time to mature. She was determined to put a stop to it. "A month? That must be an exaggeration. It was ordered just last week, wasn't it?"

"All your gowns were made for another, Giselle. *Madame* Broussard charged extra for each of them because of that."

"Then you lied when you say I have such a small waist? What else have you hidden from me?"

"The dresses all had to be taken in, Giselle, I swear it!"

Isabelle spoke quickly and then crossed herself. After all the years Giselle had relied on her, she felt insulted.

Her eyes narrowed. "I'm waiting."

"Isabelle," Louisa said, "go and fetch the dress. I'll speak with her."

Giselle swiveled on her chair and gave Louisa her sternest look. Louisa smiled. Giselle needed practice if she ever planned on scolding a servant. Giselle sighed.

"So tell me. What's so mysterious about my new clothing, Louisa?"

"Your papa...sent the bill with the shipment."

Giselle sucked in her breath in shock and dismay. "Oh no! He didn't! He couldn't! That's unheard of! How could he have done something so degrading? So *bourgeoisie?*"

Giselle was aware that tears of shame colored her words, and that Louisa heard them, but it was an incredible insult to make her new family pay for her trousseau. Giselle couldn't believe the *comte* was that undignified.

"It's true," Louisa said. *"Monsieur* Navarre received the bill this morning. The servants have been whispering about it all day — when they aren't gossiping over the *duc's* plans of attending this fete, that is."

"Oh...how can I show myself to them?" Giselle covered her face with her hands. Papa sent her to her new husband and refused to pay for her clothing!

"Giselle, you will attend this dinner with your head high. Well...as high as possible, considering your height."

"I am not amused," Giselle replied from behind her fingers.

"The clothing has been paid for many times over, Giselle," Louisa continued. "The entire Berchald family owes its escape from debtor's prison to you. They could have gone to the Bastille. If it hadn't been for your dowry—"

"I've already heard the tale, and I don't care. I hate my father! I hate him! I never want to see him again."

"Does that mean...you won't annul your marriage after all?"

How did she know? Giselle wondered.

"Of course not." She tried to sound vehement, but failed. She disliked her husband intensely, but she hated her own father more.

"Well. That's settled, then. And you can't sit there all day admiring your reflection," Louisa said. "Time is wasting. I look forward to seeing you in this latest creation. You'll stun everyone."

"Especially since they're paying for it," she grumbled.

"No, Giselle. *You're* paying for it. I daresay you haven't finished paying yet, either."

She was much too astute. When Giselle pulled her hands away from her face, the woman wouldn't meet her eyes.

CHAPTER NINE

"*Monsieur* Poinre was right, *Madame* la *Duchesse.*
You're so beautiful, and ever so small. It's a pleasure
to assist you, I vow."

Giselle narrowed her eyes, smiled her thanks to Gerty,
and then looked away. The maid knew about the bill for
payment. They all did. Giselle shouldn't be surprised
at the way news flew about the castle. She'd lived too
long in seclusion. Although she knew little about the
world about her, little was known about her, too.

Everyone probably knew what she'd been asked to
do with Etienne, too. That was a disgusting thought.

"She's right, Giselle," Louisa said. "But you need
jewels. I'm certain the family has a selection. Gerty,
could you see that the Berchald jewels are placed at the
duchesse's disposal?"

Gerty curtsied as Giselle looked back at her reflection.
Why hadn't she thought of commanding that? Would
she never learn to be mistress of her own castle? And
Louisa was wrong. It would be impossible to enhance
her appearance. She looked astonishing. A necklace
couldn't make much difference. Her hair was high atop
her head and pristine white, making her look
dazzlingly pale. The dress was a masterpiece of
needlework, too.

The material's pattern of pink and white stripes had
been sewn at the bodice so that only the pink showed.
The white stripes were revealed at the waist. The darts

in her bodice must have taken days to sew, but it was worth it. The dress was everything she could have hoped, but a bit lower cut than she was used to. Although the others beamed their approval, she felt shy at the neckline.

Giselle hadn't been blessed with much bosom, and it had never mattered before to her, but the corset Isabelle had laced her into pushed everything toward the bodice's lace edge. Giselle had never seen cleavage displayed as hers was. She couldn't imagine what Navarre would think when he saw—

Oh...why was it Navarre that occurred to her first? It should be Etienne, but something always brought Navarre to mind. It was perverse...but it was very delightful, too.

Immense panniers had been strapped atop her petticoats, holding Giselle's gown out so far at the sides, she could only go through a door sideways. The cage-like affairs were fairly weightless, and even bounced if she did. It might be fashionable, but it felt strange. It did make her waist look even smaller than it was, though. If anyone noticed that after her neckline.

There was a polite knock at the door. Neither woman moved. They all seemed transfixed by Giselle's reflection. The knock came again.

"See who's at the door, Isabelle," Giselle commanded.

She couldn't tear her own eyes away from herself. She didn't look like herself at all. Was that what the designers of *haute couture* had in mind? Giselle tipped her head to one side and then the other, and decided she wasn't as flattered at the image as she had once been. She would rather look more like herself.

"*Monsieur* Navarre requests entry, *Madame,*" Isabelle said a moment later. "He brings a selection of jewelry for you to choose from."

Giselle's heart stopped. Isabelle's even tone helped restart it. Navarre was here? He would see her and she'd yet to acclimatize herself to the neckline! She wore almost nothing at her bosom! And worse. She could actually see the tops of her breasts turning a rosy shade. She took several calming breaths, before she dared speak.

"A-a-allow him in."

She stammered. Louisa caught her eye in the mirror and Giselle looked away quickly. It wouldn't do for anyone to suspect how she felt. And that's when she went white. She could actually feel the blood drain from her face. She couldn't label anything. *No.* She did not have feelings. Not for another man. Etienne was her husband, and she shouldn't even think of another—

"Giselle?"

Navarre's voice broke through her thoughts. Giselle turned toward him and gaped.

Magnifique!

There was no better word for him. Navarre had his hair pulled back in a queue, and a froth of white lace at his throat. His thigh-length coat was made of dull yellow sateen, while black knee breeches looked sewn to his thighs. And she already knew they were muscled and lean. Giselle focused on the floor beneath his shoes.

"I brought the Berchald emeralds, sapphires, and of course, the Star of Savignen diamond. My ancestor, Jean-Claude, bought the diamond and named it after the vineyard, although he had no idea the Berchalds would someday own it. That was a strange idea of his, wasn't it?"

How he could ramble on, without the slightest tremor to his voice? Perhaps his emotion didn't match hers. Perhaps he didn't think of her, at all. Giselle trembled through the instant flash of pain through her breast and hoped no one noticed. And then she swallowed, and looked up at him.

And the world stood still. A huge rush of noise whooshed through each ear, cancelling out sound, and it was replaced by a low buzz.

He had beautiful eyes, dark blue, bordering on amethyst, and shadowed by those long, lush lashes. But she already knew that. There was something else. Something she didn't know enough about to name. Giselle's eyes widened as he licked his lips, before sucking in the full lower lip. Shivers ran her, raising gooseflesh, and Giselle sent the command, but her mouth didn't listen. She actually pursed her lips.

Oh...sweetness! Heavens!

Her breath quickened, making even that small, almost-not-there bodice feel too tight. Restrictive. Oh, this was wicked. It was depraved and immoral, too. But nothing stopped the delicious tremors that hit her legs and weakened her knees. And that's when she was extremely grateful for the skirt's fullness. And the panniers, as not one soul would be able to tell! What she wouldn't give to be in his arms, experiencing those lips. *No!* She mustn't think that. It was evil, and yet nothing about this sensation felt wicked. Every sensation felt more exciting than the last. Enticing. Stimulating. Thrilling.

Oh. This was horrid. She had Louisa, Isabelle, Gerty, and two retainers watching. And even that failed to stanch the emotions coursing her. Navarre cleared his throat and spoke from what seemed a long way away.

"I didn't know which dress you'd be wearing, Giselle. Your maid should've warned me."

His eyes dropped. A nerve twitched in his jaw, and Giselle felt herself respond, as if her bosom pulsed toward him, aching for his touch, caress and kisses.

"The emeralds are out of the question with that gown," he continued, although his voice had deepened to Giselle's ear. "But the diamond is almost as well-known. Savoy, bring the tray." He gestured, and a dark-haired man stepped forward to Navarre's side. "Savoy is the keeper of our vault, Giselle. If you need assistance in the future, send for him, not me."

She hadn't sent for him, but was it such a *faux pas*? The question made her feel vaguely ill. As did the realization that it was Gerty who'd devised this to happen. Giselle turned to examine the perfect square diamond set in a necklace of smaller stones. Named after her dowry, it would be the perfect choice for her pink and white dress, but something held her back. Perhaps it was the sheer size of the setting. She was too small for such a necklace.

"Let me see the sapphires." She spoke in a whisper.

Navarre flicked his glance to her, imprinting heat everywhere, and then he looked over Giselle's right shoulder. With that one glance, she felt as if flames roared through her, filling her ears this time with a loud, melodic humming sound. She vibrated as it filled her, overpowered her. Owned her. Terrified her.

She gulped.

Oh no. No. No.

She was in love!

As horrible and as disgusting as that might be, and as morally wrong and degrading, the certainty was still there. Carried through her with every heartbeat. Nothing had ever seemed so wondrous. Extraordinary. Thrilling. Giselle felt like a flower under the touch of the sun. She couldn't believe it. She'd never felt so gloriously, perfectly, stunningly alive.

And somehow she had to hide it.

She looked down to the sapphires. They were a perfect match to Navarre's eyes. Perhaps it was due to the red velvet cushion beneath them. She couldn't be sure, but the purple deepened the blue stones to the hue of his eyes. Giselle loved the stones the moment she saw them. She wondered if he'd known that she would.

"I'll wear the sapphires, Navarre."

Giselle ignored the impulse to look toward him, knowing how many watched.

"*Tres bien.*"

He spoke formally, as if bored.

"If you'll turn around, *Madame,* I shall do the honors and clasp the necklace. There's a matching tiara, a bracelet, and two rings."

"*Merci,* Na...arre."

Giselle split his name. And it shook. Oh dear. And she was trying to prevent that very thing! It was impossible! And then she watched him pick up the stone with fingers that trembled. Giselle's lips curved, and she had to hide that, too.

There was a cluster of tiny stones at the center, like little grapes. Giselle watched in the mirror as he hooked it. His fingers were icy cold against the back of her neck. Giselle lifted her eyes to meet his in the glass. Her skin was probably sensitive from heat — she was blushing, and that could have accounted for it — but nothing accounted for a spark that bit into her flesh and made him leap backward at the same time.

Stunned purplish eyes gripped hers, and she no longer cared how many others were in the room. They were invisible. She loved him, and he had to feel the same toward her! She knew it from the way he scrunched his eyes closed, and the look of pain that flickered across his cheekbones before he opened them again.

"I...must see to-to...Etienne."

He stammered the words and stepped back, out of her sight. Giselle turned in time to see him bow. She hadn't noticed before that he hadn't powdered his hair. That was strange, but she was glad. She loved the golden color. She loved everything about him! Isabelle held the door open as he swept from the chamber.

"Oh. My. This is interesting, Giselle."

She turned to Louisa as she picked up the tiara. It was made of smaller stones laced together with golden filigree, like the necklace. Two larger, egg-shaped stones hung from either end.

"These are meant to fall behind your ears," Louisa noted. "I've never seen such a design. Thank you,

Monsieur Savoy, but I don't think the *duchesse* will need the rings or bracelet."

Giselle let Louisa dismiss the man, although that should have been her decision. But Louisa was right. The color of the sapphires would jar against the striped skirt.

"Perfection!" Louisa announced once the tiara was in place. "When you first chose those stones, I almost interrupted, but it's clear you know your colors. Nothing could become you better. I can't wait to see the *duc's* face when you are presented."

The duc?

Giselle bit her tongue. Who cared about Etienne? She was aching to see Navarre again. She couldn't help it. She loved him. The emotion was fraught with a passion and intensity she'd always dreamed existed. And now that she'd found such wonder, it must be kept hidden? Oh, but that was going to be difficult. She longed to shout it from the rooftops, it felt so beautiful. So wonderful. So amazing.

The waterfall of sapphires fell to the juncture of her new cleavage. She knew she looked desirable. Giselle could hardly wait to see Navarre again, so she could gaze into his eyes, feel the flickers of heat, tremble, and even pretend to kiss him.

She danced down the hall, listening as the rustle of her new finery accompanied every step. It wasn't until she reached the top of the staircase that she felt shy. Giselle lifted the front of her skirts as she walked, and was glad her new shoes had heels. She wasn't used to wearing them, however, and she had to take the stairs carefully. She couldn't even bend forward enough to see where she put her feet.

Such strange fashions the aristocracy wears. Menservants awaited her at each set of double doors opening them wide for her promenade. If they hadn't been there, she'd have had to stop, turn sideways, and take little, mincing steps to proceed. It was silly.

Wasteful. She'd rather wear the plain dresses of her incarceration than such nonsense as this.

Oh. That last was a lie! And she knew it. She had never felt more beautiful, or looked more eye-catching. It was the most important thing in her world at the moment that Navarre thought so, too. Giselle couldn't imagine how she'd feel if he considered another woman was more fair. Her steps halted at the entrance to the large dining room, while the menservants bowed on both sides of it.

Navarre and another woman?

Oh no. No. That would be terrible. But likely. He could never be hers. He was probably betrothed. Aunt Mimi said nothing of it, but that didn't mean anything. The agony of thinking he belonged to another made Giselle catch her breath with stifling the cry. He couldn't belong to another woman!

Giselle lifted her head, and focused on the ceiling high above, blinking rapidly to stop the moisture in her eyes. Love was too new, fragile, and illicit. She was barely coming to terms with how it felt to experience it. This new emotion was too raw.

"Madame Giselle, the *Duchesse* du Berchald!"

Giselle was announced and immediately noted that Navarre wasn't there. But Etienne was.

"Ah, Giselle," her husband spoke loudly. "You are looking splendid. I see you wear Navarre's sapphires, though. I must speak with the boy."

Navarre's sapphires?

"Come closer, my little wife! I certainly can't come to you."

Etienne laughed at the end of his words. Giselle watched as Esmee tried to humor him by laughing, too. It didn't help. Etienne was obviously drunk. If nothing else, the condition of his clothing announced it. Giselle watched Aunt Mimi approach, pleasantly surprised to see they were of a like height due to the new heels.

"Giselle. Dearest. You look wonderful. I'm certain there was never a more beautiful *duchesse* in the entire line. Perhaps that'll be enough...."

She bit off the end of the sentence, while Giselle smiled.

"Merci. " She inclined her head at the flattery, and felt the egg-shaped sapphires bobbing against her ears. "But tell me, Aunt Mimi, how my appearance can be enough to help?"

Her mouth was speaking, but her mind was leagues away. *What did Etienne mean, Navarre's sapphires?* she wondered.

"Etienne is being...difficult," Aunt Mimi said softly. "We were hoping you might be able to...soothe him somehow. The guests will arrive soon, and...."

The words stopped.

"Perhaps I can keep him from drinking more wine?" Giselle supplied.

Aunt Mimi's lips tightened and she nodded.

"I'll do my best," Giselle whispered.

The other woman smiled.

"Come here, Giselle! Let me look at you! You look much different when you're awake!"

Etienne slurred the words, and Giselle blushed at the crude comment.

"You are looking handsome also, Etienne." She bent at the knees and held the sapphires in place with a hand while she dipped a curtsy. It wasn't to hold the necklace in place as much as shield her décolletage. She felt his gaze anyway, and detested it. He wasn't to look at her like that. It made her queasy. His gaze felt evil and disgusting and wrong.

It also dissipated the heavenly aura she'd been experiencing. And all of it was so wrong. She wasn't to feel anything for Navarre. She should feel it for Etienne. But how could she force her heart to listen? Perhaps the thought of Etienne touching her was her punishment. The *Bon Dieu* was certainly making it vile. She couldn't allow it. It would be wrong.

She loved Navarre.

She might be legally bound to Etienne in a ceremony from almost fifteen years in the past. Nothing could change that, but her heart would never accept it. She couldn't let Etienne touch her. She'd never be his, because she knew now she belonged to—

Navarre was announced behind her, stopping everything. And a moment later, came another announcement, this time of the *Comtesse* d'Antillion. Giselle took her time turning around, hoping to compose herself before letting her mama see her. It would never do if the *comtesse* thought the marriage unsuccessful.

There was too much light in the room of a sudden, and Giselle felt her face frozen in dismay as Navarre approached, her mother behind him.

"Navarre!" Etienne said loudly. "I see you talked my wife into wearing your sapphires. Is there nothing my dearest brothers won't take from me?"

Giselle's eyes went wide and she gasped. Navarre narrowed his eyes. Beyond that glance she didn't dare look again. It was too dangerous, especially with her mother watching.

Giselle gestured for a chair to be brought for her, so she could act the part of adoring wife. She hoped she was doing the right thing.

"I'm pleased to see you looking well, *Monsieur* le *Duc*," the *comtesse* said. "And Giselle, I almost didn't recognize you. You look splendid. And I must tell you, my dear, how your dear papa pines for word of you."

Giselle smiled. She longed more to weep. Her face felt ready to crack.

"The *comte?* " Etienne burst out laughing. "Set his mind at rest, *Madame le Comtesse.* My wife is pleasantly surprised by her new, so-virile husband. Aren't you, *Ma Cherie?*"

His fingers touched her arm, sending an unpleasant chill through her. Giselle swallowed past the lump in her throat.

"Of course," she murmured and smiled glassily.

CHAPTER TEN

"Why do they call the sapphires yours, Navarre?"

Navarre gestured for her to wait as he finished chewing his mouthful, but it was a wasted movement. She knew every breath he took, every bite he put into his mouth, and each time he swallowed.

Etienne was at the far end of the table, behaving better, probably due to Navarre's influence. The wine decanter at the *duc's* elbow had been refilled with grape juice splashed with a touch of vinegar. Navarre and Giselle had tensed the first time Etienne drank from it, and then relaxed at the same time. Giselle didn't need to look toward him to see it, she felt it. It was strange how attuned they were.

Her mama was midway down the table, out of conversation range. Giselle was grateful. The meal she'd been dreading hadn't turned out that way, at all. She knew why. Because Navarre was on her left again. Close. Almost intimate. The evening was actually quite wonderful. Giselle hardly tasted the courses before sending them away. She could've been served straw for all she knew. It was impossible to eat much in her ensemble, but she wasn't hungry for food. And Navarre gallantly said nothing.

Giselle knew what she was hungry for. Her thoughts must've interpreted themselves more than once, because sometimes Navarre flushed becomingly against his lace jabot. Giselle placed her elbows on the aged lace of the tablecloth and waited for him to answer her question.

"The sapphires have been known as mine, ever since I bought them as a gift for my intended bride. Almost four years ago," he replied.

His answer created instant pain. And then it burned. Why had she been so stupid? She didn't want to know. She longed to rip the necklace off and throw it to the floor. Tears flooded her eyes, and she blinked rapidly to stop them. She couldn't cry. Not now. Not with her mother attending.

"I didn't mean to make you cry, Giselle."

"I'm...not."

She had to look away and watched the crowd of diners blur and clear with each blink. This was stupid. Of course he was betrothed. What aristocrat wasn't? She'd suspected as much already. And it really shouldn't matter. It shouldn't make her heart ache or her throat dry. She was married, anyway. She had no right to him.

"Do you want me to finish my story?"

Giselle watched as the woman at Navarre's other side dipped her fingers into her goblet and stroked her eyelashes. Perhaps she wanted Navarre's attention or the man at her other side. Giselle wondered how she could watch something as mundane as another woman primping, when it felt like Navarre held her heart in his palm and was squeezing it.

"No." Giselle sniffed quietly, fortified herself, and looked back at him. "Yes."

"*Je t'adore,* Giselle."

Navarre said it softly, reaching for his wine glass with an arm that blocked the others from view.

Giselle's heart stopped, and then it felt like it moved, lodging near the sapphire waterfall at her throat. Her eyes went wide. Stunned.

He adores me?

She couldn't comprehend that she still sat upright, while the murmur of conversation flowed about them. She should be soaring. No. She must have heard it wrong. That was the only explanation.

"Did you hear me?" he whispered.

She moved her gaze to his. She couldn't speak. She watched him smile and then hide it behind his lace-edged napkin. She'd been wrong. Her spirit wasn't just soaring. It was rocketing.

"About the sapphires. My fiancée threw them at me, making certain everyone near her apartments in Versailles Palace knew how much she hated me. Do you know why?"

His fiancée hated him?

Giselle shook her head, the only movement she felt capable of making, and then she looked past him. The woman at his other side toyed with her gown, pushing the shoulders farther apart to exhibit more of her bosom. The effect on her dining companion was to be expected, because he couldn't take his eyes off her. Giselle was disgusted at what she was watching, and tried to turn the emotion on herself.

She was little better.

She moved her gaze, looking beyond the elaborate centerpiece of fruit to find Etienne watching her. Giselle swallowed as Etienne raised his wine glass toward her. Even as inexperienced as she felt, Giselle recognized the gesture as a mark of ownership. She felt ill. Chilled.

Perhaps she should talk to her mother and tell her how intolerable the *duc* really was. Perhaps the *comtesse* would save her. But how could Giselle annul the marriage that saved this family? And after her father's action of sending the bill for her clothing, why should she?

It was a vicious quandary. With but one answer. She couldn't speak to anyone. Too many lives would be altered...but what a horrid price she had to pay!

She watched Etienne dribble the grape juice on his jabot, and Giselle shuddered.

"What is it?" Navarre asked. "Is it something I said? Pray forgive me. I shouldn't have spoken as I did."

Giselle turned back to him, tensed for the effect his gaze would have, but he wouldn't look at her. He was carefully staring at a spot over her head.

"The woman who turned down your...gift? She must have been possessed, Navarre. If only...it had been..."

Giselle was near tears again. *If only it had been me,* she finished in her thoughts. She'd have wed him a hundred times over. It would be a heaven she could barely comprehend to know that at night, when the moon cast its spell, it would be Navarre with her....

Dark blue eyes drilled into hers. Giselle gasped at the intensity in his. She couldn't finish her thought. She was amazed she wasn't swooning.

"Perhaps my littlest brother can enlighten you, *Madame* la *Comtesse!*"

Etienne' s loud voice came through the spell about her. Navarre snapped his head around. Giselle used the opportunity to hold her own lace-edged napkin to her lips.

"The *comtesse* asks why I've been secluded," Etienne explained. "Perhaps you have an answer for her?"

Giselle looked to her mother. It didn't appear the woman asked any such thing, or if she had, she had quickly recanted. Giselle had never seen her mother looking so uncomfortable.

"Perhaps it's time you retired, Etienne."

Navarre pushed away from the table, flinging down his napkin.

"Why should I?" Etienne continued. "Is it my fault Jean-Claude tried to kill me? Well? Was it?"

No one spoke in the shocked silence that followed.

"Excuse my brother, ladies and gentlemen."

Navarre gestured toward the wine, and Giselle heard polite chuckling at the inference.

"Drunk, am I?" Etienne shouted as he shoved his chair away from the table. "Well, dearest brother, I'm not so drunk that I can't remember how my saddle was tampered with. I would have to be very drunk indeed, to forget that."

"Say farewell, Etienne. I'll have you taken to your chamber."

Navarre stood over him, his voice low, yet filled with authority. Giselle was surprised to see Etienne's chin fall forward. He looked like a little boy being punished.

"Forgive us, please." Navarre bowed to the group, but his gaze didn't seem to reach Giselle's end of the table. "Come Etienne. I'll fetch a footman."

He pushed the wheeled chair toward the stairs. Giselle stared at them like everyone else, and then she moved. She realized her place was with her husband, and Giselle walked quickly to catch up.

"Footmen!" Etienne complained, slurring the words. "I hate being carried, Navarre. That has to be the worst. How did I ever let you talk me into this? I'm sorry." His shoulders slumped. "What I wouldn't give to be able to walk there by myself, just once more. Is that too much to ask?"

Giselle's eyes filled with tears at the agony in his voice. And she realized he was crying, just like the first night when she'd eavesdropped. Navarre must have sensed her presence. He turned with such misery in his eyes, Giselle stepped back.

"Go back to our guests, Giselle. Now."

"Giselle? Tell her to go away! At once! I won't be pitied!"

Etienne's voice was raw with torment, making his command even more hurtful.

"Go. Salvage the party, Giselle," Navarre said softly. "I'll be back shortly."

She opened her mouth to argue, but something held her back. It wasn't her husband. Etienne was slumped forward in his chair with his arms humbly folded across his lap. It was the sum total of all that was happening. She shook her head, but Navarre wasn't looking.

She had no choice. Again. She turned back.

There was something strange about her room when she woke. Giselle couldn't quite place it. She wondered if it was the hairstyle Louisa refused to dismantle. She needed a more malleable companion.

Giselle sighed.

Such a thing would never happen. She loved Louisa, and the woman knew it. Louisa had been there for her when her own mother wasn't. Louisa listened, argued, cajoled, and made Giselle see sense a thousand times over.

There was nothing sensible about the monstrous turban she'd wrapped about Giselle's head, however. Louisa had clicked her tongue as she'd arranged the covering to make certain, '*Monsieur* Poinre's artistry isn't disturbed.' That was stupid. Where was she supposed to go with such a coiffure? She couldn't even find her way out of the castle on her own.

Giselle rubbed at her eyes and scowled into the darkness. The cage above her head was probably responsible for her sore shoulders, and her bad temper.

And Etienne's door was closed.

Giselle lifted her head to study the connecting door. It wasn't much, but she was grateful Etienne hadn't come into the room the night before. It was bad enough she had to play-act through what felt like hours while her mama questioned her. The *comtesse* hadn't come right out and asked if Etienne and Giselle had consummated their union, but she didn't have to. Giselle had known what she meant.

Giselle groaned aloud at the memory. It didn't stop it.

"Tell me Giselle, my darling one," her mother had addressed her.

Darling one? Giselle had stared at that. Her mother never would have spoken such an endearment if the *comte* were present. For the first time, Giselle felt the immense distance that was between them. She wondered how could a woman allow her only daughter to be treated like Giselle had.

But she already knew the answer — her father.

"How goes your marriage?" the *comtesse* had continued. "Things are sometimes difficult for two people...wed as young as you were."

Giselle had sat stonily and waited for Mama to embellish her words. Navarre hadn't returned, and she wasn't sure how she was supposed to salvage the evening.

It was obvious she was the main attraction. Even Esmee and Aunt Mimi were staring at her, and they should know better. So Giselle sat, a champagne glass in her hand and waited for her mama to finish her words.

"I mean...he's different from what I remember. Can he...I mean, is he...still capable? After all, I am your mama, and the Lord knows I have some experience in these matters."

Navarre still hadn't come down, and Giselle wondered what was keeping him.

"Your papa spoke to me last night about the...situation. He's at Versailles Palace, you know. Awaiting an audience."

"No." Giselle turned away so the *comtesse* wouldn't see her expression. "I didn't know."

She immediately knew what was being inferred. Her papa was petitioning the king for an annulment. Not for Giselle's sake. But because the *comte* wanted Savignen Valley back. It was crude of him, but he'd already proven that emotion toward the Berchalds.

Giselle sat there, wondering what she should say. It would be so simple. She could return to her tower... and everything would go back as before.

"He's so worried about you, Child."

Her papa? Worried about Giselle?

"He asked me to speak with you of it. He would be here himself, but you know how men are about such things. Always the property and negotiating it is with them. I wonder sometimes, how they expect...."

Giselle ceased listening. Navarre had appeared at the top of the stairs. She couldn't have prevented the quickening in her pulse any more than she could have stopped breathing. And that's when she knew.

She couldn't let the *comte* get the annulment...but how was she supposed to feign love for a husband she detested? It wasn't possible. She wasn't deceitful enough to speak such lies. And then Navarre entered the room.

All her inner turmoil fell to nothing. She no longer questioned anything. It was simple. If she hadn't been affianced and wed to Etienne, she would never have met Navarre. Never known this feeling. This...quickening of the senses.

Her escape was right in front of her. Waiting. All she had to do was say the words. Giselle's lips opened so she could breathe better.

Love was too strong.

She'd turned back to her mama and smiled shyly, and with that came an easy lie. "Etienne is every bit a man, Mama. Truly. Now, if you'll excuse me?"

Giselle crossed to join Navarre at the landing. She counseled herself to show nothing, although any lingering guests might think her worried over Etienne as well, wouldn't they?

Giselle stood at Navarre's elbow as they said farewell to those guests who were leaving. She only glanced up twice to see if he'd look. He didn't. She was disappointed. She hoped it didn't show.

Mama was leaving. Other guests had rooms for the night. Esmee, Navarre and Aunt Mimi stayed at the doors, waiting for those who were staying to seek their chambers. Giselle wondered why. She wasn't going to bed without some answers.

Giselle didn't recall what words they spoke. She watched as Esmee hinted at further invitations, while Navarre bid their guests *adieu* and kissed the ladies' hands.

"That was horrid," Esmee said finally as the family entered the blue salon and the doors were shut behind them. "Wretched. And I never want to spend another evening covering for him. How can you allow—?"

"Not now." Navarre stopped her angry words with the same low tone he used on Etienne.

"Then when? I've spent years saving the Berchald name, and he ruins it in one evening! I don't know how I can face—"

"I said, not now!"

Esmee's lips set, and she glared at Giselle before turning aside.

"Come sit beside me, Giselle."

Aunt Mimi patted the blue striped settee. Giselle looked from her to Navarre and then Esmee. Nothing was spoken, but they were deciding something. She could sense it. And this was maddening! Giselle looked at Navarre again and he finally met her glance. Her heart lurched, differently than before, as she read the emotion in his eyes. It wasn't love. It was misery. And pain.

"Go to her, Giselle." He gestured to his aunt.

"But Navarre...I must know if it's true." Giselle blinked away the moisture that had instantly coated her eyes.

"Not now, Giselle." He turned away and started walking toward the doors.

"That's not fair! I lied about the state of my...my marriage...." the words were choking her, "and you say not now? To me? Then, when?"

He stopped and the sigh that ran his frame was easy for her to spot. It lifted his shoulders.

"Tomorrow. After luncheon."

"Tomorrow? But—"

"I will not speak of such things now. Not here. I usually ride after luncheon. I will be available to you then. You can accompany me if you like."

If she liked? She was to ride. With Navarre? Alone again? Her heart was giving her trouble as it went faster, while her breath was a match. She had to concentrate in order to answer without giving anything away.

"Very good."

Giselle saw Aunt Mimi's nod at her answer through the corner of her eye. She was amazed the words came out as dull and bland as they did. That was two lies in one evening. . And there would be a heavy penance to pay. But maybe...just maybe...it wouldn't come too soon.

CHAPTER ELEVEN

Giselle rubbed at her eyes. She'd surprised herself by sleeping deeply. The connecting door still puzzled her, though. But not enough to continue looking at it. Her neck ached, and the headboard felt so hot against her back, it started a sweat at the back of her neck. So hot... So...alive.

Mon Dieu!

Giselle flipped over to face Etienne, frightened at the sight of her husband, and he knew it. She couldn't disguise it. She pulled at the sheets to cover herself, her mouth gaping as she started shaking.

"Bonjour." He greeted her and then he smiled.

Giselle went icy, the sensation depleting her strength. Sapping her will. Stilling her thoughts.

"Do I still frighten you, little one?"

Etienne reached for her as he said it. Giselle jerked back, toppling over from the unaccustomed weight of the turban-wrapped hair. He found her amusing. Laugher filled the room.

"Oh, come, Giselle. I won't harm you."

He moved closer as he spoke, using his arms and shoulders. Giselle lifted her head as she felt the mattress moving, while her jaw dropped. And then her eyes went wide. Oh no! Etienne's upper torso was thick with muscle...and nothing else. He was naked in her bed?

Non, non, and *non.*

Giselle lunged for the edge, tossing the bedcovers at him in her haste. She heard his chuckling again.

"You're very beautiful, Giselle...but I'm certain you've already heard that before, especially from my littlest brother, eh?"

Giselle was grateful the room was dark. He couldn't see the guilt flood her. The morning glow behind the draperies shed just enough light to reveal his nakedness against the white sheets.

Tiens! She hadn't looked away fast enough.

"You can run, but I can't chase you, you know."

He leaned back against the headboard, his arms behind his head as he said it. Giselle knew he was studying her. She didn't look again to see it. She felt his regard as an unpleasant shiver up her back.

She'd also been stupid with her nightgown. She had several thicker ones. Anything would have been better than the filmy thing she had on. He had slept in her bed, and she snuggled against him as if he were the headboard? Giselle felt ill at the thought, and then went cold all over.

"It's warmer back here with me."

"Why...are you here?"

Giselle started searching for her dressing gown as she asked it.

"Why? I'm fulfilling your request, of course. My rooms are being cleaned. Isn't that what you instructed?"

He chuckled again. It wasn't funny, and the dressing gown seemed to have grown more sleeves. Giselle turned both of them right side in, before finding another one. She tossed it aside, barely stopping her cry of frustration. She also stopped the rash of words. She hadn't considered the consequences of her command. She'd been testing her authority over *Madame* Dessard. She never intended Etienne to actually sleep with her. How could she have?

"Come, Giselle. Stop this nonsense and come back to bed. It's warmer in here. With me."

She shook her head.

"You weren't so cold to me before you woke. You found me quite comfortable. You snuggled against me. I know. I watched you."

He watched me?

How could she bear it? It felt like she'd betrayed the most beautiful thing she'd ever experienced – her newly discovered love for Navarre! And yet, she'd snuggled against Etienne...and didn't even know it?

She should have said something to her mama last night. That's what she should have done. Perhaps Papa would relent and let her rejoin the family after all....

No! Giselle thought. The *comte* didn't deserve Savignen Valley back. But what else could she do? What?

"Come back to bed, Giselle. See sense. It's quite cold out there. You can't hide it, you know. And I'm still a man. I can tell. You might as well be naked."

Giselle's face flamed as she crossed her arms about herself. Only a blunt, uncouth barbarian would say such a thing! She knew the sound she made resembled a snarl, but it was more. It was a wound to the heart. She'd betrayed her love for Navarre!

"You must obey me, Giselle. You do know that, don't you?"

He was trying to cajole her now? He might as well save his effort.

"I said I watched you, and it's true. I've been awake most of the night, thinking. I made a spectacle of myself last night. You have my word it won't happen again."

"I don't believe you."

The words were out before she could stop them. Giselle was amazed at her own daring.

"Why not?"

Because drunkards can't hold to promises! She longed to shout the words, but held her tongue.

"Come along, Giselle. My patience isn't that long."

"You drink too much," she said bluntly.

He laughed, and Giselle narrowed her eyes. It seemed Etienne was enjoying the situation.

"So? I can't walk, either. Pity about both. Anything else?"

"I don't know you."

"True enough. I hardly know you either. What of it? You're still my wife, and I'm your husband. You've womanly curves, too. I appreciate that."

Giselle gasped. "You're—That's so—it's...lewd." She was flustered, and the words sounded it.

The room grew lighter, and she saw him clearly as he leaned forward. "Lewd? Interesting word choice. I don't think I mind that you find me so. Truly. So, you've found a few of my defects. I have them. Who doesn't? If you look beyond them, you'll see I'm just a man, all the same. A man who happens to be your husband. I grow tired of repeating myself. Come back here. Now."

He no longer sounded pleasant, he sounded menacing, and just last night she'd likened him to a small boy? That had been naïve. She backed a step, and then another.

"Do you wish me to fetch a servant to make you obey? Or perhaps I'll summon my brother. Navarre will see to it that you do your duty. He'll see to it that you join your husband. He has no other choice. Is that what you want, Giselle?"

The moment he said the name, Giselle stopped. And then she started walking back to him, forcing one step after the next. Having that threat carried out was the worst thing she could imagine. She wondered if Etienne knew that.

He wouldn't quit staring as she reached the pedestal and stepped up. She had to turn aside from the blatant masculinity of his chest. Her eyes filled with tears. Her heart thudded, and each beat sent pain. She blinked rapidly at the velvet texture of her coverlet.

"You see? That wasn't so hard, was it?"

She couldn't answer. If she did, he'd know what she was trying to staunch.

"Now...if only you'd do it willingly, and not at the threat of my little brother's presence, all would be well, *non?* You'll work on that?"

Giselle nodded.

"Tres bien. Come closer now."

She shook with the effort, but leaned into the mattress. Wads of material in her hands kept her steady as her eyes overflowed with tears.

"Now give me a kiss."

She couldn't even face him and he wanted a kiss? He wanted her to touch his lips with her own? Giselle slammed her eyes shut to the horror of it, and didn't care that the tears slid off her chin and down her throat.

She'd found purgatory, and it wasn't part of any afterlife. It was here. Now. The Bible and the priests hadn't been succinct. Giselle's hands crushed the velvet into her palms and she concentrated on how that felt. Any sensation was better than feeling the touch of Etienne's lips against hers.

She'd have to cancel her riding plans with Navarre. She couldn't face him. Not now. Maybe never. A knot formed in her throat, choking her. A roar that sounded like thunderous rain pounded through each ear, so loud she almost didn't hear Etienne's snort.

Her eyes opened. He hadn't moved at all. He didn't expect her to crawl up into the bed beside him, did he?

"You're still a maid?" he asked. "What stupidity is this? You asked for me, Giselle. I thought it meant—." He stopped and ran his fingers through his long, blond hair, and then glared at her. "This is impossible! I don't want a sacrificial lamb I have to deflower! What fool would? I'm not even certain I can function, and now you toss this in? I certainly can't if you shrink from me. What were you thinking? I need a woman, not an unfledged girl! I need passion and heat, not tears and virginity. *Merde!*"

Giselle heard the pain in his voice and looked away. He didn't want her virginity? Only a fool would? What did that mean?

"I don't know what I was thinking. Or why. And I already have two sons — Jacques and Rene. I don't need you! As God is my witness, I don't know why I'm even here. Be gone from my sight! This moment! Go! I don't want maidenly fears. I don't want pity. And I can't abide tears! Go! Let me rest in peace."

His voice grew loud and bitter the longer he railed at her. Giselle didn't wait for the end of it. She tripped in her haste and fell to her knees beside the pedestal. She drew a quick cross of thankfulness on her breast before fleeing, pushing past rows of ball gowns to search for a place to hide in the wardrobe where she could sob in privacy. She didn't care if the servants found her there.

It would serve the *duc* right.

There were too many people in her wardrobe room.

Giselle told them twice before Louisa finally had Gerty leave. Giselle wasn't listening to any of their entreaties, either. She didn't care how the *duchesse* should behave. She knew what she wanted. She wanted her hair washed out, an ensemble set out for riding, and some answers.

"This would have been more convenient if you bathed in your chamber, Giselle," Louisa told her. "I can't imagine why we must make do with this enclosure. We are being pressured by your clothing, and you might splash. What would happen to your dresses, then?"

"I don't care."

"*Mai oui,* you're stubborn today."

"Call it what you will."

"This is a wardrobe chamber, Giselle, not a bathing room. It's so small we're tripping over each other to serve you."

"Send Gerty and the others away then. Isabelle may stay."

"You can't make do with such a small staff, Giselle. Especially with this coiffure. It'll take time to undo. What possessed you to—"

Giselle interrupted her. "I will not issue my orders again, Louisa. I will not argue them either. I bathe in here. Then, I'm going riding. Etienne isn't going to watch me. And unless you want the rest of the household to know why, you'd better make sure all these people are sent away. Away! Do you hear me?"

"It shall be as you wish, *Madame le Duchesse.*"

Louisa bowed formally and dismissed Gerty. Giselle knew tales of her bathing in the wardrobe room would grow until they'd think she'd used a closet. That was a misnomer. This room was easily as large as her tower in Chateau Antilli, and would have been convenient except for the dresses cluttering both sides of the available space.

"And shut the door after her!" Giselle shouted.

She heard Etienne's laugh. He was disgusting. Revolting. Confusing. He said he wanted a woman, but what did that make her? And who were these sons of his? She couldn't ask Gerty, Isabelle, or even Esmee, who arrived next after being told about Giselle's demands by Gerty.

Giselle didn't care. She was going riding with Navarre, and she would get the answers she deserved. If they were too horrid, she would leave. They could keep Savignen Valley. And good riddance. Giselle would join the convent of St. Mary in Bordeaux. *That's* what she was going to do.

She didn't tell Louisa her plans. That would just start another sermon on how she needed to live more and pray less. Giselle must not have been praying enough. Etienne was her penance. She shuddered just thinking of him.

"Is the water too cold, *Madame?*"

Isabelle held out a towel as she asked it.

"*Non.* I'm letting my imagination run amok again. What time is *Monsieur* Navarre riding? Has he said yet?"

"At four, *Madame.*"

Isabelle was avoiding her gaze. She wasn't calling her Giselle, either. Giselle knew why. The entire household was probably under the assumption that she prepared herself for an assignation with Navarre. Giselle lips thinned. She no longer cared what they thought.

"Bring my dress, Isabelle, and don't waste any more time."

Giselle was curt. Annoyed. They must have suspected as much, for no one spoke again. And if anyone questioned anything, she was ready to snap at them, too.

CHAPTER TWELVE

Navarre probably looked as incredibly handsome as always in his red breeches and black frock coat, but Giselle ignored him as she stormed down the steps. She came to a stop beside the beast she was to mount. She'd have been terrified of one as big as Navarre's but hers looked more like an overgrown puppy. It was uninspiring against the stylish gown Isabelle had laced her into.

She didn't care about such things as her appearance anymore. She hadn't even checked in the mirror before she left. How could she? Etienne was still there. Drinking. From a lounging position in her immense bed. Surveying the chambers as if he belonged there.

Giselle looked down at herself. The gown was tight against her cinched-in waist, the skirt wasn't full, but it was voluminous, and gone was the high, powdered arrangement of her hair. She was grateful for the comforting weight of her bun against the back of her neck, although the elegant hat on her head was as unwieldy as *Monsieur* Poinre' s creation from the previous day.

"You look splendid, Giselle."

Navarre smiled down at her, and she glared at him until the smile left.

"Put me on the horse, Navarre, and get me away from this horrid castle."

"Horrid? What has happened? If Etienne has—.

"He has done nothing, but I refuse to talk near these walls! They tell too many tales. And I refuse to be gossiped about any further."

"Very well."

He lifted her easily, and Giselle tried to squelch the instant reaction to his hands about her waist. She was angry with him, too. He was a Berchald. And the entire family was perverse, not just Jean-Claude.

Still, she felt the heat of a blush at his touch. She needed more material about herself to protect herself from the experience.

"Since you haven't ridden before, I'll lead."

Giselle nodded and tried not to watch as he mounted his horse right beside her. She'd assumed it wasn't possible to gasp in her corset, but she was wrong. Despite what everyone thought, she wanted answers from him, nothing more.

It was a pity her heart wasn't listening.

Giselle's hands on the saddle horn trembled. It would help if Navarre wasn't sitting so straight in his saddle right in front of her...or if the queue showing beneath his hat weren't so golden-blond...or if his shoulders weren't so wide. His hips so slender...

Her horse started off. Giselle choked back the cry of surprise. It would never do if he thought her frightened, and after a few steps, she realized that she wasn't. This riding was no worse than the cabriolet had been, only a bit stranger. She moved backward and forward with the animal's gait, pleased with herself.

"Do you have any preference on time or how far you wish to ride?"

They reached the gate. It was a different entrance than the one they used when she first arrived. Giselle looked through the opening at gray stone that stretched out to line the road for some distance. A few trees shaded the lane, and she held her breath in wonder as they thinned. Finally, she saw the size of her own dowry.

"You didn't answer me, Giselle. Giselle?"

Navarre turned in his saddle, so much higher than her on his big horse. Giselle couldn't see his expression in the shadow thrown by his hat, but he could see hers. She could tell by his next words.

"Ah. The valley. It's beautiful, isn't it? Very productive, too. We have the best yield in all of France. I have an excellent overseer, too."

"I?" she queried.

"Well...Etienne doesn't show much interest in any part of the Berchald estate, so I do." He shrugged and turned back around. "If you wish to tour Savignen Valley, it will take until nightfall."

"I came for answers, Navarre, not sights."

"That is what I assumed. I'll start a trot. Let me know if we go too fast."

Let him know? How was she to do that?

As soon as the animal started moving faster, Giselle bounced, feeling as if each movement might send her over its head. She hung on for what seemed hours, before Navarre slowed.

"There. That is our race course. You see?"

He pointed to his right as they walked toward a fenced area. Giselle glanced at what could be a racing course or not. It was difficult to tell, for the area was greatly overgrown.

"Designed by the tenth *duc,* it was to be three stretches followed by a series of jumps over there. Do you see them?"

She saw what Navarre was referring to. The obstacles were constructed of widely spaced poles. Some had fallen. Some supported the shrubbery that grew around them.

"It looks bad, Giselle, but Etienne ordered no one to touch it after the accident."

He stopped, and Giselle's horse drew alongside him without her influence. She patted its neck gratefully, hoping Navarre wouldn't spot her trembling.

"The accident...it happened here?" she asked.

"*Oui.* I was...about fourteen. And the one thing I loved was being with Etienne. He was my hero. I know he's different now, but he wasn't always so difficult. He was an outstanding rider, too. I used to hold my breath in wonder at his expertise. He was good at whatever he tried, though. He was everything I wanted to be, and more."

He sighed and moved his finger to the jumps. "See that one, the third? Etienne wanted that one set even higher. It was a difficult jump, even for him."

The top pole was still attached to one side, although a vine claimed it. It looked to be well above her head.

"Higher?" she asked.

"*Oui.* And he made it, Giselle. I recall how wonderful it looked, too, just before he flew off. The horse didn't knock off that top rail. Etienne's body did. I ran to him, but he refused to let me help. He ordered me to get transport and a doctor. He said he couldn't move.

"That's when I saw that he still had the saddle between his legs. The cinch was cut almost cleanly in two. It would have broken under any strain, let alone a jump like he'd just done. Someone had tried to kill him and nearly succeeded."

Giselle put a hand to her throat. *Etienne told the truth last night?* She was in shock. It sounded in her voice.

"Jean-Claude? Then...why was nothing done?" Giselle asked.

"Imagine the scandal to the family. And the loss of the vineyard if Etienne's disability became known. We couldn't chance it."

"The Berchalds allowed an attempt at murder to go unpunished? I can't believe what I'm hearing. I can't."

"It was Etienne's decision, Giselle. He sided with our mother. That's why she accompanied Jean-Claude to Versailles Palace, and stays with him there."

"Your mother?"

Giselle looked from the rail to Navarre and back at the railing. She couldn't stand to see the bitterness etched on his face.

"Only by keeping a close watch on Jean-Claude does she keep Etienne safe."

"This is incredible. *Non!* Worse. I never heard of such devious behavior. How could she let it go unpunished? Doesn't she love Etienne?"

Navarre smiled down at her, making her feel naive and young.

"Jean-Claude is as much her son as Etienne is. How could any mother choose, Giselle?"

She opened her mouth and shut it again. She knew very little, especially of a mother's love for a child. How could she? She couldn't remember receiving it. The thought reminded her of Etienne's taunt that morning.

"Navarre? Who are Jacques and Rene?"

She startled him. He lurched backwards, almost falling from his horse. It should have made her smile, but it didn't.

"He told you of them? *Mon Dieu!* The man has no sense. He's a mean-spirited, rude, satirical—" He bit off his words. "Why, Giselle? Why would he tell you of them?"

She looked down at her hands on the saddle pommel. Licked her lips. Forced her voice to work. "He—he said...I'm not woman...enough. And since he already has two sons...it's not worth his trouble."

"He said that? *Tiens!* He's a brute, as well. I don't know where he could come up with something like that, Giselle. You're every bit a woman, and so much more, I don't know where to start. You're beautiful, engaging, witty, everything a man hopes for...."

His voice lowered, as if he worried someone might overhear. In the open near a race-course? Chateau Berchand couldn't reach here, could it?

"He says...no fool wants...a—a maiden."

"What? No! He didn't! He couldn't!"

"And he said...I lack passion. I may. I don't even know what...it is."

She looked up at him, and saw anger, disgust, and along with that, abject longing. Giselle knew what the combination had to be, because she felt the exact same emotions.

"I have something to show you, Giselle," Navarre finally said, in a tightly controlled voice. "And it's some distance. Hang on."

They set out across the vineyard. All she paid attention to was holding on. She couldn't believe he'd go so fast on her first ride. She should have known where he was taking her, too. The Minot farmhouse loomed through the trees after a span, and she didn't even question it.

"You ride very well, Giselle," Navarre said. "I should have expected it. Did it frighten you unduly? I hope not, for I'm not accustomed to going at such a slow trot."

Slow trot? She shook her head. He turned back around and shouted toward the house.

"Minot!"

It wasn't *Madame* Minot who stepped from the door. It was a slightly smaller version.

"Ah. Desiree. I'm pleased you're home."

"Monsieur Navarre! We...didn't expect you! Mama should have said something." She wiped her hands on her apron and looked around so furtively that Giselle looked, too, although she didn't know what they were looking for.

"Of course you didn't. I just thought of it. I have brought the *Duchesse* du Berchald to meet Jacques."

Giselle thought the woman might faint. Navarre must have thought the same thing, for he leaped to the ground and ran to the porch. Giselle watched with interest. She was already assigning meaning to

Navarre's words, and instinctively she knew she was right. Desiree must be this Jacques' mother. Giselle stifled the instant distaste. If Etienne preferred a woman her size, no wonder he called Giselle a girl.

"Jacques isn't available, *Monsieur*. He has chores. You know that. But you say nothing of Rene. Why?"

The woman whispered, but Giselle heard her. She leaned towards them, and her horse actually followed the unspoken command by stepping closer.

"Etienne may be blind, Desiree, but I am not. Send for Jacques. And Rene, if you like. I care little at this point."

Navarre shrugged, dismissing her, just as laughter diverted Giselle's attention. Three boys came into the clearing. The sticks on their shoulders and the string of fish the smallest held showed where they had been.

"Monsieur du Berchald! I'm pleased to see you again." The tallest, easily distinguishable as Etienne's bastard son, swept into as courtly a bow as any Giselle had seen. He had the coloring and height of a Berchald, but was nowhere near as lean. Instead, he was almost as wide as his mother.

He turned his attention to Giselle. Eyes as blue as Etienne's regarded her. She gathered she would be shorter than he, although she was mounted, forcing him to look up at her.

"Bonjour Mademoiselle. I'm very pleased to meet you. Jacques Minot, at your service."

"This is the *Duchesse* du Berchald, Jacques, not a *mademoiselle"*

Giselle wondered if the hard note in Navarre's voice meant anything. The boy looked at his uncle, then back at her.

"Pity," he remarked and shook his head.

Giselle almost laughed.

"This is Rene Minot, my brother," he continued. "Rene? *Madame,* la *Duchesse* du Berchald. She's very pretty, *non?"*

Giselle looked at the boy bowing before her. He didn't favor a Berchald at all, unless it was Jean-Claude, whom she had yet to meet. Giselle looked to Navarre, who was watching her intently. And then she knew what he was trying to tell her. Giselle nodded. It was obvious Rene couldn't be Etienne's son. Only an invalid, locked in his castle would believe it.

"Navarre? Would you be so good as to assist me down? I would like to wash up, if it would be no trouble."

Giselle ignored Jacques' eager hands beside her and waited.

"Of course, Giselle. I'm certain Desiree will show you to the comfort room. Desiree?"

Navarre reached her and pulled her into his arms. She'd forgotten how it felt to be carried by him. So close! So warm! The arms about her tightened, and she turned away. It was as impossible as before, perhaps more.

Her hat made it difficult for him to hold her close, yet he did. Giselle leaned away so that the tulle border wouldn't scrape his face. She didn't meet his glance, though. That would have been too intimate.

The porch came too soon. Navarre held to her until she stood, looking at the decking as her face reddened.

"So sweet," he whispered before turning.

Giselle gulped.

"Mama, look at the fish we caught. Grandmama will be pleased with Bernard, won't she?"

"Bernard?"

Navarre asked it as Giselle moved toward the door. It was too sordid a truth already. She didn't wish to know more.

"Bernard? This is *Monsieur* Navarre du Berchald. From the castle."

"Greetings, Bernard. I haven't seen you about before. Have you a *pere?*"

Giselle slid through the door, trying not to listen. Still, she heard as Desiree answered.

"It's none of your concern, *Monsieur* du Berchald, who fathered my son, or who I spend my time with. You pay well for Jacques and Rene, and that's all you do. You know what will happen...."

Giselle found the comfort room before she heard anymore. She regarded her face in the mirror for a few moments before splashing cold water on herself. It was strange, but she didn't look any older. She felt it.

Navarre was ready to assist her to remount when she came back out. Giselle tried ignoring him. His hands seemed to burn through the material, and his breath teased her ear. She was determined, though. He was a Berchald. And she was finished with them. She'd made her decision while watching herself in the Minot's mirror. She knew she'd never appeal to her husband, and she couldn't continue being so close to his younger brother with how she felt.

That left the convent of St. Mary. It was her only choice. She almost looked forward to it. It was a relief to have it settled.

CHAPTER THIRTEEN

They rode down the road for some distance before Navarre spoke again. He was riding just in front of her, and turned his head to speak over his shoulder.

"Well. There you have it, Giselle. That was Jacques. Etienne's illegitimate son. I must apologize for the other. I didn't expect our visit to turn so...."

"Ugly?" she supplied the word.

He nodded without turning.

"It's hardly surprising anymore, *Monsieur*. I'm beginning to expect ugly secrets every time I'm alone with you."

He spun at her words, but didn't speak. Instead, he simply sat there, rolling with his horse's gait, regarding her with a strange expression. Giselle returned it, not realizing she'd held her breath until he turned back around, allowing her to exhale.

Merde, but he affected her. It wasn't fair. Or sane. Or smart. It still happened.

Navarre picked up his pace without asking. Giselle suspected it was to get the entire experience over with. She should be grateful. She wasn't. This was the last time she'd be alone with him. She'd made her decision. The convent at Bordeaux wasn't going to be any easier to bear if she prolonged time with him.

But how could she get her heart to listen?

They left the road, heading into the trees. Probably to save time. Rid himself of her sooner. The woods grew denser. Darker. The trail started to climb, and he still didn't alter the pace.

"Where are you taking me, Navarre?"

"The arbor," was his terse answer delivered over his shoulder.

"What's that?"

He didn't answer.

The trees thickened until Giselle had to lean close to her mount's neck for fear her bonnet would catch on a branch and pull her from the horse. Navarre was being impossible. The entire trip was a mistake.

And it got darker. Giselle frowned. She opened her mouth to ask again, then shut it as they reached a small clearing. It was as overgrown as the race course. Secluded. Private.

Navarre slid from his horse and looped the reins around a vine-covered branch.

"Where are we?" Giselle whispered.

His face was unreadable. "I told you. The arbor."

He gestured at a dark shelter hidden in the shadow. Giselle saw a divan tucked inside. Her eyes went wide and her heart thumped mightily as she realized what the arbor was used for.

Non. He wouldn't dare! And she wouldn't let him. Would she?

"Why are we here, Navarre?"

He reached for her. Giselle clung to the saddle horn. She'd made her decision. There was no room for this. His hands touched at her waist, heating through the silk of her riding gown. He rubbed his thumbs along her sides, creating even more warmth.

This couldn't be happening. She should stop it.

"I won't harm you, *ma petit*. I vow it."

He smiled, and Giselle was lost. It wasn't a lunge, but it was close. Her cry was lost in the trees about them as she moved her hands to his shoulders. And then she slid down his frame until she stood right beside him.

Touching.

Leaves rustled as a hint of air brushed through the bower. Giselle had never felt the like. This can't be happening! *I can't let it—*

One of his arms pulled her to him. With the other hand he reached for her chin, lifting it until she looked at him.

"Trust me, *ma petit.*" He whispered it.

She shouldn't. She should be pushing from this embrace and screeching her anger at this manhandling. She should be affronted by his actions. She should be doing anything other than catching her breath in anticipation.

Sweet heaven. She couldn't help it. She loved him.

Someone should have warned her it was an impossible emotion to fight, and no convent walls were strong enough to constrain it.

He sensed her answer. Giselle knew it as his lips curved into a smile, and she saw the flash of teeth. His forefinger held up her face as he lowered his.

Giselle closed her eyes, absorbing the scent of greenery filling her senses until it combined with his smell. His lips trailed down her nose, and Giselle whimpered with the disappointment. She couldn't stand for it again. She wanted more than a chaste kiss. She wanted...

"I love you, Gis—"

She stopped his whisper by reaching up, and yanking his head down. The move slammed her lips to his with a shockwave that rippled and then elated. He groaned and she joined it, not feeling his fingers on her hat ribbons until it fell down her back. Pins followed, and her hair tumbled down next. She struggled for each breath, tasting him as he was her. Gulping. Moaning. Thrilling. And her entire body felt it, lurching against him time and again. Closer. Crushing her belly against his hardness. She'd never felt so wanton or sensitive or responsive before.

"Easy...love."

His breathing was harsh as he lifted from her lips. And he was waiting when she opened her eyes. This was insane. Evil. Horrid. What had compelled her? Giselle looked into his eyes and felt the instant stab of tears.

What was she doing? He was out of reach. He always had been. He always would be. *Oh, dearest God.* She'd just kissed her brother-in-law! She was wicked, depraved, and immoral. Evil. Everything she'd called Etienne...

But she was worse. She wanted more!

"Don't cry, Giselle. Please?"

He lifted her, and she clung, wetting his shirt as she sobbed with a blizzard of emotions that all blended: shock and pleasure; disgust and thrill; horror and bliss.

Navarre sat, keeping her atop his lap. She guessed they were within the leafy shelter. She refused to look up, even as her tears gave way to sniffles.

"I...am sorry, Na...varre." She wiped at her cheeks.

"For what, *ma petit?* Kissing me? But that was my doing. I couldn't help it any longer. And...it doesn't always have to be ugly secrets with us. It—I go too fast. It wasn't your fault I brought you here. It's not your fault that I couldn't hold in my desires. But it *is* your fault for being so perfect, adorable, innocent, and very passionate. Etienne is blinded by his disability. I needed to prove it to you."

Giselle stiffened. "Is that why you brought me here...to educate me?" She tried to keep her voice steady as fresh tears filled her eyes.

"*Non,* my sweet. I'd never assign such a word to it. I love you, Giselle. You hear me? I love you. I've tried to ignore it. I've tried to fight it. I want you to know this. I wish it wasn't so, but at the same time, I know that it is. I can't change it. I felt it the moment you gripped my arm in the cabriolet. Do you remember? You were so small. So frightened. So perfect. You made me feel...I couldn't describe it then. I still can't.

"I want to hold you as closely as possible, kiss away your tears, and share the passion you definitely have. Educate you? Oh, my darling...I'm only thrilled that Etienne finds you lacking. *Non!* I mustn't think that! I mustn't. I've counseled myself, Giselle. I've prayed. I've tried to follow what I know to be right. This is complete madness...and yet look at me. Holding you when I mustn't. Speaking what should stay unvoiced. I must get you and my brother to see sense...when it's something even I can't see."

Giselle was kissing his throat as he spoke, making him choke on the words. She loved the faintly scratchy feel against her lips. She loved everything about him! And he loved her!

"I...love you, too."

She whispered it against his earlobe and felt him shudder at either the touch or the words.

"Don't say so, Giselle. I forbid it. It's enough that I have to live with this torment. How can I ask another to share it? Especially the one I love?"

He sighed deeply. Giselle lifted her head and held his in her hands, making him look at her. There was pain, torment, and love in those unique eyes. Her heart felt each one in turn.

"Listen to me, Navarre. Listen. Did I ask to love you? *Non.* Will I ever feel the same for Etienne? *Non.* Will I regret finding out...that you feel the same? *Non.* It will be all I have for comfort. Don't you understand?"

"I wish I didn't, and yet I cannot say that! You are too innocent to answer such questions! And I am a brute for making you. I beg of you, Giselle. Forget this. Forget I said what I did. Forget—*Mon Dieu!* What am I asking? I can as soon forget what just happened as quit breathing. I am a knave."

"No, Navarre."

"*Non?* What do you call it when I make love to my brother's wife? There is only one worse sin, Giselle. I'm afraid of what else I'm capable of. And now, we must go. We mustn't stay here. Not like this. Not...together. Forgive me for bringing you."

"Do you wish forgiveness for the kiss...too?"

Fresh tears flooded her eyes as she asked it, and Navarre's eyes appeared moist, too. Giselle couldn't bear to continue looking, and yet was unable to look away.

"I cannot answer that, *ma petit*."

"Why?"

"To know you share this torment is worse than living through it alone. Don't ask anything more of me. I'm too much of a coward."

"Well, I won't forgive it, even if you do ask. It's all I have. And I'll dream of it when no one else knows, too. Nobody can take that from me."

"Oh, Giselle."

He pulled her close, and she breathed deeply, matching every one of his. The way he said her name affected her as much as his tremors.

"This is madness, my love. You know that, don't you?"

She nodded against him.

"You must help me."

"How?" Giselle pulled from him.

"Try not to be so desirable."

Giselle giggled. "How...am I supposed to do that?"

"And never come riding with me again. No matter how many times I may beg you, say no. Don't be alone with me, either. Ever. Always make certain there's someone else about."

"Then you have to make yourself less handsome."

She'd surprised him. It was on the look on his face and in his voice. "You find me that? Truly?"

"I think you're the most handsome man I've ever seen."

She was blushing as she said it and had trouble meeting his eyes.

"Oh, Giselle, my love. This is not helping."

He was hugging her to him again.

"Come. We lose daylight, and I'm not a proficient enough lady's maid to redo your hair. Forgive me for that, as well. I lost control for a bit there."

Giselle ginned so widely, she felt her mouth might tear. He wasn't proficient with hair? That was wonderful. She couldn't share him with another woman; especially one such as Desiree. It was wonderful too, that he had lost control.

"It is no matter, Navarre."

Giselle leaned to kiss the tip of his nose before sliding from his lap, and returning to the horse, searching among the deadfall for her pins. She didn't need an assist. She'd done it before. Yet, everything felt different. As if she'd gained new sensitivity. Her hair felt slick and erotic. His hands about her waist as he reseated her felt like they left marks. And the sensation of the hard saddle against her *derriere* was almost impossible to withstand. And yet she must.

He handed her the hat. Giselle retied it and then watched him toss a leg over his mount. He had very long legs. Muscled. Strong. Lean. What she wouldn't give to feel them against hers...

"Don't look at me like that, Giselle," he said. "Or I won't be responsible for my own actions."

He was teasing, yet he wasn't, and she couldn't look away. He bent to retrieve her reins. Giselle watched the material in his jacket move, wondering what it would be like to feel his bare chest pressed against hers, as well.

"They will never believe us innocent, Giselle, if you continue that."

He was chastising her, but smiling as he did so. Giselle was grateful the sun was setting. She nearly unbalanced herself looking back at the arbor, but it was worth it. The sun's last rays touched the tips of the dark-green vines. The sight was etched into her memory and her senses. She still smelled Navarre on her, too, and she lowered her head to the ribbons at her chin.

He loves me, and I love him.

She longed to shout it, but it was just another secret the castle would have to hide. It was darker beneath the trees as twilight closed in, and Giselle looked about her. It was good it was dark. That's where their love belonged. It was evil. Lustful. Sinful.

It was completely dark before her tears started up again.

Giselle was so lost in crying, she thought when they stopped that they were at the gate. She opened her eyes to see Navarre come out of the gloom with a handkerchief in his hand.

"Don't cry, Giselle. I beg it of you."

"Then you shouldn't have given me this."

She held it to her nose and caught his scent. That added to the void building within her, the one blacker than the night all about them.

Navarre walked around the horse and lifted a hind leg.

"What are you doing?" Giselle mopped at her tears as she asked it.

"Removing a shoe. That way, Swift Night will limp, and our story will be believed."

Swift Night? Her mount? Giselle almost laughed. And that was a relief . "What story?" she asked.

'Your horse threw a shoe in the vineyard. We've been delayed immensely because of it."

"You're very good with stories...Navarre."

Saying his name even caused a reaction. Giselle fought to stop the shivers.

"Well, I wasn't always the paragon of duty you see before you, my love. I had to have a story for my mama, didn't I?"

He must have sensed her lurch of pain as she realized what he meant. He needed a story for being late coming back? Perhaps it was because he was seeing someone like Desiree?

"Giselle, you worry for nothing. I've never loved another. Nor wanted to. How could I after my fiancée threw me over for Jean-Claude's vaunted attractions?"

"Jean-Claude? Your brother? I...don't understand." And she was reeling. Giselle bent forward over the pommel to keep her balance.

"My betrothed is a very beautiful woman. Headstrong. Spoiled."

"What has that to do with it?"

"She's an only daughter, Giselle. Her *pere* gives in to her every whim."

"But a betrothal is binding."

He shrugged. "So they say. Who am I to question it? Do I look desperate enough to enforce it when she wants life at court and *him*, not the chateau with me?"

"But....Jean-Claude?"

"Who can understand women? Look about. I have little to offer. She found marriage to me wasn't to her liking just yet. Jean-Claude is the heir-apparent to the duchy. He could buy her carriages, dresses, and jewels that stun the eye, not 'pea-sized sapphires' such as I offered."

"She couldn't wed with him, though," Giselle said. "I don't understand."

"Jean-Claude has many attractions to the ladies, Giselle. I, for one, cannot fathom what they are. All I know is *Mademoiselle* wanted life at Versailles Palace as his mistress more than she wanted me."

Giselle heard the disgust in his voice, but couldn't answer. The latest secret was too much to assimilate. Jean-Claude...and Navarre's betrothed? She preferred being Jean-Claude's mistress to a wife? What sort of woman was so stupid?

'There. I've finished. Swift Night will have a strange gait until we get home."

"He won't be in pain, will he?"

Giselle stroked the little horse's mane. Navarre chuckled.

"That must be what makes you so different, Giselle. It makes me long to kiss any unhappiness from your mouth, and to see you smile. You have such a generous spirit. No other woman would care, but the animal's suffering is your first thought. *Je t'aime, ma petit.*"

His voice dropped to a whisper, then he turned from her and remounted his horse.

"Just as I love you."

She wanted to shout it, but that would never do. Ever. They resumed riding. Swift Night did walk oddly, but the castle gate loomed in the darkness within moments. And that meant her ride was over.

All of it.

CHAPTER FOURTEEN

"I can't believe the trials you've gone through, *Madame*. Look at this gown! It will take all day to press out the wrinkles, and your hair! I hope I can get a comb through it," Gerty continued.

Giselle bit on her tongue and resolved that if anyone said another word, she might scream.

"Giselle, are you certain you won't dress in your chamber?" Louisa asked.

She refused to answer. She knew Etienne was in her bed, surveying the room like a king. Louisa was being wise, but Giselle was beyond listening. Louisa wanted the *duchesse* to act with propriety, not to give Gerty more to talk about.

Giselle sighed. She refused to let Etienne watch her dress. It felt like sacrilege.

"Which nightgown would you like warmed, *Madame?*" Gerty asked. "This one? Or would you like one a bit more...concealing?"

She held up another filmy nightgown decked in lace. In her other hand was the one Giselle wanted. Made of heavy cotton, it was tied at the neckline with a pink ribbon. Giselle didn't let the maid know the answer.

"See that a supper tray is sent up for the *duc* and me, Gerty. See to it at once."

"Very good, *Madame.*"

The maid bowed and handed both gowns to Isabelle, whose inclusion into the wardrobe room made it more stifling. When Isabelle held up the cotton one, Giselle nodded. They knew her too well.

"Thank the Lord you're finally seeing sense." Louisa was using her lecturing tone. "The talk has been about nothing but you and Navarre. How can you be so blind? Even if you become a mother, they'll suspect it's his child!"

"What…did you just say?" Giselle gasped.

"You heard me."

She turned and stormed from the room while Giselle narrowed her eyes. There was no point in arguing with her about it. There would never be a child.

"She shouldn't have said that, Giselle."

Isabelle helped her into the nightgown as she spoke. Giselle was so grateful for its concealment, she nearly hugged the maid.

"You'd never do anything as evil as they whisper. I told them so."

"*Merci,* Isabelle. And could you leave orders that the *duc* and I are not disturbed?"

The smile that lit her face warmed Giselle, and she needed it. Cold squeezed off her breath almost as she spoke. She *was* capable of the things being whispered, but she refused to repent and seek God's forgiveness just yet.

She'd set aside her decision to join a convent for the time being. Navarre's embrace in the arbor was too enticing. She wasn't prepared enough. Aspiring nuns didn't melt into their brother-in-law's arms and steal kisses when no one was looking.

Giselle wished that was all she was guilty of.

She wanted more. Her entire body was aching with denial, and there was no one she could unburden herself to. If she had to stay from Navarre's presence forevermore, then she had to have one more kiss. Just one. She'd confess all, if God granted her just one. She wouldn't ask for more.

Isabelle wouldn't have believed what her mistress was wishing for as she watched Giselle join Etienne in the bedchamber. Giselle had trouble believing it, herself.

"It's about time you decided to entertain me," Etienne said. "Dismiss your woman and come here."

Giselle ignored his complaints and smiled as Gerty brought in a tray of food. Giselle was wrapped in a thick robe, concealing which nightgown she wore. It was odd, but she watched as Gerty tried to decipher it before she left, following on Isabelle's heel.

Such a strange household.

"Bring me a little bit of supper, too, Giselle," Etienne said.

"You've already eaten." She replied and bit into a croissant.

"Then bring me some wine. I'm thirsty. Giselle? Didn't you hear me?"

It was pleasant to ignore him, and she had Navarre's love to thank. It was like a warm blanket about her.

"Oh...I don't think so. You've already had too much to drink."

She glanced at him. His jaw dropped, and she stifled a laugh.

"What has Navarre done to change you so? I'll wring his neck, I swear it."

Giselle regarded him from across the room as he slammed his fist into his palm. She was no longer frightened of him. Her heart lightened as she realized it. He didn't scare her and he couldn't threaten her. She had Navarre's love protecting her. She'd never go near Etienne again, and he couldn't force her.

"Navarre? He took me to see Jacques and Rene," she informed him. "I also met Desiree, and I'm not impressed by what you consider womanly, Etienne." His name came out more sarcastically than she intended, and she bit into her roll again.

His mouth opened wider in shock. She enjoyed keeping him off balance.

"You met...Desiree?" He choked on the words.

She turned aside to hide her grin. "Oh. Yes. Since she's almost as large as her mama, I could see I'll never appeal to you."

"Desiree? Large? I don't believe you."

"So? That hardly concerns me. She also has another little bastard to add to her brood, a boy child named Bernard. She wouldn't tell Navarre who fathered the child, but it was probably the same as Rene."

That was a dangerous thing to say, but Giselle didn't care. He no longer frightened her.

"Rene's my child! How dare you question it?" He was almost purple with rage.

She turned to face him. "I dare, because it's true. I also don't care how many illegitimate children you support, Etienne. I won't bed with you. I refuse. If you try and force me, I have two options — I can join a convent near Bordeaux, or I'll let my papa seek the annulment he so desperately desires. Am I making myself clear?"

He lifted up his arms and made fists as he glared at her. Despite her earlier self-assurance, Giselle found him very intimidating. If she hadn't been in the arbor with Navarre, she probably would have been a trembling wretch under that gaze. As it was, she barely managed to suppress an unpleasant shiver.

Then he surprised her.

Giselle's eyes widened as he fell back onto the pillows and laughed aloud. It was her turn to be shocked. She was still speechless when he lifted his head.

"I believe we'll get along fine after all, *Madame* la *Duchesse,*" he said in a low tone.

Giselle was surprised at the look in his eyes. She put her hand to her throat at what looked like...interest? Lust? Her aggressiveness made him desire her? She gulped at the thought.

"Why...if you'll join me up here, perhaps I can perform after all. Come. I look forward to testing it. Come, *Madame.*"

"Didn't you hear what I said? You disgust me, and it isn't your disability that does so. It's you!"

"Ho. Ho. This is exceptional. Come, Giselle. See sense. You are wanting a man, and I want an heir. Admit it. Whatever happened to you appears to have opened your eyes to carnal pleasure. It will be a pleasure to initiate you. Come. Your anger arouses me more. I've never seen such womanliness."

He lifted the covers beside him as he finished. Giselle grabbed up her rosary and ran for the wardrobe room, bolting the door behind her. He was disgusting. The food in her stomach threatened to erupt at the thought.

Etienne got aroused by her anger? That was revolting. Jean-Claude couldn't possibly be as bad. And she intended to tell them all the moment it was light.

"I can't imagine why Navarre insists on moving to the Dower House."

Giselle's fingers stumbled on the keys of the pianoforte as Aunt Mimi continued her conversation to Esmee. It took two more chords before she recovered sufficiently to blend the notes again.

"It's been closed up so long it'll take an age to make it habitable again. It was never as lovely or as imposing as the castle, anyway. I wonder what the boy's up to. Oh Giselle. You play divinely. I can't think where you learned such talent, or from whom."

Giselle glanced up and smiled. "My tutor was a man named...*Jacques.*"

She waited for either of them to react to the name, but there was none. It seemed Giselle was the only female with knowledge of Etienne's illegitimate son. That should surprise her. It didn't.

"He was certainly a master. Are you playing his music?"

"*Oui*," she answered.

That seemed to satisfy them, and while she listened for a few more moments, neither woman said a thing. Navarre was moving away from her? *Non. He couldn't be so cruel.*

Could he?

Giselle's fingers slipped again. This time she caught it before any discordant notes. Although the pianoforte had only been invented in 1709, by the year of Giselle's birth, no noble family was without one. The Chateau Antilli had two. There was an ornate, white one on display in the music room, and an older, carved wooden one that Giselle had been trained on. It wasn't as elegant, but the notes sounded so sweetly that Jacques exclaimed when he heard them.

Giselle closed her eyes. Reminisced. She'd been about eight, maybe younger when the tutor had first arrived. Louisa had already made certain Giselle knew rudimentary scales, and Jacques had been impressed.

"This instrument is *tres belle, Mademoiselle.* Forgive my rudeness, I keep forgetting. You are no *Mademoiselle,* are you? Please continue, *Madame* Giselle. I've never heard such lovely sounds. I've been writing down some notes, and I'd love to have you practice them for me."

He gave her a sheaf of brown paper mottled with black dots. Giselle didn't recall what happened to the original score, but she memorized it and played it for years afterward. The man had been a musical genius.

"He's never mentioned a preference. I suppose it is lonely for him. Why did he not speak of it before now?"

Aunt Mimi's words invaded Giselle's reverie, causing her fingers to stumble again. She concentrated on her playing, instead of their words. Inanimate objects rather than feelings.

The instrument at Chateau Berchand didn't play as well as her old one, but it was still generous sounding. The notes softly sought each corner of the immense room in which the ladies sat, but it wasn't loud enough to hide Aunt Mimi and Esmee's conversation.

About Navarre.

She shouldn't listen. It was inviting heartbreak. She should stop playing. Retreat to a quiet corner. Hide. But that would never do. No one must ever guess the emotion she was hiding.

The keys misted before her eyes. She was grateful she could play from memory. She closed her eyes again and let her fingers move for her. Jacques' music had never sounded so lost. Giselle didn't recall when she changed to another of his compositions. She'd played it for him whenever he requested it, but she hated it, because it made her cry.

"Perhaps it's for the best," Aunt Mimi said softly. "Gossip must never cast such a shadow on the Berchald name, you know."

She worries about gossip with Esmee, a woman who married so far below her station that she was disowned? She gossips with her about Navarre and me? How can I bear it?

There would be Mass that night. And that really would be the end. Giselle had begged *le bon Dieu* for just one more stolen kiss, but it wasn't to be. Navarre was leaving her, moving somewhere where she wouldn't torment him. She should be grateful.

She breathed deeply, shaking through the sobs she dared not utter. Dared not even admit. She may understand why, but that didn't make it easier.

"Navarre will come to supper, won't he?" Esmee asked. "It will be rude of him not to when I have planned the settings. Did he tell you?"

Giselle held her breath and waited for the answer.

"You've heard how he raves about Chef Aaron's meals. He won't miss it."

They didn't know. Navarre tired sometimes of heavy sauces. He'd said as much that first day. During their lone supper. At the Minot farmhouse.

"He really should have said something."

Giselle couldn't finish playing. The memory of Navarre's words on the day they'd first met, or what had happened since, was too immense. Her hands hammered a discord from the deep octaves of the keyboard. "Pardon me, ladies," she said. "I don't feel well."

She sensed Esmee's concern, although Aunt Mimi simply looked at her blankly. Giselle guessed she was pale, but she wasn't crying. That was taking an act of will to accomplish.

"I must have overexerted myself yesterday. I...I've never ridden before."

"You will be at supper? I've planned—"

"If I am unable to attend, Esmee, you will be the first I inform."

Giselle turned swiftly toward the door. She'd heard Esmee's gasp at the curtness of her reply, but she didn't care. She couldn't care. Caring meant the ocean of ache she was holding back had value. She climbed slowly to the second floor, her legs feeling leaden and sore. She stopped at the landing, rubbing at her thighs as she considered her options.

She couldn't go to her own chambers. Etienne was still there, and he ignored her request for him to return to his own rooms that very morning.

Giselle had awakened, feeling suffocated by the robe wrapped tightly about her. She'd still slept in it, fearing Etienne would somehow reach her through the locked door to the wardrobe room. When she peeked out, she saw him sprawled across the bed again, as if he'd tried to move and failed. Giselle was grateful she had locked the door.

She allowed Isabelle to finish dressing her, and it was almost done before the maid and Louisa knocked for entry, anyway. Giselle ignored Louisa's clicking tongue. The governess must've sensed something, because she didn't say a word.

Giselle wondered now, where it was safe to go. There were only two choices, really: her room or Etienne's. She shook her head at her own stupidity. No one would think to look for her in the *duc's* rooms, and she could lock the connecting door.

She walked into the ducal chamber. The room looked much better after being thoroughly cleaned and aired. She looked over *Madame* Dessard's work. The floor had been polished until the wood shone, and the rugs scattered about were pale gray and fluffy. The room was very bright. Once again she wondered why Aunt Mimi had allowed her room to be so dark and gloomy. Giselle had no answer, and she really wasn't searching for one.

She quickly locked all the doors.

All signs of dust were removed. Even the coverlet on the bed smelled of sunshine, as did the rest of the room. She walked onto the balcony, looking over the valley as Etienne had done. It was immense, lushly green, and highly productive — enough so to start a war.

It seemed Giselle had simply exchanged one jail for another. The bars of her new prison lay in splendor before her — Savignen Valley. She gripped the twisted metal of the railing, hard enough the design that the iron-worker had pounded into it, bit into her palms. She didn't feel it. She couldn't even feel the warmth of the sun.

The sunlight seemed cold and bleak. Life was cold and bleak. The future matched. And that was what Savignen Valley was to her.

Giselle didn't bother to wipe at the tears blotting her bodice as coldness seeped into her. This must be her penance, and it was everything she'd dreaded... and more.

"Giselle?"

It was Navarre's voice. Calling to her. Now she had
to hear him speaking? Her penance was brutal.

"Why are you out here? And where's Etienne?
You're crying? Why, Giselle?"

The hand at her elbow convinced her, and her
laughter was clogged with sniffles. It wasn't in her
mind. It truly was Navarre. Here. In the *duc's*
chambers. With her. Alone.

It seemed God hadn't deserted her after all.

She turned to face him and buried her face against
the front of his shirt. And she wasn't ashamed! There
would be time enough for that later. Years of it.

But for now? She quivered through another breath
before she felt the answering pressure of his arms.
Enwrapping her.

"My love. My darling. Giselle."

She heard his endearments through a haze. She
looked up. He looked unwell. Older. His eyes shone
with such emotion, hers flooded with tears again. She
fought them. She didn't want to cry again. She had to
be able to see him and memorize everything about this.

"Forgive me, *ma petit,* for adding to your guilt." He
released one arm to wipe away a tear with his finger.
Giselle watched as he glanced at it and then looked
away, over her head. She felt his other arm loosen.

Guilt? He thought she cried for guilt? She tightened
her arms until he would be forced to pry her away.

"You must let me go, Giselle. Please? I can't stand
for this. Don't you see?"

She could, because the chest she leaned against
shuddered as he concentrated on the valley in the
distance.

"Navarre?"

At her whisper, his arm left her completely. Giselle
watched the small lines around his eyes deepen.

"Navarre, look at me."

His jaw tightened, sending a nerve into prominence.
But he moved his eyes to hers.

"What would you have of me?" he asked.

She didn't know. She started by tugging at the back of his shirt until it was free of his breeches. She had to feel him, and had no idea where that plan of action had come from. Her fingers reached flesh, moving over muscle, getting scorched by the contact. And she felt damp, as if a wellspring erupted within her. She arched her body against him, watching his eyes darken further although his skin turned pale.

"Giselle, you must stop this!"

His arms reached behind himself to pull her away.

"Kiss me, Navarre."

Giselle was blushing furiously as she asked it, but she held on. His eyebrows rose in disbelief while his eyes went wide.

"Must I...beg it of you?" Her breath came in ragged gasps. "Navarre...please?"

He groaned before bending to her, crushing his mouth against hers. Giselle's lips, as if following some unknown instinct, molded about his. Her thighs pressed against his, her belly brushing against the strangest lump, and that aroused her still further. Louisa hadn't told her enough! Giselle dug her fingers into him as he moved her lips apart, flicking and then exploring her mouth with his tongue. Her legs gave out and his hands encircled her waist if he knew.

Giselle was lifted against him, her moan surging through them, making his hands tighten until they almost hurt. And it was delicious. Sensuous. She teased the roughness of his upper lip with her tongue, tasting him, and giggling at his reaction. He pulled away as if stung.

"Mon Dieu, Giselle, but I am on fire. You don't know what you do! You must stop! I must make you—! We can't be alone! This can't happen! *Merde!"*

Giselle wrapped her legs about his hips, balancing herself so she could bring her arms forward. She pulled the rest of his shirt free as she went. The strangeness of his stomach muscles drew her fingers along them, like playing an instrument.

"Giselle, you must stop! You must!"

She lurched upward, supporting herself by leaning on his shoulders, bringing his mouth toward her breasts. He was forced to hold her in place, because she kept slipping, and she giggled at the feel of his arms beneath her. Even through her clothing, she was singed. Burned. Scorched.

"You vixen!"

They moved into Etienne's chamber. Giselle couldn't believe the sensations put into play as he walked. Someone should've told her. Her most private area was ablaze. She was being consumed by it.

The chamber looked even brighter. Giselle closed her eyes to the glow of it.

"Giselle! Open this door at once!"

Navarre stopped at the loud knocking on the connecting door. Giselle recognized Louisa's voice.

"You can't hide forever! And it is time to dress for supper. I can't imagine what has gotten into you. You can't hide from your responsibilities. How many times must I remind you?"

Giselle started to giggle at the lecturing words, and then she stilled. Navarre bent forward, sliding her to her feet. He held his finger to his lips for silence. His shirt was unfastened, the ends trailing to his thighs where she'd pulled it out. She couldn't stop looking. His thigh muscles were easily discernible through the thin material of his breeches. As was the outline of something no one had told her of.

Giselle slapped both hands to her cheeks.

"Giselle! I know you're in there. Answer me."

"I must go." Navarre whispered it into her earlobe, and then he kissed it. And despite the horror of the situation, Giselle shivered at his touch.

"Will I see you at sup?" She grabbed one of his hands.

"Of course. I wouldn't miss it. Until then, my petite love."

He brought her hand to his mouth and kissed her fingers. Giselle closed her eyes at the sweetness. The tenderness. The ache that was just beginning. It was agony to know that this was the last time she could let him kiss her. Even her fingers. She wouldn't be able to stand it, otherwise.

When she opened her eyes, he was gone. It was just as well. Louisa was still pounding at the door, and it was Mass tonight.

She would have a lot to confess.

Giselle had promised God that she'd have nothing more to do with Navarre if she was granted just one more kiss— and such a kiss! She touched her lips with fingers that felt like they belonged to someone else.

"Giselle!"

"I'm coming. Stop that noise immediately."

She glanced in a mirror and stopped, wide-eyed and horrified. She didn't dare answer the door until she looked this disheveled because she'd just awakened from a nap, and not Navarre's lovemaking.

CHAPTER FIFTEEN

Giselle tripped on a stair, but it wasn't because her dress was too long, although it was. She recovered and smoothed down the skirts. *Madame* Broussard must have really rushed on making this one, for the length was too long, and the bodice was loose enough to be unseemly. Giselle didn't care how it fit, however. Her concern was seeing Navarre again. The thought made her blush hotly.

How could I have been so wanton? Acting like little more than an animal?

The entire time it had taken to finish her toilette, Etienne had watched from the bed. Giselle had avoided his eyes in the mirror, but she'd done as he bid. He wanted her to wear this dress. He also wanted her to wear the sapphires again. Perhaps that was why he'd chosen a gown so blue, it was almost black. The blue ribbon threading through the skirt and sleeves had such a purplish hue, Giselle felt her heart twinge painfully when she saw it.

It was as if Etienne was making certain she knew who she belonged to...and it wasn't his brother.

The staircase to the ducal chambers had a landing midway down, splitting into two separate staircases. From that vantage, one could look over the foyer below and choose which direction to finish. Giselle usually took the one to her right since it led to the most-used chambers. Almost defiantly, tonight she chose the opposite. She squealed when an arm grabbed her from the seldom-used Red Salon.

"Navarre!"

She had time to whisper the name just before his lips met hers. And as wondrous as it felt, she had to stop it. She'd promised God, and He'd fulfilled his part. And she couldn't let this happen ever again—

The moment she tried to pull away, his arms tightened. How was she to feign disinterest when she couldn't prevent her own body from weakening, clinging to his? He felt it, too. Navarre lifted his head and chuckled against her cheek.

"Darling. Giselle."

His whisper was low, making her entire body tingle. She'd never be able to stop him if this continued. She pulled from him, but it was a loss so acute, she started shaking.

"Why do you move from me? I'll make certain no one knows about us. You must learn to trust me."

Oh no! This is terrible!

"I've thought of nothing else all afternoon, Giselle. You enflame me beyond reason. You're the most desirable, beautiful, exciting—ah! Words fail me."

His whisper was so full of joy that Giselle's throat constricted.

"Na... varre."

She needed to explain, but the intent in his eyes made it go awry. His name had started on a harsh note, and ended on a cry of sound. She had to look away.

"Such passion! Oh, Giselle! You no longer need to question what it is. You definitely have it. I still can't believe it. Come closer."

"No, Navarre. Please?" Giselle held up her hands.

"Non?"

He stopped the instant she spoke. The look on his face was akin to a slap. Giselle looked up at him, wishing for less intimacy than two candles lighting the space, but perhaps that was too many. Her eyes widened as she stared at him, and she watched him do the same.

They were dressed alike!

The blackish coat he wore closely matched her bodice, the lace edging his jabot was the match to her ribbons, and his breeches were made of the same satin as her skirts. Giselle didn't understand why Etienne made her wear this dress. It made no sense.

"It appears my tailor spent some time with your seamstress, doesn't it? This is interesting. I wonder...."

Navarre turned from her. She watched him walk to the window casing to stare out into the night. Perhaps he was looking at her reflection in the glass. She wouldn't know unless she went to him, and that was something she dared not do.

"Did Etienne choose your dress, Giselle?" He spoke to the glass.

She nodded.

"Strange, that. He specifically bade me to wear this suit. I don't even like it. I think I know why. Do you?"

She shook her head, waiting for him to finish. The candlelight reflected on the sheen of his breeches.

"He's not stupid, Giselle, far from it. That's what he's saying." He sighed and turned back to her. "Do you know what I'm referring to?"

She shook her head again. The lump in her throat hadn't budged.

"He has guessed how we feel. I shouldn't be surprised. He's not impaired, just immobile. And I bear full responsibility."

"Oh, no!"

Giselle clasped her hands to her cheeks cooling the heat. She hadn't considered that, at all.

"Calm yourself. He can't know everything, darling. We'll just have to be more circumspect in the future."

"No, Navarre, *non*. You...you don't understand." She was choking on the words. The lump wasn't helping, either. "What happened in his chambers can't—it was—I can't let you...."

Giselle blushed as he raised his eyebrows. She knew why. It was a silent query to recall who had attacked whom.

"You must understand, Navarre! I can't—um. I begged God...for just one more kiss," she stammered, blaming the ball of tears in her throat for the raspy voice, "before I go...to confession. I had to have one more! Just one. Don't you see?"

"You didn't want a chaste kiss, Giselle. I may not have Jean-Claude's experience with the ladies, but even I know the difference."

Giselle couldn't bear to look at him. His expression was that of a man who tasted something bitter and wanted to spit it out.

"I...I..."

Her voice halted, and it was just as well. She was choking on the words, anyway. Why was it so difficult to say the word passion? How could she make him see? *I was carried away by passion. I didn't mean to. I didn't know.* And now that she did...the future was impossible to look at.

How could she make him see?

"You toyed with me, Giselle. Admit it."

"No!" Her horror colored the word.

"You used me to satisfy your...shall we say...curiosity?"

"No, Navarre! It wasn't like that."

She crossed the room to him and grabbed an arm. He made it sound evil. Corrupt.

Exactly as it was.

"Enjoy Chef Aaron's skill, Giselle. I find I'm no longer hungry."

He shrugged her off his sleeve and walked away. Giselle didn't cling to him or call him back. She knew what was happening was the right thing...so why did it feel so wrong? She couldn't stand to be near him and not touch him. She already knew that. It would be better if Navarre wasn't about, tormenting her with the impossible, wouldn't it?

Wasn't this what she wanted?

What had she done?

Giselle called out, but the door shut softly behind him. And when she reached it, he'd gone. And she had no one to blame but herself.

"I was certain Navarre said he was coming to supper this evening, didn't he, Esmee?"

Aunt Mimi asked it. Giselle toyed with laughing from her lone place at the end of the table. But didn't. She was too close to crying.

"Perhaps he took ill, or that dratted house of mine takes more of his attention than it should. I can't imagine why the boy insists on moving there. Chateau Berchand is his home."

Giselle was grateful nobody addressed her. She doubted her ability to respond. She didn't even remember leaving the Red Salon. She'd blown out the candles, and stayed for several long moments in the dark. That part she recalled.

Dark was better, she decided, concentrating now on the ice sculpture in the center of the table.

"It's so rude of him. I've little time to change the table arrangements already, and then he upsets everything. Eleven to dinner? Whoever heard of such a thing?"

Giselle ignored Esmee's complaints and sat through every course, although, by the time mousse arrived for dessert, she was near hysterics. Now she knew what Etienne meant when he'd said they could all go to hell. That first night. When she'd eavesdropped.

Except it felt like she was already there.

Her heart seemed to be crying Navarre's name with every beat, but it was too late. It had always been too late. She'd never be his. Only in her fantasies could she imagine it so...and those were about to end. She was going to confession. Giselle doubted she had the strength to see it through.

But somehow, and from somewhere, she had to find it.

"Marriage is sometimes a rocky affair, Giselle. I can attest to that."

"Pardon?"

Giselle turned to Aunt Mimi. She'd made a point of sitting beside Giselle after sup had finally ended, and they'd moved to the Blue Salon. And Giselle couldn't even remember how she'd gotten there.

"The late *duc* was a difficult man to learn to care for."

Giselle watched Aunt Mimi blush with a sense of detachment. The rosy shade made her look years younger. Giselle didn't know why Aunt Mimi had singled her out. She wasn't paying attention.

"I mean...things with Etienne might not always go as smoothly as one might wish."

Giselle nodded to her comment. It didn't matter anyway. She wasn't interested in continued breathing, much less wanting things to go smoothly.

"What time is Mass?" Giselle asked.

"We can go now, Child. We can be a little early. It won't harm anything. It may even help with finding our own place in heaven one day, *non?*"

Aunt Mimi put her hand on Giselle's elbow, pinching the flesh as she steadied herself. Giselle longed to tell her she needed a stouter leaning post. Giselle wasn't stable. *Navarre had accused her of toying with him.* Well...hadn't she? What had she hoped to gain by begging for his kiss— and more?

They entered the chapel.

"Here's our pew, Giselle. Oh. I see Esmee's already here." Aunt Mimi said.

She loved Navarre. Incessantly. Longingly. What use was such an emotion if it tore her apart?

He'd accused her of using him to satisfy her curiosity! No. Never.

Tears stabbed at her eyes, and she daren't let anyone see. Giselle held to the wood backrest, closed her eyes, and forced the emotion down. She welcomed the renewed constriction in her throat as the sobs subsided.

She would never have done what Navarre accused her of. She loved him. And it created an ache so vast, no one could've told her of it and had her believe it before.

"They're starting, dear."

Giselle forced her eyes open. Aunt Mimi wasn't watching her. Mimi was settling onto the bench. That was a blessing. Giselle sat.

The priest's intonation of Latin made her glance up at him. What was this? He wasn't the same priest who had heard her confession earlier in the week. Oh. This was terrible. How could she unburden her sins to a stranger?

Giselle looked sideways at Esmee and felt her heart beat just a bit faster. Of anyone, Esmee knew what it meant to risk all things for love. Surely, Esmee would know how it felt, and if love was worth it. Giselle wished she'd thought of speaking with Esmee sooner.

When it came time to confess, Giselle's throat closed completely. She couldn't confess to anything. She had to speak with Esmee first.

"Welcome, my child."

"Father."

Giselle made the sign of the cross. She tried to tell herself that it was because there was something about the new priest that was unsettling, but she knew the truth. She wasn't ready. Her love for Navarre encompassed her whole world, and she'd hurt him. She couldn't admit that to anyone.

"Forgive me, Father, but I have no sins I must confess at this time," she said softly.

"You find marriage suits you, Child?"

"*Oui.*"

That took a moment's thought. She wasn't lying. If she hadn't married Etienne, she never would have met Navarre.

"I've heard your husband sleeps in your chambers. Is that true?"

He peered intently at her through the grill and Giselle turned aside. *Why does he ask that?* she wondered. *Any servant could tell him of it*

"Yes, Father. It is."

"Bless you, Child."

Giselle was slightly stooped as she left the confessional. She wasn't able to stand upright, and didn't look too closely at why. She didn't dare. She was grateful no one was paying her much attention. Because she'd just lied to a priest!

She was bent nearly double by the time she reached her chambers, where Etienne still stayed. Yes, she'd lied, but not to subvert the truth. She had to have more time! She had to speak with Esmee first.

Giselle didn't say anything as Gerty and Isabelle prepared her for sleep. She couldn't speak. The lump in her throat wouldn't have allowed it.

Etienne appeared to have drunk himself into a stupor. Giselle was grateful for that, as well. She didn't think she could face him. She couldn't even meet her own eyes in the chamber mirror.

"*Madame* is well?" Gerty asked. Giselle waved her away.

"She would speak of it if she wasn't," Isabelle answered quietly in her usual somber voice.

"I have heard she attended Mass, and the confessional."

Giselle frowned at the way Gerty stressed the last word. *What could she know of it? What could anyone know?*

"The *duchesse* attends Mass often, Gerty. Keep your speculation to yourself. I won't allow gossip of that nature."

"I never—"

"You should leave. Now."

Giselle pillowed her head on her arms and waited for them to both leave.

"My prayers are with you, *Madame*. Good eve."

The tears started at Isabelle's kind words, and Giselle's chin sank to her breast. She was in luck that Isabelle had already shut the door behind her and wasn't a witness to such a loss of control.

Giselle found the wardrobe room by touch alone. She'd extinguished all the candles. Even one candle was too much light. It was better to be in the dark. That's where all sinners deserved to be.

Giselle cried herself to sleep, clenching her rosary to her heart as she begged God's forgiveness. She had sunk far in only five days.

CHAPTER SIXTEEN

"This is the second wing," Esmee said. "Pierre, the eighth *duc?* He hated using references of east, west and north wings, so he simplified things by naming the additions from the time they were added. A bit strange, but it stuck."

Giselle nodded, although she had little interest in the ancient stone tower they were entering.

"It's said this wing is haunted, although I'm certain that's just a tale to frighten little children."

"Haunted?"

Giselle looked about with more interest than she'd felt all morning. She wanted to ask Esmee if love was worth sacrificing everything. If she had to endure a tour of the chateau before she had a chance to ask it, so be it. However, a haunted wing was almost interesting enough to take her mind off Navarre's absence — but not quite.

"The fifth *duchesse,* Bertina, didn't die naturally. It's said she still haunts this wing, although not the first three floors."

"Why not?"

"Because she fell to her death from the fourth floor. Come. I'll show you. Watch your step near the top."

The warning wasn't necessary. It was obvious the tower wasn't maintained. Giselle followed Esmee up tower stairs that were carved into the walls. They made a continual circle going up and down. She didn't really want to go. The last thing she needed to see in her depressed state was the exact spot where the Spanish *Duchesse* Bertina fell.

The stairs were filthy. Giselle grimaced at the line of dirt on her hemline. She could only lift the front section of her skirts, because she had to hold to the wall with the other hand. She watched as Esmee had the same problem. The woman's hand was splayed along the tower stones as she climbed.

"There should be a banister here, I suppose," Esmee commented.

"Why isn't there one?"

"No one comes anymore. It would be a waste of funds, *non?*"

They reached a massive wooden door with the most ancient lock Giselle had ever seen. Esmee took a key, larger than her palm, from her pocket. Giselle had never seen such a strange looking key. She watched as Esmee twisted it in the lock and turned the handle.

Giselle coughed at the dust that flew from the wind they created the moment the door opened. It took a moment before she opened her eyes again. Blue sky and leagues of land showed from the missing side. She watched as dirt and feathers swirled out.

"It looks easy to fall from here."

Giselle commented, watching from the safety of the doorway as Esmee approached the opening.

"It wasn't always like this, Giselle. It looks like the hole has been widened on purpose. I wonder who would go to such trouble? And why?"

Giselle forced herself to walk toward the opening, although she had to swallow her fright. There were new-looking marks on the rocks. She bent forward to peer over the edge. There was a pile of the same rock very far below.

She had no idea four stories was so high.

Her tower in Chateau Antilli was as nothing in comparison. Giselle gasped and backed to the safety of the inner wall, hoping Esmee wouldn't notice. And when her palms touched the stone, it was so warm to the touch, that Giselle jerked her hands away.

"Esmee!" Her voice squeaked.

"What is it, Giselle? You look like you've seen our ghost."

She walked toward her.

"The stone! It—it's warm!" Giselle's voice rose.

"But, of course. The sun has shone on it almost all day. I'm sorry if I frightened you."

She didn't sound sorry, especially as she turned aside to stifle her giggles. Giselle had rarely felt so stupid. She crossed her arms in front of her breast, defensively.

"I don't like this tower. It's dangerous. Why hasn't it been torn down? It's not being used, and it's unsightly."

She was trying to sound self-confident, but knew she sounded as childish as she felt. She watched Esmee's lips twist before the woman gestured her back through the door. Giselle didn't think she'd get an answer as Esmee took her time locking the door again and pocketing the key.

"The *duc* takes little interest in the castle or any of the estate. Why, if it wasn't for Navarre, even our retainers would have to resort to begging."

Including Desiree?

Giselle almost asked it. She lifted her skirt with a hand that still trembled, and held to the wall with the other. She was grateful Esmee was in front of her and couldn't remark further on her misplaced fright.

"Perhaps I shouldn't speak to you in that fashion. Forgive me."

Esmee tipped her head to say it, and Giselle smiled.

"There's nothing to forgive. I need to know these things. Besides, Etienne will never hear of it from me."

Esmee was apparently satisfied, for she turned back around and kept walking. Giselle felt safer the closer to the ground they got. She wondered what a tumble down the stairs would feel like, and set the thought aside the instant it occurred.

"If Etienne won't take care of the tower, why don't you approach Na-Navarre, then?"

She almost got the name out, but something perverse and wonderful made her stammer. She only hoped Esmee wouldn't notice.

Esmee looked sidelong at her. Giselle was glad they were already at the bottom of the second addition.

"Navarre already assumes enough ducal duties, and it's shortsighted of him. I've lectured him on it often enough. The duchy will never belong to him. Berchand belongs to Etienne, and then, from him, to Jean-Claude. Unless you and Etienne...." she stopped.

"I know. Unless we have a son."

Giselle finished, although she couldn't help blushing. She had changed a lot in the six days she'd been here. When she first heard it mentioned, she'd been overcome with embarrassment. Now it rolled off her tongue like it was nothing.

"Yes. Well...there is always that, and it would change things considerably as far as Jean-Claude is concerned, but a child would do nothing for Navarre. He needs a wife and family of his own instead of always running an estate he'll never possess. He's wasting his future, and won't listen to me. Perhaps you could speak with him about it?"

Giselle was lucky they'd reached the main castle again. Esmee could have hit her in the stomach and had the same effect. Giselle couldn't breathe for a bit. The black-and-white parquet pattern of the floor wavered for a moment and she leaned against the wall for support.

"Of course, Etienne has the responsibility of finding Navarre a suitable wife, and he does little more than...oh dear. My mouth has run away from me again, hasn't it?"

Esmee didn't give Giselle time to answer. She strode to the *duc's* library, trying to cover up her words.

So that's why Navarre wasn't married, Giselle thought. *Etienne must find him another wife, and, as long as he remains a drunkard, Navarre can do as he likes,*

Navarre never had to wed. He could always be available for her to look at, fantasize over, and— Giselle refused to finish her own thoughts. He could always be at the chateau, running it from behind-the-scenes...no! She mustn't think like that.

Giselle straightened from the wall.

It was such a wonderful, but disturbing, revelation. Giselle felt elation fill her, making it easy to meet Esmee at the library door, and yet was horrified and desolate simultaneously. The mix of emotions made her giddy-feeling.

"See that Chablis is brought to the library."

Esmee instructed the servant who opened the door for them. Giselle dipped her head as she followed Esmee. She should be the one instructing the staff. She wondered if she'd ever learn to be chatelaine of her home. And then it hit her, what Esmee had really said.

Navarre never had to leave!

That was what he'd meant in the Red Salon about trusting him. He'd meant that Giselle and he could—*oh dear.*

"What of you, Esmee?"

Giselle inserted it quickly, stopping her thoughts. She couldn't stop the blush. She could only hope Esmee wouldn't notice.

"Me?"

Esmee sat in one of the straight-backed chairs, and Giselle took a facing one. It wasn't until she was seated that she noticed the obvious. The chairs were so high Giselle's feet didn't touch the floor, even if she sat at the front of it. So, she perched at the front, balancing herself uneasily on her voluminous skirts.

"Don't you also need a husband and children of your own? You can't mourn *Monsieur* Denton forever."

To her surprise, Esmee burst into laughter, and continued until she almost cried. Giselle frowned. This wasn't the reaction she'd expected. Esmee was still chortling when the Chablis arrived. Giselle motioned for it to be served. Perhaps the dry burgundy would calm her. Something had to.

"You'll think me touched, Giselle." Esmee dabbed her eyes with her handkerchief and resumed her normal composure. "But, mourn Gerard? I'd sooner dance with joy at my release."

Giselle hadn't drunk enough wine to hear such a thing. She gulped it so fast that she choked. The manservant refilled the glass without comment, although she wouldn't be drinking any more. She already felt the disembodied sensation she needed.

"You didn't...love *Monsieur* Denton? Then why did you elope?"

Giselle reached for the table to set her glass down and almost fell off the chair. She hated being in a house built for giants. She watched as the manservant hid a smile behind his gloved hand. All the servants would say she drank too much. Giselle decided she no longer cared. Let them.

"Who told you that I had?"

"Aunt Mimi. I'm sorry. I didn't know it was a secret."

"It's no secret, but it's not something I'm proud of, all the same."

She walked over to the bookshelf and looked over the novels as if selecting one. Giselle waited. It was clear Esmee wasn't going to be able to answer any questions about love.

"Gerard was dashing enough, I suppose," she began. "He even had noble blood on his father's side."

Ah. He was like Jacques Minot, Giselle realized.

"My uncle was a stern man, and a penurious one. He had me practically chained to the chateau. If it had been left to him, I would never have met any eligible men. None. That would have been fine with him. No marriage for me meant no dowry spent. Perhaps you can understand?"

Giselle nodded, but Esmee wasn't looking.

"They couldn't stop me from needing new clothing, though. That's how I met Gerard. How do I explain it? I was young and looking for an escape. He was looking for a way into respectability. I suppose we both got what we were looking for."

"What was he like?" Giselle asked.

"Nothing like you'd imagine from such a tale. Truly." She turned to Giselle and shrugged. "He was rakish-looking, rarely barbered and bathed, but dressed well. And, he was forbidden territory. It was exciting to sneak away to be with him. We might be caught. Punished. It added an edge to our clandestine meetings. I don't suppose you know what I'm speaking of, but it was there."

Giselle worked at maintaining her color and a blank expression. She knew she'd succeeded when Esmee turned back toward the books and continued speaking.

"I thought I loved him, but I didn't. How could I once I found myself living in squalor? We couldn't afford much. He couldn't pay for a maid to help me. I had to clean floors on my hands and knees, Giselle. It was a time of complete horror.

"And people looked down their noses at us. I can't explain how it felt, but I shudder to remember. Gerard was a milliner, by trade and an *artiste* with his creations, but there was no one to help, so I had to sell them. Imagine standing for hours while the *noblesse* tried on hats. I had to listen to their comments as if I didn't exist. Ugh. It was horrid."

She finished looking at book titles and came to sit down again. She almost caught Giselle glancing over at the manservant lingering near the door. Esmee spoke as if he weren't there, just as she'd finished describing. Giselle decided she didn't want Esmee's advice, after all.

"Gerard took sick one winter. Perhaps we could have done something different. Perhaps we should have paid the coal timely. Who can say? It was a joy to be released, Giselle. I didn't even mind being relegated to a position of poor relation. At least I was back in the chateau, and back in my own world, among my own kind."

Among her own kind? Giselle couldn't meet her eyes. She had no idea Esmee was harboring such disgust for others. She wondered what Esmee thought of Giselle's affection for Louisa and Isabelle, and knew she wouldn't ask. But one thing was certain. Esmee had nothing of value for Giselle.

"But come, Giselle, let's talk of something else. I've certainly been morbid today. First there was the ghost in the tower, now my distaste of Gerard. I'm no grieving widow, am I? Don't answer that. I can see it in your face."

"I'm sorry."

"Don't be. It's ancient history. But come. Perhaps you'd enjoy planning the next supper party? We can invite eligible parties for Navarre and me if you like."

She chuckled at her wit, but Giselle didn't find her the least bit amusing. She wasn't going to plan a party, or anything else of that nature. She was going to order a bath and cleanse the morning's experiences away, and then she was going to pray.

She only hoped it would work.

It didn't take long to realize the futility. It seemed nothing Giselle tried brought any comfort. All her prayers seemed to gain her was more time on her knees. It had been two days and as many nights since

Navarre had left. Giselle was barely able to contain her grief, and it only worked as long as there was daylight. Louisa mentioned doctors again, as if a physician could cure what ailed the *duchesse*.

At least Etienne moved back into his chamber, and Giselle could cry each night in the huge, lonely bed without having anyone gossip about it. No one knew how much her heart ached. Giselle had no idea she possessed the ability to suffer like she was.

It was all she could do each day to pretend her heart wasn't breaking and that she'd slept well. Only her pallor gave her away. She was certain of it.

It was a fragile charade, though. She nearly burst into tears when Aunt Mimi asked her to sponsor a ball — not a small one, but a huge affair, attended by as many acquaintances as could be persuaded to leave Paris and Versailles for a weekend in the country. The thought appalled Giselle. She'd be sobbing long before she entered the ballroom.

"You can't cling to shadows much longer, Giselle," Louisa said. "You have a household to run, and the chef speaks nonstop of your cruelty in returning his dishes untouched."

"What do you want, Louisa?"

Giselle asked it in as even a tone as she could and turned away to look at the wall. She knew Louisa stood at the base of her bed-platform, her hands on her hips, surveying the bed. She didn't need to see it.

"Perhaps I'd like to seek other employment, *Madame*. It's clear I'm no longer needed here."

Giselle's eyes filled with tears. It wasn't enough penance that she lost Navarre? She had to lose everyone she loved?

"Go ahead. I can't stop you."

It was meant as sarcasm. It failed miserably. Giselle buried her face and shook with the sobs she'd reserved for the darkest hours of the night.

"Giselle, my sweet, don't cry. I'd never do anything so cruel. I promise." Louisa wrapped her arms around Giselle as she once did when Giselle was too young to understand her own father's dislike.

"You don't understand, Louisa. I love him. I do. I can't change it. I've tried." Giselle's words tumbled over each other.

Louisa chuckled and smoothed Giselle's hair. "Well...I suppose it was inevitable, considering. I've rarely seen such a man, and I'm not young and beautiful like you. *Monsieur* Navarre is a very lucky fellow, I would say."

Giselle started from her shoulder and stared.

"What? I surprise you? Oh, please, Giselle. Credit me with eyes, and the ability to see into your heart. You might be able to hide your emotions from the others, especially that drunkard husband of yours, but you can't hide them from me. Dry your eyes. We must decide what to do about this love of yours. Here."

She handed Giselle a face cloth, freshly wrung. Giselle didn't bother to ask why Louisa had it.

"That's better. Now. I daresay when you see this Navarre again, you don't want to look old and haggard like me, do you? Of course not."

Giselle didn't answer, but her tears stopped. The cloth felt cool and soothing against her eyes, too.

"We could plan this outrageous weekend ball your Aunt Mimi has been pestering you with, *non?* That should give her something to occupy herself with...and it would give everyone something better to do with their time than gossip over the *duchesse's* fragile health. In the meantime, how would you like a little jaunt to Paris?"

"Paris?" Giselle pushed up from the bed.

"Of course. I don't see why you cannot choose your own gown for this type of affair, and we can arrange for *Monsieur* Poinre to do your hair again, *oui*? It sounds exciting just thinking of it. You'll have to take your maid and companion with you, of course."

"Of course." Giselle smiled.

"I've visited the Paris *shoppes* before, Giselle. I probably need more thread with which to sew, don't I? Besides Isabelle mentioned the lack of good tatting thread here, and you know how particular she is about her lace."

"I...hadn't thought of it." Giselle gazed out the window. Had she really been so self-centered and selfish? She was as bad as Esmee,

"And with all the designers there, we can certainly find something unique with which to stun a certain nobleman I could name."

Navarre. His image came to Giselle, and she felt her heart sink. She actually felt the motion, and it made her vaguely ill. Navarre had accused her of toying with him once, and now she was planning on doing it again? Her shoulders drooped as she remembered what he thought of her. He'd never come, regardless of the fete they planned, or her *couture,* or her feelings. He'd never come.

"You go too fast, Louisa. I don't see how—"

"He'll come, Giselle. He knows his duty, and, unless the *duc* stands beside you to welcome your guests, *Monsieur* Navarre will have to do it."

"You don't know him. He's so proud, so stubborn."

"Which is why he'll come. Trust me, Giselle."

"Oh. If only...." Her whisper trailed away, and she wiped at her eye before Louisa saw it.

"Can I order the carriage for the morning? It will take some time to reach Paris, and I'm not sure where the Berchald house is in the city."

"You think he'll come? Truly?"

"He's proud and stubborn. You said so, yourself. Those attributes will make him come. You'll see. He's a Berchald, Giselle, and his duty is to stand in for his brother. He'll come. I promise."

"Then, order the carriage. See if Esmee has the directions, or Aunt Mimi. Oh, Louisa, tell them of our plans! I won't be able to sleep with the excitement."

"That's an improvement to your usual reason, I would say."

Giselle couldn't think of a witty response before Louisa left. And she had to admit the woman was right once again.

CHAPTER SEVENTEEN

Aunt Mimi was thrilled with Giselle's change of heart. Perhaps she thought it due to her persuasive talents, and that made it even more pleasant to plan. Giselle didn't dissuade her. The dowager *duchesse* readily agreed to take care of all the arrangements, leaving Giselle's time free to visit Paris and to shop. Esmee was a ready companion, too.

The trip to Paris was accomplished with so much good humor, it seemed to have taken no time at all.

Giselle clung to her side of the Berchald coach as they neared the city. The noise of so many people overwhelmed her. She was afraid it showed. She'd never seen such crowds before, and she suspected Louisa wasn't as self-assured as she tried to be, either. If it hadn't been for Isabelle's quiet demeanor, Giselle would have been trembling, but she needn't have worried. The coachman knew the way, as well as Esmee. Giselle paid attention as Esmee pointed out several landmarks.

The Berchald house was on a very exclusive street and was much quieter than the rest of the city. Giselle was grateful for that. She was tired from the travel, although it was but mid-day. She hadn't rested, but it wouldn't have been possible. Sleeping in the coach would have been difficult, and she hadn't wanted to close her eyes once they reached Paris.

"The duchesse?" a manservant said. "We've but just learned of your visit. You've been prompt. Follow me, please."

Louisa and Isabelle were at Giselle's heels as she followed Esmee and the man into a high-ceiling salon. Even here, it appeared the Berchalds built for giants. Word had been sent ahead, but the staff appeared surprised to see them. Giselle frowned as candles were lit and dust covers were removed so they could sit down.

"Perhaps you could see to some refreshments after our long journey, Garon. It is Garon, isn't it?" Esmee asked.

"Oui, Madame Denton. I'll see if something can be prepared for you."

The servant tipped his head in a slight gesture. Giselle watched him.

"Prepared? We sent word ahead of our arrival, Garon. Did it not arrive?"

"Oui, Madame."

"Then this display is inexcusable. Please have the housekeeper shown in."

"We aren't used to visitors, *Madame."*

"I will not repeat myself, Garon. The housekeeper?"

He gave Esmee a thin-lidded look before bowing from their presence. Giselle couldn't shake the feeling of his insolence. Perhaps it was the way he stiffened when Esmee spoke, but she guessed it was something more. It felt as if they were the intruders, and the staff actually owned the house. Giselle wondered if he was this insolent because it was Esmee speaking...and due to her misalliance, she no longer had the power to command? Or...was he this insolent to everyone?

"You sent for me, *Madame* Denton?"

The stiff-necked, white-haired woman who entered had the same hard note in her voice as she curtsied.

"Actually, it was I, *Madame,"* Giselle spoke up. "It seems notice of our visit didn't arrive in time for the staff to prepare for it."

"*Madame* la *Duchesse.*"

The housekeeper's curtsy was as brief as the one she'd given Esmee. Giselle's eyes narrowed, but it was Esmee who spoke.

"The *duchesse* finds the lack of servitude in her own house to be annoying, *Madame.* We can only guess it is due to your influence. I can only hope it's but newly-caused."

"My duty is to serve, *Madame,* I apologize for any lack the staff may display. I will speak with Garon."

Giselle watched her as she spoke. Far from looking apologetic, she looked more like she was barely controlling her anger.

"Very good. The *duchesse* would like to rest now. We are all wearied from our long journey. Are there enough bedchambers that can be aired quickly?"

"You don't wish refreshment, now?"

"They can be brought to our suites just as easily. I am not used to repeating myself, *Madame.* I would not like to do so again."

"It will be seen to, of course. If you'll follow me?"

Giselle watched the woman flick her eyes to the barely-uncovered furniture, and Giselle flushed. She guessed what the woman was thinking about the wasted effort, and it embarrassed her. She was as thoughtless as Esmee, ordering dust-covers removed and not even sitting on the uncovered furniture.

The duchess' suite was as warm and inviting as the one in the castle was cold and solemn. Giselle looked about in wonder. It was exactly what she would've expected from Aunt Mimi, all pink and white. Even the furniture was painted white.

"Why is this room so bright?" she asked the housekeeper, who had never ceased watching her.

"The former *duchesse* was responsible for this room."

"The one at the castle is so dark, though." Giselle spoke without thinking, and Isabelle gave her a warning glance.

"I believe the rooms at the castle were decorated because of a condition a former *duchesse* suffered from, *Madame*. She couldn't abide light. It made her head ache."

"But, Aunt Mimi—I mean, *Madame* Mimi surely would have changed it?"

"The workings of the aristocracy are beyond my reasoning. The dowager *duchesse* was very happy here, *Madame*. Will there be anything else?"

Giselle felt like she was being chastised and then dismissed. It was a horrid feeling. She longed to make the woman stay, just so Giselle could be the one deciding when she could go, but that was stupid.

"*Non. Merci, Madame*. Good eve."

The woman seemed surprised at Giselle's kind answer. Giselle wondered if that was why they were all so sullen. Was being a servant such a hateful existence? She would ask Isabelle, but it could wait.

Giselle fell asleep dreaming of the dresses she would choose, the jewelry she might try on and the shoes she'd buy. And still, Navarre's face haunted her.

It was still an issue as the next day progressed, Giselle following Esmee and their servants through the Paris streets. And at every shop she visited, she was announced at the doorway with a pomp she disliked.

'The *Duchesse* du Berchald!" each proprietor effused. "It is a pleasure to have such a beauty in my pitiful *shoppe*."

Giselle had decided by the third such greeting that if one more man mentioned his pitiful *shoppe*, she was going to hit him with her new pelisse. At first she had been flattered, then she had blushed, but by the fourth such greeting, she was bored with it. The response they got from her now was a quick smile and a nod.

Esmee ordered so many new things, Giselle quickly lost track. To everyone's dismay, all that caught the *duchesse's* eye was the new cloak she wore. She wasn't going to buy just anything. She knew exactly what she was looking for.

"The *Duchesse* du Berchald!" yet another storekeeper said. "It's a pleasure...."

Giselle ignored the rest of his greeting. She'd seen a bolt of material through the window that she wanted to see closer. She left Esmee to divert the man's attention and went looking. She couldn't prevent her gasp when she found it. It was silky to the touch and interwoven with such golden thread that it seemed alive.

"This material, *Monsieur*...have you made a dress of it yet?"

She knew the answer as his face fell. It felt like her spirits did the same motion.

"Oui, Madame, but I can have another crafted immediately."

Giselle set the bolt down with difficulty. The moment she'd seen the pale rose-colored material, she knew it was perfect. It was amazing how long and dull the day seemed of a sudden. She lingered a gloved finger on it, before turning.

"Then there is nothing else of interest, *Monsieur*. I bid you—"

"Wait, *Madame* la *Duchesse!* It hasn't been delivered yet. Come quickly. If it becomes known that I sold *Mademoiselle* Frerre's dress to another, she'll have me run out of Paris."

"Mademoiselle Frerre?"

Esmee choked on the name, but Giselle ignored her. She was already following the man. The dress he showed her was well worth the trouble, too. She held her breath. The material was cut on the bias, and seemed to swirl like a whirlwind upward from the floor. The lace he'd stitched onto the bodice, sleeves and underskirt was such a deep green it was almost shocking in contrast. It reminded Giselle of the arbor as she last saw it.

"I'll pay double what she offered," Giselle said. "As long as there's no matching material on your shelf. Do we understand each other, *Monsieur?*"

She was surprised with her own insistence. She guessed that was what made Esmee's mouth open and close, too. Giselle wasn't used to commanding anyone. She was surprised at the heady feeling.

The man clapped his hands. "It will be as the petite *duchesse* asks. The bolt of material will be delivered to the Berchald estate this evening, along with the dress. I'll attend to it myself. There is still the matter of the accessories that *Mademoiselle* Frerre chose. Do you wish those, too?"

Giselle ignored the others and followed him. If the woman had taste enough to have such a gown designed and sewn, her accessories were probably well worth the time, too. *Besides,* she told herself, *this Mademoiselle Frerre wasn't likely to need accessories for a gown she 'd never own, was she?*

Giselle was thrilled with the selection. The mass of petticoats the mysterious woman had chosen were as beautiful and unique as the dress. She couldn't wait to try it on, and have it taken in, but that could be done at the castle.

She was exhausted by the time they left the dress *shoppe.* She had spent a fortune, but it was worth it. She had no idea shopping was so tiring, and she was grateful Esmee didn't say a word.

Aunt Mimi was up to the challenge. By the weekend for the ball, the castle's guest rooms were full. Even the *Comte d'*Antillion had come. Giselle wasn't looking forward to playing an adoring wife for her papa, but she'd do whatever it took to see Navarre.

Etienne promised to attend and also promised Navarre that he'd stay from wine for the entire day. Giselle had Gerty to thank for that gossip, for if

Navarre ever came to the chateau, Giselle never saw him.

It had been almost three weeks since she'd gone to Paris. Each day felt like an eternity of loneliness passing. Giselle was surprised to feel that way. She was surrounded by people, yet so alone, she might as well be sequestered in her tower at Antilli.

She hadn't known being lovelorn felt exactly like the poets had written. There was no measure for how it felt. Each day added more to the pain. Sometimes, it felt like the weight of it, growing in her breast, was impossible to ignore. She'd double up with it, and hope no one noticed. And the fittings continued, the arrangements grew apace, and the chattering swirled about as if nothing were amiss.

Giselle would look about her sometimes, wondering at their ignorance. Love wasn't anything like she'd dreamed it would be. It was an agony of emptiness that only the thought of seeing Navarre made bearable. If it weren't for the daily fittings of her gown, Louisa's chatter, Gerty's gossip, and Isabelle's attention to prayer, Giselle would have been a sobbing wretch long before the day of the ball arrived.

The entire day, Giselle stayed hidden in her chamber. Only Louisa and Isabelle were allowed entrance. She'd kept her dress a secret from most of the staff, especially anyone who might tell Etienne. The night was going to be perfect. She was desperate for it to be so. She'd envisioned it so often, it was like it already had happened, only better.

It was still ahead of her.

The last thing Giselle wanted was to match Navarre again. Etienne's little tricks wouldn't work on her this time.

Monsieur Poinre was prompt for his appointment, and he spoke of her luck. He had at least six ladies waiting after Giselle, but he wouldn't pass up the chance to work with the beauteous, *petit duchesse du*

Berchald again. He'd spread tales of her beauty. She was good for his business, he told her. He nearly balked when she told him she wanted her hair dressed but not powdered, though.

She watched Isabelle hide a smile at the man's reaction.

"You'll be naked without the powder," he complained. "How can you possibly wish to look so? I won't be responsible for it. You'd better not tell anyone that I was. I cannot believe this! *Mai oui,* you are stubborn! The aristocracy! They have no sense. They take arsenic powder for their complexions, and then when they have the whitest, most pristine skin, they will not even apply powder to their hair to show it off. No wonder the masses talk revolution. It is beyond comprehension."

"I will not change my mind, *Monsieur.* I want it dressed but not powdered. It will look wonderful. You'll see."

He sighed in resignation. "I have the worst luck. I pass up several appointments in order to dress the Duchess du Berchald, and I cannot even tell anyone of it!"

He almost convinced Giselle to change her mind, but she already knew the gown would look wonderful against the reddish strands and white streak in her hair. She also knew she didn't need artifice against her skin. The hairdresser was right. She had a clear, unblemished complexion was just right for showing it off. She also knew the neckline was made for showing off the large emeralds *Monsieur* Savoy had shown her what seemed a year ago. She'd already asked Louisa to have them available that morning.

"You look enchanting, *Madame,*" Gerty said after the hairdresser left. "I'm to see that you attend the *duc* in his study the moment you're finished."

Gerty's words made Giselle's hands tremble. She hid them with the motion of gathering her skirts. She thought she wasn't frightened of Etienne anymore, and was demonstrating how false that was. She didn't want to see him, but it was unavoidable.

She looked at Louisa, who nodded unnecessarily. Giselle set her shoulders. She didn't need the reminder. She knew where her duty lay.

"Very well, Gerty. I'm ready. Thank you, Isabelle. Your needlework is beyond description."

It had taken the maid hours to sew Giselle into her dress. It had to fit without a wrinkle, and it did. The swirl of material rose from the floor and was cinched in at the waist. There it rose to cling to her skin until the green lace framing her bodice, and creating the back collar, completed the symmetry.

The mysterious woman hadn't designed with modesty in mind, however. Giselle's corset wasn't helping the situation. She had to keep her head high to prevent her own breath from tickling the exposed skin. Giselle gave herself one more glance in the mirror before shying away. Her appearance couldn't be faulted, she knew that much. She'd known how the dress would look, and she'd simply have to get used to exposing so much of herself. It was the fashion, after all, and she wasn't disappointed.

She hoped Navarre wasn't, either.

She grimaced as they approached the study, but with Gerty in front of her, it wasn't seen. Giselle composed her face as they approached the manservant outside the door. He looked amused as he opened the door and announced her.

Giselle's jaw dropped as Etienne wheeled from behind his desk, and she had to force it shut. She refused to believe the proof before her eyes. It wasn't possible. But somehow, his breeches were made of material from the same bolt of cloth. His dark-green jacket was only a slightly darker hue than Giselle's lace. They were perfectly matched.

"I heard you ordered the emeralds, Giselle." He smiled.

She looked away.

"They are a perfect choice, my dear. And if you'll bend down, I'll clasp the necklace for you."

She looked back to him, her face feeling frozen and stiff.

"No? Very well. Do it yourself." His proffered hand fell into his lap.

"How did you...? And, why...?"

"Giselle, Giselle."

He clucked his tongue. Giselle's back straightened.

"My valet is Gerty's brother. Simple. *Non?* As to why...?" He set the jewelry case on the desk beside him. "We are on show tonight, are we not?"

Giselle had to learn how to manage the games this household played and before she grew any older. It felt like she'd been dealt a hand in a game where no one had explained the rules of play.

"You do look a bit feminine, Etienne, but it is an effective statement, I suppose. I congratulate you."

She picked up the necklace and turned to the wall mirror to clasp it. The stone was heavy, and the facets wouldn't catch much light from where it fell, but that couldn't be helped. The chain was made for a larger woman, like everything else in the castle. Giselle blushed. The chain wasn't doing anything to keep one's eyes on her face. Quite the opposite. The chain was pointing to what extra cleavage the corset created. She opened her mouth to request Gerty's assistance in shortening the necklace, and then she squared her shoulders.

It didn't matter what anyone save Navarre thought of her. She turned back for the ear bobs.

"You promised you wouldn't drink."

She watched him gulp from a bottle while she looked at the mirror. Then, he tossed an arm across his mouth, wetting the green-colored material. It was a crass gesture from an uncouth man, but she already knew that about her husband.

"Oh...I promised a lot of things, Giselle. As have you, I might add. Our wedding promise, for instance. And the right to your body in my bed. Do you wish to continue this train of conversation, my dear?"

She shook her head.

"You're ready to greet our guests, then?"

Giselle knew it was her heart sinking, and her belly gurgled warningly. She didn't know how to contain the disappointment, but there was nothing for it. Etienne was going to be beside her as they greeted their guests. Louisa had been wrong. For once.

She watched Etienne negotiate his chair through the doorway, although he needed help turning it once he gained the foyer. He looked unsteady and a bit uncomfortable. He had more than nine years in which to learn to maneuver his chair, yet he seemed to be starting just that night.

She was never going to be able to pretend all evening.

CHAPTER EIGHTEEN

The entire evening was flat, her future looked even flatter, and Giselle knew it probably showed in her eyes. She couldn't believe her own stupidity, although she should, by now. No matter how she prepared herself, or what she planned, it wasn't to be. Navarre was as far from her as ever.

She sighed dispiritedly and looked out, over the crowded hall. She didn't wonder why none of the attendees seemed to notice her depression. They were all much too interested in Etienne.

Giselle listened as they mouthed vague platitudes such as missing Etienne at court, and how could he be so greedy as to keep his charming personality from them, and how soon could they expect him to take his place at the King's side, all of it false. Flat. She grew more disillusioned by the moment. She might as well be a doll for all the interest she felt.

And then Giselle's papa was announced, and everything went crystal clear and very real. Etienne was overly amorous in his praise of his wife. Giselle blushed at his words. Etienne fooled the *comte,* though. They both watched as he left them, entering the ballroom with a stiff stride.

Aunt Mimi had the room decorated with leaves tinted fall colors. It resembled a harvest night. Even the chandeliers had wheels of orange paper hanging from them, giving the light the same tint on the revelers below. Giselle watched her papa walk to the banquet table, reminding her of her earlier obstinacy. She wished she'd eaten the light luncheon Louisa had suggested hours earlier.

And she wondered how something so mundane could keep her interest.

"We are doing splendidly, aren't we, Giselle?"

She looked over at Etienne. His head reached her shoulder. She smiled slightly. *Yes,* she thought, *we are fooling everyone.*

Etienne met her eyes and winked. Giselle turned away before he saw her real emotion.

"The *Comte* la Maison, and his daughter, *Monsieur* and *Mademoiselle* Frerre."

The moment the name was announced, Giselle whitened. *Mademoiselle* Frerre? The creator of her dress?

"Charmaine? It's a pleasure to see you again. And *Monsieur* le *Comte.* Have you come to try and renew the betrothal?"

Betrothal? Giselle repeated it to herself. They sounded like they were talking through a dense fog, although they were right beside her.

"It would be about time, I think. I swear Navarre talks of nothing else."

Mademoiselle Frerre was Navarre's betrothed? No. It couldn't be. Such a coincidence wasn't possible. Because if it were...that meant she was also Jean-Claude's mistress! The white and black tiles underfoot blurred as she realized how close to swooning she was. She seemed powerless to stop it.

Etienne wasn't aware of his wife's reaction, for he chattered on as if he'd said nothing of moment. Giselle heard them now through a ringing blur of sound that seemed to originate in her own ears.

"Well? Shall I have the solicitor draw up the betrothal papers again? Say the word, Charmaine, and he's yours."

Take deep breaths, Giselle. Deeper. She leaned against the back of Etienne's chair and fought off the darkness at the edges of her vision. And Esmee never said a word? Giselle thought Esmee had some fondness for her, but she'd left her in ignorance. *Why?*

"Your generosity is misplaced, Etienne...and of little moment."

"How so?"

"Because I have little need of Navarre, of course. Where is the boy, anyway?"

"He'll be by shortly. I'm certain of it. He was looking forward to attending my function, wasn't he, darling?"

Giselle took one more deep breath. The floor was no longer roiling beneath her feet, although the hand holding to Etienne's chair was white about the knuckles. It took a bit of will, but she replaced the look of shock that was probably about her face with an innocent one. If acting was a Berchald trait, she'd do her best to learn it. Right now.

"He doesn't speak...of such things...to me, Etienne," she remarked finally.

"You should speak more of his future and less of yourselves, then, I would say." Although he was smiling, Etienne's eyes were hard. Giselle couldn't hold the gaze.

"You always did have too much to say, and yet say too little, Etienne."

Charmaine narrowed what were gorgeous, moss-green eyes as she spoke. Giselle's eyebrows rose. It was obvious she wasn't used to having attention diverted.

"You wound me to the heart, Charmaine. I swear it."

"Nonsense, Etienne. You haven't got one."

"Are you always this pleasant, Charmaine? I begin to see Navarre has made a lucky escape, I think."

"Navarre cannot hold my interest, Etienne. You, of all men, should know that. He is but an infant...but you are not, are you?"

Her voice purred. Giselle heard her clearly, even though she bent near Etienne's ear.

"You flatter me easily, but you always were a vixen, weren't you?" he replied.

She laughed. There was a hard edge to it, and Giselle winced before assuming an innocent look again.

"And, this must be the *duchesse* I've heard so much about, especially from my dressmaker in Paris. I believe you met up with him?"

Mademoiselle Frerre stood, and turned her attention to Giselle.

"I may have had the pleasure," Giselle replied tonelessly.

"That must make this meeting with me even more pleasurable for you, *non?*"

Giselle tipped her head to one side. "But, of course, *Mademoiselle.*"

"Oh, please!" Charmaine laughed again and touched Giselle's arm with her fan. Giselle flinched, and knew she hadn't covered it in time as the woman pursed her overly-full lips. "You must call me Charmaine. I insist. We're going to be such friends. I can tell."

She didn't wait for an answer. She simply turned and walked off, heading for the ballroom. Giselle slowly released the breath she'd been holding. Etienne snorted beside her.

"Friends? Don't trust her that far, Giselle. The woman is a snake in disguise. She is a stunning one, though."

Etienne's warning me? She concentrated on his strange words instead of *Mademoiselle* Charmaine's beauty. The woman was more than beautiful. She was breath-taking. Giselle couldn't imagine what she must have looked like when she tried on Giselle's gown. With Charmaine's red hair, white skin, and green eyes, she would have captivated all eyes in the room. In her black velvet bodice and green silk skirt, she still created quite a stir.

"Thank *le Bon Dieu* they waited until last," Etienne said. "I'm parched. How about you, Giselle? Would you join me in a toast to our success?"

He tried to move his chair, but it wouldn't budge against the restraining block on the floor. Giselle waited for a manservant to remove it.

"She doesn't powder her hair." That was stupid, but the first thing that came to mind.

Etienne chuckled. "Are you fishing for compliments, Giselle? You'll have to look somewhere else. Charmaine has long been acknowledged as a court beauty. She'd as soon powder her hair as she would toss over Jean-Claude."

"Jean-Claude? Your younger brother, Jean-Claude?" Giselle asked, feigning ignorance.

"I need a drink. If you won't see that I get one, I'll find one myself."

"But—"

"I'll leave you to your musings, Giselle. Ask someone else for our sordid history, or take Navarre to task for not apprising you of it earlier. That should give him something better to do than stand at the stairs staring at Charmaine. The boy should be over her by now." He turned to his servant. "A brandy for the *duc! A*nd be quick about it. *Garcon! A* drink."

Etienne moved away, loudly calling for his drink. Giselle didn't hear or see. The moment he gave her Navarre's location, she sought him out. Although it was true that he watched the festivities from the stairs leading to the minstrel's gallery, he wasn't watching Charmaine.

He was gazing directly at Giselle.

He'd lost weight. She could tell. His plum-colored jacket fell from his shoulders and he had dark hollows in his cheeks. Her heart lurched. Her pulse sang. She'd never seen anything that affected her more. Her feet moved toward him without thought or even looking where she placed them. She couldn't tear her gaze away.

"Navarre!"

His name came out in a whoosh, as if someone had struck her in the stomach. He walked toward her so slowly that she almost went up the stairs to greet him. His eyes never left hers. Giselle knew her reaction showed in her face, and that there was nothing she could do about it.

He reached the main floor, and she filled her eyes with the sight of him, and her breast with the smell.

"You're doing well, *Madame?*"

He sounded bored as he brought her hand to his lips. Giselle waited, but he didn't kiss it. He simply held it a moment in his chin and then let it drop. She couldn't assimilate how it felt. She had nothing to base it on. Agony?

"Come," he continued. "You're neglecting your guests."

He held out his arm for her, and it wavered before her eyes. Giselle blinked as rapidly as she could, but the tears welled and continued coming until she knew there would be no stopping them. She swallowed, desperately trying to control herself, but it was useless. She looked up at him through a film of moisture.

"You'll disarrange your powder, Giselle," he told her.

"I—"

She shouldn't need the reproof, but he was right. This was no time for such a display of emotion. There were too many others watching them. She tipped her head up, as if viewing the orange wheels above them, and blinked viciously, sending her tears to seep into her hairline at her ears. Of all the scenarios she'd envisioned, this was undoubtedly the worst.

"The dowager house has many attributes, Giselle, but it is very lonely. Do you know of what I speak?"

He placed her hand on his, and she felt him tremble. It brought her head down and her eyes to his. Her breath caught, but that couldn't be helped.

"It's lonely here, too," she told him.

He finally smiled, although it didn't reach his eyes.

"You must start the dancing, Giselle. It's tradition that the *duc* and *duchesse* do so. Everyone is waiting for you." He looked over her head at those behind them.

"Etienne...doesn't dance," she whispered.

"Then, I must fulfill my obligation to the house of Berchald and stand in for him, mustn't I? Come. We will strike up the musicians."

The dance Aunt Mimi had picked to start off the fete kept Giselle circling about. She only met her partner every eighth note — she counted — but it was everything. And nothing. Navarre's eyes held her, and it seemed like every time she moved away from him, the color in them intensified. She was probably lucky with the dance choice. She wouldn't be able to attack him like before. She felt the wicked desire creeping up on her again. The passion. The craving. And there was nothing she could do about any of it.

There were so many others watching them, Giselle should have been able to dispel it. She should feel ashamed, but she didn't. It was time to feel the elation again. The despair it would lead to was too far off to worry about.

They never finished the dance. The next time their palms touched, he broke away from the contact, and stood glaring down at her. Dancers still moved about them, but Giselle didn't see them. She couldn't tear her eyes from Navarre.

He took a step to reach her, and his fingers closed on her elbow. She knew he was leading her from the floor, knew it would cause comment, and cared nothing for that. She had Navarre beside her and she refused to look anywhere else. She watched him with wide eyes and nibbled on her lower lip.

Heads turned as they walked away, but she ignored them.

"You look beautiful, Giselle. I wanted to tell you so before I leave."

His words were tersely spoken, and a nerve twitched in his jaw. Giselle watched him fill a plate from one of the tables.

"Leave?" She whispered the word as her hands sought a wine goblet.

"I only came at Etienne's request. If it had been anyone else...?" He left the sentence unfinished.

"He asked for you?"

"It's one of the hardest things I've ever done, Giselle. Do not make it worse, *s'il vous plait?*"

"Worse? How can you say such a thing?"

He shrugged. His jacket fit so loosely, she could barely spot the movement.

"I don't understand, Navarre. Why would Etienne ask for you?"

"Perhaps he realized his limitation concerning dancing. Who is to say?"

He filled his mouth as if he hadn't eaten for days. She watched him without blinking.

"Why? Does it matter so much to you, Giselle?"

He viciously shoved another bite into his mouth and grimaced like he'd tasted something foul.

"How can you say such a thing? I—I...love you, Navarre."

He stopped chewing and glared at her. And then he swallowed.

"Don't toy with me, Giselle. I won't tolerate it. Not again."

"I—I have never toyed with you, Navarre."

"Non?" His eyebrows rose as he asked it.

"No. I swear it."

"Well, whatever you call it...don't do it. I'm not man enough to let you go so easily next time. Next time? What am I saying? I'm mad to even consider it. *Merde!"*

He set his plate down and took the glass from her hands. Giselle tried to stop her shivers as he gulped it down, then she simply stood there and enjoyed them.

"My. My. If it isn't *mon cher,* Navarre."

Giselle recognized the voice. She knew Navarre did, too.

"I see you've finally gotten some age to you. What do you know? You're quite handsome. Life never ceases to amaze me."

Mademoiselle Frerre's voice turned Navarre's features to stone. Giselle felt the same way as she turned to face the woman.

"Charmaine."

He didn't even dip his head in deference. Giselle raised her brows at the insult.

"You were invited? What was my aunt thinking to commit such *a faux pas?*"

"Have a care, Navarre. I'm still accepted in polite society, you know."

She moved close to him, arching her neck in a gesture to show off its length. Giselle clenched her hands to keep from shoving the woman away.

"Polite society? You flatter yourself."

Navarre wiped his hands on a napkin to put distance between them and to snub her. He spent several moments studying his fingers before turning his attention back to her. Giselle longed to applaud his performance.

"You're a *magnifique* specimen when you're angered. I wonder why I failed to see that earlier. Enlighten me, *mon ami.*"

If she insisted on speaking in that deep tone much longer, Giselle refused to be responsible for her actions. Her nails were digging into her palms now.

"What do you want, Charmaine? My pockets are as much to let as they always were, remember?"

She laughed her mocking laugh again. "Oh. I'm not here to make you propose, *mon cher,* although now that I have seen you full-grown, it is a tempting thought."

"You over-rate your attraction, Charmaine. I see that's something you haven't outgrown."

It was a good thing Navarre had spoken when he did. His words covered up Giselle's reaction. She was close to screaming at her. Having another woman flirt so outrageously with him, right in front of her eyes was one thing, but to know it was the woman who had the most right to do so, was close to making her lose control. She was shuddering with squelching it.

It was also a good thing Navarre had taken her wine goblet away from her. She would have tossed it in the red-haired beauty's face, and not given it another thought.

"I'd forgotten how amusing it is to trade compliments with you, Navarre, but you needn't worry about my imposing on your bachelor state anytime soon. I've no designs on you. I have my hands full with Jean-Claude. He sent me tonight for a reason. I'm checking the status of his inheritance while I'm attending your little function. He's not going to like what I tell him, is he?"

She gestured toward Giselle, and they both looked at her. To her own disgust, she blushed hotly.

"Hopefully not." Navarre replied.

CHAPTER NINETEEN

Giselle no longer questioned why her chambers were so dark. She knew the reason the very next day. The pounding in her head made her thank the peaceful dimness every time she opened her eyes. Louisa was constantly at her side, making the pain bearable. Nothing could be done for the heartache, however.

Nothing.

"You never should have stayed out so late, Giselle," Louisa said. "Isabelle told me she removed the stitches from your gown at dawn. How could you be so...?" She chuckled. "I don't know why I ask such a question. *Monsieur* Navarre was there, wasn't he?"

Giselle moaned. Her head pounded. Her throat hurt. And her heart just kept sending ache that overrode all the rest.

"What is it, love?"

"No...thing."

Giselle had watched for another chance to be with him almost the entire night, but he'd avoided her. It had been a simple matter. He was eligible, handsome, charming and wealthy. There was no dearth of females willing to dance and entertain him, and keep him from his sister-in-law's side.

"May I have another cup of tea, Louisa?"

"If it helps, love, you can have anything you like. Does it hurt overmuch?"

"Only when you make small talk." Giselle lifted the edge of the wet towel from her eyes to observe Louisa's reaction.

"Small talk? I'll have you know I've got better things to do than sit at your bedside and coddle you. *Tiens!* You are so stubborn. All I ask is a hint of how it went, and what do I get? Insults."

"I'm sorry." Saying the words made her eyes pound again, and Giselle eased further into her pillows.

Louisa had finished pouring a cup of tea and brought it over to the bed. "Here you go, Giselle. Don't mind me. I just want to know how things went. Was he impressed by the gown? Was he bowled over by your beauty? What did everyone say after meeting with you? Who is this mysterious *Mademoiselle* Frerre?"

"That one I can answer. Do you remember the dressmaker where I got my gown?"

"Mai oui! What a muddle. Did she say anything?"

"Yes and no. We didn't speak about it at length. How could we? I learned she was once Navarre's betrothed."

"No! This is incredible."

"It gets worse, I assure you."

"It does?"

"Oui."

The word was whispered. Giselle winced.

"Does it hurt much to speak? I should let you rest."

"It isn't the words, it's...everything. This *Mademoiselle* Frerre is—she's—I can't believe I'm having trouble with the words."

"Let me help you sit."

The pain was worse when she lifted her shoulders, but she welcomed it, surprising herself. She deserved it.

"Not only is she Navarre's ex-betrothed, but she's also Jean-Claude's mistress from Versailles Palace. She told Navarre and me that she was spying for Jean-Claude."

Louisa stopped plumping the pillows behind Giselle's back and stood. Giselle had to imagine the expression on her face.

"Good heavens! No wonder your poor head aches. I can't imagine anything more perverse. *Mon Dieu!* No wonder they speak of him like they do."

Giselle lifted the towel. She watched Louisa sip from the tea as she sat on the side of the bed. The expression on her face was exactly as Giselle had imagined it to be, too.

"So...Navarre did have a betrothed," Louisa mused. "Gerty tried to tell me the story when we first arrived, but I would have none of her gossip. She expects something in exchange, and I'd never talk about you. Stupid woman. She should find something better to do with her time."

"*Mademoiselle* Frerre is...very beautiful." Giselle's voice dropped.

"I saw her. If you think such overblown looks are beautiful, you're touched. And if *Monsieur* Navarre thinks she's more lovely than you...well! I don't know what this world's coming to, I don't. Besides, did you not just say she's Jean-Claude's mistress? With a wife and daughter here, he can afford a mistress? I'd like to know who's supposed to pay, that I would."

"It's quite amusing, Louisa." Giselle handed her the cloth from her forehead. It had warmed too much to be soothing. "I bought the gown with Savignen gold, which is exactly what Jean-Claude would have used, too."

"Amusing? You have developed a strange sense of humor, Giselle. I can't imagine where you learned it, either. You would have covered yourself in ashes and collapsed in a righteous faint earlier."

"I was never that devout, and you know it. Oh, my head!"

Giselle sat upright to argue with her, then fell back onto the pillows. She knew what Louisa was doing when she heard the water. Louisa was re-wetting the towel with cool water. From the sound of it, she was rushing, too.

"There, love. Don't pay attention to my words when I jest. I can't imagine what that *Mademoiselle* Frerre could have done to make your poor head ache so, but she'd better not do it again. She'll have to get through me first."

"It wasn't her. It was them."

Giselle pointed at the connecting door with a hand that wouldn't stop shaking. The room was dark for a reason, and being married to a Berchald male was it.

"Them? Etienne did something? To whom?"

"He said...he planned...he—"

Her throat closed off with the stress of trying to say it, so she lay panting with it.

"He said something? To whom? That *Mademoiselle* Frerre? He didn't renew their betrothal, did he?"

Giselle rolled her head back and forth on the pillows.

"Then what?"

"Navarre."

She whispered the name and closed her eyes. Nothing worked, though. She kept replaying the scene that had her pacing the room until she was too exhausted to walk. Navarre and Etienne were planning....

She couldn't even think it.

After Giselle had dismissed Isabelle, the light outlining the connecting door made her realize it was ajar. Her head was starting to ache, but she could have sworn that door was locked when she left for the ballroom. She recalled making certain of it.

Giselle was getting as self-centered as Esmee with her own servants. She realized it when she'd come upon Isabelle napping on the small divan as she waited to take Giselle's stitches out and wrap her coiffure. That's why she'd rushed in dressing for bed, and that's why she hadn't noticed the door ajar sooner. It wasn't going to stay that way, though. Etienne wasn't entering her rooms again, ever.

Giselle lurched toward the doorway, holding onto the wrapped bundle of her hair to balance herself. She hadn't wanted the hairstyle taken apart just yet. The chateau had many guests staying over, and she might have need of dressing formally again. It was stupid, though. She wished women would revolt against such fashions.

"It will never work, Etienne," Navarre had been speaking. "Go to sleep. You'll see things differently tomorrow."

Giselle opened the door a little farther to peek.

"Of course it will work! You've lost some...some...some—enough weight, haven't you? I applaud you for it, too." Etienne's words were slurred, as if he stumbled over his own tongue.

Enough weight? What strangeness were they plotting now?

"Trust me, Etienne. She'd never believe it was you."

"If it was dark enough, and she had enough wine, she could. Besides...she's a child. She knows nothing of it."

Navarre stepped out of her sight, so she opened the door farther to see where he went. Etienne was easy to find. He was propped against his headboard, tear tracks on his cheeks. Navarre was standing at the open windows, looking out over the valley. For some reason, she wasn't worried over being caught, so she opened the door even wider. Navarre had his hands over his ears, as if to shut out Etienne's words. He hadn't changed although his hair had come undone. Giselle couldn't tear her eyes from him even if she'd wanted to.

Dawn's light silhouetted him, turning his golden hair dark red, and highlighting every bit of him for her. When he turned, Giselle ducked back into the doorway.

"You want to see me die, too, don't you? You...along with everyone else! So be it. Get out! Didn't you hear me? Get out!" Etienne covered his face with his hands as if to hide further sobs.

"Etienne, I'd do anything for you. You know this. Please don't talk this way."

Navarre approached the bed and went to his knees on the ledge. The motion brought him directly into Giselle's line of sight.

"Anything? Have I the wrong meaning for the word? Perhaps you'd better leave before you lie more to me."

Navarre put his forehead on the coverlet, and Etienne reached out to touch his head. Giselle had to swallow past the lump in her throat at the sight. She realized she was intruding. She was no better than Gerty, listening at keyholes. She moved back into her chamber. She was in the process of closing the door as softly as possible when Navarre spoke again.

"I'll talk to Giselle again, Etienne. I promise."

"Talk? I don't need more talk. I need you to bed her and get her with child! I need a son, and you can sire it better than I. How many more times must I repeat it?"

Shock stopped Giselle, and then anger. She'd known her husband was bestial, crude, and heartless, but to ask something so evil? She couldn't believe what she'd just heard.

Say something Navarre, she silently begged. She willed him to refute Etienne's request, to let him know he asked too much. Love was God's gift, not a means to prevent someone like Jean-Claude's inheritance.

Say it, Navarre!

Silence answered. She realized Navarre wasn't going to say anything against it. The anguish settled into her stomach like a stone. Navarre was willing to try and fool her? He was willing to be intimate with her as if he were Etienne? She wondered why she questioned it, when she had the proof right in front of her. She watched as Navarre sighed, lifting his shoulders with it.

Did they really think she wouldn't know? Even in the dark? They may be close in weight now, but... Giselle wiped at her mouth, brutally rubbing away the feel of Navarre's kisses. The memory remained. They'd never be able to fool her. They couldn't disguise Navarre's scent.

Bile choked, tasting like flat champagne, as she stepped into the room. The sunlight blinded her for a moment. The *duc's* rooms were bright, but there wasn't enough light to ward off the blackness of their intrigues.

"Oh. Look. It's Giselle." Etienne saw her first. "This is excellent. You see, Navarre? You won't even have to pretend."

Etienne looked at her through such reddened eyes, she almost winced. Navarre stumbled to his feet like a thief caught in the act. Giselle centered her attention on the *duc,* refusing to even glance in Navarre's direction.

She'd been fooled at the arbor, she realized. When Navarre spoke his words of love, she actually believed him. They must think her stupid as well as childish. He hadn't been in love. He'd been placing the groundwork for this plot. Giselle didn't think she could bear it, yet she had to. Navarre had simply been preparing her for the moment when he would take her innocence and make it vile. Evil. Monstrous.

They couldn't inflict a graver wound if they used a weapon. She wondered if they knew it. She recognized it was agony gripping her heart, making her aware of every painful beat.

"Giselle?" Navarre whispered.

"Don't say a word, Navarre. Not one. I've already heard enough. And I'll never be a party to such evil! Never!"

She tried to sound vilified, but her voice gave out. Giselle said the last in a whisper.

"Oh come, Giselle. Stop." Etienne said. "You won't bed with me, and I can't force you without the use of my legs. And what might happen then? You already threatened me with a convent. Or loss of the valley. What choice do I have?"

He laughed as she turned to him. Giselle narrowed her eyes.

"You are a pig, *Monsieur* le *Duc.* I realize that now. I should feel grateful you didn't plan to send Jean-Claude to my bed, although it could hardly be worse!"

Her voice cracked. Navarre sounded like he was choking. She didn't look. She didn't care. She already knew Etienne was a devil incarnate, but why did Navarre have to be one, too?

And Navarre might not even love her. She'd been blind, innocent...and too inexperienced to know better. She could just see Etienne setting this up, telling Navarre to get her to trust him, wear down her resistance...work on her weaknesses. Because one Berchald in her bed was as good as another.

She only wished it hadn't succeeded as well as it had. That tormented her even more.

"My father kept me imprisoned for a reason, and I know now what it is. He knew how evil you all are. I wish I had remained at Antilli, and ignorant of it!"

"Isn't she wonderful when she's angry, Navarre?"

Etienne smiled at her, and Giselle screeched in disbelief, using the last of her voice to berate him.

"Do you think I care if you find me wonderful, *Monsieur* le *Duc?* Well, I don't. I don't care what any member of this family thinks of me! I'd rather lie with pigs than bed with any of you!"

The last of her words tore her throat.

"Giselle, wait!"

Navarre started toward her. Giselle ran into her room and slammed the door in his face. She was trembling so viciously, she had difficulty turning the key, sealing them out, but she did.

Anger kept her pacing until she was too exhausted to see anymore. She kept telling herself it was anger, and not the pounding on the door that wouldn't quit for

what seemed like hours. She certainly wasn't stupid
enough to open it. Not anymore.

CHAPTER TWENTY

"Is your head any better, Giselle?"

It was Louisa, walking in with a supper tray. Giselle motioned her to set it down, without lifting her head.

"Oh Giselle. You poor dear. They talk of nothing else below stairs."

How could they have anything to talk about? None of them were there, were they? The thought made her head throb even worse.

"Chef Aaron has made an onion broth just for you, but you're supposed to swallow this horrid-smelling concoction first."

She lifted a goblet and sniffed. Giselle glanced at Louisa's pained expression before she set it back down.

"If I can't drink the soup until I take that...then tell Chef Aaron *merci,* but I am not hungry."

"What they don't know won't harm them, will it?"

Louisa poured the contents out the window. Even the small amount of light that came from moving the drapes hurt her head.

"Now drink your broth. Then you'll be able to tell me what this is all about."

Giselle had begun to sit gingerly and reach for the soup bowl. The moment Louisa attached a payment, her arm sank back down.

"Then, I repeat myself. I am not hungry. *Merci.*"

Louisa put her hands on her hips and sighed hugely. "Giselle, what am I going to do with you? I thought seeing your love would make your heart lighter, not turn you into an invalid again."

"He's not my love."

Giselle kept her voice flat as she said it. Then she reached for the bowl of soup with hands that shook. Chef Aaron was a master. The soup was as delicious as it smelled, delicately flavored with beef and mushrooms. Giselle drank all she could and waited for Louisa's reaction.

"Very well, Giselle. I'm listening."

"Is the same priest still here?"

Giselle leaned back onto the pillows. Everything had started to worsen once she lied to him. She needed to make amends. That was a good starting point, and she was getting heartily sick of being in bed.

"Yes, but I don't mind telling you, he doesn't inspire me. Gerty told me he's new. That could be it, but did you know that he receives correspondence from *Monsieur* Jean-Claude, of all people?"

She'd known not to trust him. This was bad. It meant she'd have to continue her silence and pray The Lord would be in a very forgiving mood when she reached confession.

"We're not going to talk of prayer, are we, Giselle? I swear that is all you do — and cry, of course."

"I only wish I could cry. I've been trying all day. Perhaps that's why my head aches so."

Louisa stared. "It is that horrible?"

"What?"

"This reason you don't love *Monsieur* Navarre anymore?"

"Dieu! If only that were the truth!"

"You do still love him, then?"

"Why don't you leave me be, Louisa? Make yourself a comforting companion, and just go?"

"Because that isn't what you need, love. Trust me. Are you finished with your soup?"

Giselle nodded. She watched as Louisa took the tray to the door. She suspected the woman was checking for any listeners. It was certainly a strange household into which she had married. It wasn't long before Louisa returned.

"I never could hide things from you, could I?"

"Why would you want to start now, Giselle? I can't help you if I don't know what is going on."

"I don't even know most of the time. How am I supposed to share it?"

"Between us, we'll know. Come, love. Tell me what has happened."

Giselle lay on her back and looked up at the embroidered crest on the half canopy that shadowed the bed. "This is a very scheming family I've married into. I didn't realize the extent of it."

"The nobility have little else to do with their time. I've heard tales from the palace that would shock more of your hair white."

Giselle sighed, and turned her head. "I doubt it."

She watched as Louisa resumed her seat in the chair beside the bed platform. Then, she picked up her sewing as if they weren't discussing anything important.

"Are you ignoring me, Louisa?" she asked.

"It's the only way I can get you to confide in me. I act like I don't care, and you finally tell me what's bothering you. I haven't raised you from a child and learned nothing, you know."

Giselle laughed. It felt wonderful to realize she still had the capability.

"So, what do you want to talk about?"

Giselle watched her place another stitch in the stocking she was embroidering. Giselle knew the stockings were for her, but she wondered why they bothered. Very few would ever see such beauty.

"Navarre. He...." Her throat choked off with the tears she'd been holding back all day. "He...said he loved me. And I believed him. I was stupid, naive and blind. I didn't know it was just an act. I should have. I realize that now."

"How do you know he doesn't?" Louisa placed more stitches as if concentrating on her work, and not what they spoke on.

"Ha!" Giselle wiped her eyes with the towel, wondering where all the tears came from now. "Because I am not as stupid, naïve, and blind as I was before, that's how. They educated me. And well."

"Navarre spoke on this with his own lips?"

"*Oui.*"

Louisa raised her brows. "He actually said he doesn't love you? I am more than surprised, Giselle. I am in shock."

"Well...he didn't actually say that. It was more—what he didn't say."

"Navarre didn't say something? And this meant he doesn't love you? What happens when the man talks, pray tell?"

"No...yes. You're confusing me."

"*I'm* confusing you? Really, Giselle." She lifted her sewing and looked it over at the same time as she clicked her tongue.

"He doesn't love me. He can't. If he did, he wouldn't have agreed with Etienne."

"I can agree with the *duc*. Does that mean I don't care for you?"

"You don't know what it is Etienne asks!"

"Your husband asked Navarre to do something, then?"

Giselle nodded.

"And for some reason, you believe if Navarre agrees with this, he doesn't love you anymore. Is that what you're saying?"

"Anymore? *Non*. It means he never did. Oh, how can I bear it?"

The towel wasn't soothing anymore, it was too saturated with tears. Giselle held it to her eyes and shuddered through the sobs.

"You expect me to believe *Monsieur* Navarre cares nothing for you? Honestly, Giselle. Even Isabelle spoke of the way he looks at you. If there was ever a case of unrequited love, that Navarre has caught it. The man is smitten. That is what Isabelle said."

"Isabelle? She wouldn't say anything like that. I don't even think she knows what it is."

"True enough. She inferred it, though."

Giselle shoved the towel into her eyes. "I don't know why I confide in you. I don't. Truly. This is not comforting."

"Isabelle did say as much. You forget we were here when your jewelry was brought, Giselle. Do you think your servants are blind?"

"No." Her voice sounded uncertain, even to her.

"Do you think emotions such as love are so foreign that we can't spot them right before our noses? Here I thought I'd raised you differently, and yet you turn out just like one of the heartless aristocrats. What have I done to deserve such a fate?"

"I am not. I can guarantee I have a heart. Here I am crying it out. Look for yourself." She moved the towel aside to show her.

"You'd best give that to me. I'll rinse it for you. I spoke the truth earlier. Isabelle said it was a good thing that *Monsieur* Navarre was moving to the dower house with the looks he gives you. That's what she said."

"Isabelle said that?"

"That man is as besotted as any I've ever seen, and you say it's acting? Well! He should be on a stage. That's where he should be."

"But he agreed with Etienne. At least...I think he did."

"Let me see if I understand this, Giselle. *Monsieur* Navarre may have agreed to something that the *duc* asked of him, something that would mean he doesn't love you and never did. Furthermore, you aren't even certain that it was something he agreed with. Am I hearing this correctly?"

Giselle's brows drew together. "I am not that confused, Louisa. I know what I heard."

"I am just trying to get it correct."

"He may not have agreed, but he didn't disagree, either."

"So, now silence means agreement? You may find that difficult to enforce, Giselle. Look at Isabelle, for instance. She's often silent, but I don't think she agrees with me when she is. In fact, I rather think she's the opposite. Do you see what I mean?"

"You don't know what it is they spoke of."

"True enough. Are you ready to enlighten me, yet?"

Louisa put the stocking down and reached for the cloth. Giselle was surprised to find she wasn't interested in crying anymore. She watched as Louisa dipped the cloth into the basin and wrung it out again.

"Etienne—"

Her voice stopped. The rest of the words clogged her throat, choking her. She couldn't even say it? If she couldn't tell Louisa, how could she ever tell a priest?

"Was the *duc*...shall we say...in his cups at the time of this conversation?"

"Was he drunk? Is that what you ask? I've rarely seen him otherwise."

"That complicates matters for me."

"For you?"

Louisa placed the cooled cloth back on her forehead. Giselle pulled it right back off.

"Your husband could have asked anything while he was in that state, Giselle. Can you assist me in narrowing down my guesses?"

"Etienne wants a son." Giselle whispered the words and felt herself going hot, and then cold.

"Ah. And since he can't give you one, he asked *Monsieur* Navarre...."

"Don't say it! I can't even think it. It's too wicked."

To Giselle's surprise, Louisa burst out laughing. She couldn't even speak the words, and Louisa found it laughable?

"Perhaps you could save your amusement for another time, when you're not supposed to be comforting me?"

"Oh, Giselle. Forgive me! It's just...I would have given anything to have seen *Monsieur* Navarre's face."

"Why?"

"Think of it. He's been fighting his...shall we say...his attraction? Yes, that's a good word. He is at war with himself, and all he does is work through it. I hear that's all he does. He won't even stop for meals, and the chef is worried. Chef Aaron is beginning to wonder if he'll ever be able to tempt *Monsieur* Navarre or the new *duchesse* with his culinary skill. The odd thing is, they suffer from the same affliction, and only I know the truth. Oh, how Gerty would pay to hear this."

"Louisa!" Giselle tried to sound as stern as possible.

"I'm jesting, Giselle. This is priceless. *Monsieur* Navarre is attracted to his disabled brother's wife, and it's making him ill with fighting it. The poor man stays away and only attends the ball because the *duc* insisted upon it."

"You know about that, too?"

"Gerty is the *duc's* valet's sister. Always remember that. She knows more about the *duc's* movements than he probably does."

"She might know—? Oh! I'll die of embarrassment."

"She doesn't know this, Giselle. Trust me."

"But, you just said—"

"She wouldn't keep it a secret if she did. That woman can't keep anything secret. Now, look. You're making me lose my train of thought."

"Oh. Forgive me," Giselle said sarcastically.

"*Monsieur* le *Duc* longs to make certain his littlest brother attends this fest. Why is that, do you think?"

"Don't look to me. I'm certain I don't know."

"Because he wants to make sure *Monsieur* Navarre knows to whom you belong, perhaps? Or better yet, he wants to make certain you know to whom *Monsieur* Navarre belongs. That could have been his intent. It's obvious he has to do something. Perhaps the *duc* knew this *Mademoiselle* Frerre would attend, and he would want the *duchesse* - that's you, Giselle."

"I am capable of that much intrigue, thank you very much." Giselle spoke sarcastically, but she was smiling, too.

"Yes. Well. Suppose the petite *duchesse* finds out that this *Mademoiselle* was Navarre's betrothed? Perhaps the *duc* believes this revelation will get you to.... How can I put this delicately?"

"Don't bother. Etienne wants me in his bed. He doesn't care if I rant and rave about it, either. He thinks I'm wonderful when I'm angry, and even.... I shudder to recall this, but he desires me when I rage at him. Oh Louisa! He's sick!"

"It seems the *duc* may have out-schemed himself this time, though. He forgot Navarre's betrothed wants nothing to do with him. She's Jean-Claude's property." She almost spat the last word.

"Then Etienne gets so drunk, he's unable to do what he hoped, anyway," Giselle said, surprising herself and Louisa. "He can't fulfill his part of the intrigue, even if I'm willing and in his bed."

"You're learning, Giselle. Now imagine that *Mademoiselle* Frerre made certain the *duc* knows that Jean-Claude won't stand by and watch his inheritance slip through his fingers. Don't tell me he didn't try and kill the *duc,* either. I already know the story."

"I won't." Giselle rose to her knees and moved into the middle of the bed.

"That leaves *Monsieur* le *Duc* in a quandary. What can he do? Who can he trust to help him?"

"Navarre!" Giselle gathered an armload of covers to her breast.

"Exactly!" Louisa pointed at her. "And, since the *duc* has already seen Navarre's attraction to you..." She winked as she said that, and Giselle blushed, "what better plan than to put Navarre into his own marriage bed? The resulting child would have the same blood, would it not? *Monsieur* Navarre resembles the *duc* quite a bit, too. Admit it."

"I'll do no such thing. Navarre is the most handsome man in the world, but as long as the child is a Berchald and is accepted as such, Etienne would be safe."

"Right! But there are complications. The *duchesse* won't agree. Therefore, she must be fooled. The man is stupid as well as disabled to think that would work, but men are stupid creatures. Don't ever say you heard me say that, though."

"Never." Giselle shook her head.

"Which brings me to the part I wish I had seen. Oh! I can't imagine how *Monsieur* Navarre must have looked when his brother offered you to him. He must have been in shock, Giselle. That's why he said nothing. He never believed you'd ever be his, and he longs to do what Etienne wants. He knows it's wrong, but his entire being begs for it."

She was making Giselle shiver, but she said nothing to stop the words.

"But he has to argue," Louisa continued. "'It's impossible, Etienne', he must say. 'It will never work.'"

"Mon Dieu!" Giselle cried it aloud and slapped her hands to her cheeks, losing the bedding.

"What?"

"He was saying as much when I first listened. Oh, Louisa, what have I done?"

"You did something?"

"I stormed into the *duc's* chamber. I called Etienne and Navarre horrible names. Oh...how will I get him to forgive me?"

Giselle sat in the center of her bed, deflated beyond all reason.

"You stormed the chamber? You? I don't believe it."

"I said they might as well put Jean-Claude into my bed, since one Berchald was as good as another. I said I'd rather lie with a pig. Oh, Louisa! What have I done?"

Giselle tipped her head and wailed it to the canopy of red drapery above her.

"You said all that? Oh Giselle! I am so proud of you."

"You are?" Her head came back down.

"You play this game like an expert. For what but a little righteous anger would make *Monsieur* Navarre even more tormented?"

"I don't want him tormented."

"Oh please, Giselle, you wanted much worse, earlier."

That much was true. Giselle opened her mouth and then closed it again.

"You only need to choose the place, Giselle. If I'm not mistaken, your love is, right now, thinking of what he could have done differently, and what he should have said. I don't suppose your head is feeling any better?"

"*Oui*, and I'm starving. Would Chef Aaron send something more substantial up, do you think?"

"Bend your destiny to fit your needs, Giselle. That's my advice, and I don't often give it."

Giselle's eyes went wide. "You almost sound as if you think I should.... *Merde!* I still can't say it!"

"Listen to me carefully, Giselle du Berchald. From the first moment I saw you, I lost my heart. It was a good thing, too, for I failed to follow it earlier. If I had...? Well, that's a long story. I was once young and in love, too, but I didn't have the courage to follow my own heart."

"We're speaking of adultery here, Louisa. Are you honestly suggesting I surrender all hope of heaven?"

"Did your mouth say the vows? If you must think on it, remember that. Well, did it?"

Giselle smiled as she watched Louisa plant her hands on her hips. It was such predictable behavior even if her advice did border on heresy.

"I'm saying nothing, Giselle. You must follow your heart, not me. I can only tell you what you reap if you don't follow it. Once you get as old as me, all you have are regrets. And the older you are, the more costly they become, too."

"I'm sorry. I don't understand."

"Oh, pooh. Look at me, crying at my regrets and lecturing you when you have a handsome young man at your beck and call. Talk about a waste of time!"

"I don't think he'll accept my overtures right now, Louisa. In fact, I'm certain of it."

She chuckled and walked to the door. "You've got a lot to learn, Giselle, but I've monopolized your time long enough. Isabelle will still be fretting over your head pain, and I have Chef Aaron to flatter with your order."

The door shut behind her. Giselle got up and went to her window. She felt weak, but at least her head wasn't pounding anymore. She felt like she'd just been bathed and was waiting to be dried off. She shook off the fancy as she watched the edge of Savignen Valley. The trees were touched on their crowns by the setting sun. It was a peaceful sight, and she desperately needed some peace.

CHAPTER TWENTY-ONE

"Would you rather go through the third addition or the cellars today, Giselle?" Esmee asked. "We haven't seen either, yet. But, since it's such a lovely day, we could tour the gardens. The eighth *duchesse* laid out a lovely maze, and it's one of our showpieces."

"I think I'd prefer the stables, actually," Giselle replied.

"The stables?" Esmee's eyebrows rose almost to her hairline. "They will be muddy this early in the day. I'm not dressed for it, either."

Giselle shrugged and returned to the book of sonnets she'd taken from the Blue Salon. The words should have been memorized by now, but she wasn't reading them.

"Are you certain? The maze would be better, I think. It's finally been groomed. It takes nearly a week to complete, and we have to wait until the shrubs are thick enough. It's truly lovely."

"Why do you bother asking me, if you're not going to acquiesce to my wishes?"

Giselle spoke to her book. She wondered if she dared peek to see how Esmee took that particular speech, but decided against it. Esmee sighed.

"Very well, Giselle. I'm no expert on them, though. It would be better if Navarre were to show them to you."

Giselle tried not to show her satisfaction by bringing the book closer to her nose. *Louisa was right again.*

Giselle could learn to manipulate people with the best of them.

"I suppose I could wait for Navarre to show me. I don't know how long that might take, though. I really would like to see them today."

Giselle knew very well that it would take some bit of accomplishing to get Navarre to show her anything. She'd known this morning when Gerty brought in her breakfast tray, and she'd been so optimistic, too!

She'd been sending sealed missives to Navarre for two days now, and all he did was return them unopened. It was maddening. She thought she'd finally succeeded last night, though. She'd had Louisa address it and give it to a manservant to deliver.

That it was returned unopened on Giselle's breakfast tray had almost brought her to tears again.

"Have I offended you in some way, Giselle?" Esmee asked.

"Me? Offended? Oh, please, Esmee, why would you ask such a thing?"

She read a stanza four times and still didn't know the words. It was more interesting to listen for Esmee's reaction.

"You seem...different today," Esmee said slowly. "Forgive me, Giselle. I'm letting my imagination run amok. It has been since the ball. I don't suppose you've noticed, with the way you've been attending to Etienne lately."

Now...who could have told her such a thing? Giselle didn't know why she asked herself the question. She already knew the answer. Gerty was forever gossiping, and Giselle was playing the adoring wife whenever Gerty was about.

"I'll send for Navarre to show you the stables...but don't be surprised if he ignores my summons, too."

Esmee looked at Giselle from the doorway with an unreadable expression, and then she left, closing the door softly behind her.

Giselle slammed the book shut. Everyone about her seemed an expert at intrigue, while Giselle was such a novice it was almost a crime. She wondered what had given her away. The book fell to floor as she stood and walked over to a window, narrowing her eyes on the sunlit lawns.

She should have simply toured the maze. The door opened behind her.

"*Monsieur* Jean-Claude du Berchald!" a servant announced.

Giselle held in a gasp as she swiveled, but she couldn't prevent her next reaction. Her mouth dropped. Her eyes widened. And her heart joined in with a faster rate. Even though she was standing, it wouldn't make any difference. Jean-Claude exceeded his brothers in height and wore heels on his pointed shoes, too. From across the room, Giselle had to look up at him.

"The *Duchesse* Giselle," the manservant finished as he closed the door.

Giselle heard it through a fog. It felt, and sounded, like the words came from very far away. Everything in the room faded. The only thing she was capable of absorbing at the moment was Jean-Claude du Berchald.

Oh heavens!

The man was absolutely stunning. He was probably wearing court attire, but he could've arrived from a ball, as well. His coat was fashioned of ice-blue brocade, heavily embroidered with silver, his breeches were silvery satin, and his legs were encased in white hose.

It should have looked absurd. It didn't.

He had a small mustache, but it didn't hide full lips. Since he was wearing a powdered wig, it was impossible to tell if he'd inherited the Berchald coloring. The shade of his mustache didn't help. It was dark brown. Giselle considered herself a novice at male beauty, but knew instinctively that it didn't matter. Jean-Claude was an awesome specimen. And he knew it. One eyebrow was lifted inquiringly at her reaction, one leg was posed in front of the other, and he smiled slightly.

And then was walking toward her, and there wasn't anything she could do about it. Her eyes went even wider as he stopped before her. Giselle had to crane her neck to continue looking at him. She couldn't move her gaze away.

"I'm enchanted to meet you finally, my dear, dear sister."

He bent at the waist to raise her hand to his lips. Giselle was grateful she still had her lips open as she sucked for one breath after another.

"You're probably wondering why I bother wearing heels," he continued.

Giselle didn't answer.

"Well. I wear them because I want to make certain I'm noticed."

She snorted.

"I know. It shouldn't be a problem, *oui?*"

He didn't relinquish her hand. He tucked it into the crook of his arm and moved them toward the settee, taking long, slow steps. Giselle's feet moved without conscious volition. She couldn't have stopped him, anyway. She hoped he wasn't planning on sitting beside her. She didn't know if she was ready for such close contact.

But how could she have prepared for that?

He swiveled gracefully for a man his size, moved her hand into his, and had her seated before she gained another breath. He then hooked a chair with his foot and pulled it beneath him so it was there as he sat. Without looking. If she hadn't seen it happen, she wouldn't have believed it. He hadn't even let go of her hand the entire time.

She was grateful he wasn't sitting beside her, yet timid about it at the same time. He was probably closer this way. He swiveled his hand, sliding her fingers to rest atop his own, and then he touched his lips to each fingertip, one at a time. Giselle hadn't a prayer of stopping a blush.

"Charmaine told me of your beauty."

He had paint on his face. The line where it ended at his neck was obvious. That explained the contrast of his facial hair. There were black lines around his eyes, rouge on his cheeks, and he had some sort of red paint on his nails.

All of which should have disgusted her. She'd wondered what the people at Louis, the Beloved's court looked like, had received a basic education from *Monsieur* Poinre, but it wasn't preparation enough. She realized that, now.

She had never felt so admired, feted, or adored. If he'd been blessed with the Berchald eyelashes, they were swallowed in the black paint he'd lined about his eyes. That didn't stop their impact. Eyes the exact shade of Navarre's held hers and Giselle forced herself to swallow. It was like being too close to fire. It burned and yet drew her simultaneously.

She saw what held *Mademoiselle* Frerre, and Jean-Claude had entirely too much of it.

"Yet she told me nothing at all." He held her hand and her gaze, and spoke with such sweetness she shivered. "And you're so petite! I've never seen anything so... hmm. What can I say? Beautiful? *Non.* Too boring. Enchanting? *Non.* Over-used. There is no word capable of describing you. But I know now why the *comte* kept you hidden."

To her shock, he tightened his thumb and tipped her hand over. And then he kissed her on the wrist! A long, lingering kiss! Another shiver ran her. Chilling. Disquieting. It wasn't a pleasant experience, anymore. She wondered what had changed.

He released her hand, and sat back, inhaling deeply, well aware that Giselle was watching. She hadn't moved her eyes. She might have forgotten to blink.

"Ah...that smell! Fresh country air. I had forgotten how...."

He winked at her. Giselle was appalled at another blush, but couldn't tear her gaze away. Jean-Claude didn't need the heels. He was impossible to miss, and equally impossible to ignore.

"...disgustingly healthy it smells. Too many conflicting aromas for me."

He pulled a small box from his jacket pocket, placed a pinch of white powder under his nose, and sniffed it in. Perhaps that was the arsenic she'd heard of. The thought must have transferred to her expression because he explained.

"It's snuff, my dearest. Would you care for some?" He sneezed against the lace at his wrist and then held out the box.

Giselle pulled back and her eyes moved down from his. He had the same Berchald nose. And he was wearing a black patch. She hadn't noted it earlier because of his mustache. He'd placed it beside his nose. She noted the shape. A tiny spider. She didn't have the expertise to look away quickly enough.

"Oh. I've frightened you. Forgive me. I sometimes have that affect...although usually on innocent young maidens, I admit."

He'd leaned forward again to study her, making the chair creak a bit with his weight. Giselle blushed again. Ignominiously. Stupidly. If she kept reacting like this, he'd never believe she and Etienne had—

"Jean-Claude! You should have warned us before you came."

Esmee interrupted, breezing through the door with Gerty behind her, carrying a tray of delicacies. Jean-Claude appraised them silently. Giselle watched as even Gerty colored and dropped her eyes. He had that affect on all females?

"Esmee. You haven't changed — always rushing in to save others from my presence. She does that often, you know."

He said the last as an aside to Giselle before he stood. Now that she wasn't being threatened with the full extent of his charm, it was easier to breathe. He dwarfed Esmee, making her look small. He was easily the tallest of the Berchald men, even without his heels. His powdered hairstyle only added unnecessary height.

He caught her staring as he turned back to his chair, and Giselle looked to her lap. Her first impression was wrong. He didn't look as handsome as Navarre, after all...although it was hard to be certain with all that paint.

"Did Mother travel down with you, Jean-Claude?"

Esmee asked it as she poured tea. Giselle was grateful. Her hands would shake so badly, the cups would have clattered.

"You know I can't go anywhere without her, Esmee. It's a curse."

The last sentence was another aside to Giselle, as if she were in league with him. She smiled stiffly.

"I sent a summons to Navarre, Giselle," Esmee continued. "I'm certain we'll hear back before long."

She handed Giselle a cup and saucer. She concentrated on holding it without a hint of tremor.

"Summoning Navarre?" Jean-Claude asked. "Whatever for? Is he still so caught up on my vineyards he has no time to greet his prodigal brother? Really, Esmee, I'm surprised. You should have sent word the instant my grooms arrived. I gave you all morning advance notice."

Giselle was reeling, and yet nothing moved. She still sat upright in the settee, careful not to move. It was bad enough that Jean-Claude called the vineyard his, but the fact that Esmee knew he was coming, and hadn't said a word, was somehow worse.

Esmee may have been looking at her, but Giselle stared at the wall over Jean-Claude's right shoulder.

"Navarre has moved to the dowager house," Esmee said, finally.

"That wreck? Why?"

"Perhaps you should ask that question of me, Jean-Claude."

Etienne spoke up as he was wheeled into the room. The wheels squeaked slightly as he neared. Giselle watched as the chair was put beside her. Etienne held out his hand. She gave him hers. It was like ice reaching heated stone. The tiny squeeze she received made it even warmer.

"Oh. Look. I'd heard you were moving about, Etienne. I didn't believe it. How things change, *non?*"

"It was about time," Etienne replied. "I don't drink tea, Esmee. Perhaps you'd see that a bottle of Chablis is fetched. Tea is so wretchedly weak. Jean-Claude may even agree with me, wouldn't you, dearest brother?"

"Thank the saints! I was starting to wonder if you'd quit drinking, as well. And I could hardly ask your oh-so-beauteous, little wife, now could I?"

Jean-Claude set his cup down. Sunlight touched on his fingernail paint. Giselle quickly moved her glance to Esmee, watching her hesitate before leaving. Giselle wondered why. Was Jean-Claude likely to hurt Etienne with her sitting right beside him?

"And now...perhaps you'll tell me why you came back to Chateau Berchand, Jean-Claude? You know the provision of the agreement. You don't come back. I can't see what Mother is thinking to allow—"

"Spare me the lecture, Etienne."

Jean-Claude's sweet tone had vanished. This new one started an unpleasant quiver. Giselle looked to her lap, wishing she was anywhere else.

"You knew very well that the moment Charmaine informed me of this little wife of yours, I'd come back. You promised you'd never see her, let alone take her to your bed. Take care who you accuse of breaking his word."

"Etienne promised...*what?*"

The words escaped her before she could stop them. She looked first to Jean-Claude and then Etienne. She watched her husband turn red, and drop his eyes. Giselle couldn't believe it. She was reeling again, and the cup was clattering atop its saucer with it. She'd been purposely left at Antilli! There seemed no end to the intrigues in this family. Etienne had feared her presence would bring Jean-Claude. And he'd been right.

"Etienne. Brother. Is it possible you didn't even tell your petite *duchesse* why you never came for her? I'm surprised at you."

"No more than I am myself."

Etienne squeezed her hand again. Giselle looked back to her tea. It seemed safest.

"You expected me to do nothing, when the duns are at my door almost every day?"

Jean-Claude spat out the words and stood, rocking the chair with his move, and taking her gaze. She couldn't help it. He had such a commanding presence. His size. His dress. His comeliness. The force of his personality. Whatever it was, Giselle felt it, and leaned back in her chair to order to continue watching him.

"You aren't the *duc,* Jean-Claude."

"No. Pity. But I am the heir."

He walked to the window she'd been standing at. Even its height didn't make him look any smaller.

"What will you do?" Etienne asked.

Giselle held her breath.

"Do? Oh, please. I won't *do* anything, dearest brother." He chuckled and turned back to them. "I'm visiting for a while, that's all. Versailles can be so stuffy, and I can't tell you how I've missed the fresh...country...air."

He kept her gaze as he drew out the last words, as if daring her to contradict. And she was still staring, somehow mesmerized, unable to look away. He smiled slightly and then winked, as if they were fellow conspirators. Giselle swallowed, feeling gauche and stupid, caught and netted, ensnared and vulnerable. No wonder he wore a spider motif!

"Ah, the wine!"

The door opened, taking his attention from her. His exclamation greeted Esmee's return. Apparently, she'd brought Aunt Mimi, as well. Giselle didn't turn to check.

"Jean-Claude!" Aunt Mimi exclaimed. She must also be the one clapping her hands. "How can my favorite nephew come for a visit without telling me?"

Giselle hadn't moved her eyes from watching him. And he knew it. He acted like her attention was expected. Warranted. Deserved.

"I'm flattered. As always. Mimi." His bow was exaggerated, matching his tone.

"I received an answer from Navarre, Giselle," Esmee said. "He says our head groom is well-versed in anything you might wish to see. Giselle?"

Giselle shook herself slightly before turning back to the room. Every hair on her neck whispered in disagreement. Because now Jean-Claude was behind her and slightly to the left.

"Giselle sent for Navarre?"

Aunt Mimi asked it. Esmee answered. Giselle was still assimilating how it felt to have Jean-Claude near, but not in sight. It was unsettling. Disturbing. Bordering on fear.

"Of course not. She merely wished to tour the stables. I sent for Navarre."

The pressure on Giselle's fingers increased for a moment before Etienne released her hand.

"All this talk of Navarre and stables. Surely, there are more interesting things to discuss."

Jean-Claude walked through her vision, and selected a glass of wine. She watched as he drained his glass as quickly as Etienne usually did. Something Navarre said came back to her. From her tour of the portrait gallery. *Drunken, debauched, and wicked...*

"*Non?*"

He answered himself when no one else did. The then he sighed. Heavily. It was extremely visual, moving a large chest and shoulders with it. And Giselle really needed to look at something else!

"Then perhaps the charming *duchesse* wouldn't mind if I accompany her on this stable tour. What do you say, Giselle? I'm overdue for entertainment of this sort, anyway."

He looked directly at her, and Giselle barely suppressed the reaction. A shudder.

"But of course, Jean-Claude," Esmee said. "We can make an excursion of it. Someone should apprise Navarre of your arrival, though. Perhaps that will change his mind on accompanying you."

"Won't that take some time?" Giselle asked, without one bit of forethought.

Everyone looked at her. She forced herself to show nothing.

"To reach the dower house?" Esmee laughed lightly. "Honestly, Giselle. Aunt Mimi's house is just on the other side of the maze. It takes a few minutes to reach if you know the path. I should have told you earlier."

Giselle couldn't believe it. She'd spent the entire afternoon trying to best Esmee at intrigue, and she could've been talking to Navarre! She felt everyone watching, but felt Jean-Claude's stare most keenly. He was entirely focused on her. The feeling was even more disquieting.

Somehow, it felt like even he knew of her failure.

Esmee had offered to show the maze deliberately. Because she'd been told Giselle was trying to reach Navarre. How she must have chuckled when Giselle refused. Giselle lifted her cup to her lips and swallowed some tea while everyone waited for her reply. She set it back on the saucer. Nothing rattled. That was gratifying. And then she looked up and spoke with as bright a tone as possible.

"Think nothing of it, Esmee. Truly. It's nothing. If I wanted to know where the dower house was, I would have asked."

"Oh course, Giselle. I only meant—"

"I grow tired of this," Giselle interrupted, placing her tea cup and saucer on the table. "I said I wanted to tour the stables, and so I shall. And if Jean-Claude stands ready to escort, we'll be on our way. Jean-Claude?"

She stood and walked toward the door, waiting for him to catch up.

"Of course, my dear."

He refilled his wineglass and brought it with him. Giselle forced herself not to look up at him as he neared. And then loomed above her. She should've donned shoes with heels, but it wouldn't have done much good. Her chin came to his silver belt buckle.

"Wait for us, my dears," Aunt Mimi called. "I wouldn't dream of missing this."

Giselle watched Aunt Mimi rise. "Esmee?" she asked.

"No. No. You go. I'll stay and chat with Etienne. I'm certain he has no more interest in the damp and smells than I do. The stables are much too odorous this time of year." She shuddered. "*Au revoir*. Have a wonderful tour."

Wonderful tour?

Giselle heard and felt Esmee's amusement and there wasn't one thing she could do about it.

CHAPTER TWENTY-TWO

Giselle knew she should've waited for Louisa. She shouldn't have relied on Isabelle. All the maid did was slow her down. And she needed an explanation for everything! Isabelle wanted to know why Giselle was interested in the maze. She wanted to know why Giselle wasn't resting for dinner. She wanted to know why the stable tour hadn't been enough air and exercise.

And for once she wasn't keeping her own counsel.

"I can't believe you need another walk," she said. "Haven't you walked enough today? This will gain nothing but trouble for you. Come, Giselle. Let us go back before it gets dark. We'll be missed."

"Must you argue further, Isabelle? You remind me of the time, yet slow me down. That will make me late for dinner."

The maid's lips thinned, but she didn't reply. Giselle's skirts touched the grass as she entered the maze with Isabelle at her heels. She knew Isabelle still disapproved, but she'd finally stopped her questions. Giselle was thankful for that.

Now...which way?

The stables had been muddy, and if it hadn't been for Jean-Claude's misery, Giselle would've cried with vexation at Esmee. As the woman foresaw, the mud combined with other smells were atrocious, but Giselle had avoided the worst of it. Jean-Claude was heavier and wore his heels, and it was amusing to watch him lift each foot, curl his lips, and force himself not to complain. Perhaps that made the time pass so swiftly, and not the plans she was fomenting.

She had just under three hours to prepare before she was expected at dinner, which, due to Jean-Claude's arrival was swelling to over twenty participants. That should just give Giselle time to negotiate the maze and find Navarre.

Her imagination didn't think past that, to what would come once she found him. She didn't know how, or if he'd receive her. But he had to! She had to make him see she was crazed with heartache when she spoke. She thought it was something the two men had planned from the first.

No. Wait. She couldn't tell him that.

"Isabelle?" Giselle spun. The space around her was empty. "Isabelle?"

Oh! She should have waited for Louisa, but she ached with need for Navarre's arms around her. Giselle had to be honest with herself. She didn't just want his arms. She wanted his arms, lips, all of him.

She hadn't thought it through, and Isabelle didn't know her true reasons. If Isabelle knew Giselle wanted to meet Navarre and why, she'd never have agreed to come. And now, that she had, Giselle had second thoughts. And third ones. Giselle shouldn't have brought her. She'd never be able to speak freely with Navarre with Isabelle hovering over them.

The corridor she was in ended. Giselle stared at the hedge in front of her nose for several moments before she realized it. Then, she looked up, but that didn't help. The walls of the maze were very high, but she expected as much. They'd been groomed for the Berchald family. Of course it was built for giants.

Giselle turned around and started back the way she came, for it looked familiar. She caught her arm on a stray branch and heard the lace rip from her elbow.

Then there came a rustle from behind the hedge wall to her left, but it hadn't been caused by her actions.

"Isabelle?"

Her whisper was loud. It was growing darker in the corners of the maze, and no one else knew she was there. Giselle peeked around the corner before stepping out. The statue that greeted her made her squeal. She put a hand to her mouth to stifle it. There was no reason for such fear. There were statues at other corners. She walked closer. It was of Diana, the Greek goddess of the hunt.

Had she seen it before?

Giselle had been so caught up in what she would say to Navarre, she hadn't paid any attention to where she walked. There was another sound to her left, and she walked toward it. Perhaps it was Isabelle.

But why didn't she answer then? Was someone else out here? Perhaps baiting her with more intrigue? It could be Esmee. She'd probably find it amusing if Giselle got lost looking for Navarre. But wait! It could also be Jean-Claude.

Giselle backed from the strange rustling sound and ran into what might be a statue of the Greek god, Mercury. She didn't know the mythological gods well, even though Louisa had lectured her on them often enough, but the wings on the statue's heels showed who he was.

Oh, why had she come now? She should've waited until tomorrow. Navarre would be informed of Jean-Claude's visit, and she wouldn't be wandering this maze, not knowing where she was.

She ran into Diana again.

Giselle's hands went to her mouth to squelch the cry. Oh! This was impossible! She was lost in the maze, and only Isabelle knew where she was. But Isabelle could be lost, too. And...*Jean-Claude could even be stalking me!*

Giselle ran blindly, passing another statue she couldn't name, and then reached another dead end. Her heart constricted, her breath caught. She felt faint. Dizzy. There was little room in her corseted dress for panicked breathing, but that wasn't the problem.

Someone was following her. She was certain.

She was having trouble breathing. Giselle clamped her hands to her stomach and tried to suck in air as quietly as she could, listening intently as she did so. Concentrating to hear above the thud of her own pulse. The only other sound was a bird call from high above.

Oh. Thank the Bon Dieu.

She'd been stupid. This was proof. If Jean-Claude were out here...stalking her......there wouldn't be anyone to stop him. Why hadn't she thought it through? He could easily gain his inheritance back...by getting rid of her. That's why Aunt Mimi accompanied them to the stables without one comment about the mud. She was protecting Giselle. They all were, and how did she repay that?

By getting lost in the maze.

Giselle had no one to blame except herself. She turned back the way she'd come. It was difficult to hear above the sound of her heartbeat. Nothing looked familiar, but she'd been running, without marking a path. She peered around a corner and stopped, sucking in another breath. She was at the edge of the hedges, in the vast open space that was the center of the maze. She knew what it was because Antilli had just such a layout, where Giselle had played when she was very small. This one contained a small fountain, a large tree, three stone benches, and Navarre.

He sat on a bench, facing her, but his head was in his hands so he didn't see her. Giselle knew she'd been mistaken earlier. Navarre had no comparison. She'd forgotten how much he affected her, too. She realized it as her heart raced, this time for an entirely different reason.

Evening dress couldn't have been more attractive on Navarre than the homespun breeches he wore. His stockings were torn, and Giselle smiled as she looked him over. His lower half was splattered with mud, his shirt sleeves were rolled to the elbows, and his hair hung loosely to meet his sleeves. He was still the most handsome male she'd ever seen, Jean-Claude included.

She was almost to him before he looked up, and her heart stabbed her when he did. Because she'd caused the dark circles beneath his eyes, and the pain in their depths.

"Giselle?" he whispered.

She pushed between his knees, placing his head at her neck level. He looked up at her. Giselle finally got to run her fingers through his hair, filling her palms with the long, silky strands. It was as delightful an experience as she'd imagined it would be, and she put her face against it, breathing deeply of the clean, fresh aroma. She had forgotten how wonderful he smelled.

And then she felt him respond. He wrapped his arms about her thighs, and Giselle could swear she felt them, even through all her petticoats.

"My love."

She whispered the endearment before lowering her mouth to his, touching him, and teasing open his lips.

He groaned and Giselle trembled. She'd forgotten that sensation, too.

"Giselle, you must stop. You don't...know what you do."

He was panting, and she canceled his entreaties with kisses. A shudder ran through him, shaking her with it. Large hands moved from her thighs, past her buttocks covered with yards of material, to her waist. Then she felt him moving up the boning of her corset to cup her breasts.

She moaned, and felt her flesh swelling to fill his palms. His touch hardened then, almost paining her before he wrenched his mouth away, and his hands fell.

"Navarre?"

Giselle clenched locks of his hair, making it impossible for him to pull away easily. She liked being able to look down at him. She felt in control, although she knew he could change it at any moment. It was a heady feeling.

"No, Giselle. Please?" He looked away, pulling strands of hair from between her fingers. "I'm a pig, remember?"

"*Non!* I'm stupid, Navarre, and young. I didn't know what I was saying."

"No, Giselle."

He sighed and lifted his hands to hers. She knew he was going to be able to untangle her. It was a matter of time despite how she tightened her fingers.

"You were right. And I didn't even guess—"

"Don't finish that!" she stopped him. "You're not a pig. You never were. You're noble. Honorable. Chivalrous. I wouldn't love you so much otherwise."

His breath feathered across her throat, but his hands stopped trying to pry hers away.

"You don't understand, Giselle," he told her throat. "I *wanted* to do what Etienne asks. I can't tell you how much I long for it. So you see? I am a pig."

"No, Navarre." Giselle pulled him closer. The situation was exactly as Louisa told her. "You're not a pig. That was what made me most angry, I think."

Her voice dropped to a whisper as she managed to get the words out.

He looked back up at her, confusion filling his eyes. Giselle caught her breath at the light in them. She'd been fooled, earlier. Jean-Claude might resemble Navarre, but his eyes were a far cry from the soulful depth of Navarre.

"You make no sense, Giselle. Please? Release me. I must go."

He tried to untangle her. Worse, he was using his thigh muscles to push her from the space between his legs at the same time. The loss of contact made tears fill her eyes, and he flinched.

"Giselle, don't cry. Please? It's best I stay away. You must know that much. I can't stay near you anymore, and not think of—! Oh God. I am a pig."

She had to make him understand, but it wasn't easy. And she had to speak quickly. She bent forward and pressed her lips to his forehead. At the touch, he stopped moving.

"Navarre, please listen! I wasn't angry at you, or even at Etienne. You must understand! I love you. Completely. Totally. Until there is nothing else. It's the only thing I know for certain, anymore."

"You know so little, Giselle. How can you say that? You were right to speak as you did. I've been thinking about it a lot these past few days. I should've spoken earlier and told Etienne he was uncouth to suggest such a thing, let alone wish me to entertain it. See? You were right. Now, please. Let go."

Giselle took a deep breath before she lost her courage.

"I spoke as I did to hide my own desire for it, Navarre! Don't you see? I had to cover my own reaction. I didn't know any other way."

She whispered the last words to the sky. She couldn't stop the tears as she was totally honest with him. Giselle didn't dare look down. She finally admitted she wanted him, and was ready to give up her hope of heaven for it. There was no place left to hide.

Navarre's hands still touched hers, although he seemed to be stone. She didn't know what else to say. She'd bared her soul, saying something hidden even from herself. But for what?

Nothing.

"Giselle. Look at me."

She shook her head and sniffed. She couldn't possibly look at him.

"Giselle, please? I beg it of you."

"I can't, Navarre! I'm so wicked! And...no one understands."

"Wicked?" He chuckled again, his breath teasing her throat. "Giselle, we aren't wicked. We're caught in a trap from which there is no escape. I adore you so much I fear sometimes I'll go mad from it. Still, nothing changes. I can't sleep and I can't eat. My every thought is of you. Nothing assuages it, either. If I stay away, what happens then? I can't eat, I can't sleep, and then I can't even think. Nothing changes, Giselle, nothing. You belong to Etienne...and not to me."

She pulled one hand free to wipe away tears before they dropped off her chin.

"I want you, Giselle." His voice dropped to a low rumble of sound. *"Dieu!* I want it so badly, it eats at me. But I won't do as Etienne asks. And you won't either. That's not wicked. It can't be. Being wicked cannot possibly feel this bad." He sighed, and she felt hair moving across her skin as he turned his head away. "I'm explaining it badly, aren't I?"

"No."

"Then why won't you look at me?"

"Because it hurts too much!" Admitting that brought on a fresh flood of tears. They blurred her vision and clogged her throat. "I never should have come! I'm sorry, Navarre. So...sorry."

"Sorry?"

He pulled her down onto his lap, and wrapped his arms about her, holding her close. Secure. Protected. And Giselle sobbed even harder. She buried her face in his shirt front and wept bitterly.

"You have to stop this before you take ill again, my love. Then I'll blame myself for it. I'll have to send your notes back unopened and be a terror to my servants. You must think of them if nothing else. No? Then think of me out here without even a dry shirt!"

Giselle giggled. Perhaps that was the reaction he'd wanted. She moved away from his chest so she could see him. "I love you, Navarre."

"I know." He smiled, putting small lines about his eyes. "I know it just as l know the sun will rise tomorrow and the next day. It's what keeps me sane, I think. No, I lie. The only thing I know for certain," he leaned back until he was against the back rest, "is how right this feels."

His voice ended, and the arms around her tightened until she felt certain the boning in her corset would be imprinted on her skin. She didn't stop him, though. She relished the sensation of his strength.

"You must go back now, Giselle. You'll be missed." His grip eased, but he didn't release her. "And you must take care never to come here again."

"Don't make me do that. Please? When can I come? Where, then?"

"You know the answer to that, Giselle...just as I do."

The haunted look was back in his eyes, and hers filled with tears again. *Stupid, useless tears!* He was right. She did know the answer. They were caught in a painful trap, and these avowals of love did nothing but make the wound cut deeper. She realized then exactly what love was. It was up to her. She'd do anything to take the look of pain from his eyes.

But none of that made it any easier.

Giselle shuddered once more, gulped, and forced her emotions down, although her belly rebelled. She fought that, too. She refused to be ill. She stood shakily, and he let her go. And then she walked from him, focusing on the fountain while she waited for her tears to dry.

"Oh. I appear to have dirtied your gown, Giselle. I hope you can think of an explanation the others will accept."

She swiveled back to him. She wondered how he knew. He wasn't even looking at her. He was staring at the ground between his feet again.

"I toured the stables today, Navarre. That's enough of an excuse."

She spoke impersonally. Of stables. As if this weren't the last time they dared to be alone together. And it wasn't anger separating them this time. It was duty. And honor. And integrity.

She could learn to hate those words.

"The groom was a competent guide?"

Giselle backed from him, unable to bear listening any further. She was supposed to stop crying, not start up again. A hedge stopped her, and she realized she didn't know the way out. She didn't dare ask Navarre to show her. She wouldn't be able to bear it. If she remained with him much longer, she was afraid she'd be on her hands and knees begging him to do as Etienne wanted.

"Jean-Claude...didn't think so."

Giselle tried to smile, hoping it sounded in her voice. When he stood abruptly and stared, she knew she'd failed.

"Jean-Claude?"

Giselle put her arms out to stop his approach, but he lunged toward her. She couldn't bear anymore. It wasn't humanly possible. Giselle turned to run away, but the hedge at her nose stopped her.

"Jean-Claude toured the stables with you? He's here? He can't be here!"

She opened her mouth to answer, then stopped. If she spoke at all, he'd hear the grief she was stanching. It was too raw. Too visceral.

"Answer me, Giselle!"

He had reached her. She felt him right behind her. She nodded.

"When did he arrive? Why wasn't I informed? Doesn't Esmee realize what might happen if I'm not there?"

Giselle took a deep breath and turned, tensing for the effect of his eyes. She wasn't disappointed. Confusion, anger, surprise, and pain showed so clearly she could almost touch them. If she was grieving, so was he, just in a different fashion.

"Jean-Claude is evil," he continued speaking. "Truly. He's twisted. He doesn't have any thought to right or wrong. He thinks only of himself. He's dangerous! *Dieu!* Someone should have told me!"

"Perhaps you should read your missives before you return them." Her words were garbled. Indistinct.

He glared at her for a moment, and then grasped her to him, cradling her in arms that felt wonderful. It was horrid, wicked and wrong, but Giselle couldn't lie to herself any longer. She breathed deeply of his chest where it was pressed against her cheek, and thanked the *Bon Dieu* for such a gift.

"Oh, Giselle. This is bad. I can't stay away now. It's not safe. But it will be difficult! Do you understand? One hint of how we feel for each other and Jean-Claude has a weapon."

"*A* weapon? I'd say he has several already. He's very handsome and he's very charming. And he uses both as weapons."

Navarre pulled away and glared down at her.

"I can't believe you just said that, Giselle. I can't. Of all women, you should know how I detest—"

"I was teasing, Navarre."

Giselle giggled, and then sniffed. It was better than her tears.

"Teasing? Oh. Well, it's not amusing."

He set her from him, and looked at her for long moments before he shook his head.

"Go now. Tell Esmee not to expect me for sup, but I'll be back in residence tonight. I promise."

"Do I have to tell her?"

"She bothers you, my love? Very well, but I can't think it would be easier to tell Etienne. He'll know you were with me."

"Do I have to speak of it?"

"Have your companion do it, then. But for now, you must go."

"Very well. But...Navarre?"

"*Oui?*"

"I don't know how I got here. Or the way out."

"You're lost...and yet you found my hiding place? *Le Bon* Dieu works in strange ways. Come, Giselle. Take my hand. I'll show you."

He offered her heaven. She stepped back.

"Oh. You're right. Follow me, then. But stay close."

CHAPTER TWENTY-THREE

Giselle struggled with the linens and untangled her legs from her nightgown. Still, she felt suffocated by heat. There was no other word to describe it, and she didn't know what to try next. One window was already open from the last time she'd awakened.

Navarre wasn't the subject of her dreams, either. Etienne was. Giselle sat for a moment to reflect on the last one. She'd dreamed of Etienne laughing. Crying. Drinking. And then he'd been struggling. The last was the worst. She shuddered. He'd been screaming for help.

The heat sensation came again, growing to roasting level as she dwelled on Etienne's screams. Giselle pulled the cloying cotton from her legs. There was nothing for it. The night was stiflingly hot, and her dreams were filled with Etienne. She might as well check on him. And if that didn't work, she'd change into one of her filmy nightgowns.

The feeling of heat intensified as she unlocked the connecting door to Etienne's chambers. Giselle looked over her shoulder. It felt like there was someone with her, but that was ridiculous. The entire thing was.

Etienne hadn't come down for supper. He hadn't been missed. Supper had never been so stilted. Aunt Mimi and Jean-Claude did most of the talking, while Margot had sat looking like she'd seen a ghost.

A ghost?

Giselle clutched a hand to her throat. That's where she'd felt this heat before – the tower. With Esmee.

"Stop, Giselle. You're frightening yourself."

She said it aloud as she stepped into the *duc's* chambers, almost expecting to meet up with the long-dead *Duchesse* Bertina. Or worse. A drunken Etienne. Entering his room was worse than stupid. His covers were messily tossed about, and Giselle almost turned away. It appeared like he was having the same kind of night that she was, nothing more.

He wasn't there, though. That was odd...

The window casement was shut tightly, and Giselle knew he'd never leave the room unaided. She didn't know where he kept his wheeled chair, but, the moment she started searching for it, all the warmth vanished.

Giselle rubbed her hands together to ward off the sudden chill. It was ridiculous, temperature didn't change that rapidly. She was being silly, but why was the chair missing, then? She knew how rarely he used it. He wouldn't get up and roll about the halls at night...would he?

Warmth returned the moment she had that thought. She no longer ignored it. Somehow, she knew exactly where he was, and that he was in mortal danger!

"Help! Someone help! Navarre! Esmee!"

Giselle's screams went ignored until she yanked on Etienne's servant bell. The valet answered quickly. She stupidly noticed that he didn't favor Gerty much.

"Summon *Monsieur* Navarre! Go now! Get help! Etienne has fallen from the second-wing tower! Go! Don't stand there staring, go!"

She shoved him toward the door, his mouth open.

"What is it, Giselle?"

Esmee was the first to reach the ducal chambers. Giselle grabbed her arm and pulled her toward the main foyer. "Etienne's in danger. Where is Navarre? Navarre!" She saw him run into the hall below them. "Thank the *Bon Dieu!* I've been so worried."

She rushed down the steps to him, remembering at the last moment not to go into his embrace. That would have been disastrous with all the observers about. Light flared about them as torches were lit.

"What's all the noise about?"

Jean-Claude asked it, as he walked into the gathering as if the family normally assembled in their sleepwear in the middle of the night. Giselle also noticed that he came from the hall that led to the haunted tower. And that was the opposite of his own apartments. Her eyes narrowed.

"Etienne's missing, and I know where he is," she announced loudly. "Esmee! Remember when you showed me the haunted tower where someone removed some rock? Well? Don't stand there looking at me like I lost my mind! Go save him!"

"How do you know it's not already too late?"

Jean-Claude reached for his snuff can as he spoke. Giselle couldn't believe it. If she had doubted Navarre's character appraisal of the man earlier, she was more that naïve. She was criminally negligent.

"The tower's been tampered with?" Navarre asked. "Esmee, why didn't you tell me? Quick, send a man around to check at the base of it. And Jean-Claude. Don't leave. Stay with the women while I go."

He almost knocked down Louisa as he turned, and Giselle could have hugged her when she saw the dressing gown she carried. She'd been running through the halls in her nightgown. But she didn't care. She wasn't ashamed. Etienne's survival was all that mattered.

Giselle waited until Navarre disappeared from the hall, three men running at his heels before she turned back to face Jean-Claude. He finished inhaling his snuff and brushed the remnants off his jacket as if he'd asked her the time of day and not how she knew. He smiled down at her.

Giselle raised her chin. She'd thought him the most stunning male she'd ever seen. She wasn't far off. He was what she'd been warned of by Isabelle and the fat priest for years. She knew exactly what she was looking at now. He was described in any number of Scriptures. She just hadn't believed that such evil would come packaged so magnificently.

She'd been a fool.

"It's not too late, Jean-Claude."

Warmth enfolded her as she spoke. She had no need to fear him with the *Duchesse* Bertina helping her. Giselle didn't even question it.

"How can you know that, my dearest little *duchesse?* You've been sleeping."

Jean-Claude's eyes slid insolently down her frame and back up again. Giselle was grateful for the robe's concealment. She hugged the neckline against her. She didn't have to be experienced to know what he left unsaid.

"You leave her alone, Jean-Claude."

Esmee spoke up before Giselle could, championing her. Perhaps she'd misjudged Esmee.

"I'm not speaking to you, Esmee, my dear. I'm speaking to the petite *duchesse.* Someone should ask her how it is that her husband lies dead from a fall, and she's the only one with knowledge of it, shouldn't they?"

"Etienne hasn't fallen yet." Giselle answered with so much authority, she wasn't surprised to see Esmee's mouth gape open. "And I'm not the only one with knowledge, but you already know that, don't you?"

There was an audible gasp about her, and Giselle watched Jean-Claude stiffen. His purplish-blue eyes became calculating and cold. Giselle would be trembling at the intent in them if it weren't for the cocoon of warmth wrapped about her.

"He hasn't fallen, you say? Hmm. I find that difficult to believe."

"I don't care what you believe, *Monsieur*. He hasn't fallen. You were premature."

Louisa pressed against Giselle's arm. And then a servant entered the hall and started shouting.

"*Merde!* Bring a torch and some rope! Be quick!"

There was a collective gasp as activity burst about them. Giselle didn't move her gaze from Jean-Claude. She watched him watching the servants. There was disbelief on his face and she knew exactly what he was thinking. It was a powerful feeling.

"Go see what's happening, Louisa."

Giselle sent her off without taking her eyes from Jean-Claude. If he hadn't still worn his face-paint, she could have known for certain, but he seemed to have paled.

"The *duc* is dangling from the tower! They're attempting a rescue!"

Louisa was back with the message. That time Giselle was certain. Beneath his mask, Jean-Claude had definitely whitened.

"Dear God, Jean-Claude," Esmee said. "How can you stand there and pretend to us? To me?"

Giselle refused to look away. She stared at him unblinkingly. Jean-Claude had been in the castle less than a day, and he already tried to kill Etienne. Her mouth was dry and she knew she was in shock, and yet nothing broke through the warmth and security surrounding her. Strengthening her. Protecting her.

"What is it? What has happened?"

Marguerite, *Madame* du Berchald, walked into the foyer to ask it. Nobody answered.

"My maid told me Etienne has had an accident. Is this true, Esmee? And Jean-Claude? What are you doing out of your chambers?" Her voice sharpened on the last bit of her query.

He's been busy trying to kill his brother, Giselle answered in her thoughts.

Madame du Berchald had claimed illness kept her from joining them for supper earlier — but she looked perfectly healthy as she stood before Jean-Claude.

"I asked you a question!" she hissed.

"So you did. And perhaps I'll answer it, *Maman*. Perhaps not. But the one thing I won't do is stand about in the hall like a peasant."

"We'll retire to the Red Salon. See that wine is brought." Esmee said.

Giselle took her eyes from Jean-Claude in order to inspect her mother-in-law while Esmee directed the household. Marguerite didn't look as old as she should, but perhaps that was the paint she also wore. Although she was smaller than Esmee, she still overshadowed Giselle, and her dressing gown was more splendid in design than any ball gown.

"I can't take my eyes off you for a moment, can I?"

Giselle heard the whispered words to Jean-Claude as they took what seemed to be their assigned places in the Red Salon.

"*Moi?* The word you received was inaccurate, Mother. Etienne has experienced an accident...and according to the *duchesse,*" Jean-Claude said, "he didn't fall. She still hasn't explained her knowledge of it, have you, Giselle?"

"Giselle!" Their mother turned to Giselle. "We meet under horrid circumstances, *non?* I wasn't feeling well earlier, child. Pray forgive me, and explain. What is this Jean-Claude speaks of?"

The warmth in her voice didn't reach her eyes. Giselle realized Marguerite was acting. She wished there was another explanation, but knew she was right. And Giselle was getting as jaded as everyone else.

"There's never a good time for attempting murder, *Madame,*" Giselle answered coolly.

Louisa gasped beside her.

"There should be no listeners to this sort of conversation, *Madame* la *Duchesse.*" Marguerite's voice carried a note of reproof. "Perhaps you could see we aren't disturbed?"

She was speaking to Louisa, and Giselle's eyes narrowed.

"Forgive me, but Louisa is my companion. She stays. I awakened abruptly to the certain knowledge — call it a dream, if you like — that my husband was in danger. I knew it for a certainty when I went to check. I can't tell you how faint I am at this moment. Why...if Louisa weren't at my side, anything might happen."

Giselle sat on her chair and placed a hand to her forehead while she feigned a near collapse.

"A companion? You're too young for such a thing. Even I have no need of one."

"You didn't have my upbringing." Louisa's hand squeezed Giselle's shoulder. She knew that was an indication that she wanted to leave. "Perhaps you've already met my father, the *Comte* d'Antillion?" Giselle asked.

"Everyone knows the *Comte* d'Antillion and his hatred for us. I fail to see—"

"Us? *Madame.* Please. I have been a Berchald since the age of six. Louisa, could you check the rescue? I can't sit, speaking idly, while my husband's in danger."

Louisa passed the footman with the wine on her way out. He set down the tray and left while not a word was said.

"You expect me to believe that the *comte* turned his feelings against his own daughter?" Marguerite asked.

Jean-Claude uncorked the bottle and downed his goblet twice before turning back to them. Giselle kept her eyes on him the entire time.

"I can't see why you wouldn't believe me," she replied sweetly. "You must know how easily a parent can ignore one child's well-being...over another's."

Esmee's reaction was close to a scream, while Giselle sat as straight as possible and continued her steady regard of Jean-Claude.

"Perhaps I could use a drink, too. Jean-Claude?"

Giselle was still watching Jean-Claude. That's how she knew Marguerite accepted a goblet from him with hand that visibly shook. And even to Giselle's untrained eye, it looked like their mother cringed from him. That was surprising.

There wasn't a servant in the room to open the door when Louisa knocked, so Giselle gestured Esmee to do it. She smiled at the other's bad grace.

"You have news?" Esmee asked her question from around the door.

"Yes, tell us this news and get it over with."

Jean-Claude downed his third glass of wine nonchalantly as if they were attending a party.

"Begging you pardon, but my message is for the *duchesse* only," Louisa slid past Esmee and into the room.

Giselle stood quickly, feeling sudden terror fill her. Etienne couldn't be dead! She refused to think it. Etienne's death would leave Jean-Claude as the head of the family. And now she knew why everyone feared that.

"What's the message, Louisa?" Giselle felt the other Berchalds gather at her back.

"It's not good, Giselle."

Beside her, Giselle felt Marguerite stiffen at the familiarity. She ignored her. Marguerite would do well to clean her own household before she censored Giselle's.

"The *duc* has suffered injuries to his back. And his legs are broken."

"He won't even notice that." Jean-Claude said, voice sounding bored and disappointed.

Giselle whirled and glared at each of them in turn before she spoke again. She didn't recognize the commanding tenor of her voice when she did, and she saw the surprise on the other's faces, as well.

"Shall I receive my message in the hall?"

They backed away from her like a pack of animals, although it was a slow movement. Their action actually surprised her. She turned back to Louisa.

"He has suffered an injury to his head, too," Louisa continued in a low voice. *"Monsieur* Navarre doesn't know how bad it is, or if the *duc* will survive the night. I'm to take you to him while we wait for the doctors."

"My husband requests my presence. And only mine," Giselle informed the others. Esmee was the only one that didn't look surprised. "You'll be informed of his condition when I know it."

She climbed the same staircase on which she almost fainted that first night. This time there wasn't any hesitation and no weakness. The largest manservant she ever saw opened Etienne's door for her. As a guard, his position wouldn't be questioned, but it was a sad day when the *duc* needed guarding in his own house.

Navarre stood from the bed when she entered and reached for her hands.

"How is he?" she asked.

"I'm frightened, Giselle. He was hanging by just a bit of his blanket. Jean-Claude hadn't counted on the bedding becoming entangled on a jagged block. I don't know how it happened. By rights, he should be dead."

His eyes filled with tears, and Giselle held his hand tighter.

"Will he...?"

"Live? I don't know. Come. See for yourself."

Navarre drew her to the bed. She stepped up onto the platform as he lifted the linen off Etienne's face. Although she tried to control her emotions, she couldn't help crying aloud. An ugly gash bled from his forehead, and the scraping along his face, neck, and chest made her eyes fill.

"It was very difficult getting him back up. I tried to be gentle. As it was, it took Jean, the guard at the door, and his brother, who stands guard in the lower hall, to help. I didn't know Etienne was so heavy. My arms still ache, but I have no right to feel pain if he dies. I should have been here! I should have attended sup. I could have done a thousand things different to prevent this!"

"No, Navarre. The only thing that could've stopped Jean-Claude was making certain he was punished the first time."

"Impossible!"

"The entire situation is impossible. How can you say that! Look at him! He was almost killed! He might have perished if the blanket hadn't caught. You said so, yourself."

"We almost lost him anyway! The blanket was ripping when we got there. I don't understand how you knew he was in danger, but it was you that saved him, Giselle. If ever I doubted my love and respect for you, I was a fool."

Although there was only one candle on the dresser, she had plenty of light to see. Giselle felt her heart pulse as she read his eyes, filled with anguish and love. And then he turned away, back to his brother.

CHAPTER TWENTY-FOUR

Giselle didn't know which was worse — Navarre's constant pacing, Etienne's thrashing, or the bleeding the doctors insisted on performing. She asked Navarre not to allow that, because it had taken the entire first night to stop the bleeding from the gash on Etienne's temple, but they didn't listen. The doctors treated her like she was an ignorant woman.

By the fourth day, when Etienne still hadn't awakened, the Berchald family physician sent for a specialist from Paris. There was nothing further he could do. He suspected Etienne had sustained further injury to his back, too. Nothing could be done, but he wished to make sure. He asked Giselle if she understood.

The head wound had all of them mystified though. It was more severe than any of his other injuries. It appeared as if the *duc* suffered a blow to the head before his fall down the stairs.

Down the stairs? What other lies were they telling?

"Make sure the *duc* drinks this liquid," the doctor told her. "It will alleviate any suffering. It isn't the legs that he'll need it for, he'll not feel that. It's for his head. I just don't know...."

The doctor clicked his tongue and left her. Giselle watched as he whispered the details to Navarre so Giselle wouldn't overhear. She knew what they were discussing. She'd overheard them before. Etienne's back was severely pulled out of placement. Perhaps not as bad as they suspected, but if he wasn't already paralyzed, he would be now.

Then the specialists came, and Giselle wanted to toss them out the moment they attached leeches to Etienne's feet.

Somehow, Navarre got Etienne to swallow the special broth, and it did soothe him. It dawned on Giselle that Navarre wouldn't let anyone close to his brother, not even the guards. It worried her. She wondered what would happen when Navarre collapsed from his schedule.

He wouldn't listen to her suggestion, though. Giselle offered to sit with Etienne while Navarre napped.

He rejected the offer, saying she was too frail and much too innocent. Giselle wasn't interested in changing her husband's clothing or his dressings, just in keeping Navarre from collapsing.

It wasn't until the specialists left that Navarre finally allowed her to help. He didn't wish to, but Giselle had tiptoed into the *duc's* chamber one morning to check on them and was surprised to spot Navarre slumped across the platform while Etienne thrashed about.

"Navarre! Fetch him!"

Etienne moaned it as he tossed off his covers and ripped at his bandage. The blackish-yellow color of his forehead made her wince. It was a good thing he wasn't fully conscious yet. The pain would have been terrible.

"I can't hold much longer!"

The bandage slipped down into his mouth and he gagged, so Giselle stepped up onto the pedestal to adjust it. Etienne was lucky he hadn't lost an eye as deeply bruised as he was. Giselle's mouth hardened into a thin line as she saw it.

"Jean-Claude?" Etienne asked. "Why would I want him? He's a girl. He wouldn't want to climb with me, but Navarre will. Fetch him, I tell you!"

"It's all right, Etienne," Giselle said softly. "Here. Let me help you." She lifted his head and dribbled some of the medicine onto his lip, waiting until he swallowed.

He sounded lucid enough, but he mumbled often, sometimes about incidents so far in the past they were forgotten. She glanced at Navarre as Etienne slouched back against the pillows.

Navarre was still sleeping, so she smoothed Etienne's covers back into place. Not once was she able to take her eyes off her love. One arm was flung out and propped against the bed post, and his legs were fanned out. Even with his mouth open and dark circles under his eyes, he was beautiful.

Giselle put a cover over Navarre next, and eased a pillow beneath his head. Aside from a grunt, he didn't show she was even there. That was fine with her. He couldn't argue about her if he slept.

She settled into a chair and waited for Navarre to wake. Henri, Jean's brother, stood guard outside the chamber. The door was locked tightly, but she was still alert for intruders. Navarre hadn't left the chambers since the accident, and she knew how deeply worried he was.

But she'd have traded places with him. She envied him the solitude.

Throughout the past week, she'd attended to castle functions as if Etienne didn't hover near death, but it was wearing on her, especially when she had to face Marguerite and Jean-Claude.

The previous night, over dessert, Marguerite had asked how Etienne was, as if she cared. Giselle suspected the true reason. She was asking so she could provide Jean-Claude with the information.

"Tell us, Giselle," Esmee had said. "We've heard nothing. For all we know, he could be gone."

"Oh. He's not dead." Giselle had glared at them and pushed back her chair as she stood. "And I won't let him die, either!"

Her grand exit was ruined when she'd reached the doors and couldn't budge them. She'd had to wait for a servant to assist. Behind her, she'd heard the sounds of amusement. And that's why she raced the stairs, tears of humiliation staining her cheeks.

"*Monsieur* Navarre?"

A discreet knock at Etienne's door made her rise, but Navarre only shifted his weight and went back to his dreams. Giselle smiled as she walked through the antechamber.

"What is it, Henri?" she asked.

"*Madame* du Berchald requests again to see her son."

He sounded strange through the door, but she refused to open it. Giselle leaned her forehead against the painted wood.

"My husband can't receive any visitors, Henri."

"You can't keep me from him forever, Giselle," Marguerite said.

Giselle unlocked the door and opened it a crack.

"I demand to see my son, and no monster of a servant will stand in my way! I'm his mother!"

"Henri has his orders, *Madame.*" Giselle drew herself up to face their mother, although she barely reached the woman's mouth.

"Please, Giselle. Please? I beg it of you. I'm his mother. You can't keep me worrying this way."

"Henri, please have *Madame* du Berchald shown into the *duchesse's* chambers. This display is unseemly. I will join her there when I have time."

Giselle closed and locked the door, drowning out Marguerite's gasp as the key turned.

"What has happened?" Navarre asked groggily. "Why was the door open, Giselle?"

Tousled hair streamed down both sides of his face, and a light brown beard covered his chin and upper lip. The effect was still stunning. Giselle opened her mouth to tell him, but no words came out.

"Who were you talking to? Has something happened to Etienne?" His eyes widened and he turned back in panic.

She stopped him with a hand on his arm. "Etienne sleeps comfortably enough, Navarre. He only had one episode while you slept."

Giselle blushed. She didn't know why. Navarre had also been asleep while she studied him. No one would ever know, would they?

"I slept? And you didn't wake me?"

He reached for her, pulling her within the embrace of arms so tender, Giselle's heart fluttered.

"Why would I wake you? You're very handsome when you sleep, Navarre," she whispered.

His chuckle against her ear sounded strange through his chest.

"I slept, and you watched me? Not Etienne? You're not a very good nursemaid, not that I'd trade you."

"Etienne slept, too." Giselle leaned away to argue.

"I'm teasing, my love."

He shouldn't use such endearments. It started a wellspring of want, pain, and desire within her. If she had to pretend disinterest, it wasn't very helpful. Besides, his mother probably listened at the connecting door.

"Your mother." Giselle gestured toward her own rooms. "She asked of Etienne."

His face hardened, aging him. He released her and stepped back. "See her if you must. I won't need you to spell me until this eve. *Merci.*"

She watched him walk over to Etienne, and her eyes misted. Even Marguerite's youngest child turned from her. Why wouldn't the woman do what she must?

Navarre put his hands above his head and stretched. Giselle stood at the doorway, watching him. He must not realize that Giselle still stood there, as he then bent forward, and began doing some strange series of exercises.

It was quite visual. Interesting. And stirring. And it had to stop. It would never do for Marguerite to guess her feelings. Giselle was inviting an enemy into her camp, and she mustn't forget it. She went to the connecting door to her chamber, unlocked it and had it relocked before Marguerite spoke.

"Thank you, Giselle! Thank you!" Marguerite began before Giselle turned around. "I have been so worried."

"Pardon me if I don't believe you."

Marguerite must have spent time trying to guess the best way to approach her daughter-in-law. It showed. Giselle watched the woman assimilate the answer before trying again. Giselle twisted her lips and raised her eyebrows.

"Giselle, my dear, please. I can't sleep for worrying. He's my son, yet you deny me."

Giselle spent an extra bit of time arranging her dressing gown before sitting in a chair. She motioned Marguerite to one, too. The woman had drawn the drapes, letting the morning glow dispel some of the chamber's gloom. Giselle wondered what else she had tampered with while she waited.

"You're about very early, *Madame*. That must be different for you," Giselle finally replied.

"Early? Late! What does that matter? I've been unable to sleep, I tell you!"

She rubbed her hands together in an agitated fashion. Her drawn appearance could be the product of sleepless nights, or the absence of her facial paint. Giselle didn't know which, so she waited.

"Giselle, please understand. I'll never rest if Etienne dies. I can't possibly describe a mother's love to you until you've experienced—"

"Spare me the emotional entreaties, *Madame* du Berchald. It's much too early for such."

Giselle watched as Marguerite sat back and stared as if seeing her for the first time. The woman's eyes filmed over with tears before she turned away. But that could be an affectation, too.

"As to your words? You're right. I can't understand a mother's love, and since Jean-Claude is doing everything in his power to prevent such an event, I probably never will."

"You don't like me very much, do you, Giselle?"

She sounded on the verge of tears. Giselle narrowed her eyes before answering. Marguerite didn't sound like someone fishing for a weak spot, but Giselle knew her limitations when it came to intrigue. That's what came from being surrounded by masters of it.

"I hardly know you, *Madame,*" she finally answered stiffly.

"Yet you've already formed such opinions. You judged me before we met, didn't you?"

"I...I can't say that for certain, *Madame*"

"Don't call me that any longer. I prefer Marguerite. Being called *Madame* as coldly as you say it almost breaks my heart."

Giselle barely stopped herself from snorting. It was clear Marguerite was yet another expert.

"I remember how thrilled I was when I first met my husband, Giselle. He was a very handsome man, tall, blond. Very masculine. You've probably realized that from my sons, haven't you?"

Giselle tried to still the blush at being quizzed with such a question, but she was being nonsensical. She could be reacting to Etienne's description for all Marguerite knew.

"Unfortunately, he was more interested in his *coquettes* in Paris and was wed very much against his will. Almost the instant our signatures were on the marriage register, he left me for his other life. He only condescended to visit me when his relatives forced him to. Do you know what that's like, to love deeply and be tossed aside?"

She stood, as if the thought still caused her inner turmoil. Giselle watched her pace to the wardrobe doors and back. Giselle had some idea of how it must have felt.

Non, that was a lie.

She couldn't imagine how it would feel if her love for Navarre was unrequited. Tears flooded her eyes at the idea. She was in luck that Marguerite wasn't looking.

"The entire time I carried Esmee, my husband taunted me about my size and my bloated shape, as if a woman in my condition wasn't supposed to look like that. He was as stupid as he was handsome, and he was gloriously handsome, Giselle. Even more so than his sons.

"No. That's not true. My little Navarre bears an uncanny resemblance to him, except for his hair color. I don't know where that came from. You've probably noticed how dark he is in comparison, if you notice such things."

She gave Giselle a piercing look. Giselle fought turning redder. She'd have to be blind not to notice Navarre.

"I can't describe how disappointed everyone was when I produced a girl."

Giselle almost told her she didn't have to, then stopped.

"I suppose I should have been closer to her when she was born, but how could I? I was disappointed, too. I shouldn't have been. With her birth, my husband had to visit even more often. It seemed to take forever to conceive again, but it wasn't for lack of trying."

She looked over at Giselle, and it was her turn to redden.

"That child was still-birthed. The shame nearly killed me. I had no one I could trust, and none that cared. My husband stayed with me then at the castle, though, said loving things to me, and made me fall even deeper in love with him. And all he wanted was an heir. I should have known it, but I didn't."

She sighed and moved her view to the window.

"I thought he'd given up his mistresses. I was happy and foolish. I didn't know then the games that people play with each other. I had to learn. I see you don't believe me, and you should. Do you know why?"

Giselle shook her head.

"You're young, you're beautiful, and you're wed to the Berchald heir, just as I was. It's not an easy position. I know. You have every reason not to let me see my son. I've been a bad mother, but I never had a chance. I swear it. Don't you see?"

Giselle shook her head again.

"I lost Etienne the moment he was born. How can I explain it so you'll understand? My husband's brother, the *duc,* so wanted an heir for Berchand, that he surrounded Etienne with servants and guards. I was the outsider. I was unwanted by my husband, and unneeded by my own child. I'd never felt so alone. There are no words for it."

A sarcastic reply came to Giselle's lips, but she didn't speak. Marguerite sounded like she was speaking the truth. And even if it was a lie, it made an interesting story.

"Why are you telling me this, Marguerite?"

Marguerite smiled shallowly. Perhaps it was the morning light, but Giselle saw all the lines on her face. She could believe the woman hadn't been able to sleep.

"I should have transferred my feelings to Esmee. She was a beautiful child of five. Looking back, I see I failed at being a mother to her, too, but all that changed when Jean-Claude was placed into my arms."

Her face took on such an expression of love that Giselle put her hand to her mouth to silence the gasp.

"My husband may have missed me, or he may not. He came back to visit me when Etienne was still small. Healthy. He was such an engaging boy. Even at a distance, I was so proud of him, but not as much as my husband was."

She laughed bitterly. "That would have been impossible. As far as *Monsieur* was concerned, Etienne was perfect. No one paid any attention to me as I carried Jean-Claude. It was horrid. His birth was the hardest, and his hair was so black when he was born, I feared my husband would disclaim him. It made me more protective of him. Looking back, I realize I must have gone a little mad. I felt such joy at my Jean-Claude. There was never a more blessed child. In appearance, height, and those fabulous eyes...he had no equal, but you already know of that. Anyone who meets him is enthralled. And he needed me when no one else did.

"My husband went back to his life in Paris, but I wasn't lonely anymore. I had Jean-Claude to protect and nurture. It's strange, isn't it? No one questioned my ownership of him. My little Esmee was hidden away in her schoolrooms, Etienne was feted, adored and dressed for show on every state occasion, but Jean-Claude was *mine*."

She came back to sit, facing Giselle, and the earnest expression on her face seemed real enough.

"I spoiled him. I see that now, but he has so much...what would you call it? Guile?"

"Charm." Giselle gave her the word she was searching for.

"There, you see?" She clapped her hands and nodded at Giselle. "You've noticed it, too, haven't you? He can turn my anger around with so little effort. He's unique, I tell you."

"He has tried to kill his own brother, Marguerite. And he'll try again."

"You think I don't know that? I've been in an agony of worry. I can't believe he would do something so evil. I can't. May God forgive me."

She shook, and her head sank to her hands. Giselle's eyes widened.

"How is my child, Giselle?" she whispered, looking up. The tears on her eyelashes weren't forced, they were real.

"Navarre watches over him."

"Ah. My littlest. Navarre. He was such a quiet child. It was hard to tell what he thought. I was in luck my husband visited me long enough to bring my little Navarre into the world. He's quite special, isn't he?"

"I..." Giselle couldn't finish it. She didn't have a prayer of stopping her blush this time, either.

"I don't suppose you've noticed. He's quiet, and so very intelligent. Behind that quiet demeanor, he senses everything. I wasn't a good mother to him, either. I had to leave him at a young age. I had to keep Etienne safe, and I just couldn't turn on Jean-Claude. I can't do it even now. Oh God! What am I to do?"

She reached over and gripped Giselle's hands as she pleaded with her. There was torment in her purplish eyes, and Giselle made up her mind.

"Come. I'll let you see Etienne. But don't be shocked by what you see. He's living in the past when he talks. The doctors aren't sure how disabled he'll be when he wakes."

"But he lives?"

Giselle didn't answer. They must have suspected she was hiding Etienne's death. As they entered the room, Navarre bolted from his chair and glared at them with bloodshot eyes,

"What are you doing?" he snapped.

"Oh, Etienne! My darling! I'm so ashamed!"

Marguerite ignored Navarre and sank onto the ledge beside the bed to cry into the coverlet. Giselle turned away. Navarre could guard Etienne from Marguerite if he wished. Giselle believed her story.

"Oh, his face! *Mon Dieu,* Navarre! I can't stand to look."

"Jean-Claude wasn't gentle. The blow to his forehead left Etienne unconscious before he was moved. I don't think Jean-Claude meant to kill Etienne that way, but he almost succeeded, didn't he?"

"I can't bear to think on it. Oh, what am I to do?"

It took a moment for Navarre to answer her. His voice was solemn and devoid of emotion when he did.

"Only you can decide that, Mother."

Marguerite looked up with an agonized expression. Giselle backed to the door. She didn't want to hear any more. Navarre could keep Etienne safe from his mother, if he still thought it necessary. Giselle was glad she didn't have the woman's conscience.

CHAPTER TWENTY-FIVE

"Navarre, I've told you repeatedly not to ride without me," Etienne said loudly. "What do you want to do, kill yourself?"

His voice grew stronger as he mumbled, and Giselle shook Navarre awake to help her. She had tried by herself, to keep Etienne from thrashing about during the previous night's musings and got a bruised knee and lecture from Navarre for her trouble.

"You're too small, Giselle," Navarre had said. "Wake me next time. I insist."

Navarre had almost shouted it at her, and she deserved it. Etienne had tossed her onto the floor, making a loud thump that had brought Navarre from his chair. Giselle didn't have time to stand up before Etienne started up again.

"I know you're only eight, Navarre. Stop that crying and get back on. Thunder tosses everyone who rides him, not just you. If you don't stop crying, I'll send you to the nursery where you belong!"

Navarre had flushed up to his neck and earlobes at that. Giselle had giggled. It was like hearing a replay of his most embarrassing moments.

"Etienne," Navarre had said, "you must rest. Here, try this." Navarre had lifted his brother's head. They were both amazed when he gulped thirstily at the liquid.

"This wine is bitter," he complained. "Send another bottle and then leave me. Who are you, anyway? I haven't seen you about."

Giselle had leapt to the platform as Etienne tried to focus on Navarre with his good eye. He had sounded like his old self.

"Navarre, you say? He's but a whelp. Get off me, blast you."

Navarre had held on, although it looked like Etienne would be able to toss him off any moment.

"Why are my legs tied? I insist you untie me. Don't look at me like that, young man! I demand to know what's going on...what's going on...with...."

He'd slumped back onto his pillows, and frowned.

"You're Navarre? Impossible. Give me more wine, and stop that infernal noise."

And then he'd burst into dry sobs, but he no longer fought to get up.

"Navarre!"

Giselle shook him harder this morning as Etienne tossed a pillow to the floor. In the drapery-filtered light of dawn, Navarre looked more ashen than ever. Giselle motioned him to the bed.

"He's moving again," she whispered.

"Stop whispering," Etienne said. "I'm not deaf, just disabled."

Navarre and Giselle looked at each other in surprise. And then they both turned simultaneously to the bed. Etienne regarded them with his good eye.

"Navarre, you look terrible. What have you been doing to yourself? Drinking? You're too young for it. And Giselle, fancy seeing you in my bedchamber. That may mean something, but my head hurts too much to ponder it. Have you two been—*Merde!* I've got the worst headache of my life. Why didn't you stop me from over-drinking, Navarre?"

"Over...drinking?" Navarre choked out.

"Etienne! You're awake!" Giselle said. "You don't know how wonderful that is!"

"You're touched, Giselle. I usually do wake up, sooner or later. What mystery is there in that? Why can't I see, Navarre?"

He tried to look at his hand through his bandage. Giselle giggled in relief. He was awake and he was lucid. *The* Bon Dieu *be praised!*

"You had an accident, Etienne." Navarre lifted a goblet and poured the liquid into it. "Drink this, and I'll explain."

"How can I have an accident? I never go anywhere without assistance. Do you have a fever?"

"Just drink this."

Navarre helped him sit up. Etienne was as weak as a baby. He drank the liquid, although he coughed on it twice.

"Now get out. Both of you," he commanded. "I long to sleep off my drunk, and you dawdle at my bedside. Go."

He lay back and shut his eyes. His even breathing was the only sound in the room as Navarre stumbled off the platform.

"He's awake, and he hasn't lost his wits," Giselle whispered. "Can you believe it, Navarre? I'll say a prayer of thanksgiving. Wait until I tell the others."

Navarre ignored her and walked to the windows. Giselle followed him as he stepped out onto the balcony. The sun scattered its light about the valley like a painter coloring his canvas, but Giselle didn't see it. She watched with concern as Navarre's shoulders fell forward. He gripped the rail so hard his knuckles turned white.

Then a tear struck his hand. Giselle ran to him. She held to him from behind, clamping her hands about his stomach as he silently sobbed.

"Oh, Giselle. Forgive me."

He took a final, ragged, shuddering breath that nearly made her lose her grip. She tightened it instead.

"Forgive you? For what? Loving your brother? Bringing yourself to collapse with nursing him? I've never witnessed such emotion, and it makes my heart swell. I'd as soon leap from this balcony than forgive you. I adore you."

"Ignore me for a bit, then. Allow me some time to compose myself."

"Compose yourself? Oh, Navarre, you're the most masculine thing I've ever imagined existed. I refuse to ignore you."

He turned in her arms, and Giselle looked up the open collar of his shirt to the sparkling amethyst of his eyes. And masculine seemed too weak a word.

"After hearing of my youthful exploits and now dealing with my tears, you still think so?" he asked. "I'm surprised at you, Giselle.

He clicked his tongue at her, and she loved it.

"You just need some sleep, Navarre. You've been awake too long." She fluttered her eyelashes at him.

"You think to flirt with me when it's all I can do to keep my hands off you? Woman, you play with fire." He growled it at her. The rumble came through his chest. "Come. We need to go back inside. We can't be seen like this."

She held him a moment longer, then reluctantly released her grip.

"Father, could you spare me a moment?"

Giselle watched the new priest's plump face as she approached him. He was pleased with the attention, she could tell.

"I'm here to serve," he replied.

Giselle gathered her nerve. "Is it a greater sin to break a commandment, or to follow the commandments and let another perish, because you wouldn't break one?"

His face fell.

"That's a theological question. I'm not certain I have the knowledge or experience to answer it."

He was right about one thing. He wasn't very experienced. He looked younger even than she was. Perhaps that was what made Giselle trust him implicitly the moment he'd been sponsored by the Berchald family.

The other priest had been dismissed after Navarre had rested, and that had taken two entire days. One of the servants had spoken up. They'd seen the other priest in the second wing near the tower. At the time, it was assumed he was trying to exorcise the ghost. Now, the suspicion was he'd been working on the tower.

It was enough proof for Navarre. Giselle was pleased the other priest had been replaced. She liked the new one. He was easier to talk to, but he still hadn't heard her confession. It was too soon, and there was more at stake.

She knew now what she was up against, and Jean-Claude seemed to go out of his way to make certain she knew.

"I'm curious, child," the priest said, making Giselle tense, "how can anyone assign a value to a life? If breaking a commandment saves a life, can our Father really be unmerciful? You've asked me something I must consider carefully. Will you give me time to answer?"

She nodded slowly. She didn't have any time. Etienne had asked her yet again that morning if she would have a child by Navarre. When Giselle had asked him what Navarre's reply was, Etienne shrugged and said, "He'll do as you wish."

There was purgatory on earth. It was in Chateau Berchand. There was also paradise. Giselle wondered which she was going to find, and wished she wasn't so fanciful.

It was almost a sennight since Etienne awoke, and he couldn't believe the extent of his injuries. He had been truly frightened over his face, and Giselle had watched him view it. Still yellow and green, the bruise extended to his mouth. It would be a long time before his flesh healed enough to enable him to go without a bandage. And he still couldn't see out of the damaged eye.

What should I do, and who else can I ask?

Giselle wondered why she still lied to herself. She already knew what she was going to do. She just wished she knew why. Was she accepting Navarre to save Etienne...or because she couldn't bear to say no?

"Bless you, my child."

Giselle waited as the priest murmured words over her head before rising from her knees. She couldn't fool the *Bon Dieu* and she knew it. She had to be honest with herself, and with Etienne, if she was going to do as he asked.

She had a sense of purpose as she climbed the steps to her own chamber. It was still there when she turned the handle to Etienne's chambers and walked in. She saw both brothers were there, and she started speaking before she lost her nerve.

"Etienne, I need to speak with you. And Navarre? Don't go. I need you speak with you, too. It's good you're both here."

Giselle flushed to the roots of her hair as they looked at her.

"I've been praying, Etienne, about what you asked...me to do. I know how serious it is, but...." She wrung her hands, stammered, and felt like a fool.

"But what?"

He had the wrong impression of what she wanted to say. Giselle realized it as his shoulders slumped.

"I can't accept Navarre...." She blushed furiously, and her palms were slick with nervous sweat. She licked dry lips and tried to force some moisture into her throat, "...to my bed, un—"

"Damn it, Giselle!"

"Let me finish." She held up a hand to stop Etienne. Navarre had turned to look at her, too, but she couldn't meet his eyes. It was harder than she'd envisioned it would be.

"Go on, then." Etienne's good eyebrow was raised. She glanced at it before moving away. She couldn't meet his gaze, either.

"You...and Navarre. You must know...that I will—I'll do it. I'll accept Navarre into my bed, but not simply because...not just...." She swallowed hard. "It's not just for you, Etienne."

Her voice dropped to a whisper, and it no longer resembled the self-assured tone she'd started with. "I'll do it, because...Navarre and I...we...."

Giselle was backing slowly toward the connecting door and she looked at the floor, and then the ceiling. Anything was better than the men's eyes.

"I want to. It's not just a question of saving you, Etienne, it's because I...." Her voice stopped. She couldn't finish it out loud, after all.

Etienne chuckled. "You'll do it because you think it will be enjoyable? Is that what you're saying? Well, it usually is, Giselle. Or Navarre will be doing it wrong. You're such a child, sometimes."

She couldn't stay a moment longer. She barely made it to her bedchamber before bursting into tears of humiliation. Giselle knelt beside the bed, her knees on the platform, and she lifted the bottom edge of the coverlet to her face. Her belly was reeling, but her mind was numb. She longed to pray, but knew she wouldn't. She had made her decision, and it was going to be night soon.

"The talk is all about the latest, Giselle." Louisa opened the drapes, and Giselle covered her eyes against the sunlight. And then lifted her head.

It's morning? She slept? Navarre didn't come?

What new game was this?

"I thought it was a bit much for *Monsieur* Navarre to spend all his days and nights guarding his brother, but.... Here I am, running on when I've got a bath and ensemble to prepare for you. Come in, Gerty. Step smartly. See to her, Isabelle."

Giselle's mouth opened as Gerty came in. Giselle watched while Gerty fussed with the hip bath and nodded graciously at the first wardrobe selection they held out. The activity about her seemed at a standstill, and Giselle looked at them for a moment before knowing what it was. They were awaiting further instruction. *"Merci,"* she said. "That will be all."

Isabelle and Gerty paused at the door before curtsying and leaving.

"Now, what's this about Navarre?"

Giselle shoved off the bedclothes and watched as Louisa eyed the sheer nightgown she'd worn. Louisa didn't ask, however. And Giselle wouldn't have answered. They both knew she detested the flimsy attire.

"It seems your brother-in-law feels the *duc* and his little wife," she paused at the title, and Giselle looked away, "need to revisit their privacy. I admit my mouth dropped open when he spoke of it, not that I was listening at keyholes, mind you."

"I would never think that of you. Go on please."

Giselle didn't need another lecture on nosy servants. She needed to know about Navarre.

"Let me see...*Monsieur* wasn't alone. He was announcing his intentions to anyone who would listen. Seems he believes he has intruded for too long on his brother's life. I can't tell you how those words made my dander rise. Even his sister questioned it."

"What did she question? What?"

"Monsieur Navarre is relocating again to the dower house again. They think he's mad. I think he's mad. He can't leave Etienne at Jean-Claude's mercy. The

reason I know this part is because that *Madame* Esmee muttered it to herself as she passed me."

"What? The dowager house? I don't...understand."

"You don't understand? Why is it you're dressed in that, then?"

"It was the first thing I grabbed."

Giselle looked down at herself, surprised for the moment at how quickly the lie had come to her. And how well it left her lips.

"Navarre moved out last night, Giselle."

"Navarre? But, why?"

"That's exactly what I'm trying to tell you. It created quite a stir below stairs, too."

Louisa let Gerty back into the room with more water for the bath.

He listened to her bare her soul...then he left? Giselle thought she felt humiliated the previous day. She'd been naive.

Etienne must have lied about all of it. He was probably laughing about it in his bed chamber at this very moment. That was the only explanation for Navarre's odd behavior. Navarre hadn't said he'd abide the *duchesse's* wishes. Instead, he ran from them.

"You mustn't dawdle all day," Louisa said. "There's still a chance to speak with him about it at supper. I understand everyone will be there. They've arranged a dinner party."

How would she ever get through supper? With Navarre attending?

"Thank you, Gerty," Louisa said. "I'm certain the bath is the perfect temperature for the *duchesse*. That will be all."

Gerty looked at Giselle for confirmation. Giselle looked away. She was incapable of speaking or meeting anyone's eyes. She had admitted her lust in front of both Navarre and Etienne. She was mortified. Supremely embarrassed. Ashamed.

"Giselle? Your bath?"

"Leave me be, Louisa. Please?"

"Why do you still worry?" Louisa asked. "He may be at the Dower house, but it's only the width of the maze away. He, most certainly, is preparing to see you again. I can pass a note to him if you like. I've been told that if you stay to the extreme left in the maze, you won't get lost. Not that I tried it — I wouldn't dare. Still, I'd chance it to get a note to him if you like."

Giselle shook her head, watching the red on the bedspread shimmer like it had the previous night in the sputtering candlelight. There was no point in contacting Navarre. He was probably thinking up an excuse to avoid her. She couldn't tell Louisa of it. She could barely stand to live through it herself.

"You aren't going to luncheon, are you, Giselle?" Louisa sat on the edge of the bed.

Giselle turned away. She couldn't meet her eyes yet, either. "I'm not hungry."

"Something horrendous has happened, hasn't it?"

Giselle shook her head and concentrated on the ball of material in her fists.

"Will you tell me about it?"

"Nothing's wrong, Louisa, I'm just tired." Giselle released the bedspread and lay back against the pillows. There would be no benefit in sharing her humiliation.

"Very well." Louisa sighed and stood.

Giselle imagined Louisa looking down at her, her hands on her hips, and her lips pursed in thought. She knew she wasn't far wrong.

"I'll tell the staff of your new malaise. But rest assured, Giselle, you can't hide from your duties forever. The entire household needs an example set, and that Jean-Claude needs to be put in his place."

Put Jean-Claude in his place? That was laughable. She'd be as proficient at that as a newborn kitten. And now, she didn't even have Navarre.

CHAPTER TWENTY-SIX

Louisa hadn't been succinct. Which was odd. Giselle realized it as she entered the drawing room later that evening. She narrowed her eyes on the scene.

She knew she looked like the *Duchesse* du Berchald should. She'd allowed Isabelle to curl her hair, although she hated the hot iron and how long it took. She'd had also donned Louisa's embroidered stockings, although no one would see them. She only wished she felt as self-assured as she looked.

Jean-Claude lounged across a settee as if prepared for sleep, not an eleven-course meal with guests. Esmee looked uncomfortable. Giselle glanced at the manservant and narrowed her eyes further.

He looked slack and unkempt, as well. It wasn't that his uniform needed washing or wasn't buttoned correctly. It was the stubble on his face and the smirk on his mouth. It was clear Giselle had been neglecting her duties. She didn't need Louisa to apprise her of it, either.

"Good evening, Esmee," she said. "You look elegant as usual. I'm proud to stand beside you and greet our guests. Jean-Claude...." Giselle walked to the center of the room to look down at him. "...we're expecting the mayor this eve. You will retire to your chamber and dress appropriately?"

To her shock, she saw there were insects moving about in his wig. Giselle quickly averted her eyes. She'd been told he shaved his head. But she hadn't known the wig was a vermin-filled powdered confection. Then again, he'd always been towering above her.

"I'm perfectly aware of our guests, my dear sister...Giselle." Jean-Claude lowered his voice after pausing on Giselle's name, but he sat up. "It's just so horribly boring here. Still, I mustn't complain."

She watched him open his little container and use more snuff, dusting his jabot off after he finished. He was disgusting. She wondered how she'd ever thought him attractive.

"I was just telling Esmee she should accompany me to Versailles when we return," he continued. "There's so much more to do there."

More lives to tamper with? More plots to hatch? More careers to ruin or murders to plan?

"I look forward to seeing your evening attire, Jean-Claude. You may be excused."

He stood, although he took his time, and dwarfed her. Giselle kept her chin high as she met his gaze.

"Do I detect a rebuke, dearest little *duchesse?*".

Giselle smiled tightly. "I'd never aspire to such, Jean-Claude. *Au revoir.*" She moved sideways to let him reach the door around her skirts. "We look forward to your presence at supper later, don't we, Esmee?"

Giselle kept her eyes on his and felt Esmee nod mutely to one side. She didn't realize how tense she was until Jean-Claude swept out of the room.

Once the door slammed, she turned on the manservant. "And now you will find a replacement while you, too, prepare for our guests. You may hope it won't be a permanent replacement. That will be all."

He nodded and walked out quickly.

"Oh, Giselle," Esmee sounded strange. "You were magnificent. I swear I didn't know what to do. I thought I experienced enough embarrassment when Etienne dined downstairs."

"What has Chef Aaron prepared for this evening?"

Giselle wasn't really listening. She had to think. Jean-Claude was evil, filthy, foul-smelling, and something else — he was cunning. She'd spoken out against him already, and the look in his eyes promised retribution. And she didn't even have Navarre—.

"Bonjour, Giselle. You look wonderful this evening. My compliments."

As if she'd conjured him up, the moment she thought of him, he greeted her. Giselle composed her features before turning.

"It's lovely to see you again…Navarre."

What began as a simple greeting ended on a sobbed note. Giselle barely restrained it. Esmee was watching, and so was the manservant who opened the door for Navarre to enter. She had no choice. She looked at him.

He was wearing harlequin red-orange breeches, white stockings, and a black frock coat. His dark blond hair was neatly tied back, and a small diamond stick pin sparkled from his snowy jabot. Tears blurred her vision, and she blinked them away. She knew he was the most handsome man in existence, so why did it always take her by surprise?

"You're well?" He bowed over the hand she hadn't realized she'd held out.

This was monstrous. Jean-Claude was due back any moment Marguerite, Aunt Mimi, and our guests will be arriving, and she couldn't even quell the quivers that touched the garters holding Louisa's embroidered stockings in place above her knees. The warmth of his storm-colored eyes touched hers, and Giselle looked aside quickly.

"Well enough. *Merci."* She whispered her answer to the blue-flecked wall and found room to breathe again once he dropped her hand.

"It's wonderful of you to condescend to join us this evening, Navarre." There was strong sarcasm in Esmee's words. Giselle watched him walk toward her to bow formally before he answered again.

"I wouldn't have missed this evening for all of France, my dearest Esmee. Not even for all the world."

There was a strong lilt in his voice as he said it, and Giselle pinched her hands together to avoid holding them to her cheeks. She suspected she was as pale as Bertina's ghost, and she still had to face all the evening's festivities.

"I had no idea you held our fine mayor, Ambross, in such high regard, Navarre," Esmee continued. "I placed him in your normal position beside Giselle. I can have him moved closer to you, if you like."

"No!" Giselle said abruptly. Navarre started, and she blushed when he looked toward her. "It's too late to change the arrangements, Esmee, and I'll find conversing with the mayor enlightening. Please don't change a thing."

To her surprise, Navarre chuckled, then turned back to Esmee. "It's all arranged then. Is there a cordial available? I feel parched of a sudden."

He poured a small amount of brandy into a snifter and swirled it to coat the glass and disperse the aroma. The movement looked sensuous, and Giselle wasn't certain of the meaning of the word. His long, slender fingers wrapped about the glass stem, then his lips pushed against the crystal, and his throat moved as he swallowed.

Giselle swallowed too, sucking on her bottom lip as she watched. She was even more thankful he wasn't going to be sitting beside her. She was in danger of being mesmerized. It was shameful, and yet it was exciting, too. She couldn't look down fast enough when Esmee cleared her throat.

How was she to get through the evening, and it had barely started! Years of training in the intricacies of proper dining etiquette saved her. She realized it as the meal progressed. She kept stiffly upright in her chair and acted the perfect hostess, although Ambross was a complete bore.

But it wasn't the mayor that she was posturing for.

Jean-Claude had usurped Etienne's place, facing her, and Giselle caught his gaze on her often. Each time, she studiously ignored him. She was more than grateful that Navarre wasn't beside her. He'd been right. If Jean-Claude suspected how they felt, he'd have a terrible weapon.

It was a wearisome affair, and Giselle was relieved when it was finally over.

They adjourned to the Red Salon for after-dinner drinks. She sat with a glass of wine in her hand and waited until she could escape upstairs. She was worse than weary. She was exhausted. She hadn't known pretentious behavior was so draining.

Giselle had acted well, though. She'd done her duty with an exactitude that Louisa couldn't fault. She'd made sure Jean-Claude dressed appropriately, and that the servants deported themselves correctly. Everything seemed to be in place. Even Esmee kept up a steady chatter as if entertaining a suitor, and not the mayor.

"I find the entire affair a waste of my time," Jean-Claude said, drawing everyone's attention to his complaint. "Here I am, the prodigal son returned, and my esteemed brother, the *duc,* doesn't even attend his own gathering and converse with me."

"Perhaps he hasn't recovered from his injuries enough, yet," Esmee said in the silence that followed Jean-Claude's remarks.

"I heard of His Grace's unfortunate accident. Is he well?" Mayor Ambross' many chins waggled as he asked it.

Giselle decided to drink some of her wine instead of simply holding it.

"You'll have to ask the *duchesse* that, my good man," Jean-Claude said. "I haven't been allowed in to see him, although Navarre mentioned his recovery this very morning."

Despite her best intentions, Giselle whitened at the reminder of Navarre's desertion. The sip of burgundy pained as she choked it down. She looked for a place to set her goblet. That had been foolish. She couldn't possibly swallow around the lump that was settled into her throat. She'd already proved it during dinner, when she pretended to eat and hoped the mayor wouldn't notice.

"If you're asking of Etienne," Navarre spoke for her. "He's recuperating well. It will still be some time before he can join us again. He has asked for his privacy, and to be alone with his *duchesse*. I believe she bolts the doors. I'm certain Etienne regrets missing your company, Ambross, and I know I speak for him when I extend the invitation for a later date."

Although he spoke to the mayor, everyone knew who his words were for. Giselle watched Jean-Claude gulp his wine.

Some of Navarre's words had been meant for her, too. She was being instructed to bolt her doors, allowing no one to enter. Even Navarre.

She'd forced herself not to look at him all evening, but her resolve broke. Navarre stood, leaning against the mantel, his open coat draping to his knees, and the diamond stick pin catching light from the candelabra. His dark blond hair was pulled back so severely, it made his nose look even longer. He was avoiding her glance by studying the liquor in his glass.

He didn't need to tell her about duty. It was one of the words she hated anymore.

Navarre hadn't mentioned how beautiful the view was in the moonlight. Perhaps he hadn't seen it that way. Giselle shoved the drapes all the way open and pushed on the window latch, opening it. Her room didn't have the full view of Etienne's, but she saw the side of the valley. It was enough. And if she wanted a better look, she could always go back into his chamber.

Giselle leaned over the balcony, looking at the blackness below her. Isabelle had tried to argue with her, but Giselle had insisted the door would be bolted after the servants left. Henri had looked up and smiled from his chair in the hall before Giselle shut and bolted the door.

The pale blue dress she would wear the next day was sent to the kitchens for ironing, but for once Giselle wasn't happy to see Gerty sent off with it. It had left her alone with Louisa. Giselle knew Louisa expected her to explain things, and she had left disappointed. Giselle was determined to remain silent.

She reached up to undo some of the pins in her hair, knowing Isabelle would raise her eyebrows at Giselle's actions in the morning. They'd spent a lot of time curling, pinning, and arranging the *duchesse's* hair to look elegant tonight. Giselle should have felt grateful, instead of being so horribly lonely.

There was a sound in Etienne' s chamber. Giselle turned to it for a moment, but it wasn't repeated. She could check again, but both times she had, the bolt was still in place, and he slept heavily.

Moonlight threaded through the mist, while the trees bordering the vineyard cast a long enough shadow to reach the gardens below. It was beautiful, cold and austere, as if awaiting the warmth daylight would bring.

Giselle shivered. She should've wrapped a dressing gown about herself before venturing out onto the balcony, especially since she wore one of her sheer nightgowns again. Louisa smiled when Giselle had told Isabelle to leave the stockings in place. It seemed silly, now. Perhaps she had wanted to feel feminine and beautiful in the immensity of her own bed. It was a wasted effort. The only thing the bed looked was large and lonely.

How could she face an entire lifetime of this?

Giselle knew now what emotion made each breath shallow and quick-paced as she studied the view. It was a desperate sort of longing. She longed for Navarre's kisses and ached for his touch. With almost savage hands, she ripped the lace at her throat and yanked her ribbons free. This was an unbearable emotion, and it would always be so.

She had the nightgown opened almost to her breasts before her fumbling made it impossible to continue. The night blurred, and she clenched at her stomach. It burned as she forced the sobs back, and even that didn't work.

Giselle stifled the deep whimpers and folded in half as she did so. If this was a foretaste of her nights, she'd rather die.

"It's too cold out here, Giselle, my love."

Navarre's whisper? Here?

"Why do you weep? I've come, and I find you not in the warm bed awaiting me, but shivering with cold on the balcony. Giselle? Darling?"

Hard arms lifted her against him. Navarre's arms. He was here! He'd come!

Giselle pressed into him, shuddering while he held her. He moved them back into the chamber...placed her on the bed. Navarre had come to her!

"You must let me go to shut the window, love."

"Non! Please don't make me!"

Giselle peppered his face with kisses, her hands pulling the dark cape from his head.

"Very well."

He chuckled, and reached for the tie at his neck that she was attempting to undo. His motion shoved her fingers aside.

"Non, Navarre, don't leave me." Her whisper was frantic.

"Leave you? Oh, no. Not tonight."

He lunged onto the bed beside her, filling the mattress so that it looked normal-size. Giselle wiped hastily at the moisture on her cheeks.

"I adore it when you look at me. Did you know that?"

She would've answered, but he bent his head to her neck, and she could no longer think to speak. Giselle squealed at the touch of his lips against her skin, and she gripped his hair in hands that seemed to belong to someone else. Hot breath touched her throat and slithered over her shoulder. She caught her breath.

"So sweet. So feminine," he whispered. "Sometimes, I find it difficult to believe you exist beyond my dreams. *Dieu!* I cannot believe I am here, and I actually have you. Here. Right now. In my arms."

"Oh, Navarre. I love you. I need you. I love you. I do."

Giselle kissed his hair, forehead, and nose. She needed to feel his lips against hers. She was almost insane with the desire to feel his kiss.

Mon Dieu!

She couldn't contain the sounds of ecstasy that flooded her when he gave her what she wanted, seizing her mouth with his. The roughness of it ignited her. Giselle hooked a leg around his waist, pushing up and into him. His clothing rubbed and teased her, tormenting the barely covered flesh of her thighs. Giselle heard her nightgown rip, and then Navarre's chuckling echoed through her breast.

"I love you, Giselle."

He lifted his head then, and she wasn't going to allow that sort of distance between them. She lunged up to him again, and he rolled, pulling her to a straddling position atop him. *Sweet Mary!* This new position sent heat. And vibration. And she wanted more. Giselle worked at the lacing of his shirt, her hands shaking so violently, they didn't cooperate.

He wasn't helping, either. Heat from his palms seared her waist. Giselle almost had a lace free when the touch of his hands moving up her sides altered everything. Large fingers fit about her breasts, molding and rubbing, while she arched her back to get even more sensation. More friction. More...amazement. The lawn fabric of her nightgown stretched beneath his fingers as he brought her nipples into sore darts that tormented. Shocked. Stunned. Almost frightened.

"Navarre?"

"Kiss me, Giselle."

He pulled her down, using her flesh to hold onto her, bringing her mouth to his, and giving her all sorts of sensation in all sorts of places. His thumbs toyed with her nipples, his tongue danced against hers, and his hips bucked into her most private area, each time sending thrills. Shivers. And nothing stopped her moans as they blended with the deep rumble of sound coming from his throat.

"Giselle...my love. You must...let me shut...the window now."

His whisper was gulped through kisses, shoved between breaths. And she wasn't letting him go. Not now.

"But I'm not cold."

He chuckled and rolled, placing Giselle on her back again, beneath him. Her legs somehow wrapped about his thighs. His legs between hers. And his hips...oh! She was actually squirming with little lunges that connected. Teased. Tormented.

And then he lowered his head placing the tip of his nose against hers. His hair was unbound, or perhaps it hadn't been tied before. It hung from him, tickling her neck.

"I don't fret the chill, love. We'll be making our own heat. But sound travels. And that...I do care about."

CHAPTER TWENTY-SEVEN

There were only four candles lit in the candelabra, and Giselle watched them as he fussed with the draperies. There wasn't much light, but it was too bright, of a sudden. What happens is so loud, he worried? She had the covers about herself before the light sputtered, moved by his presence.

"Giselle? Turn around, darling."

She shook her head and clutched the covers tighter to her. Two large hands grabbed her shoulders, pulling her toward his chest, placing her right against his heat. And he was no longer wearing leather. Hard thighs molded to each side of her. Arms wrapped around her, and she swore the chest she was leaning against trembled.

"I love you, Giselle," he whispered. "I love how small and feminine you are. I love your hair unbound like this, too."

He bent forward to reach her ear.

"I can't tell you how often I've dreamed of this...to see you, and hold you. Now that I am, it's unbearably sweet."

He set his head atop hers. Giselle's eyes were wide as he trailed his forefingers down her arms. Goose bumps rose at the touch.

"You see? You feel it, too, don't you?"

He lifted one of her hands to his mouth and touched his tongue to her palm. Giselle squealed.

"Navarre, I don't—. You must...."

"Oh. Never."

He lifted her other hand to his lips. His legs tightened about her squirming, locking her in place. Her cries turned into moans. She twisted. And his bare chest came into focus. She stopped moving and raised her eyes to his.

"Navarre?"

"*Oui?*"

She snatched her hands and reached for him, running fingers over his chest, shoulders, neck. The slightly rough texture of his chin drew her, and then she touched his full lower lip. Giselle answered him in kind as his mouth curved into a smile.

"Your eyes darken when you touch me. Did you know that?"

She shook her head and licked her lips.

"*Merde!* What you do to me."

He hissed the words in seeming-agony as he gripped her to him, lifting her for another kiss. Lips, raw with need, caught hers with bruising pressure. And Giselle returned it.

He lifted his head, breathed harsh and quickly for several moments and then looked down at her. And then smiled again.

"*Tres belle,* Giselle."

"You're...very beautiful, too...Navarre." Giselle stammered the words with shyness, but kept her gaze on him.

"Men aren't beautiful, Giselle."

He raised one eyebrow. She watched the candlelight glisten off his eyelashes as he blinked.

"*Non?* Well, you are."

She reached to touch him again and watched his intake of breath. He had a smattering of brown hair between his chest muscles, and she rested her hand there, feeling his heart beat tap at her palm. Her eyes widened as his nipples tightened...right before her eyes! Oh, this was absolute magic, pure and simple.

"I love...you."

Giselle choked on the last word because a hard lump surged against her hip, making her start. He grinned, raised his hands, and started pulling at her nightgown lacing. The thighs about her tightened at the same time.

"Navarre?"

"*Oui?*"

He didn't look up from where his fingers untied one ribbon after the other, pulling them apart with a rhythm that somehow matched how her breath caught, edged out, and caught again. Giselle watched his face. Then his fingers brushed against her belly, spreading open the nightgown, and that time she jumped with the contact.

"So sweet. So feminine. So...beautiful. I find it difficult to believe you're real...and that I'm here. Right now. With you.'"

His words were as erratic as his breathing, and Giselle's lip curved. He raised his eyes to hers, then, and the smile died on her mouth.

"I'm real, Navarre."

"So you say." He raised one eyebrow.

"Do I look like a fantasy?"

"Oh. *Oui.* How did you guess my thoughts?"

"Because they're the same as mine." She blushed.

"You fantasize about me? That is...uh. That's.... Oh, Giselle! What you do to me! You have no idea, either, do you?"

"No. Yes. No. All I know is that...you're going to make me yours tonight."

"Oh yes. Totally. Completely. Forever."

He slid the nightgown off her shoulders. It felt strange...and yet exciting. Wicked. Sensual. She held his gaze a moment longer before he looked down. Giselle saw him catch his breath.

"Oh. *Love*. You truly are too beautiful for words. I cannot! I will not—! We have all night! I mustn't rush it. I mustn't—"

"Navarre?"

Her whisper stopped his words, and she watched him exhale. It looked erotic. How it felt was even more so.

"*Oui?*"

"I love you."

He reached for her, and cupped his hands about her. And then he lowered his head. And kissed a nipple. Giselle's cry echoed about them as she gripped his hair, her fingers clenching about silky strands. Waves of fire-laced spikes flashed from where he suckled. Crashed to her most private area, and then spread outward, sending more heat in waves.

"Navarre, help me! I beg it of you!"

He chuckled at her torment, lifted his head, and used it against her neck, pushing her onto her back. And settled between her thighs, partially covering her. From the waist down. He held up from her, delineating the muscles in his arms. His upper chest. His abdomen. And the candlelight was so bright! She saw...

Oh my!

She glimpsed a leg and something else so foreign it startled and almost frightened. Giselle's eyes went wide. He was so large. So heated. So strong. Everywhere.

"You definitely have passion, my love. Never doubt that. So much woman. Such beauty! *Merde!* I can't believe I am here!"

His lips met hers, branding her with more than words. And she helped him, running her hands up his sides and back down again over and over in a palsied fashion. While he pumped his hips in little motions, sending sparks with every minute touch of that strange part of him. On her inner thigh. Higher. Her lower belly.

His groan deepened, and then his arms started shaking. He lifted his head, and huffed each breath toward the headboard.

"Actually love…you are almost *too* much woman."

"What?"

"I must be gentle. I must go slow. I've no experience in this, and—. Oh my God! What stupidity made me say that?"

Her mouth dropped open, and then she was kissing his jaw. His cheek. His nose. She was his first? Oh, for the joy! She knew exactly what the emotion was. He was hers! No women like Desiree or Charmaine could ever take that away from her, either.

"You must stop that, Giselle. You must—"

His words ended in a garbled noise as she pressed her lips to his throat. And the shudder that ran his frame moved hers with it.

"Giselle! So sweet. So fragile. Help me, love."

The words were deep. Guttural.

"I don't understand, Navarre."

"I know, sweet. I know."

He angled his head into the space above her shoulder, using the position to balance himself and free his arms. She was frightened, and her eyes filled with tears at it. She felt him tip his head sideways in order to look at her.

"What is it, darling?"

Giselle shook her head.

"I won't harm you, little one. It would be like crushing a flower. But…you're so small, don't you see?"

She refused to open her eyes just then. The tear she tried to hide rolled out from under her eyelid.

"Don't cry, darling. Please? I can't stand it."

"But I'm frightened, Navarre! And I don't even know why."

He kissed her tear trail.

"I love you. I'll try and be gentle. It won't be easy, though. I've wanted you so much, and waited so long. That's not a good combination right now."

His hands wrapped about her hips and yanked her against him. She gasped as he lowered his lips to hers. The strange lump of him slid along her belly. Stabbed between her thighs. Back to her belly. Thighs. Back. Over and over in motions that matched his hips. She felt him lift her buttocks, parting her legs more, his muscles tight everywhere, and then there was nothing but complete and solid pain.

Giselle screamed, but the sound was captured in the caverns of his mouth.

He pulled up from her and pushed up again, lifting his weight. She hadn't realized how crushing it was until it was gone, along with his warmth. She couldn't think. All such ability seemed stolen from her. Her apex was afire. He was branding her! Every twinge he made only added to it.

"You must help me, Giselle. You're too small." He shoved again, and she cried loudly, and arched her neck, giving the sound room. "Wrap your legs around me, darling! Push down. Now!"

She tried to lunge away instead. He was too strong. Too big. And he was hurting her.

"No, Navarre...no. Please, no. You must stop. Please?"

A sigh touched her cheek. And then everything on him shook, including her. The mattress beneath them even shuddered with it. And then he lowered his weight back to her, pushing out her air.

"I can't do this, Giselle."

The pain left, along with his pressure. But instead of feeling relief, she felt bereft. Alone. Cold.

"Navarre?"

"I refuse to hurt you, *ma petit.*"

He tried to roll away, but she tightened her legs.

He sighed. "Let go, Giselle."

She shook her head.

"You're too tight, and your fear makes it worse. You're fighting. Not helping. Now, have pity and let me rise."

Despite how she clung, he shoved away, reaching the side of the bed. He stood, and then he was walking away. Leaving her.

"No, Navarre! Wait! Please? I won't fight. I'll....help."

The last was whispered. It was as if she unleashed a beast by the sound he made, as he swiveled and snarled at her.

"I am a man, Giselle! Not a toy. You cannot beg me to stop, then tell me otherwise when I do. I cannot believe I managed to halt it now! I'm desperate, I tell you! Don't you understand what you do?"

"Please?" she asked.

She heard his heavy sigh, and then he was approaching. Giselle moved into the center of the bed as he crawled onto the mattress, lifted his torso, put his hands on his hips, and then tipped his head, as if studying her. She didn't know if he was angry. She'd never seen him angry...but she'd never seen anything like what he'd put on display, either. Far from frightening her, it was doing exciting things. Tantalizing things.

"This is what a man looks like, Giselle. Yes, I'm big. And yes, you're small. But it will fit. It has to be your maidenhood making it hurt. It won't always be so. Do you understand?"

He was still angry. The red tone in the center of his chest showed that, and Giselle's lips parted. She nodded.

"You won't cry?" he asked.

She shook her head.

"Then come here."

He opened his arms and she scooted into the space he'd created. He lifted her at the same time his mouth met hers, and nothing had tasted so sweet! His hands were rough this time as they rubbed her breasts, arms...thighs. Giselle lay back against the pillows again, bringing him to her, and this time she helped him. She did her best to welcome him. Despite everything, tears filled her eyes. He saw them, but she didn't cry out — she didn't dare.

She tried to endure it without complaint. She held to him as he filled her, branding her with an agony she didn't know existed. It burned. Tormented. She had to force herself not to beat at him. He was blurred. She opened her mouth to beg for mercy, but he forestalled her.

"Look at me, Giselle," he interrupted her. "Look and don't look away."

Blue and violet eyes held hers, resembling storm-filled skies, just like the first time she saw them. Giselle had never seen them so soft and tender.

"I love you." He whispered it and pressed his head against the headboard. "Are you ready?"

"For what?" she asked.

"Wrap your legs about me," he answered. "Now. Tightly. You do trust me, *Oui?*"

She nodded, although it took an act of will to do it. Everything was raw and painful.

"Navarre? I love— *Dieu!*"

Her words were lost in a shriek as he grabbed her hips and rammed, fully possessing her. Filling her. He stopped the cry with a kiss, this one containing the flick of his tongue. Another. And then Giselle was matching him, losing reality in the enticement of his mouth. His lips. His tongue.

He moved, sliding the swelled part from her. The pressure eased. Giselle had a moment to sigh her relief before he rammed again, bringing it right back. She would have tried to shove him from her then, but he was having none of it. He gripped her buttocks with hands that were probably going to leave bruises, as was the frantic motion of his mouth against hers.

And then he did it again. Sliding from her only to thrust back into her. Out. Back in. Again. Over. And over. Little grunts began emanating from his throat, matching his movements. Sliding out. Ramming back in. Out. The mattress started rocking in accompaniment. The bed frame joined in next, creating a rhythm of creaks and groans and then it held her moans.

And still his body pumped into hers.

A stray spark flit through her lower belly. It came again. Stronger this time. And again. Adding to his motions as they started increasing in tempo. Harder. Faster. While the structure about them rocked with it. The inner spark came more often, each time gaining intensity. Duration. Strength.

It altered as Giselle began shoving against him. Locking her ankles behind him for stability. The spark no longer ended. It just kept growing. The rhythm got even faster, swaying the mattress with it. And Navarre's grunts weren't little, nor were they spaced out. They were matching every thrust of his body into hers. The depth. The scope. The heat.

It was still hot, but it was a different heat. Scorching. Fiery. And then the most amazing sensation flooded her, whooshing to inferno level, and even that wasn't enough. Her legs strained to match his rhythm. Her fingernails caught on the ridges of his back and shoulders.

"Oh Giselle. Oh, love. Oh...love. Giselle. Love."

He lifted from their kiss, mouthing a litany of words in accompaniment to their motions. Sweat slicked the air, coated their bodies, meshed their joining. The motions got faster. Harder. More erotic. Smell further excited her. He pushed up from her, gaining a position in order to pummel her body with his. And Giselle exploded.

She grabbed a breath and slammed her entire body up into his. Lightning was hitting at her. Stunning her. Overtaking and encompassing her. And her ears were filled with a thunder that sliced the night, encompassed her hearing, overrode her experience, and claimed her body. Giselle clung to him while the cacophony of sound dimmed, replaced by the heavy thud of her own pulse.

His arms shook, and then it transferred to his body as everything went taut. Rigid. He lifted his head, arching backwards while his body vibrated in spasms that lifted her, too. The space above them reverberated with the deep rawness of his long, drawn-out groan. It ended in laughter just before Navarre collapsed, rolled onto his back, and pulled her atop his chest, where Giselle rose and fell with each breath.

"Oh Giselle. *Je t'adore. Merde!* I've never.... I had no thought to—I love you. I can't believe it!"

She felt exactly the same way. Navarre whispered more endearments to her once his breathing calmed. Giselle listened to each beat of his heart as she struggled with her sobs. She knew it was the wrong time to cry, but nothing stopped them.

Navarre lifted his head when he felt them.

"You're crying?"

He was smoothing the hair from her face as he spoke and his whisper tore at her heart.

"I cry, because it's so beautiful, Navarre."

"You do? Truly? I didn't hurt you overmuch, then?"

She shook her head and wiped quickly at the moisture before it dripped off her nose. She couldn't believe herself. She'd just had the most incredible experience of her life, and she had eyes swollen with tears and a red nose.

"Ah, Giselle, my love, you're wondrous. That was wondrous. I can't believe it! Everything is amazing. I've never felt so amazing. Etienne had better plan for a dozen children, and I'll tell him of it on the morrow."

He chuckled at his joke before turning on his side. He settled her into the niche he'd created at his front.

"I love you, Navarre." She whispered it into his throat.

"And I you, *ma petit.*"

He kissed her ear. His breath touched her cheek, and his warmth enfolded her nearly everywhere.

A dozen children?

Sounded wonderful.

CHAPTER TWENTY-EIGHT

"Open the door, Giselle!" Louisa called. "The entire staff is awaiting you."

Giselle should have guessed who was behind the infernal pounding at her door. Then again, she was the one who'd bolted it.

"You'd better see what they want," a bored, male voice said beside her. "I certainly can't do it."

Giselle gasped and lifted her head from the pillow.

"Good morning, Giselle," Etienne said.

Chills ran her back at the memory of what Navarre and she had done. In the exact same place where Etienne now reclined. Giselle slid from the bed and raced to the water closet. And the chamber pot. She was afraid she was going to be ill. It didn't help that Etienne's laughter accompanied her actions.

"Giselle! I don't want to break down this door!" Louisa shouted.

Giselle swished a wet cloth across her face with a trembling hand and tied her robe more securely. She wore one of her heaviest ones. Navarre had dressed her in it before he left. After another session of lovemaking. At almost dawn. She was blushing as she crossed to the door, knowing Etienne watched her.

"Ah, Louisa! You've been so loud, you woke my...husband."

Giselle stumbled on the word, and at the sight of Gerty directly behind Louisa.

"The *duc?*" Louisa asked.

"*Oui.* He sleeps at my side...as you can both see."

Giselle moved aside to let them in. The women looked at Etienne. He replied by waving his fingers at them.

"Yes. Well. I suppose *Madame* will want breakfast. Gerty?"

Louisa sounded strange. Gerty was staring wide-eyed. Etienne wasn't having any problem with the situation. He stretched out, folded his arms behind his head, and then grinned. By the way Gerty was shifting from foot to foot Giselle guessed the maid couldn't wait to tell everyone this news.

"That sounds nice. Yes. I'd like my breakfast. And a bath brought up, too."

"A...bath?" Louisa was still acting stunned.

"Perhaps Gerty will see to it, instead."

"Gerty?" Louisa asked.

"Gerty, see to a breakfast tray for the *duc* and myself. Fetch Isabelle, too. You may go now."

Gerty swiveled and started running. Giselle's lips twisted. She knew her supposition had been right. And she shouldn't quibble. It was according to plan. If none gossiped over Etienne's presence in her chamber, they might spend their time gossiping over who sired Giselle's babe, when there was one.

She blushed and had to duck her head for a moment. If there was no babe, it wouldn't be due to any lack of Navarre.

"Isabelle?" Louisa whispered.

"Perhaps you'd better sit down, Louisa."

"Dismiss your woman, Giselle. And come back to bed. I miss your warmth."

Louisa saw the look that accompanied Giselle's shudder, but that didn't stop it. She might be learning to play-act like any other Berchald, but Louisa would be hard to fool.

"I shall come back to you...darling." Giselle rolled the word across her tongue like it was nothing. She was rather pleased with herself over it, too, "but only if you keep your word not to drink today."

"My what?"

Louisa looked a little pale, and both women watched Etienne' s temper tantrum as he pounded on the covers. He just managed to look and sound silly.

"Oh look. Our breakfast has arrived," Giselle said. *"Merci,* Gerty. Perhaps you could see now that my husband's valet is summoned?"

"It's already been seen to, *Madame."*

Giselle wondered at her own naiveté. Of course it was already seen to. Informing her brother of the duc's location would have been the first thing Gerty did. Giselle narrowed her eyes.

"Tres bien. You're very competent this morning, Gerty. My compliments. That will be all, then."

"I don't need my valet!" Etienne folded his arms and glared as Giselle helped Louisa to the door.

"Please see that Isabelle has a bath brought for me, Louisa. I'll wish to speak with you later, too."

"I daresay you do." She shook her head as she left. Giselle returned Henri's nod before closing the door behind Louisa.

"Now. What is that nonsense of my valet?" Etienne said. "I'm perfectly capable of getting back to my chambers myself. I didn't need anyone to get here, did I?"

"Well, then...." Giselle surveyed him from across the chamber, assuming the same type of affronted expression he wore. "I look forward to seeing you do just that. Do you need your chair?"

She poured a cup of tea and sipped it, ignoring him no matter how difficult it was. Her legs and thighs were sore, and she blushed again. It was so near. So dear. So amazing. She closed her eyes, breathed the tea aroma, and let the memory wash over her. Making love with

Navarre had been unbelievable, and she felt the renewed satiated feeling.

It was difficult to brand such a beautiful thing as evil.

"What brings that sort of look to your face, I wonder?"

Etienne said it snidely, and Giselle opened her eyes. He was wheeling himself from around the bed. She watched him for several moments.

"Are you still here?" she asked finally.

He made some exclamation she didn't try to decipher, stopped at the chamber door. "Tell my brother not to get too used to usurping my property. I may be half a man, but I'm still a man. Understand?"

Giselle nodded. She didn't trust her voice.

"He must be a no lazybones, by the look on your face. Give him my compliments, will you?"

She screamed the reaction, and threw her cup of tea at the closing door. Etienne found that amusing. She knew what he was trying to do. He was trying to manipulate her into feeling guilty. Despite the fact he'd begged her. Giselle was determined not to allow such a thing. She'd made her decision. Nothing about what happened with Navarre had been anything other than heavenly. She closed her eyes again. That way, she swore she could actually smell Navarre.

She wouldn't have awakened, but Navarre's movement near dawn pulled the covers off her, and she tried to cling to him.

"Don't leave me," she'd mumbled.

He'd kissed her lightly on the nose.

"Imagine the scandal, Giselle. Especially after I've gone to all this trouble. Do you think it easy to slip through the maze at night?"

She'd giggled.

"You think it's amusing?" He'd sat on the edge of the bed, his outline vaguely visible. "Perhaps you should visit me instead. Except you'd probably get lost, and then what would everyone say?"

"I shudder to think of it," she whispered.

"Help me find my shirt. I can't leave it here. This room is so damnably dark. Why in the blazes—? Ouch!"

Giselle had laughed as he fumbled about and opened the drapes, letting the first blush of dawn into the room. She shouldn't have, but he was in such disarray. His hair was a riot about his head, and his breeches were on backward.

"You should put on something before you walk about, Giselle."

Her eyes had widened as he neared, and she crossed her arms modestly, before realizing how stupid that must look.

"Not that I'd complain..."

His breath had raised the gooseflesh on her arms, although he simply stood there. He wasn't touching, just looking, and her blush warmed her more than the bedding could.

"You must stop this enticement, Giselle," he complained. "I'm so sore, I may not be able to visit you again for a time."

"What?"

She'd grabbed at him, pulling his arms around her as she trembled against him. Now that she knew what loving meant, it wasn't possible to think he'd not come again.

"I'm teasing, my love. It's not my soreness that bothers me, it's yours. You must let me know, during supper if you like, if you can...or if you can't. I'm explaining this poorly, aren't I?"

She shook her head before meeting his eyes.

"It will be light soon. I must make certain you're dressed. Choose a more concealing gown. There's no question now, you know. You're mine. I can't bear to recall how you looked last night, and no one, not even Etienne, is to see you that way. Ever."

He'd touched a finger to her chin, lifting her mouth to his.

"You're mine, Giselle. Mine!"

Their lips stopped his words, and she'd sagged against him. The beat of his heart warmed her, filling her palms with the texture of it, and then he stepped back.

"Go back to bed, love. Dream of me."

Giselle had settled onto her belly against the pillows, watching as he tied on his cape and pulled the hood over his head. She stretched, lifting her *derriere* into the air a bit. She would do as he asked, and don the thick nightgown...but not yet.

He was almost to the connecting door to Etienne's rooms.

"I love you, Navarre." Her voice barely made a sound, and his back stiffened.

"*Merde,* but I can't bear the thought of leaving!"

He'd lunged across the bed and pulled her into a hug so tight, she almost fought it.

"The hours ahead of me now? They will seem like days! I know I'll see you at sup, but that's much too far away. Oh, how can I bear it, Giselle? I slept away the day to be awake all night long with you. And what happened? I slept." He smiled, then sighed. "What have you done to me to make it so? Life, she is cruel, *non?*"

Giselle was trembling so much at his observation, she couldn't answer. She knew exactly what he meant. She never felt more protected or loved. She was where she belonged, where she was meant to be, and there was nothing bad or wicked or wrong about it.

A noise out in the hall had Navarre lifting his head. They both had held their breaths as the sentry set down his chair in a new place.

"I must go." There was the slightest touch of his lips to her hair, and then he was gone.

Giselle had listened, without knowing how tense she was, waiting for Jean or Henri to shout the alarm outside Etienne's door. She didn't realize no sound of alarm was given until a shaft of sunlight lightened the floor where Navarre had stood. Thank goodness! They couldn't be caught now! But, how could she face the hours ahead?

"We could always tour the first addition, Giselle," Esmee said. "I couldn't take you there before, but that's not a problem now."

"Really? Why would that be?" Giselle lifted her blue skirts with a hand that trembled.

"Why, because it's Navarre's wing, of course."

She should have known. Giselle steeled herself to meet Esmee's gaze with a blank expression. Esmee smiled as if harboring a secret. Giselle felt her heart drop. And then Esmee turned back around and led the way.

Giselle forced her legs to climb the staircase to Navarre's rooms. She had no idea lovemaking would leave her so tired and sore. The throbbing in her legs threatened to drop her more than once. She also had several thumb-sized bruises on her inner thighs. She knew Isabelle had seen them, too, but her maid didn't say anything. She never did.

"Navarre chose this wing, because he loved the idea of the secret passages it was rumored to hold."

"Secret passages?"

Giselle was four steps below her, and moving awkwardly. Esmee didn't seem to notice. She waited with the same smile on her face that she'd had all morning. Giselle wondered if it was Esmee's turn to guard her from Jean-Claude. She should probably be grateful they cared.

"*Oui.* Navarre was always full of stories, even as a child. He was very inventive. I didn't know whether to laugh or follow when he dragged me down these halls."

Giselle reached the landing and looked about with obvious interest.

"'Look, Esmee,' he'd say. I'm certain they're here. If I turn this cornice-piece, a secret staircase will be revealed behind this panel.' He knocked on the walls, searching for a hollow sound. 'You hear it, Esmee?' he would ask."

She knocked on the wood panels as she talked, walking slowly toward the three doors at the end of the hall, imitating Navarre as a boy.

"'I'm certain this wall has a space behind it, Esmee! Listen! Do you hear?'"

"Did he ever find any?" Giselle came closer, lowering her voice at the same time.

"Can you keep a secret, Giselle?"

Esmee bent to Giselle's level. Giselle nodded. Esmee crooked her finger at her and pushed open the first door.

Oh! I shouldn't have come!

Giselle was immediately wrapped in Navarre's scent. If Esmee had turned she would've caught Giselle sagging against the doorframe.

"Oh. Look at this! He should've had maids attend to this room yesterday when he left." She shook her head at the sight of Navarre's unmade bed with the quilt tossed aside and the sheets dented where he lay.

"Brothers," she snorted. "They're all cretins. I wash my hands of them."

She walked to the fireplace and gestured over her shoulder for Giselle to follow her. Giselle eyed Navarre's four-poster bed, the filmy sheeting of a canopy spread all about it, and her legs shook beneath her skirts. She had trouble walking across to Esmee.

"If you run your finger along here...there's a little button-thing. Like a bump the woodcarver forgot to remove. It was...right here. Oh. Here it is."

She'd run her hand along the bottom of the fireplace mantel, and the panel beside her dropped back into the blackness. Giselle's gasp of surprise was covered by the sliding sound.

"Where does it...go?"

Her voice stumbled on the last word. Esmee had just given away Navarre's secret. He didn't use the halls to reach Etienne's bedchamber. He used this passageway.

"Just about everywhere, I assume. I don't know. I never explored it. Navarre would have my head for showing this to anyone. Why, I don't think he knows that I remember it. It was a very long time ago."

Giselle glanced at Esmee uneasily. She'd lived long enough in this household to realize that Esmee was trying to tell her something. The unpleasant chill she felt was worse than the one she'd experienced that morning from waking beside Etienne.

Giselle looked at the floor. Esmee was letting her know that she knew the secret. Giselle flushed with shame. What had felt so wondrous and heavenly the previous night suddenly felt lustful and damning in the daylight.

Giselle clenched her hands at her side. Well, what had she expected? Even if it was heavenly and wondrous, her love for Navarre was still a sin.

"Should we explore it and see?" Esmee stuck her head into the space while Giselle watched. "It's not that dark, Giselle. I see daylight through some cracks, too."

Giselle waited until Esmee pulled her head back into the room before peeking in, too. She didn't see any cracks.

"Should we follow it and see where it leads?"

"No." Giselle shivered.

"Why not? It might even lead to the *duc's* chambers. What a surprise that would be. What do you think?"

She knows!

Giselle choked on her reply and stepped into the passageway to disguise her reaction. She was too naive for such word games and too emotional to act a part. She wished Esmee would simply quit baiting her. It would be more compassionate.

"It's very dark, Esmee."

Giselle reached out to gauge how wide the passage was and squelched the scream as her fingers touched warm stone. She wasn't about to speak of it, for Esmee would simply ridicule her again. But there wasn't any sun in here to warm anything.

"Wait while I light a candle, Giselle. I can't wait to see...."

The panel slid easily back into place, cutting off her words. Giselle was left staring into the blackness without time to even gasp. The warmth of the stone was all she found soothing, and she spread her hands about it at her back.

"Giselle!"

She barely heard Esmee's words, but the noise of her pounding against the panel reverberated through the passageway.

"Giselle! Oh, Lord! What am I to do? Don't move. Giselle!"

Esmee's voice faded as she moved away. Giselle blinked the self-pitying tears back. Esmee was leaving her after sealing her into the wall. She didn't question it. She should've suspected it, instead of following blindly.

Warmth surrounded Giselle then, calming her panic, and she turned to face the outer castle wall. Esmee had been right, and now Giselle could see there were tiny slits assembled into the stone that let in a hint of light. She waited for her eyes to become accustomed to it.

There was no reason to panic. If Navarre found a way out as a child, she could do it as an adult.

"All right, Bertina." Giselle whispered it, feeling silly. "Show me the latch."

There was a narrow flight of steps climbing to her left. Another set sank into the blackness on her right. Giselle looked from one to the other. The heat was definitely at her back though, so she turned around.

There was a vague outline of the panel, and it had a peep hole. Giselle rolled her eyes as she saw the height of it. She should have known if the Berchalds had a secret passageway, it would be built for giants, too. Giselle had to stand on tiptoe and lean one side of her face against the wood in order to see out of it. She was surprised to see Esmee' s frantic movements at the mantel, and Esmee was crying.

"Esmee?" Giselle pounded on the panel.

"Giselle? Oh, God! I'm so sorry. I can't get the button to budge now. Are you all right?"

She instinctively knew she'd misjudged her sister-in-law. When Esmee had championed Giselle against Jean-Claude, she should have been listening with her heart, and not her imagination.

The heat intensified at Giselle's cheek, and she pulled back as it got hot.

"Stand back, Giselle. Can you hear me? I'll be right back."

Giselle ignored the instruction. She concentrated on following the heat source along the inside of the door. Her fingers scraped against wood, and then a tiny bump moved.

Giselle barely ducked in time as the panel opened. Esmee was on the other side, swinging a chair toward the wall. It struck the stone wall at Giselle's back, and bounced into the back of her legs, and that's what buckled them.

CHAPTER TWENTY-NINE

"*Mon Dieu!* Are you hurt? Oh, Giselle, I told you not to move."

Giselle stayed on her knees, laughing so hard she couldn't answer at first. Esmee had lifted one of the heavy chairs and swung it. That was surprising, and then it got more so as Esmee grabbed her into an embrace and hugged her.

"You're all right? Truly? Etienne would never have forgiven me if anything happened to you. I'm so sorry."

Giselle patted her back awkwardly.

"It's all right, Esmee, see? I'm fine, and, not counting the chair, there's been no harm done." Giselle pulled away and motioned toward the chair. Esmee made an attempt to smile. "I can't believe you lifted that," Giselle said, "but I hope you can do it again. Come. We'd better put it back before someone comes."

They tugged to get the chair out. Giselle was amazed that any woman could have lifted such a heavy item. It took so much work getting it back into place, that once it was done, she sank into it gratefully. And then looked over at where Esmee sank onto Navarre's bed.

"I am so sorry, Giselle. I hope you forgive me. I was only going to spy on Etienne. I thought it would be amusing. I've heard about this morning, and it made me very happy. Since you came, things have gotten much better. I never meant for you to be trapped in there. I swear it."

"Perhaps it was my movement that closed the door. You're not to blame."

"You're sweet to think that, but I should have made certain it was safe before putting you into such danger."

"It wasn't that bad, Esmee. Truly. And I was lucky."

"Yes. You are. You and Etienne are so lucky. Sometimes, I wonder why I still exist. For that's all I do, you know."

Giselle watched Esmee go to the windows and open Navarre's drapes, revealing an edge of the maze. So...that was how Navarre got from the dower house, too — the maze ended almost on his doorstep.

"Why do you say that, Esmee?" she asked. "I can't manage without you. Aunt Mimi dotes on you, and Navarre would...uh...I'm sure he would be lonely without you."

'That's just it, Giselle. It's lonely for him. And me. Oh...I know what you're thinking. It's impossible to be lonely in such a beautiful chateau. But I think that's your love for Etienne coming through. And the fact that it's returned. I know. I'm in love myself."

"Pardon?" Giselle couldn't think of anything else to say.

"I know you don't trust me, especially after the ball. I wouldn't trust me, either. But how could I tell you that *Mademoiselle* Frerre was Jean-Claude's mistress? I didn't want to ruin your happiness. And you were so happy. I saw it. I think everyone else did, too. That was when you first fell in love with him, wasn't it?"

She looked at Giselle for confirmation. Giselle didn't move. It felt like blasphemy to lie. Esmee smiled.

"It's all right. You don't have to answer. I know. I saw it. Everyone did. It was easy to see how much you cared for each other."

It was? She must be better at intrigue than she thought.

"I even saw to it that you matched. It was the least I could do, with you wearing *Mademoiselle* Frerre's gown. It was a perfect gesture, too. I congratulated myself. You looked so happy. You still do...and I'm jealous of it."

She strode to where Giselle sat and swooped into a pile of skirts at her feet. And then she reached for Giselle's hands, surprising her.

"I beg you, Giselle, before it's too late for me. Please? I need your help. I've heard he searches the village for a wife, and I can't see another in that position. I love him too much. I never thought I'd feel this way."

"Who, Esmee? Who searches?"

"*Monsieur* Ambross. Didn't you see the way he looks at me? I almost swoon."

"Ambross? The mayor?"

When Esmee had been flirtatious with the mayor, it was because she loved him?

"I know what you're thinking." Esmee released Giselle's hands and looked away. "He's not particularly assuming and isn't as handsome as Etienne, but there aren't many like my brother, are there? And I'm almost too scandalous for him to consider. I was disowned, I'm not young anymore, and I might not be able to have children. The list against me plays in my head until I want to scream."

"Esmee." Giselle touched her shoulder, and Esmee turned tormented eyes to her. "You're every bit a marital prize. I can't see why he wouldn't be delighted at the prospect of wedding you. He's not blind, and you are a beautiful woman. Besides, you're a Berchald. A nobler bloodline would be difficult to find."

"But I have no dowry."

"That's easy to arrange."

"Etienne has to do it, though, and I can't even get in to see him."

"Oh, Esmee!" Giselle felt giddy with the relief. She'd been so busy with her own life, and putting secret meanings behind everyone's words and actions, she missed everything. "I can speak with Etienne. We must plan another soiree, too, one which Monsieur Ambross won't decline. Didn't Na...varre intimate that very thing last night?"

Giselle stumbled on the name. *Had it really only been last night?*

"Oh, Giselle. I can't tell you how happy this makes me! Perhaps it's not too late for me after all. What do you think?"

"I think we've done enough exploring for one day."

"You'll speak with Etienne?"

"Of course." Giselle stood and waited for the trembling in her legs to subside. "I'll do it the first moment I can. I promise."

"And Navarre? You'll speak for him, too?"

"Navarre?" Giselle was in front of her or Esmee would have seen the expression. Giselle barely managed to keep her voice even.

"Oh come, Giselle. He can't spend his entire life taking Etienne's place about the estate."

She was innocent of the meaning Giselle gave her words. The spurt in her heart stopped her for a moment.

"Hasn't he spoken to you about it?" Esmee asked. "I felt certain he would, by now. You two seem very close."

Giselle watched Esmee shut the door behind them. She didn't trust herself to answer.

"I know him best, I think," Esmee continued. "And I'll tell you another secret."

She bent down to Giselle as they reached the stairs. Giselle clutched the railing and forced herself to study the black and white flooring below them. Otherwise, she was afraid she might swoon.

"I think Navarre is in love, too! Wouldn't it be wonderful? Would Etienne arrange a...what is it called? Oh yes, a double wedding? Navarre is quite a catch, you know. Any woman would find him an acceptable...."

Giselle didn't hear the rest of her words. For the first time since she came to Chateau Berchand, she fainted.

"You gave us quite a scare, young lady."

Louisa's hands had to be the ones moving the cloth on Giselle's forehead, although she didn't feel ready to open her eyes and verify it. She was in bed, but the linens smelled of Navarre so strongly she didn't want to open her eyes for another reason. The sheets shouldn't have that scent.

Where was *Madame* Dessard? Such ineptitude wouldn't do. Giselle had instructed them to have the linens cleaned as she'd bathed this morning. And then she'd had to suffer the blushes as the maids exclaimed over the bloodstains on the sheets.

"You're lucky that *Madame* Esmee is as stout as she is. I shudder to think what could have happened if you had fallen, Giselle. It's only by the grace of *Dieu* that doctors haven't been summoned already. The staff has noodles where their minds should be."

"What are you talking about now? So, I fainted. Is that so rare?"

"It is when the staff believes you're expecting a Berchald heir. And brings everyone on the run to *Monsieur* Navarre's chamber."

Giselle's eyes flew open. "I'm in his bed?"

"*Oui.* That was where *Madame* Esmee placed you. And then she came for me. You'd think you were dying the way some of the staff acts. And that Gerty is the worst. No child makes itself known so early. I told her as much when she fetched me."

"Oh, Louisa. I'm so confused." Giselle lifted the sodden rag from her forehead.

"You're confused? When you'd rather die than accept the *duc*?"

'Things aren't as they appear, Louisa. I can't say anymore. Help me up."

"Oh no. You aren't to move until *Monsieur* Navarre arrives. He'll move you back. Esmee insisted on it. I think she was just forestalling Jean-Claude's assistance with it. Since he offered."

"Where's Giselle? I heard you fainted, my love."

Navarre pushed his way to her, oblivious to Louisa, who stood right beside him. He lifted Giselle's hand to his cheek and leaned against it.

"I'm well, Navarre. Truly."

Giselle pulled her hand away, while Louisa did her best to look away.

"I'm to see you to your chambers. Don't tell me you'll walk, either. After all, I enjoy holding you. And just this morn, you said I could sleep."

Giselle supposed he thought he was whispering, but the smile Louisa was hiding let her know Navarre spoke too loudly.

"Navarre...."

He put one arm under her knees and lifted her. She gripped to his shoulders, trying to keep from clasping both arms about him.

"You should eat more, *Madame,*" he announced loudly. "You weigh nothing. Get the door, my good woman."

Louisa opened the door, and Giselle hid her face against Navarre's shoulder when she saw how many servants lined the hall.

"She'll be fine, Esmee. She just needs some rest, she says."

He spoke loudly enough for everyone to hear. Giselle closed her eyes, held to his neck, and tried to memorize how his coat felt against her.

"I can't hold you much longer, Giselle," he whispered into her ear. "You must know what you are doing to me."

She blushed, and hid against his neck.

"Can someone see that the door is opened ahead?"

He spoke in a rough tone. She knew why. She felt everything coming alive on her with every prolonged moment in his contact. But her desire wouldn't be as apparent as his was.

"Of course, my lord."

Isabelle did his bidding and waited for them to pass before shutting the door on the rest of the onlookers.

"My thanks, Navarre."

Giselle held to him a moment longer than necessary once he lay her on her bed. It was difficult to let go.

"I'll see you at sup, still?"

She tried to act unaffected as if they were sharing tea, and not remembering. She glanced at where he'd shown her such joy, and then back at him. When she tried to look away again, she failed.

"Unless I sleep through it, *Madame,* which isn't as far-fetched as it sounds."

His eyes went to the lace of her bodice before sliding down her body. She hadn't considered the light blue morning-gown an enticing ensemble, yet that's how she felt. She matched the shudder that ran down his frame. She'd never felt such undiluted longing, and knew he experienced it, too.

Oh! This was terrible. Isabelle was watching them from the doorway, hovering near to show Navarre out.

"What am I saying?" He reached for her hand and brought it to his lips. "I cannot stay away. And it is useless to sleep. I close my eyes, and you're beside me. Why do I bother describing it? Dismiss your maid, darling, and let me show you."

He didn't know what he asked. Or how wondrous it sounded!

"Can I get you anything, *Madame?*"

Isabelle spoke loudly from the door, interrupting, and reminding them of their duty as efficiently as any chaperon.

"No, thank you, Isabelle. *Monsieur* Navarre is just leaving."

He walked from her before Giselle finished speaking, taking all the warmth in the room with him. Giselle turned into the pillows so Isabelle wouldn't see her expression. She had no right to be bereft. She knew he'd come back that night, sneaking through the secret passage in his chamber to make love to his brother's wife.

Navarre had changed clothes from that afternoon, although Giselle couldn't have said for certain what he'd worn. In evening attire, he eclipsed even Jean-Claude. Giselle spent some time comparing the two. Navarre wore dark-brown velvet breeches, a light tan jacket, with a shirt and jabot of the finest beige-colored linen. He was pure masculinity, but she already knew that.

Jean-Claude was wearing medium-blue striped silk breeches, a lace-edged ecru-shaded jacket, and if Giselle wasn't mistaken, his shirt had a purplish tone. Perhaps it was the contrast to Navarre that made it so, but his facial paint with a crescent-moon-shaped patch near his mouth and a large wig on his head made him look silly.

She was in luck, they were dining *en famille*. Margot hadn't attended, leaving only six for the affair. Even with a small audience, though, Giselle felt the tension from sitting beside Navarre.

She hadn't worn a ball gown, panniers, or large hair style, because it was just a family meal. As shocking as Isabelle had thought it, Giselle had refused to wear a corset, too. Her figure hadn't changed the slightest, but she wanted to tease Navarre. She must have been too innocent to know the consequences.

"I understand Etienne has recovered from his accident, Giselle," Jean-Claude said.

"Excuse me?"

He interrupted her from contemplation of Navarre's upper lip, and it took a few moments to comprehend what he asked.

"I understand Etienne...visits you?"

It was unbelievably crude of him. Giselle smiled behind her napkin and considered what the news meant to him. Gerty already told her Jean-Claude wasn't welcome back at Versailles without a substantial sum of money. The fact that Etienne's marriage had been consummated must have given Jean-Claude fits of anxiety.

Still, it truly wasn't amusing. Her smile faded. Jean-Claude was probably more dangerous when he was desperate, but what could he do? Henri and Jean both guarded the ducal chambers, the doors were bolted tightly, and no one was allowed in without the *duchesse's* permission.

"Why yes...Etienne does visit me," she replied finally. "I'm gratified you considered it worth noting."

Navarre shifted beside her. Giselle fought the urge to glance at him.

"I'm simply considering my future, Giselle," Jean-Claude replied. "It will be difficult to put aside my, shall we say, aspirations? If Etienne produces an heir."

"Oh, I don't believe *if* will be the issue, Jean-Claude. I think it will be more a matter of *when*."

Giselle's amusement colored every word. Jean-Claude jumped visibly, and Navarre sounded like he was choking. Marguerite smiled hugely and Esmee giggled into her napkin. Aunt Mimi blushed, but she looked pleased at the same time.

"I see." Jean-Claude pushed back his chair. "I find it too stifling to finish this meal. If you ladies will excuse me? Navarre?"

Giselle watched him walk away, teetering a bit on his high heels. He was a presence even dressed as he was. She knew where he was headed, and didn't envy Margot at all.

"If doesn't come into the question?" Navarre whispered it to her as he bent to retrieve a dropped fork, waving away a footman as he did.

"I'm not wearing anything beneath my gown," Giselle whispered back, covering her mouth with her napkin as she did.

"What?"

He jerked upright, and wide, blue-violet eyes glared at her. He was furious. He almost threw the fork at the servant, while his hand shook. And she had done that to him? *Incredible.*

"We can get workmen on it, can't we, Navarre?"

Giselle watched Navarre's eyes narrow before he turned to look down the table at Esmee. Giselle was reeling in place at the look he gave her.

"What...needs...work?"

He pronounced each word carefully, and Esmee shrank against her chair.

"The tower that Etienne fell from," she replied finally.

"See to it, then."

He turned away from her, and she sighed in relief. Then Navarre grabbed his wine glass and glared at Giselle over the rim. Her eyes widened as his fingers turned white on the stem. She didn't realize what she did to him. Hadn't he already said as much? She didn't hear the sound, but the stem fell to the table, separated from the goblet. Several dark drops of blood immediately followed.

Giselle's hand went to her mouth as she realized Navarre didn't appear to have even felt it.

"Navarre! You have hurt yourself!"

Marguerite's cry brought a footman from the wall, cloth in hand. Still, Navarre glowered at Giselle. His nostrils widened. She knew she was turning white.

"Merci." He spat the word at the footman and wrapped his own hand without breaking his gaze at her. Giselle knew the others were staring. She needed

to invent some story to such a show of anger. But what? She could say she'd suggested a bride for him?

No, that would never do. She had to avoid that subject for fear Etienne would hear of it and start thinking. He could have Navarre married off easily...just as soon as Giselle conceived.

She couldn't believe her train of thought!

"Navarre."

Marguerite pushed back her chair before the footman could assist her and walked toward them. Navarre must have been aware of it, but he refused to relinquish Giselle's gaze. He forestalled his mother by flinging his napkin to the table, shoving back his chair, and with one last glare at Giselle, striding from the room. Relief swept through the rest of the diners while Giselle clasped her hands in her lap and concentrated on controlling their shaking.

"Do all my sons react so to you, Giselle?" Marguerite smiled.

Giselle swallowed to gain time. *"Oui,"* she replied, "although Etienne takes a bit longer to run from me."

Everyone laughed, including several of the servants. Giselle knew Gerty would be upset at missing this latest tidbit of gossip.

"I think Giselle spoke too soon, didn't you?" Esmee asked.

"About what?" Marguerite asked.

"Navarre has been acting a bit strangely. Giselle and I talked of it earlier, didn't we?"

They were looking at her. She was frozen in place.

"We think Navarre may finally have another interest beside Chateau Berchand duties. Isn't that right?"

"I—" Giselle began, but no sound came out.

"We think he might be in love," Esmee continued. "Isn't that exciting?"

"With whom?" Aunt Mimi asked it from behind Marguerite.

"Did he say, Giselle?" Esmee asked. "That's what you were speaking of, wasn't it? Come. Confess. Who is it?"

"I—"

This time there was a bit of sound, but her words stopped anyway. What could she possibly reply? Yes. He was most certainly in love. *With me.*

"Would you ladies excuse me as well? It's been a very tiring day. I should have dined with Etienne, I think."

Giselle was feeling a reaction so intense, she feared she might be ill. She couldn't possibly sit calmly discussing the possibility of Navarre having another lady. She simply wasn't up to the task. Giselle walked from the room without assistance and ignored any looks the servants might be giving her, too. This was all her fault, and while she was sorry, she was exhilarated as well.

Teasing him had been very gratifying, even if she couldn't tell anyone of it. It had been immensely warming, too. She'd never seen such blatant sensual desire. She could hardly wait until he came to her.

CHAPTER THIRTY

It was difficult to climb to her room with the shivers racing her legs. Giselle was grateful that Louisa, Isabelle, and Gerty were still eating below-stairs. She needed the solitude.

Locking the bolts took some time, as did lighting the candles from the one she carried. When she finished and blew it out, she saw Navarre's bulk detach itself from her drapes.

"Navarre! You'll be seen!" Her hand went to her throat.

"I don't care, Giselle."

She backed from him, until a dresser stopped her. Jars rattled on the dresser's surface when she bumped into it.

"Navarre."

Her hands slapped against his chest as he reached her. It didn't stop him. Punishing lips secured hers and pushed her until her back met the wall behind her.

"You intoxicate me, Giselle. You make my blood boil. You make my control break and my senses sharpen until nothing else matters. I've never had a woman before, and I can't believe it! I crave it. Shake with it. I'm on fire for you, and yet you toy with me!"

"Navarre, no! Wait! Not like this!"

He ignored her plea and lifted her to the dresser top, splitting her legs with his hips, shoving her skirts aside to put velvet clothed thighs against hers. His mouth twisted, drawing her glance.

"*Non?*"

His head dropped. Giselle whimpered as he tongued her neck and finished by nibbling her ear. His hands had moved to her waist, to hold her and then yank her to him, shoving her right against him. The hard part of him rubbed against her moisture, hard and ready, even covered by velvet. And the contact tormented. Teased. Titillated.

"*Non?*"

The touch of his tongue against her throat gave her chills. Tremors.

"You want me to stop, Giselle? Truly? Then say so. Don't just react to a man teased beyond his limits. Do you understand what I'm asking?"

He shoved again at her, brushing velvet against her apex and she was ready to scream it.

"Well, my love? Do you want me to stop? To leave you to the loneliness of yon bed? You must tell me now...while I still possess the power to go."

Giselle lurched upward, sealing her lips to his. A groan surged through them. She restlessly pawed his hair loose, barely able to breathe through the kiss.

"Is that a yes?"

"Oh yes, Navarre. Yes!"

She fumbled with the knot of his jabot for a moment, before he tossed her hands away.

"You tease me with visions of nakedness and now torment with slowness? *Non.* I think not."

He lifted her. Giselle wrapped her legs about him and clung. And then the linens of the mattress met her back. And then he pushed back from her. His eyes drilled into hers, causing such a roar in her ears that she almost missed the knocking of the maids.

"You answering that?" he asked.

She shook her head. He grinned.

"You'd better shed that dress before I get there, then."

His jacket spilled from the chair he tossed it to. His shirt followed.

"Your dress, Giselle?"

"Navarre, I...."

Her voice stopped at his motion of untying his breeches. Giselle had to look away. She couldn't watch. She could scarcely make her hands function.

"I still frighten you?"

His chuckle brushed her earlobe, and she concentrated on that, rather than the movement of his fingers on her dress hooks.

"You really aren't wearing anything else. What a vixen you're turning out to be."

His whisper ended with the firm pressure of what had to be his lips against her back, and she squealed as it tickled.

The dress did rip when it got caught at her waist. Giselle didn't care. All she wanted was Navarre. Holding to her as he explored. Imprinting his ownership everywhere he touched. He kissed the small bruises on her thighs and licked her inner knee until she screamed at him to stop.

And then he yanked her to the edge of the mattress, using the pedestal to join them. And it wasn't shock filling her moans. It was gratification. Satiation. Ecstasy. And all of it orchestrated by him.

"Giselle! Love! Giselle! Love!"

The words became a string of them, placed into existence to match his rhythm. Every thrust. Every time he pulled her toward him and then pushed away. The bed joined in again, rocking and swaying to each movement as Giselle cried with bliss again and again. And this time when he tightened everything and yelled his pleasure to the ceiling, she watched. Glorying in each palsied surge. Each twinge. Every heavy breath. Imprinting it on her memory. Stored. Saved.

The man was beautiful. Everything about this was the most heavenly of experiences. She was so lucky. She loved him.

"Aunt Mimi, may I ask you something?"

"Why...anything, Giselle. I so rarely see you out anymore. Not that I would wish things any different. I must tell you how pleased I am to hear about you and...Etienne."

She blushed and Giselle almost did, too. Her blush wouldn't be from shyness, especially after what Navarre and she had done every night for over a week. Giselle closed her eyes for a moment and held her breath and reminisced. It was paradise to be in his arms, loving her with every quiver of his body. Exploring every inch of his. And what might happen next. She caught herself impatiently waiting for sunset anymore.

She opened her eyes again. Such thoughts weren't going to accomplish her goal, and she'd been lax with her promise already.

"I'm worried about Esmee." Giselle sat below Aunt Mimi on an embroidered footstool and whispered her secret.

"Esmee? I didn't think you had time to worry about anything except...oh. My. I shouldn't bring it up, but I can't help it. It's just wonderful how you young people have taken to each other. I can hardly wait for the news." She blushed again.

"Yes, well...," Giselle cleared her throat. "All that aside, I don't think Esmee deserves to be shut up in Chateau Berchand. She's still so young, don't you think?"

Aunt Mimi looked at Giselle over the rim of her hoop. "Esmee made her own soup, dear. Now she will just have to swallow it."

And after saying that, she set her thin lips and bent her gaze back to her stitching. Giselle watched as she placed several delicate threads.

"But I'm so happy, Aunt Mimi, it almost makes me cry to see Esmee so miserable. Don't you think she deserves a husband of her own? And maybe...a family?"

Now, she was as red as Mimi. This was ridiculous.

"If she is, it's her own fault. Esmee is ineligible, my dear. Unacceptable. There isn't a man in France who would offer for her now. I told her that when Etienne welcomed her back into the family fold, I did."

She finished her row of stitches. Giselle waited while she turned the piece over and slit the thread with a sewing knife.

"What if I knew someone acceptable?"

Mimi put down her hoop with a trembling hand, but she still wore her bland expression.

"Giselle, you worry over a trifle. Esmee can spend her days being of assistance to you in running your household, or she can join a convent. She knows that."

"But I know someone. Don't you want to see Esmee happily wed?"

"There is no one, Giselle. Esmee is happy enough as she is, I assure you."

"What of children, Aunt Mimi? Doesn't she deserve to be a mother?"

"She's much too old, Giselle. You're almost too old to contemplate a first child, but given the circumstances, I'm sure the Lord will overlook your age. You don't know how dangerous it is to attempt birth at Esmee's age."

"What if I had been asked to approach her, Aunt Mimi? What if the groom was totally acceptable and declared his intentions to her. Couldn't we overlook the past, then?"

"Another *bourgeois?* I refuse to contemplate it. I already told you, Giselle dear, there are no acceptable suitors."

"Isn't the mayor acceptable? He comes from a long line of—"

"Ambross has declared himself for Esmee?"

"*Oui*," Giselle lied.

"That's startling. Hmm. I suppose, if it's Ambross, I have no objections. Have Etienne make the arrangements."

Oh no. That was the one thing she couldn't do.

Giselle almost blurted it out. She'd already tried speaking with Etienne just this morning. It was still a mortifying memory.

"You heard me correctly, Etienne," she'd told him. "*Monsieur* Ambross and you must approach him. I suppose Navarre can do it, if you're unable."

She shouldn't have added the last, but she was tired of his arguing. Not only must she abide his presence in her bed every morning, but he looked at her now as if she were crazed.

"I believe Navarre does enough of my duties already, don't you agree?"

Giselle had eyed him over the rim of her cup and tried to ignore the furious beating of her heart. She was accepting Navarre into her bed in order to save Etienne's life. He'd begged her for that very thing, hadn't he?

"We can have a small dinner party, Etienne, with just the local elite attending. If you come down to it, wouldn't that start tongues wagging?"

"*Oui*, and if I were to do so, Jean-Claude will have his opportunity. That would be worse than stupid, and I think not. Navarre can set it up. I grow tired of this whole affair."

'I'm sorry."

The harshness of the morning light made his features appear more angular than ever. He looked thinner, too, but she hadn't noticed that before.

"Are you getting enough rest, Etienne?" she asked.

"With all the howling you two do? I'm surprised anyone in the castle can sleep."

Giselle's jaw had dropped. She didn't even feel the burn from her spilled coffee. "How dare you?"

"How dare I? Surely you should look in a mirror occasionally, *Madame* la *Duchesse.*"

Giselle had opened and shut her mouth and then shut it again. He was right. No matter how beautiful, amazing, wondrous, or loving. They were still wicked for what happened. But did that mean they were to cease enjoying it? Is that what Etienne wanted now?

Giselle had turned her back on him and gone to her wardrobe room. She loved Navarre. And that was the only thing that mattered.

Giselle looked now across to Aunt Mimi, tossing off recollection of her morning argument with Etienne. She didn't want to face her conscience. Not yet. Maybe not ever.

"Etienne doesn't feel...up to...interviews of that sort, Aunt Mimi."

"Then have Navarre arrange it. It matters little at this point. Esmee a bride? I can't believe it."

"Na...varre can't arrange it."

Despite every hold she had on herself, Giselle stumbled over his name. Aunt Mimi didn't notice, though.

"Why not? He handles everything else."

"But Jean-Claude is next in line. If Etienne can't handle the arrangements, shouldn't it fall to Jean-Claude?"

"Jean-Claude?" Aunt Mimi paled.

"Unless you do it," Giselle added quickly. "As the matriarch, you can arrange it, *non?*"

"Me? Arrange a marriage? I wouldn't know the first thing about it. I feel faint. Could you have my maid bring me a cordial?"

"I'll help you." Giselle longed to shake her. "It can't be too difficult. We simply send for Mayor Ambross and accept his offer when it comes, *non?*"

"Do what you will, Giselle. Call me when the man arrives. I can't think! It's too much to ask."

She was shaking as she stood. Giselle didn't know if it was due to her age or the upcoming interview.

Ambross looked like a man summoned to his own funeral. Giselle prayed Esmee was right about him. He had to offer for her. Giselle had to get him to. Oh, she wished Navarre was here!

"I wish to thank you for your invitation, *Madame* du Berchald."

He bowed over Aunt Mimi's hand. She blushed at the contact. He'd already done the same to Giselle, and she felt him trembling when he touched her. Giselle waved the manservant from the room and waited for Ambross to sit down.

She was helping arrange her sister-in-law's marriage — she had matured a lot in the last season.

"Monsieur, you're probably wondering why Aunt Mimi and I wished to see you," Giselle said.

He gulped and nodded. Esmee waited nervously at the top of the stairs. When Giselle had told her they'd summoned Ambross, she'd almost cried in gratitude.

"We've heard of your attachment to my sister, Esmee. Haven't we, Aunt Mimi?"

She nodded, and Ambross whitened beneath all his fat. *What have I done?* Giselle wondered.

"Esmee?" He choked and dabbed his lip with a handkerchief.

"Oui. If we're not mistaken, she would welcome your suit, *Monsieur"*

"Welcome?"

"The Berchalds are prepared to offer the sum of two hundred *louis d'ors* as Esmee's dowry." Giselle knew little about money, but that sounded about right. Francois' bride had come with a thousand, and land, too.

"Did you say two hundred?" His eyes gleamed in the folds of his face.

It's always the money! Giselle thought in disgust. *From Savignen Valley to this amount, it's all men think of when gaining a bride!*

"A fortune," he breathed.

Jean-Claude burst into the room, and Giselle almost cried out like Aunt Mimi did.

"I didn't realize you had returned, Jean-Claude," Giselle said.

Hard violet-blue eyes glared at her. Despite her intention to be brave, Giselle felt the chill in her belly.

"Evidently…just in time."

Giselle looked past his shoulder and saw Esmee's face. She looked uncertain and worried.

"Aunt Mimi just finished the betrothal of Esmee to Mayor Ambross," Giselle said. "Didn't she, *Monsieur?*"

Giselle ignored Jean-Claude and looked to Ambross, although it was one of the most difficult things she ever did.

"Aunt Mimi?"

Giselle felt the shivers caused by Jean-Claude's whisper. She couldn't imagine how Aunt Mimi was taking it. Giselle knew then she'd been right. Aunt Mimi did have the authority to arrange a marriage!

"Most assuredly, *Madame,*" Ambross said. "I look forward to seeing my fiancée at her convenience."

"Of course." Giselle smiled. "I'll see her summoned to the Red Salon. Aunt Mimi, will you pull the cord?"

Giselle dared not do it herself. She wasn't moving from contemplation of Jean-Claude. And he returned the favor. And as Aunt Mimi rose, Jean-Claude took her seat. She almost cringed away from his nearness, but caught it.

"You seem interested in giving orders, Giselle," he leaned close, "but don't grow fond of giving out my gold. Do I make myself clear?"

"Your gold? Why, Jean-Claude! Such a jester you can be." Giselle laughed, but it was brittle-sounding to her own ears.

"It's no jest, *Madame.* I warn you." His words stopped, and his eyes narrowed. At the same time, his features softened. She'd never seen such a change. She knew he was going to try a different tack, and prepared herself. "You're such a lovely *duchesse,* and yet you stay sequestered with my older brother? Why would you deny the world the pleasure of your presence like that? It isn't very gracious of you."

Giselle shrugged. "It's Etienne's wish."

"What does he have to keep your interest, *ma cherie?*"

He leaned closer, and Giselle gripped the chair arms. Oh, why did she ever think herself brave?

"Why Giselle, you're not dressed for our ride. I specifically mentioned the time. Did you forget?"

Giselle struggled to control her expression as Navarre was ushered into the salon. He walked to her and bent over her hand. His attire was perfect. He looked perfect. Healthy. Clean. No one would guess he'd been up almost the entire night, although... Now that she looked closely at him, she could see a tiny scratch on his chin, and some darkening along his throat where she'd been overly amorous with kisses.

"I must...have forgotten," she stammered.

"Pity. I was looking forward to showing you the grape stamping vats. Tomorrow, perhaps?"

Giselle nodded. It seemed like the only thing she was capable of. She couldn't believe her own reaction to his touch. Even with Jean-Claude sitting right beside her, she felt the quivers from holding to Navarre.

"And Jean-Claude. Here, still? I can't imagine what the chateau has to keep you from Versailles this long,"

Navarre continued. "I've heard they mourn your continued absence."

He released her hand and turned toward his brother. Although his voice hadn't changed, Giselle didn't imagine the threat in his stance. She knew Jean-Claude wasn't immune to it, either. Navarre looked dangerous. It was strange how that thought thrilled her.

"I find things much more entertaining here, littlest brother," Jean-Claude replied in a bored tone. "Why, you never know what might happen next. First, my eldest brother consummates his marriage, and then my sister gets betrothed. I wouldn't find it odd to hear of your own wedding plans when next I wake."

"Esmee's betrothal?"

Navarre glanced at Giselle, and he shouldn't need to. She'd told him about Esmee's feelings the previous night. He said he'd handle it, but Giselle wanted to prove herself. He should understand, if anyone could.

"I just walked in on Esmee's betrothal to the mayor, and no one had the decency to notify me in advance," Jean-Claude complained.

Giselle mumbled something about Etienne needing her and escaped from the room without looking back.

She had done it!

She settled Esmee's future and no one helped her do it. When Louisa and Isabelle saw her skipping about her chamber, even they paused in their duties. Giselle simply tipped her head and smiled wider. She knew what the change was.

She wasn't a mouse anymore.

She was the *Duchesse* du Berchald.

CHAPTER THIRTY-ONE

"We'll leave Swift Night and Judgment Day here, Giselle," Navarre said.

Who would name a horse Judgment Day?

She didn't ask it aloud, because it sounded like a bad omen, and she didn't want anything to spoil her day with Navarre.

"In case any look for us, we wandered amid the vines, but you'll have to ride up with me. Can you do it?"

He shouldn't need to ask.

"I always keep a mount here. It saves time if I've been away too long or the horse is tired. Come. I'll lift you up."

Barring the cabriolet, Giselle had never been so high in her life, and she looked down in trepidation.

"Don't be frightened. I won't let you fall. I'd fall in your stead, I swear it."

Hard thighs slid into place behind her, and Giselle tried ignoring the sensation, especially when he pulled her against his chest. Because they were touring stamping vats. Nothing more.

"Where do we start?" she asked.

He didn't seem inclined to answer for a bit. They left the vineyard behind and started up a hillside. Steady heartbeats filled her ears. His soft breath teased her neck, but still, he didn't answer.

"Navarre?"

"You can't tell?"

She shook her head.

"I'm taking you to the arbor."

"The arbor? But why?"

"Need you ask?" He chuckled.

She turned in shock. "But, Navarre, it's still daylight!"

"I know." He laughed harder, and his arms tightened around her. "You don't know how many times I've imagined this, too. I felt like thanking Jean-Claude yesterday for making this a reality."

"But...we can't!"

Giselle tried to ignore the images. It felt wicked and depraved, as bad as any animal in heat. She couldn't possibly allow it. The arbor loomed before she could give voice to her rebuttal. Sunlight streamed through the greenery. She'd never seen anything so beautiful and peaceful.

Navarre slid off the horse's back behind her, and she eyed his hands. In the dark of night, hidden away in her bedchamber, it didn't seem as real as it did at that exact moment.

"I love you, Giselle."

Her eyes filled as she looked at him expectantly standing there. If she wished it, he'd remount and leave with her. She didn't need to ask. Light percolated through the leaves, touching on the bench within the greenery beyond him. Giselle's heart surged.

She leaned forward and fell into the tightness of arms that trembled as he held her. That's when she knew he'd been holding his breath, awaiting for her decision.

"And I love you, Navarre."

Lips touched hers, softly at first, then powerfully. She grabbed his jacket lapels with hands like claws. He moved, and she clung. Vines brushed her elbows, forehead, slippers, but she paid little attention to the contact. It meant she'd have some scratches to explain, but that sounded like a small price to pay for what was going to take place.

She felt the bench at her back, the give of a stem behind her head, and above all, Navarre's weight atop her. The weave of his jacket tickled her neck as he pressed into her, dropping his kisses onto her cheeks. Her nose. Her lips.

"Oh, dear God! What am I doing?" He ground out the words against her mouth and then yanked his lips from hers.

Giselle watched him lift his head. He had the oddest expression on his face. His eyes were wide with an expression bordering on disgust. She still trembled at the feel of him atop her, the length of one leg was already between her thighs, separating them.

"Navarre?" she whispered.

He heaved a breath and stood, disentangling himself from arms that felt leaden. Giselle cringed away from the look he gave her before he turned. His shoulders lifted as he sucked in air, then he gave the loudest, most raw cry she'd ever heard.

Giselle gaped. She wasn't the only one affected. More than one bird was startled from its perch and loudly proclaimed the reaction about it.

"Mon Dieu!"

Navarre yelled the words with another cry, this one deeper in timbre and lasting even longer. It raised gooseflesh all along her as she heard it.

Giselle put her hands over her eyes. She didn't dare look at him. She didn't dare look at anyone. The rustling about her quieted and she waited what seemed a long time.

"I must apologize, Giselle."

His whisper was as heart-rending as his cry had been. She turned her head and opened her eyes. He was leaning against greenery, holding back his hair with hands that trembled. She wondered what he was looking at, out beyond the horse.

"Navarre?"

"Didn't you hear me?" he asked.

"But…I'm willing. I heard you, but I'm willing, Navarre."

Giselle didn't know how she got the words out. She watched his shoulders flinch when she did.

"I know, my love. I thought I was, too. It's just…I can't explain it. I long to see you, be with you, grow old with you…love you. And I want to be seen with you! I don't want it hidden anymore…like the deceitful secret it is."

Giselle sat up slowly, brushing stray leaves and twigs from her bodice as she arranged her skirts into the proper arrangement.

"Can you understand what I'm saying?"

She nodded, but he still faced away from her, and couldn't have seen it.

"I've envisioned you here so often…your hair unbound. Your clothing strewn about. And now that I have it…I can't do it. I love you too much."

He stopped, and she waited again. She knew exactly what he spoke of.

"I thought if I possessed your body, I'd be whole. The torment would end. I was a fool. I find it so difficult to imagine being apart from you that I've created an even greater purgatory to reside in. I'm explaining this poorly, I know. You'll have to forgive me for that, too."

He turned stricken eyes to her, and Giselle's immediately welled with unshed tears.

"I was never a poet, Giselle. I never aspired to such. And then I met you. All I know is that I love you so much, it hurts. I can't believe it at times…but I also love my brother, Etienne! And you belong to him. Sometimes I fantasize of what could be, but I'm evil to contemplate that! You will never be mine unless something happens to him. It can't be. You belong to Etienne, not to me."

He fell to his knees before her and grabbed her hands with such force she winced. He didn't seem aware of what he did. He wasn't capable of seeing her. He looked like he was being sentenced for the same crime she was guilty of.

"Navarre, please don't do this. I beg it of you."

He smiled sadly.

"You see? I explained it poorly. I don't mean our love. That is a gift from the *Bon Dieu*. Never doubt that. It's the only thing that keeps me sane. And don't you dare forget, we do what we do to save Etienne. But that does not excuse my new feelings for you. The way my heart feels whenever you're close. How it aches when you're not. It's as much a part of me as breathing. I love you so much I can scarcely recall Etienne's face! But I must. I have to. Don't you see?"

He lifted her hands and touched his lips to them, but it wasn't to kiss. He was pulling back from her. Withdrawing.

"I have to also accept the fact that your child will belong to Etienne. He'll be its father. Not me! I don't think I can even contemplate how that will feel. Do you understand? I can't imagine standing by and watching as that happens. I'm no saint. I've dreamed of us together, just as our nights have shown, but it's impossible. Etienne stands in the way."

He sighed and turned away. "But for such thoughts, I'm as vile as Jean-Claude."

"No, Navarre."

He looked up and smiled, but his eyes no longer held any secret messages for her. They were as empty as glass.

"I love you, Giselle. I always will. But I can't have you. I never could. Only at night, hidden from view, can I play-act as if I can...and play-acting isn't real! God! I wish it was."

He might not have been crying, but it looked like he was. Giselle knew what he was saying. He didn't explain anything poorly. He was a master at words. She didn't try to stop him as he walked to his horse, still grazing as placidly before them.

"Come, Giselle. It grows late. We can have no whisper attached to your child, can we?"

"How do you know I carry one?"

"I don't know. I simply hope it is so. We can't do this much longer. Seeing you here made me certain. You were so pure and untouched, Giselle. I should worship at your feet, not drag you into hell with me!"

She followed and waited for him to lift her back in front of the saddle. At least she'd have the ride back with him. Navarre had opened her eyes, and he was right. The situation was worse. Now that she knew what loving meant, how could she face it when she did conceive, and it was over?

No.

Giselle refused to think of the babe as Etienne's. The entire world could say it, but she wouldn't. She loved Navarre too much. Their child would be an extension of that love. She was certain.

"Navarre?" she whispered softly.

He didn't look down at her. He watched the leaves shimmering above them, instead. She reached to touch his throat. She had her fingers against it when he gulped, and she felt the tremble of his cry. He refused to look down at her, and she knew why. It would cost him too dearly.

"I love you." She leaned against his chest.

He grabbed her about the waist and lifted her away from him and into the saddle. She instinctively knew why he didn't put her in front of it. Because he really was withdrawing. She wouldn't even get this ride.

He walked the horse slowly, shoulders slumped and his head bowed. From her solitary perch, the vineyard looked spectacularly lush as they left the trees. Giselle tried to look at anything except Navarre's back. They were well into the growing season, and purple grapes hung from every limb, contrasting with the green leaves.

Savignen Valley was well worth any price to possess it.

Except the one she was paying.

She knew she had to tell him, and it felt like she was facing execution to contemplate it. She'd been suspicious of the success of Etienne's plot, but, after swearing Louisa and Isabelle to secrecy, Giselle hoped to have a few more days, maybe weeks.

Navarre still visited her nightly, and they pretended like nothing had changed since the arbor. But it had. It was like an unspoken pact between them. They were living in a fool's world, but she still went on her knees to beg God for a few more days.

That didn't seem too much to ask, a few more days before she had to tell Navarre of her pregnancy. The knowledge would end his visits. She'd never again catch her breath at the sound of his footstep, nor cry aloud her pleasure, nor hear his groans of fulfillment. The babe would end everything that mattered for her.

That's what he'd been telling her at the arbor. And that's what she couldn't bear.

Gerty's action while Giselle was preparing for supper convinced her, though.

"I have brought a bottle of Savignen 1736, Your Grace."

Giselle watched her uncork the bottle and set it on the night table. Giselle rarely drank anymore, and Navarre wouldn't find it of interest, either.

"Savignen 1736? Why would you do that, Gerty?"

"We save it for special occasions, *Madame.* I thought it appropriate."

"I gave no such word, Gerty. You overstep yourself."

"In that case, I stand corrected, *Madame.* Shall I have it sent back to the cellars?"

Her apology was given beneath her breath. Giselle barely heard it. Gerty suspected? That meant it wouldn't be long before her brother knew. And then Etienne. And then everyone. And Giselle wanted to be the one to tell Navarre.

No. That was a lie. Giselle didn't want to tell him, at all. She wanted him to remain in ignorance as long as possible. Gerty was still standing beside the bed, her dark eyes full of curiosity and something else. She looked like she was enjoying Giselle's discomfiture.

"Isabelle has served me so well, Gerty, I find it annoying sometimes to have so many maids. Perhaps I'll speak with Esmee when she returns. She may have need of your services."

"You don't need my services?" she gasped.

Giselle had managed to break through the maid's complacent stance?

"I didn't say that. I only intimate that Esmee, being in such straits when she marries, would appreciate you far more than I would. It's something I must think over. You may go now."

"But, *Madame-*'

"You heard her, Missy," Louisa snapped. "Take your gossipy tongue below-stairs where it belongs, and make haste! Bringing wine to celebrate? I can't believe what I am hearing!"

"Calm yourself, Louisa."

Giselle waited until Gerty shut the door to speak. Louisa sighed.

"Your secret won't stay hidden much longer, Giselle."

"I know." Giselle shook her head as Louisa poured some of the wine out.

"The *Monsieur*...he will be pleased?"

Navarre? Giselle doubted that. "The *duc* will be. And that has to be enough. Oh, Louisa...how will I bear it?"

She was lucky to have Louisa. She realized it fully then. All those years when Giselle had argued and berated her companion over her incarceration, Louisa had remained loyal and patient. Giselle couldn't imagine the loneliness of her future nights, when Louisa would be her only confidant.

Once Navarre knows....

She couldn't finish the thought.

"You should be happy, you know. This child will bring such joy to this household, and I can't imagine more beautiful parents. Just think...an *enfant!*"

Her voice dropped to a whisper, but Giselle glanced down. She must have been drugged not to have thought through the consequences before, because her belly was twisting with it, now. Her nights with Navarre were ending. She would never again whisper to him in the darkness, or feel his touch, or look deeply into his eyes, or feel his nakedness pressed to hers?

"I know." Giselle tried to smile. "It's just...."

Isabelle entered the room, struggling with Giselle's ironed dress without any help with the door from Jean or Henri. That reminded Giselle of their absence. They had been given some time to themselves. Etienne wasn't out of danger. News of Giselle's pregnancy would make Jean-Claude even more desperate.

At least, he was far away. Esmee needed a new trousseau, and Jean-Claude took the ladies to the Paris *shoppes.* He was offering his approval of their outfits. As out-of-character as that was, everyone in the castle breathed easier the moment the carriage drove out of sight.

"Do I have to attend sup?" Giselle eyed the dress Isabelle carried as if it were sack cloth. "I'm not really hungry...and I dread it."

She just wanted to sleep as she had for the past week. That was one of the things that made the women suspicious of her condition in the first place.

"I suppose the family can get by without you," she replied. "It's only Margot, some retainers, and *Monsieur* Navarre of course."

"Navarre?" Giselle's voice caught. "I suppose I can make an effort to dress then. After all, I don't want Chef Aaron sulking, do I?"

She looked from one to the other, trying for an innocent expression. Louisa contorted her face as she suppressed her reaction to Giselle's words.

"I think it's a very good thing *Monsieur* Navarre lives in a different house. That is what I am thinking," Isabelle replied. "It keeps tongues still."

"Oh, Isabelle! The things you say," Giselle giggled. "As if I would be interested in *Monsieur* Navarre. I have the *duc* to keep me company. Perhaps I'll dine in with him, instead. That will give them something else to talk about. What do you say to that?"

"I think it's an excellent plan."

Louisa nodded sagely, and Giselle longed to toss something at her.

"It will give us something to do with this celebration wine, too."

"Wine? What wine?" Isabelle asked.

"Gerty brought me a bottle with which to celebrate," Giselle informed her.

"She needs better manners, may the Lord forgive her."

"Leave it for now. I grow tired of discussing it. I don't believe my husband will have further need of wine this evening, anyway."

Louisa saw through the words, if Isabelle didn't. Etienne was doing his utmost to drink himself insensible anymore. Giselle had to banish the thought. No one would believe Giselle was besotted with him, if they could but see him.

Giselle made her decision. She would tell Navarre of their baby that evening.

Perhaps, a celebration would be in order before he left her.

CHAPTER THIRTY-TWO

It was strange how hollow-sounding her bedchamber could be. Giselle surveyed it from the safety of her pillows as she waited for Navarre. Even the sound of her breathing echoed back at her. She should have had Louisa light a fire. That way, the crackling logs would dispel some of the stillness.

So this is my future.

She was wearing the most beautiful negligee she owned. Made of ivory silk, slit past her thigh, it had a bodice sewn of the finest Brussels lace to frame her bosom. She looked at the effect in the mirror before her eyes misted over with tears. She'd never be able to wear it again. It would hurt too much.

Etienne still snored. Giselle caught a hint of the louder ones again. He'd snored through supper, too. She hadn't missed his company. He hadn't anything except sarcasm for her anymore. He was too drunk to care if she ate in his chamber with him or not. That was a small favor, but she must learn to count her blessings.

There was a slight creak of a door hinge, and then Navarre was with her.

"You didn't dine with us, Giselle," he said. "I've never been so worried. Do you ail? Should I go?"

The look of concern on his face made her smile freeze. The man was so handsome! Even dressed in nondescript black leather, with his hair hidden under his hood, he was absolutely beautiful.

He was heartbreaking, true...but beautiful, too.

Giselle's eyes filled with tears, and she cursed the emotion that caused them. She didn't want to spoil this. Somehow, this night would have to see her through all the hollow-sounding nights ahead until her child was born.

But what release would that bring? She was so stupid. And their mother had even warned her of it.

"Giselle? What is it, love?"

The bed shifted as he lurched across it, gathering her into his arms. Giselle quickly looked aside. She couldn't face him. Not until she had these accursed tears banished.

"Don't cry. Please? I can't stand for that."

"I love you, Navarre,' she whispered against the leather covering his chest.

"Ah. I think I see." He kissed her hair and the arms about her tightened. "It is your woman time. And we can wait. I've been told it lasts but a sennight. I understand, but I refuse to sleep elsewhere. Help me off with this."

Giselle held his sleeves for him as he tugged his arms free, leaving her with the shirt.

"But I've never seen you wear this before," he said. "You wore it for me? *Merde!* I can't keep my thoughts, my desires, not to mention my hands from you, yet you tempt me? Is there no end to your wickedness?"

She let him talk, loving the sound of it through his chest as she snuggled against him.

"You're nearest the light." He yawned, and she followed. "You must blow it out." He kissed her forehead and settled them into the pillows.

Giselle ran her hands down his chest, using his flesh like the keyboard of a pianoforte. His skin was smooth and warm to the touch. Then she played with the satin sheet against his waist, moving it back and forth slowly.

"Giselle, I'm warning you!"

She giggled and slid further down his side in order to explore. There wasn't enough lace at her bodice to prevent skin-to-skin contact with him, and she rubbed against him greedily. He felt hot and firm. The curve of his hip filled the space between her breasts, and her fingers slid across his thigh.

"Mon Dieu! You really are a vixen!"

Large hands gripped her shoulders, hauling her to him. The hard look in his eyes was meant to be intimidating. She pursed her lips and kissed the air between them.

"What? I tell you of my understanding, and what do you do? Torment me. Toy with me, again."

Giselle felt the hard pressure of him writhing against her belly. Was it striving against his will, then? She shook, or rather the hands holding her did.

"I love you, Navarre."

She assumed he cursed her, but the words weren't clear when spat from between his tight lips. She wasn't thinking about that. She clung as he rolled, twisting them in the bedding and pinning her beneath his weight.

His hair wasn't tied back. It fell from both sides of his face, tickling where it touched. Giselle felt the contact against her chin and earlobes as she shook her head. He rained punishing kisses on her throat and breasts.

"Navarre!"

Giselle couldn't help squealing when he licked her. Her hands clenched his shoulders, kneading the muscle there. "I can't—Navarre, I beg you, I can't breathe!"

She knew he didn't believe her, for he shook now with laughter, holding her immobile while he tickled and teased.

"Navarre!"

Finally, he shifted his weight, and Giselle gulped for air while he settled his chin into the hollow of her shoulder. His eyes sparkled with mirth. Giselle let her gaze rove over every bit of his face.

"Now will you let me sleep in peace and not tease me with your beauty?"

Giselle loved the little lines that ran from the corners of his eyes down his face. She traced one with a fingernail, pulling back when he turned his face to nip at her.

"I—I'm in the family way, Navarre," she whispered.

"Hmm?"

It was difficult to concentrate on her words when he was gazing at her. His blue-violet eyes were soft and warm with love.

"Didn't you hear me?" She expected surprise, perhaps joy. Even anger would have been acceptable. He acted as if it was nothing. She couldn't believe it.

"Why do you anger, Giselle?"

"I'm not angry. Why do you think so?"

"So the family is in the way. Do you think I can forget? It's the first thing I think of every day when I awake, and the last thing I recall before I sleep. *Non.* That's a lie. I can't go a minute without thinking of you."

"That isn't what I meant, Navarre. It's done. You and I...um. *L'enfant...the* heir. We've done it, and I'm...."

Her voice stopped as his eyes filmed over with tears. The joy she'd glimpsed was quickly overshadowed by such immense sadness, she actually felt it.

"So soon?"

Giselle felt her heart lurch when he asked, then he turned and rolled away from her. He was taking the sheets and his warmth, and she knew the real reason was to disguise his emotion.

"Navarre, you can't leave me!"

She would have held to him, but he shrugged her hand away, easing those lengthy legs back into his leather breeches. She had to stop him.

"Please? I beg you!"

Something in her voice slowed him. She watched a tremor run down his back before he pulled on his shirt, hiding his skin from her. She wondered if she'd ever see such splendor again.

"Giselle. I can't stand your pleas. I'm too much of a coward, I tell you."

"No."

He turned back to her. Candlelight brought his features into sharp relief and glinted on the single track of a tear. Giselle didn't feel brave, either.

"It's been a joy beyond words, Giselle," he whispered. "Lord help me, I knew this would come. I knew it. I thought...I was prepared for it." He wiped a hand across his face. "I can't endure the thought! Your face. Your...skin!"

He turned aside, his voice dropping to a whisper, raw with emotion. Giselle hastily wiped her own tears away.

"We can run away, Navarre," she said quickly. "We'll leave Etienne. I'd go anywhere with you. Surely you know that?"

He turned back and smiled without any pleasure. Although the light was dim, Giselle saw the lines of bitterness on his face.

"I will not do that to my brother, Giselle. Think of the scandal he'd have to face. And, even if I listen, what would you have me do? I have no skills. I wouldn't even be capable of menial labor. You want to add the guilt of sentencing you to poverty to everything else?"

"If I can be with you, and have our baby with you, I can do—"

"Enough!"

Giselle pulled back, clutching the sheets to her throat at his expression. He was shouting at her. And he wasn't finished, either.

"Not *our* baby Giselle, Etienne's! You carry the Berchald heir! If you think I desire this child, you're mistaken! I hate it, I tell you! I hate it as much as I hate myself!"

The connecting door crashed open with such force, Navarre's mouth fell open, stopping his words. Giselle was grateful. She was displacing pillows in her haste to hide. Get as far from him as possible. He hated the baby? She'd heard it, but her mind didn't accept it.

"How many times must I ask it of you, *Madame* la *Duchesse?*"

Etienne stumbled over her title. His bleary red eyes focused on her perch against the headboard. "Do you think it a pleasure to listen to you two night after night?"

"You're drunk, Etienne."

Navarre's words were hushed, but frightening-sounding. Giselle trembled even more as she heard them, but Etienne seemed unaffected.

"Drunk? Of course I am. Do you think it easy to listen while my wife adulterates me?"

Giselle gasped, earning another glare from Etienne.

"Acting like little more than a woman of the—"

"Stay your tongue!"

Giselle thought she'd seen Navarre angry before, but it was nothing to this. The red color rising up his throat, the narrowed eyes, and the lowered head seemed to be someone else. She couldn't imagine anyone more predatory-looking.

"If you value anything, Etienne, you'll go back into your chambers. Now. Before you say something for which there is no apology good enough."

His whisper terrified Giselle. Etienne seemed to shrivel in his chair.

"What do you think I'm made of, Navarre, stone?" he asked. "Do you think I care nothing for my wife? She's my wife, damn you! Is nothing sacred to my brothers? I know I'm only half a man. I see it every time the drink wears off, but does that change anything? *Non.* I'm still a man. And that is still my wife."

He turned to Giselle, and she couldn't look away. Blue eyes filled with drink and remorse regarded her. She gulped past the constriction in her throat.

"Perhaps, if I had been the one, Giselle?" he asked.

"The...one?" She was surprised the words made sound.

He smiled. Despite his unkempt appearance, she saw the man he once was. He was a handsome specimen, equally as beautiful as Navarre, just different.

"To fetch you," he added. "If it were possible for me to come—what am I saying? You know the truth. If I possessed enough courage to come and get you, would you have wanted me instead?"

Giselle couldn't see his face any longer through her tears. There was no way to answer such a question. Navarre backed from the area, leaving her range of vision. Giselle ignored his movement, for she couldn't answer otherwise.

"I'm sorry, Etienne," she said softly.

His head fell forward, and Giselle covered her face with her hands. It wouldn't have mattered who she met first. She'd never love anyone like she loved Navarre.

"I suppose I already knew the answer. But I had to ask."

The sarcasm was back in his voice and Giselle pulled her hands down.

"It's no matter, Etienne." Navarre went on his knees before his brother. Giselle tensed for what she knew he was going to say. "I won't be coming here again. It's finished."

"But you must, Navarre," Etienne said. "Forgive me, I was crazed! I still...Jean-Claude! He may...'"

Giselle held her breath.

"He'll gain nothing from your death now. He can't inherit. Giselle...." Navarre's voice cracked on her name, making her heart skip a beat. "She carries your son. It was what we were so loudly discussing."

"My...son?"

Etienne slurred the words. Giselle barely heard it over the roaring in her ears.

"*Oui.* If the *Bon Dieu* is merciful."

"This is wondrous news! It deserves a bit of cele...cele...bah! My tongue fails me. I need a glass of wine. And look! Savignen 1736. Perfect."

He'd rolled to the bedside table and grabbed up the bottle Gerty had uncorked for Giselle. After two swallows, his expression began changing. Then, he choked and spat the ruby-colored liquid down the front of his shirt.

"This wine. It's so...so bitter...."

Navarre leaped to catch him as he lurched forward. The motion knocked both of them to the floor.

"Etienne! No! Dear God, no! Giselle! The wine!"

A trail of red stained the rug at his knees. Giselle threw off the covers, stupidly noticing she still wore the negligee she'd planned to seduce Navarre with.

"Etienne! *Non!*" Navarre slapped his brother's face so hard, Etienne's head rocked. "*Non. No.* Please God no!"

He cried and kept shouting at ears that couldn't hear anymore. Giselle tripped as she stepped off the ledge, forgetting it was there.

"Don't touch the wine, Giselle!"

"The wine?"

She knelt and lifted the bottle, dripping some of the liquid on her fingers.

"It's poisoned! Etienne's dead because of it. He wanted to celebrate the news. Oh God, and I wanted— no! This isn't what I wanted, *Dìeu!* How can I ever forgive myself?"

He rocked and crooned to his limp brother as Giselle set the bottle down. She shook so hard, she tipped it over again. She had to grip it between both hands the next time.

"Don't touch it, Giselle! This is all my fault!" Navarre wailed.

Giselle thought she'd heard his cry of pain in the arbor. She'd been ignorant. This cry of agony came from the depths of his being.

"What can I do, Navarre? Tell me! Should I fetch someone?"

Navarre's arm shot out to stop her. He gripped her upper arm in a fist that would leave a mass of bruising. She winced.

"You forget yourself, Giselle."

His tone was cold. Deadly. A match to his eyes as he cradled Etienne with one arm and held her with the other.

"I'm not supposed to be here. Remember?"

He enunciated each word, everything on him condemning and brutal. She was going to be ill.

"You'll do nothing. Do you hear me?"

He let go of her arm. Giselle clapped her hands to her mouth and scooted from him. Shivers rippled up and down her back. She was ready to retch and he commanded her to do nothing?

"Give me time to reach the maze, Giselle! Listen to me, damn it!"

He was speaking harshly to her, because she was near to fainting. That was the reason, she reassured herself. She watched him set Etienne onto the floor and touched his cheek for a moment before rising. Giselle couldn't move her eyes.

"Giselle! You understand? I need time. Two...maybe three minutes. At least to reach the maze. Then call for help. Not before. You understand?"

"Navarre?"

She looked up as she whispered and saw him blanch. Against the black of his cape, he looked the shade of Jean-Claude's face paint. She thought he wasn't going to answer as he turned and walked stiffly toward Etienne's room.

"What is it?"

He turned at the door, his gaze flickering from where she was crouched to Etienne and back.

I love you.

She didn't have the courage to say it after all, but she could have sworn that he heard it. His lips thinned as he frowned.

"I didn't truly believe in hell until now, Giselle. I just wonder what it will be like to live in it."

She gasped. His words were so cold. So bitter. So hate-filled.

"Au revoir."

The door shut before his words reached her, but it wouldn't have mattered. It was good-bye and she knew he meant it.

CHAPTER THIRTY-THREE

"You're not going, and that's final."

Giselle glared at Louisa from the pillows, then let her head fall back. There was little use in arguing. The last thing she wanted was to attend a Berchald family meeting, anyway.

"You heard the doctor, Giselle," Louisa continued. "He's the expert, *oui?* Not that my own recommendation for bed rest wasn't justified, but they had to have it from a physician."

"But I need to know what's happening! It's enough that I wasn't allowed to attend Etienne's wake."

"Of course not. That child is the only thing standing between the family and that horrible man!"

"The baby's doing fine, I tell you. And I can't stay abed much longer. Isn't eight days enough?"

"You think they noticed your absence? Even his mother hasn't been here!"

Louisa placed her hands on her hips to lecture. Giselle looked away.

"Of course they noticed that Etienne's widow didn't attend. It was totally déclassé, and you know it."

"Not when you suffered a collapse."

"A collapse? Is that what they call it? Those doctors need more training."

Giselle settled back into the pillows, willing patience into her limbs. That's what they thought of her incessant screaming?

"I know the truth, Giselle, and I told the doctor of it, too."

"What did you tell him?"

"Don't take that tone with me, young lady. I would never let one hint of scandal near your name, and you know it."

"Forgive me, Louisa...it's just...I'm so out-of-sorts. I don't even miss Etienne. Does that make me a bad person? I mean...worse than I already am?"

"You're a woman expecting the Berchald heir, Giselle. That baby will be adored and cherished. And you just saw your husband die a gruesome death. That is what you are, Giselle. That's all you are."

"Oh...if only that were true."

"It is in my heart. It will be in yours, I assure you. Just you wait until they place that babe in your arms, Giselle. You'll see."

"*Merci,* Louisa," Giselle whispered.

"There, you go again with those tears. It's all well and good for a new widow to take on so, but you only have me for an audience, you know."

"It's not an act." Giselle sighed. "I wish it was."

"I know that, love. I'm just trying to lighten my sentence."

"What?"

"The doctor said you're to stay in bed and not move unless I assist you. So. Here I am. Sentenced to listen to all your complaints. Such is my life."

"If only *Monsieur* Navarre would answer my messages. Are you still sending them?"

"With dreadful consistency. He doesn't come because his hands are full dealing with all the relatives that continue to arrive. Relations? They act like vultures, pecking at each other with their tongues. Your husband's demise has given them a bit of gossip fodder, too. That, and Esmee's betrothal. You should see them around her. It's quite amusing."

Giselle smiled and tried to imagine it.

"They're also caught up in trying to ferret out this mysterious love interest of *Monsieur* Navarre. Now that, you should see. He's as tight-lipped as anyone could wish, though."

"I wish he'd come, then. Oh! Why won't he?"

"He has to give it time, Giselle. He can't simply waltz into his late brother's widow's rooms, and woo her, now can he?"

"You do think he will, though?"

"Oh, please, Giselle, grant me some wits here. Haven't I been right all along?"

"I must see him."

"No. You must rest. That's what you must do."

"I have to know what they decide, though. Navarre can't refuse this request. If he does, I'll storm into their little—"

"You'll do no such thing. *Merde!* You're so stubborn. I tell you what I'll do. I'll have Isabelle stand at the door. She will have to swallow her shyness and accost *Monsieur* Navarre for you. Will that suffice?"

Giselle nodded, thinking she had finally got around Navarre's refusal to see her. He had to speak with her now. He just had to.

She should have known there was nothing she could do to force it, however. She was beginning to think he'd really meant good-bye when he'd said it. No matter what accosting Isabelle did, Navarre wasn't going to come and see the newest dowager *duchesse.*

Louisa lifted the bolt that evening to admit Esmee.

"I've been so worried, Giselle," Esmee said. "We all have. The doctors won't tell us anything useful."

"I'm doing splendidly, as you can see." Giselle tried to greet her with a smile, but her disappointment was so vivid, the emotion had to be showing on her face.

"Thank heavens! I'm not the only one who thanks you from the bottom of my heart for the child. You don't have any idea—"

"What was said at the meeting?" Giselle didn't want to hear, yet again, how much the child meant to everyone — except from its father.

She was asking for the stars. But it couldn't be true. He hated the baby?

"Of course, it was Jean-Claude all along. He used Gerty's help, the simple-minded fool. I don't think I've ever seen Navarre as severe with anyone before."

"What happened?"

"Gerty wailed how it was all her fault. The hair stood up on the back of my neck when I heard it. Stupid woman. Of course it was her fault. We knew who brought the bottle. Then Jean-Claude spoke up in front of all of us."

"Jean-Claude was there?"

"*Oui.*"

"Who else?"

"Only Navarre, Jean-Claude, and myself. Aunt Mimi was too frightened to come, and Mother's gone. I don't know where she went. I think Navarre knows, but he's not saying."

She finished on a plaintive note, and Giselle understood how Louisa felt about her complaining. Giselle wanted to shake Esmee.

"Jean-Claude told Gerty to silence her tongue. He didn't even raise his voice to make her weep harder. That's when Navarre told him if he didn't keep quiet, he'd have Jean-Claude chained into the same tower he tried to toss Etienne from. I almost screamed."

"Navarre said that?"

"*Oui,* and more. Jean-Claude didn't say another word, either, but I watched Gerty look to him."

"What happened then?"

Giselle knew Louisa was listening from the door. She didn't blame her.

"Navarre asked who had given her the wine, although we already knew. She said *Monsieur* Jean-Claude gave her the wine. He said it was to celebrate. He promised you would come to no harm. She begged not to be blamed for the death. We couldn't even make out the last of her words, for she threw herself at Navarre's feet and started crying hysterically. It was as dramatic as any theater."

"What did Navarre do?"

"He looked at Jean-Claude and asked him what he put in the wine. I held my breath. It was useless to get any more information from Getty. She wouldn't be able to talk for a while. She looked like an infant in the midst of a tantrum. I'm surprised you didn't hear her wailing."

"What did Jean-Claude say?"

"He laughed, and I almost swooned to hear it. 'Arsenic,' he said. 'Besides, you've got no right to question me, because I'm the *duc* now, aren't I?' I can't tell you how horrified I was to realize he was right. If he becomes *duc,* we'll all perish."

"Navarre did nothing? I can't believe what I am hearing."

"Of course he did something. He told Jean-Claude of your child. It is such wonderful news, and at such a welcome time. Even if it's a girl, Jean-Claude has to wait to know for certain. So, we have a few months before we have to worry."

"I think I'm rather tired, Esmee. Thank you for coming."

"You don't want to hear what happened to Gerty?"

Louisa stopped escorting Esmee to the door. She was as intrigued at Gerty's punishment as Giselle was.

"Is she being charged?" Giselle asked.

"Charged? Imagine the horror. I've lived through scandal once already. Why, I still remember—"

"Discharged, then? She's being released without references?"

"Not...exactly."

"So, she's not being punished at all? Why am I not surprised? I don't want to hear the rest. You may leave me."

"Oh *non,* she's being punished, Giselle. I suspect before she's done she'll wish she'd been charged, instead."

"What would be justice...in Navarre's eyes...for trying to poison me and causing the *duc's* death? Well?"

"She's being sent to Mother's household."

"To Marguerite? I suppose Jean-Claude smiled at that. Go now, Esmee. You make my head ache with your talk."

"I'm sorry, *Madame,*" Louisa said. "She needs her rest. Doctor's orders."

"Navarre promised Mother will see Jean-Claude is punished severely," Esmee added at the door. "And I believe him."

"Forgive me if I laugh." Giselle turned away and waited for her to leave.

"This won't affect my engagement, will it?" Esmee asked.

Giselle was going to have to remonstrate Louisa for not escorting *Madame* Esmee out quicker.

"The engagement has already been announced, Esmee. There may be cause for shortening the mourning period. Navarre should be the one you ask. Good night."

"But, can't you do something? You have his ear. You're the—."

Louisa shut the door as Esmee kept talking.

Giselle got up late that evening. She couldn't stay another moment in her bed. She told Louisa of her decision as she checked the door.

"There are too many memories in this dark, somber room," she said.

It wasn't simply the image of Etienne's death, there were many other memories. Love-imbued nights. Navarre asleep beside her...his limbs entwined with hers. She refused to stay a moment longer. She'd move to the ducal chamber. Surely that would be acceptable if a grief-stricken widow used her late husband's rooms. She didn't ask Louisa, but she knew the woman approved, too.

Even in Etienne's room, though, surrounded by silver and black bedding, Navarre still haunted her. She couldn't sleep, and it got very hot every time she tried. All she managed to do was toss and turn.

"Merde! Help! Help me! *Mon Dieu!* Help!"

The moment Giselle heard Louisa's screams, she knew what was happening. Jean-Claude wouldn't allow his inheritance to slip so easily through his fingers. Giselle ran to the connecting door and surprised Jean-Claude. Her heart nearly stopped beating when she saw he was clad in the same type of black leather outfit Navarre used to wear. He had climbed through the open window, and he was struggling with Louisa on her make-shift cot, thinking it was Giselle.

Her strangled cry alerted him. Giselle barely had time to slam and lock the door before he struck it. The wood bent inward under the blow.

The hinges groaned as Jean-Claude struck the door again, and Giselle twisted her hands together in anguish. He would win - he always did. Then, heat seemed to swell out at her from the unlit fireplace, jogging her memory and making her think.

She ran to the fireplace, cursing the lack of light as she felt for the tiny bump that had to be there.

"I'll get you yet, my petite *duchesse!"* Jean-Claude's shouts came easily through the door. "And when I do? You'll wish you'd never set foot in my castle!"

The door ruptured just as she knew it would. The noise covered up the sliding motion of the panel beside the fireplace. Giselle stepped into the secret passageway. She heard Jean-Claude's shout of surprise as the panel closed behind her.

But she couldn't stay there. Giselle fought rising panic. The blizzard of pulse beats in her ears. Loss of visibility. No daylight was percolating through any slits, leaving her in total blackness. Giselle felt with her foot until a step stopped her progress. And that step went up.

No!

That was the wrong way. The wall at her ear trembled with a blow. She ran the other way, ignoring her own safety. She had to find the staircase. But she tripped, stifling the cry as she fell. She scraped along the stone wall, and when it abruptly ended, she bounced painfully down the opposite wall. She had a moment's panicked thought of perishing here. In this passage. With only Jean-Claude for a witness.

She slammed into a floor, grunting as pain lanced through her shoulder and hip. The breath was knocked out of her, too.

"Secret passages can't hide you, my lovely, little Giselle."

Jean-Claude's torch lit the area above her, and she nearly screamed. He'd found the door lever? Already? No. He probably tore through the panel. And what did it matter? She forced herself to her feet to run. She had a slight advantage within the walls, because they weren't very wide. Jean- Claude wouldn't find it as easy to catch her. And his torch shed a little light.

She had to get to the dower house. She had to reach Navarre. That meant she had to negotiate the maze. But she could do it. She knew the secret. Louisa had told her some time ago.

Stay to the left.

She found slivers of light, and then a peephole, and a moment later, the lever. Then she was out of the castle and onto the grounds. Even outside, it was dark. Thick with fear. Heavy with exertion. And then she entered the maze, where the hedge walls closed in on her.

She kept left, feeling her way along bushes that scratched and tore at her nightgown, then her arms. And then the skin of her belly. Yet the warmth stayed at her right side, never waning.

Right?

"Oh, Giselle! Little *duchesse*! Where are you my little, pregnant *duchesse*? You can't hide in here forever! Jean-Claude will find you, you know."

He was taunting her, creating heart-racing fright, and panic-laced steps.

"You'll never reach safety. Stupid woman! You're all stupid. All I want is my rightful inheritance...and what do I get? Little duchesses that are increasing with the newest *duc*! Blast and damn your soul!"

The heat intensified until it burned her cheek, and Giselle finally followed it, hugging a statue when she ran into it. Almost immediately, the hedge behind her rustled and swayed as Jean-Claude must have raced past.

Oh, dear God! He'd been that close? Giselle stuck a fist in her mouth to stifle the scream.

"Come along, Giselle. Stop hiding! This is a very big maze. And you are such a petite thing. And look. You didn't even bring a candle for light. I find such stupidity refreshing. Your naiveté stimulating. Who knows? Perhaps we can come to a mutually satisfactory arrangement...as soon as that bastard you carry is destroyed! What do you say to that, Giselle?"

His voice faded, and she could tell he'd stopped to listen for her. Giselle couldn't remain clutching a chunk of faceless marble forever. She had to find Navarre, and only Bertina could help her. Perhaps the *Bon Dieu* would help too, if she asked it. It had been so long since she'd prayed for something besides sin, that she was almost afraid.

"Help me, Lord," she began.

"All you have to do is lose it. I've a potion to help, too! Come, Giselle. No one needs to die!"

A stitch of pain hit her belly, making her gasp. The sound blocked out Jean-Claude's words and everything else. She cupped her hands over the place that would be her baby, filled with foreboding so violent, it iced. And then it froze.

Oh no. No. Nothing must happen to the baby! She couldn't bear it.

"Ma petit! Are you still hiding from me? You long for games? Very well. I will play along, then. It will be amusing."

Jean-Claude still called for her, using the same endearment Navarre used. Giselle had to move away from the statue. Only by moving was she safe. She tiptoed along wall after wall of shrubbery, stifling cries as twigs scratched her face, or her arms, or her exposed belly. And whenever she reached a crossing, she went right. She didn't dare follow the left.

Another pain almost forced her to her knees. She staggered through it, taking short breaths until it eased. Oh no. She *was* losing the baby! And there wasn't anyone to care. Or know. The life she and Navarre had created was being snuffed out.

And Jean-Claude would win.

Lights filtered through the bushes at her nose. Giselle pushed her face into the shrubs, narrowed her eyes, sensing Navarre and safety. He was so close, but so unreachable. Again.

Still.

"Which way, Bertina?" she whispered. "Show me the way!"

No warmth answered. Nothing. Giselle scraped along the bushes that lined the drive. What she wouldn't give for a sword. A knife. An ax. Anything to cut through this barrier and reach the security she could see, but not touch. And then she heard Navarre.

Her heart jerked to a stop, her knees gave. And her belly sent another solid pain lancing through her.

"Jean-Claude? What are you doing here?" Navarre asked.

"Where is she?" Jean-Claude demanded loudly. "You can't hide her forever."

Giselle watched him shove past Navarre, using a vicious gesture that almost sent Navarre over the railing. He caught it and swiveled, yanking Jean-Claude to a stop with a hand on his arm.

"Who? Who are you chasing?" Navarre asked.

"None of your concern."

If you've done anything to Giselle, I swear I'll kill you!"

"Save your threats for those frightened of you, little brother. Where are you keeping her, the salon?"

Jean-Claude's voice faded as he entered the dowager house. Giselle released the breath she'd been holding. She was safe, at least for a while.

Bertina had deserted her, though. Giselle knew she had to make the decision herself, so she went right once again. It was the correct one, because she crawled onto the small pebbles of the driveway as another pain laced through her back.

It couldn't be the baby if it was in her back, could it?"

"Navarre? Help me. Navarre?"

Her whisper was drowned out by the sound of an approaching coach. Giselle was forced back into the hedge as six mounted men filled the courtyard. And if she wasn't mistaken, they wore the uniform of the king's guards.

"We've come for *Monsieur* Jean-Claude du Berchald," the leading man said to Navarre's servant.

Giselle thought the man was going to faint. He slid back against the door frame as the soldier dismounted.

"Come, my good man. Wake your master."

"That won't be necessary." Jean-Claude stepped onto the landing with Marguerite directly behind him.

Giselle scooted deeper into the bushes, snagging her hair, and scraping her scalp. Marguerite was at the dower house? She didn't attend Etienne's funeral but was sheltering here?

"I am Jean-Claude, *duc* du Berchald. I take offense at this interference into my family affairs. The king shall hear of this."

"Mother?"

Navarre stepped out from behind them. Giselle tried to call out to him as she watched, but her voice wasn't cooperating. She watched as Navarre gave his mother support.

Marguerite turned to Jean-Claude, just as Giselle saw the dark stain spreading down her gown. That was it, then. She'd lost the baby. She recognized the symptoms of hysteria, making her breathe too rapidly and shallowly. She had to force it away. She gripped her hands into fists and started swallowing over and over again, whole hot tears spilled from both eyes. And then she heard Marguerite speaking. The words brought Giselle's head up.

"There is no mistake, nor is there any interference, Jean-Claude, my son. These soldiers possess a *Lettres de Cachet,* signed by the king, that bears your name."

"A *Lettres de Cachet?*" He spat out the words. "Have you lost your senses, Mother?"

"No, Jean-Claude, no. I have finally found them."

Giselle forced herself to stand and moved around the closest horse. If she didn't find help soon, she might not be conscious long enough to save herself. The pain in her side was gaining, making everyone's words blur together.

"Not the Bastille!" Jean-Claude said.

"It's more than you deserve. Did you think I'd allow Etienne's death to go unpunished? No matter how much I love you, he was my son, too."

"Etienne?"

Jean-Claude laughed, a high-pitched sound. Giselle stumbled to her knees, feeling the rocks scraping her knees. Although it stung, she concentrated on it gratefully. It would help her to stay conscious.

"I wouldn't have harmed him. You must know that. I'd be a fool to do so after your warnings, wouldn't I?"

"More lies? Take him away."

Giselle was shocked out of her own misery by the stern tone Marguerite was using. Jean-Claude was probably white under all his paint.

"It's no lie, damn it! The wine wasn't for Etienne. It was a mistake, I tell you. It was for that little *duchesse* and her bastard!"

He made a strange garbled noise, and Giselle looked up, ignoring the ache in her entire body. Navarre had hit him! One of the soldiers had to pull him off Jean-Claude, and Giselle saw the blood gushing from his nose.

"Enough!"

Soldiers surrounded Jean-Claude and shoved a gag into his mouth. Giselle suspected he might choke, yet still, she heard someone screaming. She didn't know it was her.

"Oh my God, Giselle!" Navarre leapt the stairs and ran to her. "Mother! Quickly! Send for the doctors."

Giselle felt him lift her, but she struggled weakly against him.

He hated the baby. The baby.

"Navarre...the baby," she whispered. "I'm losing...the baby."

Blackness was closing in. She could hear the jingle of the horse harness as the soldiers left with their captive as silently as they'd appeared. There was a familiar tingle at her fingertips. Her nose.

She only wished she'd lost consciousness before she saw Navarre's look of horror.

CHAPTER THIRTY-FOUR

"Be still, *Mademoiselle* Patrice, or I won't be able to finish."

Giselle sat as stiffly as possible, obeying Sister Evangeline's words. The sister was preparing Giselle's hair for what would have been the ultimate sacrifice just five short months earlier.

Shaving the scalp was a ritual Giselle knew she'd face eventually. It was a small thing, really, but vanity was such a curse. She tried to pretend it didn't matter, and after a few moments, she felt it was true. She may have been called a beauty in her past life, but no one would think so now. Not with her hair thick with dark fluid.

It didn't matter, yet tears pricked at her eyes. How odd. She thought she was done with tears as she felt the familiar burning sensation behind her eyelids.

"I have something for you, *Mademoiselle.*"

Giselle looked up from contemplation of her ragged fingernails and met Sister Evangeline's glance in the mirror. The Sister smiled and Giselle returned it, fighting the impulse to cry, instead.

"My mother gave this to me the night before I took my vows. She said it would give me something to think about during the long night ahead."

Sister Evangeline didn't have to explain. Giselle knew she was expected to spend the time praying. After fasting for two days and nights, she was to make certain of her commitment before dawn.

Sister Evangeline reminded Giselle a bit of Louisa. She held out a book. It was a slender volume and Giselle stiffened at the title — *Sonnets of Love.*

Love?

There was no such thing.

"Merci, Sister." She accepted the book, and not one inflection betrayed anything.

"I'll be right outside, *Mademoiselle* Patrice. If you have need of anything, just call."

"Thank you."

Giselle watched the door shut softly behind Sister Evangeline. Everything the nuns did was soft and muted. Quiet. Unobtrusive. As if they weren't truly living life, just existing through it.

Such thoughts wouldn't serve her now. Giselle had to stanch them. She looked at the volume in her hands, turning it over at length and wondered if she had the courage to read even a little.

She opened the cover and read the inscription — *To my love, my Evangeline.*

Giselle fought the urge to put the book down, and looked at the door instead. It seemed Sister Evangeline had turned her back on love, too. Giselle wondered why she was surprised. She dropped her eyes and read.

Pen was ne'er touched to page, With more love than I gave!

My spirit trembles, and yet.... Nothing stops the dawn from coming,

The past from rushing in. I am dead.... For I ne'ermore live.

Giselle didn't need such sentimentality now. She already made her choice. *Navarre!*

Giselle wrapped her arms around herself to stave off the agony. She wasn't going to cry. She mustn't cry. She had to be stronger than this!

Tears served no purpose. The baby was not hers to mourn. And Navarre had never been hers. It was now a fact. He was as far away as the stars themselves.

I mustn't cry!

She lost Navarre the moment she lost the child. Or, perhaps it was sooner than that — it may have been when he told Etienne the news.

What did it matter when? It still happened. Giselle couldn't afford to give in to the emotions. She had to stop any tears. It couldn't possibly matter when—

It matters when. It does.

The little book slid from her fingers as she knelt on the cold stone, bending to touch her forehead to it. She was aching to make the coldness one with her heart, and yet knew she'd fail before she even started.

Navarre!

Giselle's hands splayed onto the floor, pressing so hard against the unbending surface that she tore the skin. She ignored the pain.

"Don't leave me to this, *Mon Dieu!* Please?"

Giselle raised her face, looking over a ceiling spliced with one narrow beam. Nothing else. No answer came. Because she didn't deserve one.

God had deserted her. He wasn't there when Navarre was summoned to Versailles. He hadn't listened to Giselle's prayers when *Mademoiselle* Charmaine had visited for Christmas, laughing and chatting with the residents about her upcoming betrothal – or perhaps, what was really a renewed betrothal – all about how well all the *duchesse's* jewels were going to look on her. God wasn't listening to any of Giselle's pleas, and it was time to look at why.

She was a sinner. Unworthy. Unloved. And exactly what Charmaine said - unwanted.

I mustn't do this! Not again!

Giselle had made the decision the following morning, Christmas day, allowing only Isabelle to help her escape Chateau Berchand's walls. Louisa would never have let her go. She'd have informed the new duc, and Giselle couldn't have stood it. She couldn't see standing in the shadows watching Navarre. Knowing that when he went to his chamber, he'd be loving his wife. Charmaine. His body against hers. In that enormous bed...

"Forgive me, Father...."

She put her mind back on her vows. In very few hours, she'd no longer have a right to such thoughts. No more jealousy could taint her heart. Because God would know she was lying again.

"...for I have sinned."

Giselle's whisper broke as tears flooded her eyes, and she stifled the horror inside herself.

I mustn't cry. I mustn't cry!

"Dear God, my baby! Why did You have to take the baby? He was an innocent, and I would have given anything for him. Anything!"

The walls were deaf, too. Still, Giselle glared at them. Sister Evangeline should have already shaved her hair. Then, she wouldn't be able to pull at it in anguish, staring blindly at the strands of white in her fingers. That was amusing. Briefly. Giselle had pulled enough hair out, she might not even look freakish, anymore. Soon it wouldn't matter, anyway. Nothing would.

What did that poem say again? Something about no longer living?

Giselle retrieved the book and sat at the edge of the cot to read it. She'd been given a book of heart-felt love sonnets. Tonight. As if words could replace it. She'd tasted such love. Tasted it, and then lost it. Perhaps this book was part of her penance.

I cannot live without love, There are not days enough....

To hold my sorrow.

Giselle slammed the book shut as a vision of Navarre's features overwhelmed her, making her stomach ache with the force of her sobs. She no longer cared if Sister Evangeline heard.

If only Marguerite had acted sooner, then none of this would have happened.

Giselle held the book to her breast for a bit. She was lying to herself. She was trying to turn her pain and hate onto Marguerite. It was a useless gesture, and she knew it. Marguerite was the one who'd gained justice. The one who'd sentenced her most beloved son to the Bastille. An unnamed prisoner. A life sentence. Without possibility of freedom. Forgotten.

Oh...if only she'd done it sooner! If only Navarre didn't blame himself! If only....

The candlelight sputtered to the base. Giselle glanced at it. She had little light left. She wouldn't ask for more candles, however. She learned her lesson the first night here.

"Candle wax costs francs, dear *Mademoiselle* Patrice, and it's an expense the convent can't sustain. I'm sorry," the nun had said.

Yes, they were sorry, but that didn't make it easier. Nothing ever would. Because Giselle didn't regret Etienne's death. That sin couldn't be repented. It wasn't forgivable. And there wasn't anywhere to hide from it.

The darkness made it all worse. Giselle watched the candle sputtering with anxiety. She was afraid. So afraid. Louisa had been wrong, after all. Giselle was a coward. But in the dark, with nothing to look at, the memories were worse than unbearable. They were excruciating. God knew it, too. Giselle suspected it was her punishment.

The candle sputtered again, the flicker warning her as it wallowed in the melted wax.

"Not yet!" Giselle crouched beside that tiny bit of light. "I'm so frightened! *Mon Dieu.* I'm so frightened."

She cupped her hands about the flame, helping it live for a little longer.

"No!"

Her cry echoed after the light died, and she crept to her cot by touching the wall for guidance.

There could be nothing worse than complete darkness. It was a darkness even prayers couldn't penetrate. Darkness that made Navarre seem so close. Her eyes refused to cooperate. Giselle kept drying them on her blanket, vowing she was done with tears. Tears were for the weak of heart. She had to be stronger than that.

I mustn't cry! Nothing on earth is worth such tears.

"You cry, *ma petit?!* How many times must I beg you not to cry? It makes my own heart ache and my eyes fill. What? You don't believe me?"

Navarre smiled at her, warming the air around her until the blanket seemed unnecessary even in the cold, tiny room.

"How you've changed, little one," he told her. "In the span of less than a year, I'd hardly recognize my shy beauty from Antilli."

"Navarre, I'm so sorry about the baby. So very sorry."

His hand caressed her face, thrilling her as his fingers touched her throat and chin. And then he spoke.

"It's no matter, Giselle. Really. Because I hated it."

"You're ready, *Mademoiselle* Patrice?"

"I'm not sure."

Giselle whispered it to her reflection and waited for it to answer. She hadn't slept. It would have been impossible to sleep.

Oh, why do I keep lying to myself?

She woke with the bells, her body so tightly wrapped in her thin blanket she had to stand in order to unwind it. She was bathed in sweat, too. It took most of her cold water to wash it off.

"I've brought the razor and strop, *Mademoiselle.*"

Razor?

Oh yes. She remembered. She was having her head shaved. Because today she was joining the sisters of one of the largest convents in all of France. That is what she was doing. Because that's what she wanted.

"Come in, Sister," she said. "I am ready."

Giselle hadn't had access to pincers like the ones Isabelle had once used on her, and her eyebrows no longer arched as subtly as they used to. Her complexion would give Louisa fits if she saw it, but that didn't matter. Mottled red spots covered her forehead, and deep circles were all about her eyes. It was a good thing she was sealing herself where no man would see her again. Even Navarre wouldn't think her a beauty anymore.

Oh, why did she have to think of him? Wasn't it enough torment to have her dreams filled with him until even the hint of darkness made her heart pound in fear? Did the loss have to extend to every waking hour, as well?

"Thank you for leaving me this, Sister."

Giselle pressed the book of verse into the nun's hands. Her eyes filled, along with Sister Evangeline' s.

"Don't cry, Sister," Giselle said. "I am content."

"Mademoiselle Patrice, you possess a lovely spirit. The church will benefit from it. You have no regrets?"

"Non." Giselle looked away, unable to meet the nun's gaze as she lied.

"Very good. Please have a seat, and we'll begin. I brought sanctified water."

"Merci." Giselle dipped her fingers into the holy water in order to trace a cross upon her front.

Navarre!

She couldn't seem to banish his image. It was as if he mocked her from the mirror. She looked away at the cross above her bed, the rosary hanging beneath it, and the small window.

A knock stopped Sister Evangeline's hand before she made the first cut. A hint of impatience crossed her face before she dropped Giselle's hair — not that she'd ever let that be known. The sisters let no emotion upset their calm. Giselle wondered how long it would be before she achieved that, and if she ever would.

"Mother Superior requests *Mademoiselle* Patrice's presence, Sister," a voice called.

"The *mademoiselle* hasn't been prepared yet."

"It is of the upmost importance, Sister."

"Very well, but this is most irregular."

Giselle watched Sister Evangeline shut the door on the young novice's face before walking back to her.

"I can't think what the mother wants, *Mademoiselle,* but we must do as we are requested in this life, *non?*"

She acted so much like Louisa, Giselle averted her eyes. Her hair was hidden under a wimple. Giselle saw how dreary she would look in the future just before they left her cubicle.

Light fell on Sister Evangeline's head from the high windows. Bright. Probably warm. It didn't reach Giselle. That was all right. She didn't deserve it. It seemed God was letting her know of it, yet again. All she knew was she was cold and heartsick and worn out.

Was she ready? She doubted she'd ever be ready.

The slight scrape of their slippers against the stone was tempered by the bare hint of singing as they walked, passing rows of ancient, insipid tapestries. Giselle quickly quelled such musings. The convent was dedicated to poverty after all, removing any comparison with her past.

She thought momentarily of Chateau Berchand with all its polished halls and expensive furnishings, and the white magnificence of Chateau Antilli, then told herself to be humble. Of course the hangings bore little resemblance to what she was accustomed to. Just as the large-weave cotton chemise rubbing against her skin bore no resemblance to her silks.

The double doors leading to Mother Superior's office loomed. Giselle waited patiently with Sister Evangeline while they were opened.

"This Sister Patrice? She's very petite? With a pale streak in her hair, like so? If she's here, there is no payment enough."

Navarre!

Giselle stopped the moment she heard his voice and knew Sister Evangeline was watching. She couldn't enter the room if he was there. She couldn't bear it. She was exhausted trying to bear everything else, already.

Giselle could see his hand where he sat to one side of the desk. There was lace from his shirt cuffs grazing his fingers. She could also see a hat, a long leg clad in white hose, dark-blue velvet breeches, and silver-buckled shoes.

She made some sound and turned to run. She had to hold her hand over her mouth at the same time to hold the agony in. She couldn't face him. Not now. Not when he had everything, and she lost the only things that mattered. And she couldn't return! She couldn't bear to see him with Charmaine!

And that was what decided her.

Charmaine had arrived during the Christmas season and taken over, gracing the dining table, sitting in Giselle's old spot, and murmuring double-edged words, now that Giselle was just another dowager *duchesse*. 'Such a horrid experience you've been through. Such trauma. What a pity to lose your child, Giselle. It's a triple tragedy for you, isn't it? Not only have you lost your husband and your position, but you lost the Berchald heir, too.

'Such a shame. I won't hasten your departure from the ducal chambers, of course. But, you cannot stay there forever, now can you? Navarre and I will be needing them. Navarre and I make such a lovely pair, don't we? I'm certain the dower house will easily suit your needs. And think! You'll have Mimi for company. I understand Navarre has made it quite habitable. I know I speak for him when I offer you an assist on the move. We'll try to make it...how can I say it? Less emotional? Yes. That's it. We'll make it less emotional for you.'

And then, Charmaine had laughed.

Giselle had somehow found the courage to ride a Berchald horse. She'd left it at an inn, and then joined Isabelle for the ride on a post coach. She ran from Charmaine. She ran from all the Berchalds. And he had no right to find her!

Navarre gave chase. She heard him. Giselle realized he could outrun her before she reached her room, so she stopped. She should have known she'd fail at escaping him, just as she failed at everything. She waited for her breathing to calm as he neared.

"Giselle?"

She thought she was prepared, but a riot of shiver went all the way through her, reaching the tips of her boots and the headdress atop her head.

"Will you not turn and face me?"

She shook her head.

"Why not? I've spent a lot of time and effort to find you, searching convent after convent."

His sigh exposed her weakness, and she was glad she faced away from him.

"The least your woman could have been was specific."

Giselle smiled slightly at Isabelle's loyalty.

"Is there someplace we can go with more privacy?"

She knew what he was referring to. It was rare for a handsome nobleman to chase a nun through the halls. The thought almost made her light-headed. They had

an audience at the end of the hall ahead. She wondered
how many sisters were watching from behind them.

"There's no need for further privacy, *Monsieur* le
Duc. I have no desire..."

She had to somehow force this lie from her lips. She
had to be strong enough. She made herself remember
his words. He hated the baby. He had probably rejoiced
at the loss. That would make it easier to woo the lovely
Charmaine without any guilt on his conscience, "...to
speak with you."

It would have had more bravado if she hadn't lost the
last word in anguish. Giselle pressed her knuckles to
her mouth to stop the emotion. *He hated the baby,* she
kept reminding herself. *He hated the baby. He hated—*

"Look at me, Giselle."

She heard the tenderness in his voice, but it was
Charmaine's property in the future. She had the right
to hear such a tenor from him, not Giselle.

He hated the baby.

She composed herself as best she could. Maybe if
she made him understand she'd made her decision and
that it was useless to pursue her further, he'd leave.

And then maybe she'd be able to sleep at night.

Another lie, Giselle?

She turned and was grateful of a sudden there were
only high windows below the eaves letting in light. His
was the only face to receive illumination. That was too
much, though. Giselle held her breath to look at him,
and released it as slowly as possible. If she were trying
to pose disinterest, she was failing at that, too.

He had more lace in his wardrobe than she recalled.
She tried to think of him as foppish like Jean-Claude.
She failed at that, too. Where lace flowed from
Navarre's collar, it only strengthened his appearance.
That didn't seem possible.

His face looked thinner. Perhaps that was what made
him look so masculine despite the lace. Nothing about

those violet-blue eyes had changed, and Giselle gasped, turning all her avowals to dust when she met his gaze.

"They tell me you haven't completed your vows. Is that true?"

He stepped nearer, blocking out the light, and Giselle swore his eyes darkened. She couldn't stand for it, but she must.

"If I say it's too late, will you go?"

"Do you honestly want me to?"

He stepped closer still, leaning his head toward her, and there wasn't any room to back away. She remembered those eyelashes, how their slight shading on his cheeks made her heart pump color into her cheeks. She'd give anything to hide her blush.

"Oui." She held out her hands to keep him away.

"I don't believe you." He lowered his head, almost grazing her lips as he smiled. Giselle felt the spark leap between them when he did.

"Very well, Navarre, I admit it. I love you. All right! I always will."

Unpleasant shivers flowed down her arms as she bared her heart and turned her face away. There was a tempest of tears behind her eyes, but she wouldn't let him see it. She wouldn't tolerate his breath on her neck a moment longer, either.

"You say you found hell, Navarre?" she asked bitterly. "You don't know the extent of it. I do. I found it the day I met you. Now go, before I say something I'll truly regret. Go."

CHAPTER THIRTY-FIVE

Giselle waited for him to leave. When he didn't she had to look back at him. There was a sheen of moisture coating his expressive eyes, and hers filled, too.

"Why do you do this to me, Navarre?" Her voice croaked, and there was little time left before trembling eroded it completely. "Isn't it enough to know I'll always love you? Isn't that enough for you? Why? I admit it. I love you. I love you so much, I can't stand to see you with another woman. So much so that I've chosen this."

She gestured to the hall about them. The interested faces at the ends of the hall waited. They were foregoing their breakfast in order to listen.

"Must you torture me further?" she begged. "Isn't it enough to know you destroy my peace, my sleep, and my every waking moment? Well? Isn't it?"

She had failed again. Giselle knew it as sobs overwhelmed her. She covered her face with her hands and shook with them. Then, she wasn't alone, and her tears were soaking into the front of his jacket. She couldn't keep from his embrace. She'd never been able to. Her trembling was far shy of his, though, and she felt it like a fresh wound.

"Why do you do this?" she asked. "I already told myself you're out of reach for me. You always have been. And just when I think I can live with it, you come again. Why? It's hopeless, that's what it is, and you only prolong the hurt. Why must you do this?"

"Because I love you, Giselle."

She couldn't stand the catch in his voice. She shoved herself free.

"Love? Love means nothing to the nobility, Navarre! It's less than nothing! We have our assigned roles to play, and we do. We allow loveless match after loveless match. *Merde!* I wish I were a member of the *bourgeois.* Perhaps then you could belong to me. What am I saying? It can't be. It never could."

"Etienne was right, Giselle. You're rather delightful when you're angered."

He smiled slightly, and she turned her back on him.

"Go away now, Navarre. I have no further use for you. Can't you see? Go back to your role and let me choose mine. It's the least you can do."

She walked to her cubicle door and opened it, trying to see through the tears in her eyes.

"Do you ever wonder what he, or she, would have looked like, Giselle, deep in your self-righteous praying?"

Cold flooded over her as she realized what he asked. *Her self-righteous praying?* Giselle tore off her wimple and threw it at him, wishing it were something more substantial. She wanted something to put a crease in that hard head of his.

"Self-righteous praying? Me? It wasn't I who hated the baby, *Monsieur* le *Duc!* It was you! Do you think those words haven't been engraved into my memory? They torment me so that even my prayers fail me! Well?"

She screamed the last words at him and moved to slam the door, but he was too quick. Giselle suspected the gasp she heard outside was due more to his presence in her chamber than her words.

The same mirror that mocked her that morning reflected his face, and she wouldn't allow it. Giselle turned her back on him and his image, staring at the wall behind her cot. She saw the rosary and cross and knew she hadn't been praying enough.

"I didn't hate the baby, Giselle."

She wanted to trust the tears staining his voice, but she didn't dare. He asked her to trust him before, and what had it gained her? A lot of heartache and an ocean of tears. She forced herself to ignore the vague hope his words started within her. She could be that strong. She had to be.

"I only said that to make it easier for you. I don't blame you for not believing me, but it's true."

His voice sounded strained, as if he fought back tears, but Giselle wasn't a fool anymore.

"You lie convincingly, *Monsieur* le *Duc*. It appears to be a trait all the Berchalds share."

Giselle trembled at his intake of breath behind her, and she hoped he didn't notice. If she didn't turn, if she just controlled her reactions, he'd never know. That was her last hope.

"I needed to make you dislike me, Giselle. I only lied...."

He stopped, as if unable to continue. Giselle looked at the ceiling to stay her cry, concentrating on the vacant ceiling and bare beam overhead. She didn't want to think about the rawness of his voice.

"It was stupid of me. I know that now, but I only thought.... *Mon Dieu!* I'm not even making sense, and it's because it feels as if you've already tried me and found me guilty. I only thought that maybe if you hated me enough, Etienne wouldn't be such a horrid alternative. Not for you...."

His voice dropped to a whisper. Giselle studiously watched the beam, refusing to listen.

"...or for my child."

She turned, failing once again in her resolve. She ignored the tears that streamed into her mouth. Her humble little room had never looked so small before. The sight of him leaning against the door as if for support made it feel as if her heart fell to the pit of her belly.

He lied to make Etienne more acceptable?

"Navarre?"

He refused to look at her at first. His gaze remained on the floor. Then, slowly, eyes the color of a stormy sky reached to her. Giselle was fortunate her cot was so near, because her knees crumpled. How well she remembered those eyes.

"I want to believe you, Navarre, I do. But I'm so afraid."

"Afraid? Of me, *ma petit*? I can't bear it if you are. I'll do anything. I swear it. I've been rampaging through the entire countryside trying to find you. I think I frightened your maid into an early grave. I beg you to return with me, Giselle. I can't live like this much longer."

He fell to his knees in front of her, and she couldn't avoid him any longer.

"Navarre—."

"You must return with me! You must. I can't admit failure. Esmee pines for you. She has postponed her wedding until I find you. Mother refuses to leave her wing of the castle, and that Louisa will have my head. It's enough to drive a man mad."

Giselle longed to smile, but she couldn't. Charmaine was going to be there, too. Why didn't he mention her?

"Navarre." She swallowed to stop any more tears, and knew he noticed. "I'm sorry, but—"

"Don't finish that! I've been stupid, Giselle, and I've been a coward. I showed both when I allowed Jean-Claude access to you. I don't ask your forgiveness and do you know why? Because I cannot forgive myself, that's why. Don't look at me so sadly. Listen to what I'm saying!

"I'm no poet. I can't even write a decent love letter, but we've lost enough time. I have many faults, and I'm certain you can name even more. Is there any other reason not to accept my suit? Well? You don't answer, and I must ask myself why. Why, Giselle? Must I first approach your father? Say so, and I will, no matter how much I dislike the man. I swear it. I'll even cede Savignen back to him if you wish. Don't look so surprised, I'll do it, and do you know why? Because I can't live without you. The entire estate can't do so, and I refuse to give such a long speech ever again in my life. So tell me — will you accept my suit?"

He didn't make sense. He must have known that from her expression. As much as she longed to hope he was offering what it sounded like, she wasn't sure.

"What of Charmaine?" Giselle whispered. "She'll have something to say about your request."

"Charmaine is a harlot of the lowest order. Her name must never cross your lips again. Do you think it was easy for me in Versailles? I waited endlessly for an audience with the king. I spent so much gold trying to see him, we're almost paupers again. Do you know why? For you, Giselle. I wrote you daily, *non!* Hourly."

He sighed. "You ask of Charmaine? She can find her own way. She always does. All I wanted was one thing from His Majesty. Permission to wed. You can't imagine my fear when I returned and found you gone. And no one knew where. You can't imagine my emotion when I learned of it.

"I begged the *Bon Dieu* for one chance to see you again, to let you know of my stupidity over *l'enfant*. The only clue I had was that miserable maid of yours. She didn't make it easy. She sent me on endless empty chases. Finally, this morning, when the Mother Superior told me of your description...."

He was going too fast. Giselle put up her hand to stop him. She didn't dare fill in his words. "You...wrote to me?"

"Of course, *ma petit*. I could think of nothing except how miserable life would be without you. I wrote endlessly, but you never answered. I thought I'd go insane. I wondered if you ignored me because of my words, or my actions. I wanted to know, but you were always silent."

"I...I never received a letter from you."

"I know. Just as I was leaving Versailles, Charmaine gave them to me in a bundle. She had them intercepted. You can't imagine my fear when I found you missing. Even Louisa didn't know where you were. *Merde!* I've been run ragged!"

Beautiful, tear-damp, blue eyes beseeched her, and Giselle felt the smile tugging at her lips. She'd almost let *Mademoiselle* Frerre's intriguing ruin her own life? Charmaine had almost won. It was a horrifying thought.

"I had to petition Rome for the annulment, Giselle, and then the pontiff made me wait until the New Year before he decided."

"You petitioned Rome?" Giselle was shocked at his audacity.

"For an annulment, *ma petit,*" he said gently. "You don't think I'd allow any memory of the disastrous marriage to Etienne stand between us? Never. I shall remember him as the older brother I adored. You may recall him as you will, but I'm not chancing it. When we wed, it will be before God and all mankind, *Mademoiselle* Giselle Patrice d' Antillion. You didn't know I knew your full name, did you? You have your mother to thank for that. She's happy to have the *Duc* du Berchald remain her son-in-law. The *comte?* He will take more persuasion, I think."

"You can honestly ask for my hand in marriage?" Giselle was afraid to let her joy sound too much in her voice.

'That's what I have been saying all along. Did you listen? *Non.* What else must I do to get your attention?"

Giselle giggled and reached for him, pulling his hair from the blue satin ribbon that held it. "Marry me, Navarre. This moment."

"You don't want an official engagement soiree? Or congratulations on catching such a prize?"

A self-mocking smile twisted his full lips, and Giselle licked hers to still their trembling. "Later."

She pulled on his shoulders, but only managed to slide from the cot when he didn't move. His arms enfolded her and almost started her crying again.

"Later?"

Giselle didn't know how he managed to drag his lips from hers long enough to ask it, but it was too long.

"Do you have the papers with you?" Giselle couldn't keep her fingers from him, and she tried to ignore the play of muscles as she searched his pockets.

"The Mother Superior has them. I made certain she knew my intentions were strictly honorable. You must stop that, my love!"

All she wanted was to feel his skin against her again.

"You don't know what you do! Give me a moment to compose myself!"

Giselle stopped her motions and looked into eyes that were merry, blue, and very close. "Of course I know, Navarre." She leaned forward to kiss his nose. "I always have."

Giselle stood to watch him rise and averted her eyes as he tucked in his shirt. Just the glimpse she had of him was enough to start the hunger within her. She'd forgotten how masculine and immense he was.

"Always?"

He looked at her from under his eyebrows as he worked his hair back into a queue. He looked so beautiful, while she was a disgrace. Giselle looked down at herself. What was she thinking? She wore a brown dress belted with a cord, and her oiled hair lay flat against her head. Yet somehow, when he looked at her, she felt beautiful.

"*Oui*, Navarre. I know I tease, and I won't stop. What do you have to say to that?" Giselle giggled as she opened the door and stepped out into a large number of nuns in the hall.

"*Je t'adore.* That is what I say. Step lively, my good sisters. There's a wedding to attend. Don't look at me like that. This is sanctified ground, isn't it? There's a priest awaiting us, too. Don't just stand there. Go!"

They scattered, giggling. Giselle smiled as she watched them. She'd noticed before how women acted around Navarre, so it wasn't a surprise. He was a Berchald, after all.

"Navarre, can I take a moment to bathe? Perhaps I can find something suitable to wear, too?"

"A moment to bathe?" he considered her. "*Non.*"

"No?"

"No." He shook his head and pulled her hand.

"But I want to look beautiful for you."

Giselle stayed in the shadow of the hall. She was going to marry the man of her dreams in a sack cloth dress? Sometimes, he was very obtuse.

"You are *tres belle,* Giselle, as always. I've rarely seen anything as lovely. Besides, when you bathe today, and you're going to bathe all right, it's going to be in broad daylight."

He looked down at her. His long eyelashes shielded his gaze from her, and she must have looked as puzzled as she felt.

"Then I'll already be your husband, and nothing will stop me from being there. Do you understand now, darling? No more deceit, no more secrets, and no more lies. *Merde,* but you're a vixen, and I grow tired of your slowness. You give me no other choice."

Giselle opened her mouth to reply, but she made no sound as he lifted her and left her in no doubt of his intentions. And no one looked surprised as Navarre carried Giselle into Mother Superior's office.

EPILOGUE

"Navarre, we mustn't come here so often." Giselle's whisper seemed loud in the peaceful contentment the arbor always seemed to inspire.

"Why?"

"I think Louisa suspicions."

"Your companion is aware of this? But, I said nothing. We are touring the vineyard, remember? It will be a good year, too."

Giselle laughed. "Louisa knows, Navarre. You can hardly keep your hands from me. It's no secret to her. She's known for years."

"She knows that we come to the arbor? But, it is my secret place. Giselle. I didn't even tell Esmee of it," he complained.

"Non." She reached up to push his hat away and run her fingers through that honey-gold hair. "Not this, but she knew everything else."

"Well, don't look at me. I certainly didn't tell her."

"I did."

"You spoke of me...of us? I am surprised at you, Giselle."

"I had to have someone to confide in, Navarre. You left me nothing when you moved to the dower house each time. You don't know how dark it was for me. I don't know how I survived it."

"Oh. Then. I was demented, my love. Come here. I will make it up to you again."

"Again?"

Navarre held her close. *"Oui.* Last night wasn't enough? I shall redouble my efforts." He lifted her chin with his finger, and touched his lips to hers, and her sigh blended with his. Then, he lifted his head.

"Je t'adore, Giselle. More now than ever, if such a thing is possible."'

She blinked rapidly at the tears filling her eyes.

"Always the tears it is with you. You are in luck that I know now it's due to the beautiful things I say. Here." He handed her his monogrammed handkerchief and smiled softly. Then, he turned her so her back was to him, and they both surveyed the view.

"It is a lovely valley, Navarre."

"That it is. Perhaps I shall dower our firstborn, Claudia, with it."

"What of Evette, Jessamine, and Marguerite?"

"You shall make me a poor man with all these daughters you present to me, Giselle."

"That...matters to you?" she stiffened.

Navarre spun her so quickly, the trees above her whirled. "You know me much better than that, Giselle. Do I look like it matters to me?"

"You look like the most handsome man I've ever met."

"Oh, Giselle, I have never loved another. I shall never love another. I cannot believe how full my heart is, and yet it grows each time I look upon one of our babes. If you were to present me with nothing but daughters, I would be a very wealthy man. To prove it to you, I shall allow all my children to wed where their heart takes them. Just as I did."

"Oh, Navarre." She could hardly see him through the blur of tears in her eyes.

"Besides, I have my sons, Etienne and Pierre-Navarre, to bring in rich brides, *non?* I must speak with my neighbors."

"But you just said...!"

"I love you, Giselle. My brother had it wrong all those years ago, too. You are not wondrous when you're angered. You are spectacular! And it isn't your anger that makes it so, it's when you feel strongly about something. Come. I didn't bring you here to make parlor talk with you."

He was walking toward the divan, lifting her into his arms at the same time.

"Navarre, I'm warning you...."

"Do not take that tone with me, *Madame*. You promised me a dozen children once, remember?"

"That wasn't me, Navarre. That was you."

"Details. It's always the details with you women."

"Navarre?"

"Oui?"

"We mustn't be out too long. They'll suspicion."

"Perhaps we should wait before giving Etienne his pony. I never considered that aspect."

"Oh, hush, and kiss me. You're wasting time."

His grin was her answer, then their lips touched, and their hearts meshed.

ABOUT THE AUTHOR

Jackie Ivie lives in Alaska with her husband and three pets. She started her writing career with hot Highland historical romances from Kensington. Her eleventh, LAIRD BALLANCLAIRE, is set for publication October 2013. Keeping her head in the clouds most of the time, Jackie spends most of her time researching, developing, and writing her paranormal series - Vampire Assassin League - because there's just something about a hot vampire with a mate fixation. Jackie loves to hear from fans at http://www.jackieivie.com/

www.ingramcontent.com/pod-product-compliance
Lightning Source LLC
Chambersburg PA
CBHW061303170626
46817CB00001B/26